THE WOMAN WHO READ TOO MUCH

THE WOMAN WHO READ TOO MUCH

⟮ A NOVEL ⟯

Bahiyyih Nakhjavani

REDWOOD PRESS
Stanford, California

Stanford University Press
Stanford, California

©2015 by Bahiyyih Nakhjavani. All rights reserved.

No part of this book may be reproduced or transmitted in any form or by any means, electronic or mechanical, including photocopying and recording, or in any information storage or retrieval system without the prior written permission of Stanford University Press.

Printed in the United States of America on acid-free, archival-quality paper

Library of Congress Cataloging-in-Publication Data

Nakhjavání, Bahíyyih, author.
The woman who read too much : a novel / Bahiyyih Nakhjavani.
     pages cm
Originally written in English, this novel was published first in translation. The French publisher, Actes Sud, published it as La femme qui lisait trop in October 2007. In Italy, Rizzoli also published it in 2007 as La donna che leggeva troppo. In 2010, Alianza in Spain published it as La mujer que leia demasiado. Includes bibliographical references.
     ISBN 978-0-8047-9325-4 (cloth : alk. paper) —
1. Qurrat al-'Ayn, 1817 or 1818–1852—Fiction. 2. Women poets, Persian—19th century—Fiction. 3. Women—Iran—Social conditions—19th century—Fiction. I. Title.
     PR6064.A35W66 2015
     823'.914—dc23
                                        2014042783
ISBN 978-0-8047-9429-9 (electronic)

Typeset at Stanford University Press in 10.25/15 Adobe Caslon Pro

To my uncle, Amin Banani

TABLE OF CONTENTS

THE WOMAN WHO READ TOO MUCH

THE BOOK OF THE MOTHER

(1)

When the Shah was shot, he staggered several paces in the shrine and fell stone dead in the lap of an old beggar woman. He had been turning towards his wife's tomb at that moment, and the beggar was sitting next to the alcove where the assassin had been hiding, near the door. Even if she were at fault for having strayed beyond her allotted corner in the cemetery outside the mosque, it would have been unwise to draw attention to the fact. The killer was arrested and identified, the occasion and location were carefully noted for posterity, but there was naturally no mention of a woman in the history books. A veil was drawn over the sordid details of his majesty's death. It was more useful to evoke the failed attempt on the life of the king, half a century before, than to contemplate the actual circumstances of his assassination.

The old woman was a regular among the corpse washers and liked to claim that she had handled royalty in her time. None of the others believed her, of course; women are usually more inventive than exact and this one was notorious for her lies and her deformities. But perhaps there was some truth in it, for even the escort admitted, when questioned afterwards, that the king did stare at the beggar with something like recognition just before keeling over. Whether this was due to her words or her deeds was uncertain, however, for both were thoroughly banal. All she did was to stretch out her open palm and ask the king for alms. But since it was inconceivable that his majesty should have had traffic with such a creature and would have caused a scandal to arrest her, given the circumstances of his death, they simply kicked her in the ribs and let her go.

She had naturally protested innocence and swore on her scabs that she had no intention of importuning his majesty to death. She had only been begging for the love of God, she said.

❨ 2 ❩

The Mother of the Shah had never worried much about the love of God before the attempt on the life of her son. She had not considered it a threat until then and had simply exploited it, as she had the love of men. She had feared plots and conspiracies, naturally, and had dreaded regicide and revolution; she had been on her guard against pestilence, famine, drought, and indigestion. But while providential grace had rarely been a natural ally in her life, she could hardly have called it an enemy either, much less a rival. Before the young Shah came to the throne, the divinity had only intervened in her affairs by means of absences.

It was hardly surprising, therefore, that she should believe her son owed his titles to her efforts, rather than to accidental grace. She had taken every precaution, ever since his childhood, to protect the Crown Prince from his frailties. She had made the sickly boy consult cosmographers, submit his urine to the doctors, and tried by every means at her disposal to deflect his penchant for cats. She had planned his marriages, controlled his concubines, and governed his financial policies. In the course of his unhappy adolescence, she had even mastered the art of poisoning to confirm his political survival in the court. And by the time he succeeded his father to the throne, she assumed that the King of Kings and Pivot of the Universe had learned to distinguish between his Mother's political acumen and the love of God.

But she underestimated the threat posed by divine compassion. Some years after his coronation, the Shah of Persia was reminded, rather abruptly, of the arbitrary mercies of providence. In the fifth summer of his reign, a group of youths approached his majesty on his way out hunting, early one morning. The court had removed from the capital several weeks before, as was customary during that season, and the royal tents had been pitched on the cool slopes, north of the city; a gratifying breeze was fluttering the pennants, as his majesty rode out in high spirits for the chase. The officers of the royal equerry had gone ahead of him, so as not to encumber the sovereign with the dust of their horses. The tribal archers were escorting him at a respectful distance behind, and no one was near when the would-be assassins accosted the king, outside an abandoned orchard some *farsangs* north of the capital. The students were waving petitions in the air and crying for justice; they were calling out for his majesty to stop and hear their appeals, for the love of God. But instead of maintaining a respectful distance, as was to be expected when asking for a royal favour, they closed in and surrounded the young Shah with an air of desperation. They apprehended his rearing horse with dreadful imprecations, and began to shout absurd demands in his face. And then, to his utter surprise, they had the impertinence to empty buckshot into his royal person.

Since no one was near enough to see what happened, reports about the attempt on the life of the Shah were contradictory. Some said there had been at least six youths intent upon killing his majesty; others said there were four, and a few said that two were quite enough, given the paucity of damage inflicted. Some insisted that the young men were driven by political motives and others believed they were religious fanatics and misguided reformists. Some claimed it was a cold-blooded attempt at murder; others said it was an act of folly, driven by despair. Some claimed the shot had entered the Shah's neck; others said he had been touched in the leg; and certain swore that his cheek was hurt. Or was it his thigh? A few even murmured his majesty might have been shot in the loin. No one remembered what the petition was about.

Rumours were rife, however, by the time the sovereign was rushed back to the capital. The royal chamberlains who carried him, hollering, into his private apartments, swore that his majesty was in his death throes. Although his French physician noted, somewhat testily, that the wounds were grazes, merely, fit to fell a partridge and far too few to merit such blood-curdling shrieks, the handful of lead pellets which the cold-blooded man of science poked mercilessly out of his majesty's flesh that morning, as he lay face down and twitching, on a satin couch, were sufficient to fill a royal mind with foreboding. They warned the king of the providential grace on which his powers depended. They confirmed his fear that autocracy might not extend beyond the grave. And they reminded him that he owed his bare existence to the love of God.

But they branded his Mother's heart with hate forever. She stood barring the door to her son's private apartments, seething with rage as the physician poked and prodded. Much to her indignation, the Frenchman had insisted on her leaving the room. The ministers were pressing round to protest their loyalty to his majesty, but if she had been refused entry she saw no reason why they should be allowed inside. Besides, it was bad enough that the howls of her son could be heard through closed doors; she certainly did not want him to be seen in such conditions.

The Shah had always had a tendency towards histrionics. In childhood, his wan air had attracted the attention of British diplomats with a bent towards pederasty, and in early youth, one glance of his lustrous eyes had been enough to raise him to imperial knees and win him the Tsar's signet ring. Having transcended pimples to attain his father's throne, his posturing had become positively theatrical, but with this attempt on his life, the melodrama was turning into a farce. The sheer pettiness of his position, quite apart from its insecurity, could not have been more painfully obvious to the queen. He was crowned the sovereign of hysteria at last, she thought, bitterly.

Her imperial highness knew there was no alternative but to take charge of the situation. Her son's reputation had to be salvaged or he would lose all credibility in the eyes of the people. Although it was too soon to prove his political value, this botched attempt could be exploited to show his valour. And so she turned the Shah into a hero in order to seize the reins of power for herself. After shutting the doors firmly on the faces of his ministers, she sacked the royal chamberlains, beat the servants into silence, and gave strict instructions to the court chroniclers regarding the historical records.

She informed the court that his majesty had fought the assassins single-handedly. She claimed that he had defended himself against his assailants with solitary courage and had faced this dastardly act of betrayal against his person, nobly and alone. He had overcome, she said, as only a true king could, through divine intervention. He had been saved miraculously from assassination by the love of God.

It was the best use she had ever made of the deity. But even she could not control the ironies unleashed when providence is recruited for political ends. She did not live long enough to see her son sprawling in the lap of the corpse washer. Perhaps the love of God was more dangerous to the Shah of Persia than the love of any woman.

(3)

The Mother of the Shah did not have a religious inclination, but she had always counted herself among the chosen. Grace and providence had nothing to do with it. She could hardly have been called handsome, even in her prime, but she was distinguished by a striking pair of eyes, which, whatever God's intentions, she enlarged with kohl to considerable effect. The wife of the British ambassador, who paid her respects at the palace soon after the Shah's accession to the throne, acknowledged them, primly, in her diary, to be her highness' finest feature, and court poets, who deferred to her talents as a versifier, sang eulogies to their greenness and avoided mentioning the rest. In fact, her jaw was too square, her cheeks too broad, and her jowls too heavy for genuine praise. But the veil can flatter well as well as hide, and sycophants were naturally susceptible to her charms.

The British Envoy's wife was neither responsive to nor seemed capable of flattery. She looked thoroughly ill at ease at her first meeting with the Mother of the Shah and had a bilious air about her, the queen thought, as though she had eaten something disagreeable just before coming to the palace. She appeared to be quite bewildered by the smirks of Madame, the French translator, who was the first to welcome her in the mirrored antechamber, and who then ushered her into the royal *anderoun* where the queen was waiting to greet her.

Her highness was in no mood for visitors that day. The return of the
British Envoy from his leave of absence during the old Shah's reign had
coincided with widespread insurrections in the provinces, and the queen
regent feared that her son's new Grand Vazir was seizing this excuse to
throw his weight around. She was frankly more preoccupied with his policy
regarding these sectarians than with how she should welcome the English
bride to town. He had ordered extensive purges up and down the land;
dozens were being arrested, on his orders, and many more were still being
hunted down. One of the most notorious among them was a woman. Born
in Qazvin, educated in Karbala, and renowned for her audacity and eloquence in Persia, Turkey, and the Kurdish provinces, this rebel had already
proved to be a serious threat to the stability of the state. She had been
preaching dangerous reversals; she had been teaching new ways to read the
rules. The name and fame of her gospel was spreading rapidly. But given
the woman's popularity and the young Shah's lack of it, the consequence of
chasing such a creature from house to house and street to street was surely
just as dangerous as her cause.

The Mother of the Shah was half-eager for, half-afraid of her arrest.
The woman was influential, as famous for her poetry as she was infamous
for her ideas. She was beautiful, so they said, and of a dazzling intelligence.
Most disturbing of all, she had an uncanny gift for divination, according to
the rumours. She deciphered secrets in silences and saw unspoken desires
between the words; she read past failures in present actions and predicted
future possibilities even in vacillation. Some people swore she was a witch.
Her formidable powers had been proven by her ability to escape every
stratagem, elude every trap. Despite the many troops deployed to find her,
she had so far avoided being taken into custody. She was damnably elusive.

Although the Mother of the Shah approved of the premier's plans to
curb her influence, she was jealous of his intentions. Why was the Grand
Vazir so determined to catch this woman? Why didn't he simply ensure
that she was killed? Did he suspect her of conspiracy? But what schemes,
what plots could such a woman have on him? How could she have con-
spired against the new Vazir without the knowledge of the queen, whose

primary business it was to overthrow him? Her highness was outraged by the possibility. She was fearful of the impact of the poetess in the court. She was determined, above all, to keep her away from her son.

The queen scrutinized the Englishwoman closely as she came through the door. This one, now, she thought, was certainly no threat; this woman would never be a troublemaker. She was one of those mousy creatures who blushed easily and did not know what to do with her hands. Why was it, thought the Mother of the Shah, that Western women blushed so easily? They might be less self-conscious, she said to herself, if they wore veils. Perhaps this one was feeling particularly awkward because she was expecting her first child: she was newly married after all, as well as recently arrived in the country. Perhaps it was because she was un-acquainted with Persian customs, for instead of sitting sensibly on the ground, she had perched uncomfortably on a chair, obliging the Mother of the Shah to do likewise, and forcing all the princesses to stand as stiff as ramrods round the room. Perhaps she thought them all barbarians and did not trust herself among the natives, thought her highness, bitterly, for the country was in such a turmoil that there was even talk of revolt in the women's quarters. The Englishwoman probably did not trust do-mestics either, given the way she gawped at the Nubian, who was the queen's confidante. But in the last analysis, it may have been the fault of the Frenchwoman that she was so ill at ease. Translation is a danger-ous business, and everyone knew that Madame, with her giggles and her smirks, had sold something besides flowers in the streets of Lyon, before marrying a Persian tailor and rising to the giddy heights of royal translator in the women's quarters of the Shah.

The Mother of the Shah offered the Englishwoman a glittering smile as she settled awkwardly in her chair, which despite being put to so little use, did nothing to belie an air of antiquated weariness. Her young guest was barely in her twenties, the queen calculated, and seemed more like the daughter than the spouse of the elderly British Envoy. Her highness kept her own age less obvious. Although she was, theoretically, a widow, she cultivated the impression of being too young to be a mother, and made no secret of despising the role of wife. The former Shah, to whom she had been betrothed since birth, had never been to her liking.

The marriage between these ill-paired cousins had proven unsatisfactory to both sides. His late majesty had been more interested in his alimentary canal than in his dynastic prerogatives and, frankly, more concerned with elimination than with insurrection. His consort's penchant for beards, and her particular weakness for the growth that rippled from the chin of the Chief Steward of the royal bedchamber, had caused the latter's exile, and her subsequent intimacies with the Secretary of the armed forces had also led to the latter's disgrace. After discovering one of her infidelities, her husband had finally prevailed upon the queen to act with discretion if only so that he might never have to curtail her pleasures in the future. But in the end she had been relegated from royal consort to the ignominy of a temporary alliance with the old Shah. Her show of grief beside his grave, however, was as genuine as any widow's, and her passions had not been buried with him. Although her son's new Grand Vazir had not been her choice for premier, he certainly attracted her fancy. He also piqued her jealousy. She had been much put out by his keen interest in the poetess. It was outrageous, she informed the Secretary, shortly before the Envoy's wife was announced that day, it was disgraceful that the new premier should deploy the armed forces of his majesty the Shah just to hunt for a woman who read too much!

She hid her indignation, however, under a show of hospitality to the wife of the British ambassador and welcomed her ladyship into the room with considerable pomp. The Mother of the Shah was highly trained in performance and opposed to the fashion for candour. How else could one survive the hypocrisies of the court? Or make an impression on presumptuous foreigners? It was easy enough to lie to them, because they had such a shallow interpretation of words, but it was not always possible to impress them. They were so confoundedly superior.

After the Envoy's wife had found her perch, amid rustling petticoats and creaking stays, her highness clapped her heavily bejewelled hands and summoned a fanfare of food to be served to her honoured guest. At her signal, the curtained doorways parted and a pair of young women with polished cheeks and stiffened curls entered the room, bearing platters heaped with sweet almond cakes and tiers of fruit. These lovely ladies, sang the queen, waving away the lazy winter flies, these pretty princesses, she trilled, ordering them to pile the sweetmeats high on her ladyship's plate, are among the Shah's most privileged wives. How happy they are, and how blessed among women, she cried; what good fortune they have and what an advantage to live under the shadow of the Shah of Persia! And she yawned behind her hand.

The Envoy's wife tested the Frenchwoman's powers of translation to the full by effusing about her Britannic majesty, whose birthday had been celebrated at the Legation recently and whose powers, in the absence of more compelling proof, apparently ruled the waves.

The Mother of the Shah gritted her teeth. The last thing she wished to discuss was birthdays. She was more anxious to hide the ravage of time than to advertise its passage and was as frustrated by the range of her powers as by the constraints of her sex. She had done everything to ensure her son's succession to the throne but suspected this new premier was trying to erode her authority with this business of the poetess of Qazvin. Women weren't the only ones trying to reverse the roles, she thought resentfully, flashing another dazzling smile at her guest.

She had been a young virgin in her time, she replied airily, as well as a bride; she had seen the privileges of a sister and a mother too, and knew the meaning of being a daughter and wife. But a woman's highest aspiration in life, surely, was to be a queen; none but a real queen's hand could hold the reins of true power in the land, she added with bitter emphasis. It would have been awkward, in the circumstances, to mention the sea, given the British presence so close off the coast of Bushire, and besides, it would have spoilt the rhyme, but as she listened to the florist from Lyon wade and splash into the shallows of translation, her imperial highness realized that it didn't matter a jot whether Madame had plumbed the depths of her bitterness. The linguistic capacities of her guest were not likely to extend beyond the rhyming couplet, and accuracy was hardly required to offer perfunctory honour to the English monarch.

Her guest praised her literary skills. But although the compliments were waved elegantly aside, she did not repeat them, as expected. She did not insist on them, as required. She digressed abruptly, with an irrelevant inquiry about the rates of literacy among Persian women.

The queen was put out. What had literacy to do with literature? she asked, raising a wry brow at the translator.

The English lady, explained Madame, in Persian, was interested in how many women in this country were able to read and write. The wife of the British ambassador, she repeated with a French shrug, was begging that such souls be released from the bondage of their ignorance.

Her highness narrowed her eyes. Released from bondage? What ignorance! Was this foreigner suggesting that women were no better than slaves? The latest British interference in Persia's domestic policies had gravely impeded the slave trade at the Gulf port, and the queen had done everything possible to dissuade her son from ratifying the treaties. She believed them to be as foolish as any of the doctrines of the notorious poetess. Was the Englishwoman supporting the recommendations of the new Vazir? Or had something been lost in translation?

Madame insisted not. Her translation into and out of Persian was above reproach. But she could not vouch for the Englishwoman's grasp of French, she added with a smirk.

And so the queen brushed the comment aside with the flies with another wave of a dismissive and bejewelled hand. All the princesses knew how to read and write, she stated majestically. All the ladies of distinction in this country knew how to play the dulcimer and sing. They had all been taught the rudiments of poetry and the ground rules of religion, but education did not guarantee intelligence; poetry was pointless without political discipline.

She plied her guest with more tea as the translator intervened, and brooded on the nature of political discipline. She might not have ordered the purges in the land, but she was determined to dictate what should be done with any female prisoners who were arrested. Women's business was her concern. The common jail in town was filled with riff-raff of the lower orders but was hardly appropriate for a lady of renown. If this dangerous poetess were ever captured, she would have to be held under house arrest rather than in the prison. Since she was from a distinguished family and had already humiliated her kinsmen, it would be best not to provoke their pride still further. But in which house should she be imprisoned, pondered the Mother of the Shah? And under whose vigilance should such a dangerous woman be kept? Since he had been her candidate for the premiership, she favoured the custodianship of the Secretary of the armed forces. She believed he would obey her wishes in hope of future preferment, and would follow her instructions to the letter. Poetry was futile, she thought grimly, without political discipline.

By some irony of international dimensions, the notion of political discipline, translated into French, appeared to bring the conversation squarely back to the tedious subject of the British Queen. The Envoy's wife showed her a picture of the sovereign, and blushed again.

The Mother of the Shah despised the British monarch with her pale, protruding eyes. She could not understand how a queen could place so much emphasis on her age. She also found it inconceivable that any sovereign worthy of the name could govern properly from the childbed or set the standard for her countrywomen by reigning in a permanent state of pregnancy. She herself pursued power with the jungle instincts of the Qajar court, at the cost of her own body. She was both the wife and the daughter of a king, she told her guest, but had no need to prove it annually. Unlike other women, she did not need to multiply her progeny either, because the heredity of the Shah and his Sister, she added proudly, was doubly royal.

After the French florist from Lyon delivered this broadside in the vernacular, the queen observed that her English ladyship was suitably discomfited. Her enthusiasm regarding royal birthdays was nipped in the bud, and her questions about female literacy were effectively curtailed. Much to the queen's relief, she did not raise the subject of the purges either or the punishments they might entail, and cut her visit short after the first collation of fruits and tea. If reading led to such witlessness, thought the Mother of the Shah, then this British conspiracy would not go far in Persia. And if

removing the veil rendered one as red-faced as this poor foreign girl, then
why in heaven's name would any woman choose it?

But she was in half a mind at that moment to march out of the women's
quarters and strip off her own veil in front of the Grand Vazir. She wanted
to shake his presumptions and shock him a little. She wanted to get his attention and force him to defer to her demands. It was one thing to throw
his weight around by ordering arrests up and down the land but quite another to threaten a regent's powers in the court. He could interrogate all
the sectarians he had rounded up, if he insisted; he could administer what
he called justice, if he so wished. But the guilt or innocence of any female
offender was her affair. The Mother of the Shah was determined to have
total control over the poetess of Qazvin. It was her right to decide the fate
of this preacher of literacy. It was her privilege to choose what should be
done to this woman, for whom thoughts were syllables and deeds words,
for whom a life sentence was a cheap price to pay for her beliefs, and who
claimed that the future lay before all in equal measure, like an open book.

But the rights of the Mother of the Shah may have been less exclusive
than her privileges; her noble heritage was, in the last analysis, equivocal.
She was certainly not going to admit it to the Envoy's wife, who was being
ushered out of her room by her slave at that moment, but since her legendary forebear, the Qajar patriarch, had spawned as many offspring as there
were fleas in his kingdom, scarcely a woman in Persia was not, in some
sort, his daughter. She sometimes harboured a vague suspicion that she was
related to half the paupers in the land.

(4)

Perhaps when he was shot in the shrine fifty years later, his majesty the
Shah may be forgiven if he mistook a beggar woman for his Mother. The
last time he had seen her highness, she had been grovelling at his feet too,
and begging, uncharacteristically, for the love of God.

So much for her precautions, murmured the gossips, afterwards. A
mother's fears may prove more efficacious than her prayers.

He had not set eyes on her for more than a quarter of a century by then; he even avoided thinking about her once she died. But it had already become his policy, for reasons of economy as well as sanity, to muddle the identities of his remorseless relatives long before that. For several years after the first attempt on his life, he chose to forget he even had a sister, and in the course of the five subsequent decades, he frequently found it convenient to confuse his wives. Some swore he could not tell the difference between a woman and a cat by the end. He was evidently losing his powers of discrimination. The ladies of the *anderoun* said that his obsession with the young boy, whom he pampered obscenely in his old age, was because he imagined the wretched commoner to be himself. To confound a corpse washer with a queen was nothing, by comparison.

Besides, it was hard to distinguish between cream and whey that day, with the doors closed and the interior of the mosque so suffocating. Although a fine spring breeze was blowing outside, the press of the pious in the building was unbearable. The Shah was no doubt desperate for some fresh air. The dripping candelabras and the hanging lamps shed less light than heat, and the smell of armpits and of feet was overpowering. He may have been turning towards the courtyard just to breathe. If he seemed to recognize the corpse washer, it may only have been because his brain was addled. He may simply have confused that moment with another.

He had no time to wonder what that other moment was. Although they say the soul can read history backwards at its passing, he had no opportunity to give it a second glance. The prayers were over and he was just beginning to move towards the courtyard door after the prerequisite lull of piety, when a roaring flooded his mind and he was lost. His brain began to unravel as soon as the shots were fired, and it took hardly any time to erase the grammar of his memory. Besides, the dead do not linger long to tell of the ironies culled at that last recall; they are eager to be gone and intent upon what happens next in the story. Words had become history and prophecy combined by the time the old corpse washer held out her palm to him.

It was not as though she uttered anything grand or significant. What she began to say, just before the gun was fired, was not original.

The phrase she completed, as the echo of the shots ricocheted through
the shrine, was hardly unusual either. All she did was to remind him that
wealth, power, and lordship were his and that poverty, homelessness, and
misery were hers. For the love of God.

The words were familiar enough, the usual formula for beggars; they
were clichés so often reiterated that the Shah could hardly be expected to
remember their origins. The sentiment seemed trite enough, too, almost
meaningless, but its impact on his majesty's mind was as devastating as
the bullet, which entered his heart at the same moment. If he thought the
corpse washer was his mother, it was hardly surprising and only to be expected, because what is more banal than a mother's words, after all?

The beggar woman swore she had no ill intentions. She meant no harm,
she said, in naming God. It was not as though she had chosen the moment
of his death to remind his majesty of the one person in the world who'd
worried about it from the day of his birth. Her disrespect towards the old
queen naturally earned her another kick in the ribs.

〔 5 〕

Chaos ensued in the wake of the first attempt on the life of the Shah. As
soon as the news came that he had been shot while out hunting, the royal
camp, spread on the leisured slopes of the cool hills for the summer season,
was seized by sudden panic and took flight within the hour. Striped tents
were lowered, gay carpets rolled up, copper pots and kettles packed on pro-
testing mules, and the entire company of princes, courtiers, officers, and
guards clattered helter-skelter down the hills in clouds of hysterical dust.
The royal harem had hardly re-entered the palace doors before a strict cur-
few was imposed, on the queen's orders. The gates of the city were closed
and the cannons directed at the air in frantic preparation of disaster.

Only the British Envoy refused to budge. Although his wife sat trembling under her suffocating tent, imagining assassins behind every bush, her
husband insisted that they were safer in the camping grounds, surrounded
by their Ghurkha guards, than down in the capital and at the mercy of the
queen. No one was free from suspicion at this time, he said; anyone might

be accused of collusion in the crime. Her highness was interpreting every act as a challenge, every word as a slight to the authority of her son. She was demanding instant vengeance.

It was rumoured that one of the would-be assassins had already been slashed to ribbons on the spot for what he said and another had his brains blown out within hours of his arrest for refusing to speak. In the days that followed, the rest were beaten and summarily executed without trial, but that was only the beginning of the carnage. If godless students had tried to assassinate the young Shah, then spies and heretics might be anywhere. For weeks afterwards, grooms and guards and gardeners made themselves hoarse in the alleys, yelling for retribution. Nannies and nurses and midwives flocked out of their homes for days, screaming for blood. All good citizens filled the market squares to watch the executions, and the Mayor, who was responsible for public order and what he was pleased to call security in the city, personally undertook to find the perpetrators of the crime. He said that he owed it to the Mother of the Shah.

All through that summer, the only sound more dreadful than the drums and horns on the city walls was the rattle of the Mayor's cart in the narrow alleys as he made his way from lane to lane and house to house, hunting for suspects. Within hours of the foolhardy attempt on the Shah's life, a wretched youth, whose misfortune it was to be acquainted with the assassins, was seized by the chief of police, threatened with death, laced with liquor, and supplied with the most profitable addresses. After that, there was nothing to stop private greed from being turned to public profit. A knock on the gate was enough to prove the guilt of those behind it; a summons to the door was sufficient to confirm a would-be conspirator, and endorse his wealth. None but men whose purses weighed more than their protestations could buy themselves a reprieve, and only women of rank dared stay at home. The rest were hauled out and hounded to death, like dogs.

There had never been such a bloodbath in the kingdom. None of the attempts to quell the insurrections in the time of the old Shah had been as ruthless as these reprisals; not even the purges at the beginning of the new one's reign could be compared with what took place that year. The Mother of the Shah obliged all servants of the state to participate in the massacres in order to prove their loyalty to the throne. No one was exempt from the requirement; no one was immune. High-ranking courtiers and lowly clerics all had to share the honours, because the Prime Minister did not want to bear the brunt of the blame. Ministers and mullahs were welcomed with confectionery into the brotherhood of executioners, and sugared almonds and sweet tamarisk were exchanged for corpses on a daily basis. The butchery that summer was unparalleled.

Nor were foreigners excused. If they expressed unwillingness to contribute a penultimate stab or offer a final thrust at the breast of whoever's turn it was to take the brunt of the queen's rage, they were obliged to serve as witnesses at the executions. When the Shah's French physician declined the invitation with a laconic smile, and begged to be excused from slaughter on the grounds that he caused too many deaths already in his professional capacity, he was found poisoned ten days later. An Austrian captain, providing military training to the army, fled from the country within the week to avoid being implicated in the bloodshed, and a young Englishman, employed to translate excerpts into Persian from the Western papers, found himself writing prose that summer which rivalled the penny dreadfuls in London, just to save his skin.

Despite their endemic rivalries and temperamental differences, even the Russian and British envoys were obliged to take refuge in the safety of collective condolences after the attempt on the life of the young Shah. They presented their joint sympathies to his majesty at the earliest opportunity and protested simultaneous indignation at the outrage he had suffered, in an attempt to pre-empt any suspicion of having played a part in the plot themselves. Afterwards, the Russians barricaded themselves in the sweltering suburbs and the Colonel returned to the camping grounds, but his attaché insisted on remaining at court, in the capital. He preferred to keep an eye on her highness, as he put it, rather than providing her with another back to stab. The Viennese ophthalmic doctor to whom he made the remark retorted, rather dryly, that he would rather have had his own eyes put out than see some of the atrocities being committed in Tehran.

Bazaars were soon ablaze with bodies and walls were trophied with bleeding heads. Men were stoned, flayed raw, and shod like horses before being whipped through the streets with burning candles buried in their flesh. They were thrown into the subterranean pits beneath the palace and fed the roasted ears of their companions; they were hewn apart and hacked into pieces by the frantic crowds. The Mayor had promised the Mother of the Shah to stop at nothing. He swore that no stone would be left unturned, no effort lost in rooting out the murderers. He had promised her that he would chase these regicidal rats out of their holes, that he would leech the city, drop by drop, of treason. He would hunt the traitors down wherever they might be, he told her, even if the chase led him street by street and lane by lane to the very gates of his own house.

It was not an empty oath. The bane of the queen's life was living under his roof. The celebrated poetess of Qazvin, the most brilliant scholar and eloquent spokeswoman of her times, had been under house arrest in his private residence for the past three years, on the orders of the Shah's first Grand Vazir. It was not hard to guess why the Mayor would be knocking on his own doors before the summer was out.

❪ 6 ❫

The Mayor's house was an ostentatious building in the south of the city, situated at the far end of a blind alley leading away from the market square. The heavy studded gates of the property led to twin courtyards: a public one, large enough to accommodate a garrison of soldiers in the front, and a private one at the back, catering to the women's quarters. The courtyard of the women's *anderoun* was graced by a pair of silver birches, whose delicate leaves tinkled over the rectangular pool lined to the marbled brim with turquoise tiles; its walls abutted on an empty lot behind, filled with dark rows of cypresses and poplars. The courtyard of the *birouni*, or men's side, was squalid with mule manure and the comings and goings from the alley. There were only two other gates in the alley beside that of the Mayor's house: a heavy iron one to its right belonging to the British Legation, and a wooden one, to the left, which opened into the vacant lot.

These grounds had been leased as a garden some years before to the Envoy Extraordinary and Plenipotentiary of the British Queen. Despite the inconvenience of its location across the alley, the Legation garden was, to all intents and purposes, inaccessible to the public. Its walls were high, its wooden gate was heavily barred, and the only aperture, beside the dovecotes through which anyone could look down on its secluded paths, was a small window in the unused upper chamber of the Mayor's residence. Although British proximity would not always redound to the Mayor's credit in later years, it afforded some amusement to his women at the beginning of the reign. Before the arrest of the female prisoner, the members of his *anderoun* used to take turns peeping down from this window at the newly arrived wife of the British ambassador, as she walked under the drooping poplars and lingered beneath the cypresses behind the house.

The upper chamber of the Mayor's residence had been constructed over the kitchen quarters, on a flat-roofed terrace on the top of the outhouses that divided the public from the private sides of the building. The male and female quarters were linked above ground by a gated arch at the end of the outhouse walls and by a thick door below, in the common cellars. A flight of stone steps led down to these cellars from each side of the house, beneath the twin breezeways, but due to an inadvertence on the part of the builders, the upper chamber was inaccessible, except by a ladder, to all but the doves nesting under the rafters. It could not be used without causing offence or posing a danger, and was subsequently left empty. Since its only purpose was pretention, the exterior walls overlooking the garden were elaborately ornamented while the interior ones were left rough and raw. Despite this fact, when the Mayor's residence was gutted almost a decade after the attempt on the Shah's life, people still insisted that it was because of that upper chamber. It was commonly believed that the second storey of the Mayor's house contained a vast store of treasure.

There had already been speculation in the last years of the old king's reign about the Mayor's motives in building himself such a grand dwelling. There had been some apprehension, too, about its cost to his safety. For the second storey towered above the other sun-baked houses in the neighbourhood in dangerous imitation of the palace of the king. The vaulted cellars beneath the ornamented tea rooms were a provocation too, not only to engineering. No one else in town had ever presumed to erect so high or dig so low; no other house was so lavishly adorned with tiles from Isphahan. Even the British Legation up the alley, with its large court and fancy porticos, did not have such aspirations, despite its more extensive grounds. By the time the young crown prince attained the throne, everyone knew that the queen regent had fixed her eye on this attractive property. The only question was what excuse she might employ to seize it.

On the solemn occasion of the Shah's coronation, however, the Mayor put an end to speculation by offering his residence himself, as a gift to his sovereign. The gesture justified his extravagance, but it did not stop the gossip. It gratified the queen, too, to some extent, but also pricked her suspicions. She wondered what the Mayor's Wife would have to say about it.

Her highness' shrewd green eyes, heavily circled with kohl, observed the Mayor with keen interest during the coronation ceremonies, as he strode down the length of the reception hall to pay his compliments to the Shah. She had seated herself where she could best watch all those who approached her son, behind an ornamental screen, on the left-hand side of the throne. The Mayor was a portly man in his early sixties who had dyed his hair black according to the older fashions. He was not tall, but made up for his lack of height by a bold tread and an imposing girth, and he was rubbing his hands nervously as he walked through ranks of fawning courtiers, step by step, from chandelier to chandelier. They said his second wife was a good cook. They also said a hen ruled the roost in that family. Although he was brutal in the discharge of his civic responsibilities, his Wife was known to hold domestic sway. She had social pretensions too. He had several older daughters but only one son, a boy with fat cheeks and a shambling gait, according to the gossips, who was the same age as the crown prince and also unmarried. If the Mayor's bid to win royal favour was to coincide with his Wife's aspirations, the queen suspected that she might have to intervene. Especially if she were to have some influence over that house.

As he drew near the raised dais of the glittering throne, the queen saw that the Mayor's small, shifty eyes slid frequently towards the grizzled beard and ceremonial robes of the new Vazir, who was seated prominently on the king's right. She pursed her lips with irritation. She *was* still the official regent! And the Secretary of the armed forces, whom she had been grooming for a ministerial position, *was* standing visibly beside her! Despite the fact that the Shah had favoured a different premier from the protégé she had proposed, she did not see why the Mayor should advertise such overt deference towards the wrong side of the throne.

The Mayor had a tendency to stutter when he was nervous, and his compliments were punctuated by more than the compulsory pauses and obsequious bows. After protracted preliminaries, he offered his palatial residence to the king haltingly, with one eye lolling to the right and the other slinking towards the left of the throne. Addressing the vague vacancy between them, he expressed the hope that his majesty would accept his humble home. His sole purpose in building it, he averred, his only desire in constructing it, was to serve his supreme sovereign.

The Mother of the Shah rustled behind the screen and prepared herself to speak, but before she could open her mouth, the Grand Vazir had intervened.

Take the fellow at his word, he told the Shah. Relieve him of his house and turn it into a prison headquarters. A man like that deserves to be put in his place.

The queen was affronted. She was unaccustomed to defer to others in the presence of the court. The Mayor, she muttered, leaning towards the Secretary beside her, was not the only one who needed to be put in his place. This recently appointed premier with his grand title was a little too forward, in her opinion, a little too broad-shouldered and ornamented with pearls.

The Secretary of the armed forces bowed his assent. The new Vazir might also be a little too tall, he murmured. As her royal highness may have observed, his head rose to the level of his monarch's weak chin, even though he was seated below the right side of the throne.

The queen seethed with frustration. She wished her son would not so visibly droop beneath his diamonds. Even if he could not command power properly, she wished he would hold his head up a little higher. It was a matter of acute frustration to her that he was not the man she would have been. Bristling with silks, she leaned towards him from behind the screen.

It might be wise, she warned, to raise the status of the Mayor before lowering his pride. Grant him some kind of a title on my behalf, she hissed, before you sauce his pretensions too sourly. Remember his Wife has a tongue.

And so the Shah graciously accepted the Mayor's gift to the general acclaim of the toadying court, and raised his rank to that of chief of police, thereby simultaneously redefining his residence and maintaining his dignity. But to his Mother's dismay, he also authorized the Grand Vazir to name the exact nature of the man's duties. With a flourish of royal seals and repetition, he announced that the new Vazir would be instructing the new chief of police regarding the new captives he had arrested in the recent purges. The premier would decide which of them should remain under the Mayor's custody and which would be thrown into the common jail in town. The queen regent, he proclaimed, would be relieved of such onerous duties.

Her imperial highness sat very still behind the screen. She would not have minded throwing several people into the common jail in town, at that moment. How could her son do this to her? How dare he authorize the Grand Vazir to decide the fate of the poetess of Qazvin? His incompetent soldiers had not yet captured the woman, of course; they had been chasing around, all over the northern provinces, in a futile fashion for weeks, to no effect. But if the notorious rebel was going to be placed under the thumb of the Grand Vazir, her highness almost preferred them not to capture her at all. She would only allow that woman to be in the custody of the new chief of police, she thought grimly, if he was under her command and obedient to her wishes. But it was unlikely that the Mayor would take her orders now.

She felt terribly tired all of a sudden. What was the point of reading the future, she thought, if one couldn't control it? And where was the woman, no matter how literate, who would ever do that? The tedious ceremonies were only half over when she complained of a headache and left the throne room in high dudgeon, sending a flurry of apprehension through the court.

The abrupt departure of the queen regent, coinciding as it did with the compliments of the foreign diplomats to the young sovereign, was unfortunately interpreted by them as a political slight. Since neither Envoy could construe the gesture as undermining the other without also registering the snub to his personal detriment, they chose instead to read it as being mutually offensive. As a result, they submitted a joint protest to the Shah some days later. It was the only time in their diplomatic careers, except when they presented joint sympathies to the Shah after the attempt on his life, that the Russian and British ambassadors ever collaborated.

(7)

The corpse washer always said it was a perfect moment for the Shah's assassination. She had a weakness for coincidences, having devoted years to the pace of prayers and decay. Unlike the attempt on his life, which in her opinion occurred unpredictably on a pointless summer's day, she thought that his majesty's actual death, half a century later, could not have been more effectively timed. Instead of taking place at the hottest hour, when tempers were easily exacerbated, it happened on a fine spring morning when the linden trees were still in blossom and everyone was bored. It coincided precisely with the fiftieth anniversary of his majesty's reign.

The corpse washer had been among the crowds thronging the doors for days beforehand and had only managed to squeeze into the shrine at the very last moment. Most people were content to wait outside, waving petitions, expecting pardons. Some had camped near the mosque, scattering picnic rinds across the cemetery grounds; others had lined the avenue all the way from the shrine to the capital. The poor had flocked from the provinces weeks earlier, drawn by promises of free food, and the rich had been vying with one another for the past year over titles and tax exemptions. The public squares and buildings were ablaze with lights, in imitation of paradise or the capitals of Europe, and unsightly cripples had been swept clean off the streets some days before, for the celebrations alone were expected to beggar description. According to the gossips, cough medicines had been distributed among the clerics to lubricate their praises of the Shah, and the fountains had been enlarged to hold enough holy water for a general amnesty. It was rumoured among the corpse washers that even heretics might be granted a reprieve. For this was the high-water mark of half a century of tyranny; this was the day when the Shah might finally spread his largesse and his leniency among his subjects.

No one expected his liberality to extend as far as death, however. The corpse washer swore that the Shadow of God had not been expected to pay with his life to relieve the debts of his people, even though he was clad in black for the occasion, and as easy to distinguish as a maggot in a cheese. His brocaded jacket was braided with gold cord, his hair freshly dyed, and his felt hat decorated with spangled diamonds. His trousers of Manchester broadcloth were crisply tailored and immaculately creased, and his waistcoat fitted snugly, till the buttons bounced. His Mother would have been proud of him, according to the beggar woman. She had always advised her son to cut a royal figure in public, even if he had nothing to say.

The Shah could hardly have said anything in the circumstances. The two fatal shots that were fired left him speechless. The first tore a passage through his rib cage and the second wreaked havoc in his lungs. The old woman was just reminding him that wealth, power, and lordship were his when his heart began to thunder in his ears. And she had barely finished saying that poverty, homelessness, and misery were hers before the blood was thickening his tongue. He uttered a faint gasp as he stared at her. His mouth fell open, in dawning recognition, like one who saw his immortal soul rolling out of sight before his feet. But it was only the buttons. And then the words were reversed for him forever as they scattered helplessly across the floor.

Poverty and misery became his and over-lordship hers, as he tumbled headfirst into the corpse washer's lap and lay there, quietly. Staring.

(8)

Several weeks passed before the Mother of the Shah had occasion to speak to the Mayor in private. During her first term of regency he had met her frequently, for the fortunes of his family and the security of his position had always depended on her highness. But although it had been to his benefit and her advantage that he wielded rough justice in the capital, times were more unsettled now and omens less promising. A man could not live on titles alone. The young sovereign was hardly fit to wield the powers he had assumed, and the country was effectively under the sway of the Grand Vazir. Although this visit was ostensibly to compliment him on his new honours and confirm her approval of his appointment as chief of police, the Mayor was aware that the queen had summoned him to gauge his fidelity at a time of growing insecurity.

For rumours had begun to filter to the capital, soon after the coronation of the Shah, that the poetess of Qazvin might have been captured at last. No one was sure of where it had happened; no one could tell exactly how it had happened. There was even a possibility that it might not have happened, or that the witch would escape en route to the capital, but in the meantime, everyone, including the queen, was thinking of what would happen if and when she finally arrived. The Mayor was hoping that her imperial highness would not raise the subject of prisoners. His aim was to seize all the wealthiest merchants who had been rounded up and extort as much as possible from them under his custody. He had no interest in the women among them.

His private meeting with the queen regent took place in the presence of the Chief Steward of the royal bedchamber, who combed through his long, black beard with manicured fingers throughout the conversation. But although this made the newly appointed chief of police increasingly nervous, it proved to be no threat. The conversation was anodyne enough. No mention was made of the Grand Vazir's recent arrests. No reference was made to prisoners, whether male or female. But just as he was preparing to pay his last respects and began to back away from the brightness of her presence, her imperial highness suddenly called him back and asked him to convey her special greetings to his Wife.

The Mayor was startled. He was obliged to stammer his gratitude and bow. The queen allowed him to take one pace back and then added, after the briefest pause, that his Wife would doubtless agree that the instincts of the new chief of police should coincide with hers on matters of security. He bowed again, and mumbled compliments in a manner that would not be misconstrued. Permitting him another backward step, she remarked that as royal regent, she was keenly aware of the need for safety measures in the capital: she hoped his men could be called upon to replace the soldiers of the Shah in an emergency? He froze in his tracks once more, uncertain whether to bow or stammer some formula of courtesy that would enable him to leave without further commitment, but just at that moment she raised her voice and called loudly across the full length of the room. Since he could now extort what he wanted from the accused under his custody, she trumpeted, she hoped that the Mayor would defer to her judgement when it came to female prisoners; she was sure that his Wife would see eye to eye with her on the matter, she added. The Chief Steward combed through his beard with lingering fingers in the ensuing pause.

The Mayor hesitated before answering her highness. He knew that she wanted to thwart the new Vazir, whose orders he had to obey. He also knew that she wanted to promote the interests of the Secretary of the armed forces, who was her protégé. He was well aware, too, that she was referring to the general not the particular, as far as female prisoners were concerned. The newly arrested poetess of Qazvin was well acquainted with the sister and the wife of her ally, the Secretary, and the queen wanted to be able to control what happened in his *anderoun*. But what unnerved him most was that she was using his Wife to blackmail him over the issue. It left the chief of police in the most ticklish position. And still far from the door.

The proper thing to do, thought the Mayor, as he bowed still lower and took another step back, was to keep the troublesome woman under his own roof, if the Grand Vazir demanded it. Even though it would be a headache, he thought, straightening up nervously, and his Wife would never let him hear the end of it. The more tempting alternative, he thought, lowering his head again and retreating another step, would be to agree to place her in the custody of the Secretary of the armed forces, for the queen would control that *anderoun* in a way she could not influence his. This, he thought, straightening up with relief, would allow him to avoid conflict

with his Wife and to gain favour with her highness at the same time. But if
he disobeyed the premier and deferred to the queen's protégé, would he not
be jeopardizing his loyalty to the Shah?

The Mayor almost stumbled at the thought. He had no desire to be
hauled before his sovereign as a traitor any more than he wanted to antagonize his old patroness, if he could help it. He certainly did not want to upset
his Wife. And the last thing he wanted was a woman prisoner in the house.
But business was business. If he wanted to reap any rewards from these
arrests, he would have to conform to the rules of those who held the reins of
authority now. He would jeopardize his loyalty to the Shah, he concluded,
if he did not obey his majesty's favourite.

A fraction of a second passed before he cleared his throat and stammered his pledge of obedience to the Mother of the Shah. Would that
he might be forever permitted, he declaimed, would that he might always
have the honour of remaining a prisoner of her highness' wisdom, a slave
to her good pleasure, a captive of her will. Let the whole world defer to the
queen's judgement, whether about female prisoners or anything else, he
added. And took a deep breath.

It was a dangerous thing to do. The Mother of the Shah was acute when
it came to registering vacillation. She imagined disparagement in delay and
suspected criticism whenever praise appeared to be too faint. Now she felt
her regency tip beneath the weight of the Mayor's breath. She knew that
he expected her to bargain on the open market and was aware that there
were other buyers competing for his loyalty. But she was a seasoned war-
rior in this old war; she had her private arsenal of power. She had wanted
the female prisoner to be held in the home of her protégé, but if the creature ended up in the Mayor's custody, she knew of ways to penetrate his
anderoun too. She was well aware of the social aspirations of his Wife and
of how to exploit them. As the door opened, she repeated her expression of
good wishes to that lady. And then, even as the Mayor edged out, inquired
with irritating loudness, after his youngest born.

How was the charming youth, she shrilled, in penetrating tones. Was
he of marriageable age yet? Was he betrothed to anyone of distinction?

The Mayor glared at the carpets, tongue-tied. He would have liked to slam the door on the faces of the smirking chamberlains who opened it for him. Or else whip them out of his way, as the Chief Steward bowed him out. Everyone knew that his son was a disappointment to him; everyone knew he had a distinct lack of interest in his father's line of work. Why didn't the queen inquire after his daughters' prospects? But she was ruthless.

Please would he present her compliments to his Wife and her sincere respects and hopes that a profitable and appropriate alliance might be quickly contracted with their most respected family. The Mayor's residence must not only be remembered as a jail: his house should go down in history as a perfect place for weddings too, she sang, as he turned tail and fled.

(9)

Although no one could agree over the Shah's last words, women claimed that the shrine where he was shot was a perfect place for an assassination. The mosque itself, situated some five miles south of the capital, had been constructed some centuries before in honour of a saint, and the shrine, besides being a haven for beggars and a home for corpse washers, had become famous in more recent times as a sanctuary for those fleeing from injustice during the old king's reign. But once the laws of safe asylum were abrogated after the present Shah's coronation, the place ceased to provide either physical or spiritual immunity to the populace. It was gradually transformed from a picnic site into a morgue, and by the time his majesty's popularity plummeted half a century later, it had become an ideal place to kill a king.

The shrine was frequented, in particular, by members of the female sex because it was associated with the favourite of the Shah. He had given his heart to this concubine after being spurned, so they said, by the poetess of Qazvin, and had loved her immoderately during the first decade of his reign. Soon after the courtesan's arrival at the court, he had raised her status to chief wife, and once she had given birth to a son, he had distinguished her as mother of the Heir Apparent. His own Mother's thoughts

darkened perceptibly after that. Sex, in the *anderoun*, was normally inde-
terminate for the first years of a baby's life or else identified as female,
which came to the same thing. Mortality rates were such that children
were obliged to live beyond the age of seven to be proven boys, and it was
exceptional to name an heir apparent so young. Besides, her highness took
great offence at having her own rank and authority undermined within the
intimacy of the *anderoun* after having it threatened in court and country by
the poetess of Qazvin. She was so upset that she was ready to pronounce
the Shah's favourite a heretic too.

But the precedence was short-lived. The child's precipitous advance led
to a premature downfall, and he succumbed to a grave malady in his sixth
year. Since nothing could be done for a brain fever with political dimensions, the little boy failed quickly, his little body arching like a bow, and
stiffening with every spasm. He died between the lull of midday and the stupor of an afternoon, when the spirit looks for natural outlets, and his mother
began to cough blood from that time on. She tried to put a brave face on it;
she tried to dance for the king again and pretended a few pregnancies. But
her heart was not in it. Her laughter became caustic as she succumbed to
opium supplied by the Mother of the Shah. Since there had been little love
lost between the two women, no one was surprised when the courtesan died
within the year of her child's demise.

The Shah was absent on a hunting expedition when it happened. He
fled from the court because he could not bear to hear her last words, so the
women said. Instead of honouring his favourite with a lavish funeral, he
gave her a garish tomb instead. On his return, after the mourning period
was over, he constructed this mausoleum for her, south of the capital: a
tomb of blue-veined marble all adorned with gold, in the courtyard of the
mosque dedicated to a saint. It seemed an appropriate gesture of conjugal
fidelity. True love was priceless, after all. The widowed Queen of England
had built a similar monument in honour of her late lamented consort. So
the Shah decided to follow the current fashion for gravestones. But his grief
cost his countrymen dear. He spent more on one woman dead than on
keeping the rest of them alive.

As a result, death became an excuse for a day's outing from the capital. For decades afterwards, women flocked in droves to visit the marble tomb south of the city. They loved to gossip about the courtesan who had become a queen, the dancing girl who had given the king the dare on her own deathbed. She was doomed by marriage and undone by motherhood, they murmured; she had reversed the roles of womankind, like the poetess of Qazvin. But his majesty had loved her in spite of it. Or was it because of it, they wondered? They argued about his favourite all afternoon, while their little ones played in the cemetery.

By the end of his majesty's reign, the mausoleum had become more popular than the shrine itself and was permanently covered with the shells of cracked pumpkin seeds. If the jubilee celebrations were launched here, it may only have been because it was so easy to ensure the participation of a crowd in such a place. In fact, most women believed that the assassin had chosen to hide beside the courtyard door because he knew the favourite of the Shah would lure the king in that direction. Although his majesty built a railway line to the shrine, for his exclusive use in the last years of his reign, the velvet comforts of an upholstered private carriage and the speed of a steam engine adorned with brass were less effective than the arts of the courtesan. She was the magnet that drew him down from the capital, they said. Push and pull, push and pull, it was all games with her, sighed the ladies; it was all provocation and flirtation to the very jaws of death. Hardly anyone besides the queen could beat her at it. Since she couldn't die in his arms, it would've pleased her mightily to give him the last come hither. Hadn't he been moving towards her tomb, when he was shot? Hadn't he called out his favourite's name the moment that he died?

The debate about the Shah's last words was never resolved. The corpse washer claimed that he fell between her legs, like a turd from a mule, with his mouth still moving. There was no doubt about it: he was trying to say something just as he died. But perhaps, after half a century of empty promises, it was understandable if nobody was listening to that last grand gurgle. For no one could agree over what his majesty actually said.

Some were certain that he called out to his favourite wife when he died.

Others swore that he cried for his Mother at that moment. But the corpse washer insisted that the name he breathed as he fell in her lap was that of the poetess of Qazvin.

(10)

The poetess of Qazvin was known by a variety of names. She had been given the usual one at birth, the one given to all girls of pious family, the holy name of the Prophet's daughter. But as long as her maternal grandmother, who shared this distinction, remained alive, she was called after the first heroine to accept Islam, the Mother of Believers. Later in her career, she was crowned with golden laurels and branded with labels that shared nothing in common but their inconsistency. The governor of Baghdad praised her as a most chaste lady, while the high priests of Qazvin slandered her as a woman of ill repute. Scholars in the theological centres of Najaf and Karbala either quoted her as if she were an oracle or damned her for a witch. Some said her beauty was a solace to the eyes and her mind pure beyond compare; others called her a heretic, a murderess, and a whore. But by the time she was arrested in the first winter of the young Shah's reign, both her admirers and detractors were forced to agree that none of the traditional names of womankind could sum her up. She was admitted to be the calamity of the age.

It was an age marked by calamities, and she symbolized them all. It was a country shaken by revolt, wracked by the demand for change, but when the news of her capture was confirmed in Tehran, it shocked the whole nation. For though she was not the only woman to be blamed in history, she was the first to be arrested in the purges of the new Grand Vazir.

The soldiers tracked her down, after a whole year's search, in the far-thest corner of the realm. One cold dawn, after hunting her mile by mile across the bleak stretch of several provinces, they surrounded a small vil-lage where she had been given shelter, bribed the inhabitants with tea and sugar, and lured her maid out of hiding with a copy of the most Holy Book. They promised that the girl would be unmolested, if her mistress gave her-self up immediately. They even agreed to leave the inhabitants of the village in peace if she submitted to arrest. Although she gave in to their demands with the greatest docility in the world, the soldiers of the Shah broke their oaths on the grounds that they could not read the book on which they swore them. They torched the huts on their way out of the village and plundered the last orchards bare before they left. But they allowed the maid to serve her mistress till they reached the capital.

It was a difficult journey, at the onset of winter. The biting wind glittered with salt on the bleak plains and the paths were perilous with brigands. Soon after they started, relentless autumn rains forced the soldiers to take shelter in a miserable post house on the outskirts of a village, for the riverbed which served them as a road had turned into a mud ravine. One of the mules lost its footing and was swept away in the torrent. The fresh horses they had procured in the previous village were already lamed by stones, and the next day's weather did not promise to be fairer than this one. Tempers frayed, the soldiers grew fractious as night drew on, and when it was discovered that the wretched post house was infested by venomous bugs that covered their bodies with swollen welts, they began to blame the prisoner for their bad luck. It was all her fault, they muttered, that they were itching so unbearably. It was her fault that they were so wet and cold. Let her light her own fire, they growled, since she had quenched theirs; let her fetch her own water, since she had brought a deluge on their heads. Let her be damned for her evil eye!

When her maid braved the weather and stepped out of the rickety *howdah* to pick her way to the village well, several of the men dared one another to follow the girl. She could hardly be called a pretty creature with those scabs all over her arms, but female flesh did not need reading in the dark. Two of the boldest, seeking redress for their privations, crept out of the sodden camp and trailed after the girl through the pelting rain. Their plan was to grab her, gag her mouth, and rape her, huggermugger, in the mud.

But just as they prepared to seize on her, they heard a sudden noise behind them. Just as the girl leaned over the mouth of the well, they heard a cry, which did not come from her. It was the briefest sound, like the faint start of a word, the call of a night bird, but it chilled their blood. The trembling maid whirled round, dropping the bucket down the well with a sharp intake of breath. The soldiers froze in their tracks when they realized she was not even looking at them. Their limbs grew slack and they swallowed their oaths as they glanced behind them.

The female prisoner stood on the muddy bank, staring down at them. Her robes were wet; her braids were loose. Her head was bared beneath the rain, but what shocked them most was her naked face. Her eyes were fixed on them as they stood in the shadow of the well, and her lips were moving.

Calmly, coldly, and with terrible quietness, she began to curse them. According to the strict rules of theological debate more terrible than physical force, she cursed them. Using the dread proof by execration, she cursed the soldiers hollow: she annihilated them with oaths; she swore their lust to perdition; she damned the venality of their souls.

The two men drew back in terror. The sheer force of the woman's words flashed through the dark like a bolt of lightning and unmanned them. They turned tail and fled. She must be a witch, they muttered, to have read their intentions. The bitch was a caged tiger: her words had claws! No wonder she was accused of blasphemy, they whispered; no wonder she had been condemned for heresy. She'd proven subtle in the past, they told the others, so they had better watch out with that one; she'd escaped from her father's house once before in a bundle of dirty laundry, humped on the back of a common washerwoman. No wonder she had to be kept under the tightest security. Perhaps she was a *jinn*! The soldiers began to fear the prisoner more than they feared the Mother of the Shah. They were very careful after that, to leave her maid alone.

But during the tedious weeks that followed, that woman's strange ways began to work on them. She had raised her voice against them once, and for one reason only, but never did so again. Her meekness confused them. When they abused her, she offered no resistance but a query as to what, exactly, their words might mean. When they swore at her, during the long winter journey to the snow-bound capital, she asked them, politely, to repeat themselves, as though she had not heard them. She shamed them, and imperceptibly, their attitudes began to change.

Although they treated her with surly indifference and callous insolence to start with, they found themselves obliged to restrain their vulgarities as time passed. They had refused her the bare essentials at first and had denied her any comforts, but after she shared what little she had with them in times of want, wonder began to sweeten the tea she offered them so freely. When some among them began to limp on the long foot march back to the capital, she provided them with salves that gave reverence to their pains and drank to their health with the clear waters of sincerity. They noticed that she treated them with the same compassion which she extended towards her maid, and after a while, they were forced to behave with similar respect towards her. Her oaths had been most dreadful but her courtesies proved more dangerous, in the end.

A few were of the opinion that her tea must be drugged and suspected her dry bread to have bewitching powers. For her prayers conjured the faces of their women in the fire; her chanting summoned the voices of their children from the wind. Some even whispered that if they survived the journey it would only be because of her, for though they may have feared her ill omens in the beginning, they trusted her good angels in the end. When they were engulfed by blizzards in the mountains, a troop of spirits seemed to ride in attendance round her, bearing aloft white standards to guide them. When the bleak sun rose over the plains on wintry mornings, it seemed to carry counsels of comfort, messages of cheer which she gladly shared with them. After a while the soldiers swore that she could read the future as well as the most Holy Book, for she saw writing scored across the desert landscape and seemed to sense the king's couriers coming towards them from the distant horizons. She had a remarkable alacrity in anticipation.

When they questioned her about it, she laughed and said it was just like reading. If you only look at the word that's under your noses, she answered, you'll never see the connection with what came before and what comes next. If you only see what's happening now, you'll never understand the link between yesterday and tomorrow. Let your eyes move with the wings of a bird across the page and you'll remember the future.

Since most of the men were illiterate, she taught them how to read, step by step, along the journey. It was not easy. They reddened, at first, when she showed them how to pull the syllables apart with their tongues; they did not immediately believe her when she assured them that the letters would come together again, in a blink of an eye. They scratched their heads in wonder at the thought of holding words in their minds even as they let them go. But they swore they saw the shape of things unfolding on the mountain paths even as she chanted of them. They were awestruck to find the alphabet unrolling like a road before them all the way to the capital. The poetess of Qazvin was an excellent teacher and fastidiously clean, they said; she was fearless, and never complained of discomfort. She was like no woman they had met before.

By the time they reached the outskirts of the city at the foot of the snow-capped mountains of Damavand, the escort had fallen under their captive's spell. They were quite devoted to her and vied for the privilege of riding next to her *howdah*. They escorted her through the gates more like a princess than a prisoner, and when required to hand over their charge on their arrival, all of them, with one accord, refused to do so. They would have remained her guards even under house arrest, had she permitted it. But she turned them all away.

They had risked their reputation for her quite enough, she said. She had jeopardized their future by teaching them how to read the past so let them protect themselves, for the present.

(11)

The question as to whether royal escorts acted primarily to protect them-selves or to guard the king was a thorny one. During the protracted trial that took place in the capital after the assassination of the Shah, the ethical and political dimensions of this issue exercised the minds of those in both the civil and religious courts. If his majesty's guards were only concerned with their own safety, were they just as guilty as the assassin? If they had been motivated by a desire to protect their king, might they be considered innocent despite their failure to fulfill their task?

History had to be consulted. When the despicable youths had attacked the sovereign half a century before, the Shah's escort had been hopelessly inept. They had vaguely heard the airguns pop in the distance; they had dimly noticed the echo of shots in the dusty air; but they were too far away to understand exactly what had happened and had no idea how to react. They simply gawped through the heat and the haze at the clot of young men gathering round the Shah and stared uncomprehendingly as they attacked their sovereign. He was obliged to yell for help before his escort even bestirred themselves. It was a shocking indignity. Their incompetence was such that her imperial highness suspected their intelligence as well as their loyalty.

The case was clear as far as the Mother of the Shah was concerned: the men were culpable. Had they really been as willing as they protested to sacrifice themselves for their sovereign, then they should have proved it by their actions. But since their actions only demonstrated their lack of will, they had to be sacrificed, despite the survival of the king. Their punishment could be used to prove his significance to his people. On their return to the capital, the first thing she did was order the guards to be bastinadoed for failing the Shah in his hour of need. Even if they were not directly involved in the attempt, they could have been collaborating with regicides, she said; they might have been under the influence of heretics. And then, on the grounds that they may also have been members of the original regiment that conducted the poetess of Qazvin to the capital three winters before, she had them executed after flaying their feet.

Fifty years later, however, when the assassin fired at the Shah at point blank range inside the shrine, his escort behaved with far greater competence. The royal equerry may have failed when his majesty's life was in danger, but his guards certainly knew how to act on the occasion of his death. Even if they did not manage to save him, at least they preserved their own reputations. After the first shot, they were somewhat nonplussed, but with the second, they leapt into action. They identified the assassin, kicked the corpse washer aside, and circled their sovereign instinctively, in self-defence. No one could fault them for their speed or their proficiency, except perhaps the corpse washer, whose ribs were broken by their boots.

History is filled with screams that are best ignored. Had they been questioned for brutality, the guards would have said they were only following orders. The Prime Minister had hissed at them to shove the beggar woman out of the way this instant. He had ordered them to lift the lolling Shah back into an upright position as fast as possible, so that no one would notice, no one would guess he was dead. He had commanded them to move his majesty out of the mosque, now, double quick. As a result of their timely intervention, the king's last words were forgotten, but his limp body was instantly restored to dignity. He was wedged between his guards and marched smartly out of the shrine before anyone could notice his dangling feet.

The corpse washer expected to be arrested, momentarily, however. The escort was exonerated but she assumed her crime was worse than murder. She had been so frightened that she had dropped her veil as soon as the Shah was shot, and exposed her face to view.

❨ 12 ❩

When the poetess of Qazvin arrived at the gates of the capital, her face was hidden behind the curtains of her *howdah*. It was only on the strength of the word of the commanding officer that the gatekeepers permitted her to pass. No one saw her and no one heard her speak.

Her entourage was stopped on the other side of the gates by a group of men, brandishing clubs and sticks. The Mayor's thugs had come to conduct the new captive personally to the prison headquarters and insisted that the prisoner be handed over to them. The commanding officer of the escort protested that he had been given prior instructions to deliver his charge directly to the chief of police himself. A quarrel ensued and voices were raised, but the passenger inside the weather-beaten *howdah* still did not say a word.

After some moments, however, their harangue was interrupted by the arrival of a courtly gentleman with a special briefing from the queen. The luxurious beard of the Chief Steward of the royal bedchamber did double-service in hiding his horse-like features and proclaiming his identity, but his mandate further added to the conflict. He was opposed to the prisoner being handed over to the custody of the Mayor, with or without an escort. In outright contradiction to the instructions of the Grand Vazir, he ordered the Shah's soldiers to conduct the poetess of Qazvin straight to the residence of the Secretary of the armed forces, under his own command.

This posed a thorny dilemma for everyone. The Mayor was answerable to the Grand Vazir, whereas the Secretary, who was known to be the latter's rival, was a protégé of the queen. To prefer the demands of one to the instructions of the other involved a political risk of considerable proportions. Since the soldiers of the Shah were willing to concede to a different destination but refused to relinquish their charge to anyone else, the litter came to a complete standstill. Everyone joined in the argument, which no one could resolve. Voices rose and altercations ensued at the gates, but the captive herself remained aloof from the argument, much to the disappointment of the gathering crowds.

The flow of traffic was much impeded by definitions of authority that day. Certain said the king was the rightful ruler and had to be obeyed, once his instructions were known. Others feared his first Vazir was actually in command and dreaded the obstruction of his orders. Not a few believed that the queen still held the reins of power in court, but whether or not she was in control of the streets, the two escorts could not agree about their final destination. Since argument failed to clear the gates, it was finally decided to extend the problem through them, and a burgeoning mob crowded round the curtained litter as it wound its way through the narrow alleys, following the silent prisoner with hoots and shouts of imprecation into the town.

News of the prisoner's arrival spread like wildfire through the city. People began to flock out of the baths and the bazaars to catch a glimpse of her *howdah*. A crier ran ahead of the double entourage in an attempt to clear the streets, and when the Grand Vazir reviewed the troops with the Shah that morning, he found himself whistling to the empty air, because no one was on the rooftops to watch the military parade. Half the city had gathered around the Mayor's house and the other half were at the gates of the Secretary, waiting to see the poetess of Qazvin.

The Mayor's house was the first stop, but as the swollen entourage turned into the alley leading to the prison headquarters, it was forced to a halt once more. A third escort of twelve mounted guards, wearing the extravagant livery of the Envoy Extraordinary and Plenipotentiary, was attempting to cross the street at that very moment. The British ambassador had obliged his wife to follow the strictest regulations each time she wished to stroll in the garden. She had to sit in a covered *howdah*, veiled from top to toe, and traverse the twenty paces from the Legation buildings to the grounds across the street, flanked by a dozen mounted guards in Gurkha uniform. Their appearance was less imposing than the flamboyant entourage of Cossacks that was daily paraded round the town by the Russian ambassador, but the Colonel was acutely sensitive to questions of protocol and had determined that his wife's constitutional could serve diplomacy. This morning, however, the British escort also came to a standstill in the middle of the alley.

When she peeped through her crimson curtains to see what was happening, the Envoy's wife saw the corner of another *howdah* wedged against her own. It was a rough cart, mud-splattered with travel. She could not tell who was in it, for it was thickly draped, but she could hear the mule on which it had been strapped, loudly braying, as soldiers shouted, guards cursed, and her own escort protested. Everyone was giving instructions to everyone else. Whips cracked, rank was evoked, dignities were offended, and arguments rose to a high pitch, but no one moved in the congested alley. For in addition to the conflict of escorts, the gatekeeper of the prison headquarters was also proving stubborn. He claimed that he had been told by the Mayor not to open the gates to anyone. The poor fellow was so taken up with keeping the soldiers out that he was slow to register who he was keeping in, and the Mayor had to knock sense into the idiot's skull before he was able to force his way through to the alley.

By the time he pushed his way into the crowd, the uproar had become infernal. The Mayor, who was determined to obey the command of the Grand Vazir, was furious with his thugs for ignoring his instructions and even forgot to stammer as he bellowed up and down the alley. His Wife, who was in favour of conforming to the wishes of the Mother of the Shah and did not mind airing her opinions whichever side of a wall she happened to be on, added to the rumpus by scolding her husband loudly from within the compound. Once the gates were flung wide and the gatekeeper lay sprawling in the mud, their domestic quarrel had risen to a political crescendo.

The Englishwoman, caught between the two contending forces, was experiencing the most frightening sensations in her *howdah*. There was nothing she could say, surrounded by this fracas of yelling men and beasts. There was nothing she could do either, trapped behind the flimsy curtains of her litter. She could only hope that her husband would come to her rescue, and when that did not happen, panic caught her by the throat. Her heart was beating wildly and she could hardly breathe. Her head began to spin as prayers thickened her tongue.

The Envoy's wife had found it difficult to pray since coming to Persia. After seeing the aching throats of minarets lift high against these turquoise skies, after hearing the unearthly voice of the *muezzin* rise up above the dun-coloured domes of this city, the familiar words no longer came so easily to her. Why, she wondered, should truth be confined to bells? How, she brooded, could salvation be restricted to her whispers, when the whole world seemed to be reverberating? Was sense confined to a single syntax? Did truth reside in one language alone? In the presence of the worthy bishops of Chaldea, she merely mouthed what her husband piously intoned. And trapped in that chaos of men and mules, she felt dry to the very lips of her soul.

But just as she felt she was about to faint, a voice rose above the cacophony in the alley. The voice of a woman, different from all the rest, lifted up from the *howdah* beside her. A calm voice, closer to her than her life's vein, and equally vibrant. It soared above words and letters, it transcended the murmur of syllables and sounds. Like the call of a trumpet, like the summons of a bugle, it cleared the air of contradictions. And it pierced her heart like a prayer.

The prisoner did not say much. She ordered her own escort to give way. She instructed the Mayor's men to defer to them. And she told the British escort to step back and to await their turn. Three or four words she uttered, no more, but they gave the impression of coming from the highest authority in the land. The knot dissolved. The soldiers of the Shah stood aside without demur and the Mayor's men stepped forward, as the Legation guards crossed over to the garden. The gatekeeper, who was known to be a simpleton, cheered enthusiastically at that moment and her ladyship, jolting forward in the red-curtained litter, wept with pure relief.

The crowds dispersed with some reluctance after this anticlimax. The sound of a woman is far less gratifying than the sight of her, in the last analysis, and conflict more interesting than resolution. Since people had been cheated of seeing the heretic, they were more than ready to condemn her for being heard. In the days and weeks that followed, most agreed that a little less talk and a little more blood should have been spilt in the alley that day. Most echoed ecclesiastical opinion that the poetess of Qazvin had overstepped the bounds. Not only had she caused rather than resolved the congestion when she entered the capital, but she had no business to be ordering everyone about as though she were the highest authority in the land!

The question of authority was a hot topic in the coffeehouses that evening too. When the commanding officer relinquished his charge at the prison headquarters, he was reprimanded roundly by the Mayor for disobeying the highest authority in the land. The Chief Steward also reminded him that he had failed in his duty to the highest authority in the land. On his return to the garrisons, he discovered that his entire regiment had also been put on remand without pay for the rest of that winter, by the highest authority in the land. It was not hard to read the future then, for the queen regent never forgave those who forgot who was the highest authority in the land.

She was furious with the Mayor for preferring the Grand Vazir's instructions to her own. She threatened to cast the Secretary aside if her protégé did not protect her interests more effectively, and she sent word to the Chief Steward that she did not wish to see him until further notice. She was very upset that the poetess of Qazvin had slipped between her fingers.

When the Chief Steward presented his compliments to her highness later that evening, begging to assure her of his undying fidelity, offering the hope that she might remember his past services with generosity, and urging her to allow him to still serve her in the future, she would have dismissed him in a fit of pique. The only way he could win back the queen's favour was to compensate for her disappointments, all night long, in the royal carriage.

❨ 13 ❩

The Shah had barely expired in the shrine before he was propped up against the cushions in his royal carriage and returned to town. His Prime Minister placed a pair of dark spectacles on his majesty's nose, to maintain appearances, and sat next to the dead man, conversing with him, dry-mouthed, all along the avenue of linden trees to the capital. He also instructed the coachman to take his time, to give no sign of unseemly haste or undue urgency, and even managed to wave a stiffening arm to the cheering multitudes they passed en route, while keeping a tight hold on the puppet king to stop him from toppling over.

The arts of diplomacy are demanding. The Shah's last Prime Minister was his only one in fifty years to have survived the sovereign. The first, who had presumed the title of a Grand Vazir, was put to death by a royal order a year before the botched attempt on the life of the young king occurred. The second retained his powers during the summer massacres that followed, only to be driven from office through the machinations of the *anderoun* during the sovereign's second decade in power. The third was reduced to penury when the Shah returned from his trip to the West, and there had been a period during which the Shadow of God reverted to ancient customs and refused to appoint any ministers at all, just to spite his Mother's protégés. It was only after her death, in the third decade of his reign, that he submitted to counsel once again.

By the time the last Prime Minister was appointed, his powers of office were reduced to the attributes of an impecunious tailor, for the Shah had ensured that the cut of his cloth was wholly insufficient to the girth of his task. His only civic achievement, during a ministry marked by rising discontent, was the grand gala he organized to celebrate the jubilee of the king's interminable reign. Let your people have a party, he had quipped in the days leading up to the celebrations, so that they will no longer think of having a people's party, he added lamely. But after the assassination and during that slow, macabre ride back to the capital in the royal carriage, the Prime Minister rued the day that he had offered the sovereign such democratic counsel.

He had been having a fit of the fidgets in the shrine just before the first shot rang out. His new Western-style jacket felt tight under the arms, and the idea of spending the rest of the day in his majesty's deaf company was making him feel murderous. As a distraction, he had started to imagine various ways to kill the king. He stuffed him headfirst into a cannon as the royal escort proceeded with all due pomp towards the mosque, and he lighted the fuse with lingering deliberation as the Shah entered the building. He tied him to a pair of poplar trees as the priest intoned the prayers, and tore him limb from limb as he bent to kiss the iron railings of the shrine. When his majesty began to show signs of boredom and glanced idly towards the door leading out to his wife's tomb, he pierced his nostrils neatly with a metal hook and dragged him back at the end of a halter. He did not see why the Shah should escape from his own jubilee.

But with the first shot, the Minister woke from his reverie. At the sight of the king sprawling headfirst in the beggar's lap, he was convinced his worst fantasies had come true. It was only the tightness of his jacket that recalled him to reality and galvanized him into action. He ordered the guards to seize the assassin, get rid of the beggar, and hide the Shah from view. And then calling for air, and the doors to be opened, he shouted that his majesty was feeling faint as they hustled the king, limp and lolling, into the royal carriage. By the time he was rolling back to town in the company of the corpse, the Minister's tongue was cleaving to the roof of his mouth. He knew that if he was to avoid blame, rumours had to be repressed at all costs.

No one should know the exact circumstances of the assassination. Although the sound of the shots verified the general location, it would be best, the Prime Minister thought, to keep the visual details vague. It was shocking enough to kill his majesty, but to shoot him headfirst into the lap of a beggar was a disgrace. No one, on any account, should know about the woman. It was enough to confirm that the king had been assassinated in the shrine.

But no one should know that his majesty was dead yet either; no one should know that he had already been killed. Although he knew it would provoke the anger of angels, to say nothing of clerics, to carry a corpse back into the capital, he had to take that risk. The reason why dead heretics were thrown over moats or into wells outside the city gates was to dissuade people from retrieving them. Half a century before, the body of an English officer had been conducted into the city as if he were still alive, in order to avoid riots among the pious. To carry a wounded king back to town could possibly be an accident, but to kill him and then hustle his dead body through the gates was heresy. The Prime Minister did not want to be accused of violating religion, but what alternative was there?

In fact, the less that was known about his own role in this affair the better. He certainly did not want anyone to question him too closely about his activity in the shrine. He dreaded the grim fate of ministers before him and did not want to pay the price of serving the deaf despot to the end. The Crown Prince would arrive in the capital surrounded by old resentments and new advisers, and he did not want to be blamed for fifty years of misrule.

Finally, he brooded, white-lipped, on all that he did not know. Each time the carriage fell into a rut or jolted over a stone, the Minister's heart missed a beat. Each time the sovereign rocked or sagged on his seat, his spectacles sliding off his royal nose, he shuddered at that look fixed in the Shah's dead eye. What did a soul see at the moment of its crossing? he wondered. Was there resurrection after such a passing? What happened when one died?

Answers to some kinds of questions can only be read backwards, which may be why the Minister glanced over his shoulder so often on the way into town. He could not read the future, so he fixed his eye on the past in order to see the road ahead. And as a result he had invented a fine story by the time they returned to the capital. In fact, the story had started circulating before the carriage had half turned around. It was being bruited about already, as his subjects spilled out of the mosque, that his majesty must have had a minor accident. Just like the first time. It was said, as everyone surged back in the wake of the royal carriage into town, that he must have grazed his leg and would recover soon, as he did the first time. The Shah was in no greater danger, people averred, than when there had been an attempt on his life before. The first time.

It's usually easier to repeat an old tale than to invent a new one, but even the best told lies can prove short-sighted before the long truths of eternity. Facts were disregarded in favour of fictions fifty years before, but the women of the royal harem guessed something was amiss as soon as they were told the stories. Besides, they had invented so many tales themselves that they could tell a falsehood blindfold by then. They began to wail as soon as they heard of the accident.

Tears were a profession with the Shah's wives and concubines. They had been known to weep from sheer boredom if there was no reason for despair, but when they suspected a cause, their cries could bring down the palace walls. The Prime Minister had barely laid the corpse in the reception room before they were assailing its doors. He had not even called the doctors in for official verification, before they were demanding to know if their lord was dead. Although he had hoped to delay the dreadful proclamation until the Crown Prince had been duly informed, the royal widows demanded precedence, and long before the official news was released, their ululations were echoing across the town.

There was no alternative but to hand the body over to them.

(14)

"Hand the woman over to me!" protested the angry mullah as he stormed out of the king's reception rooms. "A husband is the only man who has to right to touch her body!"

The Mother of the Shah heartily agreed with him. A heretic's body needed very careful handling, in her opinion. And she told the prisoner's husband as much that very afternoon.

The arrival of this cleric had caused quite a stir in the capital during the first winter of the young Shah's reign. He had come in the wake of his wife's capture some few weeks earlier, and was accusing her of his father's murder, which had taken place the year before. He had petitioned the old Shah for restitution on these same grounds once already, and he was now back again, a second time, to demand justice from the new one. He insisted, as husband of the accused and as a son of the deceased—to say nothing of his rights as a member of the clergy—that he was the only person authorized to judge, condemn, and punish this woman for her crimes.

The embittered cleric hung about the antechambers of the Shah for several days, waiting for an audience with his majesty. When it had finally been granted, he was not greatly satisfied with his reception, for the Shah had heard of the case before and had no patience with the plaintiff's caterwauling. He was also fed up with the way everyone was taking charge of the female prisoner. His Mother had interfered in the conditions of her imprisonment without his permission; his Grand Vazir had assumed that he would be interrogating her like the other prisoners arrested in the purges, without deferring to his sovereign's opinion; and now here was her husband, insisting that the ecclesiastic courts should take over the case, demanding that she be handed over to the clergy. The Shah decided he was going to take over. He told everyone, in the presence of the cleric, that he could not come to any decision until he saw the woman himself.

The priest had been greatly offended. He had stalked out of the throne room, not only cursing his wife but muttering against his majesty as well. The queen had found it necessary to invite the man into her private apartments in order to mitigate the consequences of his disappointing interview. She had entertained him lavishly and undertaken to be his advocate, whatever the Shah's decision might be regarding the poetess of Qazvin. She had given him her word to support the clergy and concurred that a woman should definitely be handed over to her husband.

The Shah lost his temper when he heard of it. Why had his Mother interfered again? he grumbled. He did so wish she would not undermine his decisions!

His Mother's eyes widened, innocently. Decisions? she inquired. She thought his majesty had said that he could not come to any decisions yet.

As the Grand Vazir said, responded the Shah, loftily, her imperial highness diminished his authority by intervening like this.

The queen could not bear him quoting his Grand Vazir. She pointed out that there would have been no need for her intervention if her son had acted more wisely. When an angry husband wants to take revenge against his wife, one should avoid making a jealous cuckold of him too.

As she had anticipated, her son did not know whether to be flattered or offended by her insinuations. He resolved his uncertainty by becoming sarcastic. If a man is jealous, he sneered, it's only because the woman he marries is cleverer than himself.

It was not very clever of his majesty to send this particular man away furious with his monarch as well as his wife, the queen retorted.

Fellows like that are furious by profession, scoffed her son.

All the more reason to be wary of him, was his Mother's reply.

The man's accusations were obviously vindictive, continued the Shah. Retribution surely had some limit. That cleric's pride had been bitten, he said, and there was little one could do about the barking of a rabid dog. At which point his majesty extended the metaphor to the point of no return and in a manner that might have caused serious offence but for the excuse of youth.

The queen pursed her lips. Her regency depended on her son's immaturity, but it had to be admitted that while callowness might be permissible, vulgarity was unpardonable in a king.

There was no reason to antagonize the clergy, she told him, crisply. This man belonged to a powerful religious faction. His whole family were either bigots or heretics, so it would be safer to make a friend rather than an enemy of him. Stay out of his domestic scandals, she advised.

That's why he had sent the fellow packing, the Shah retorted, hotly. A domestic brawl did not merit a sovereign's judgement.

She knew he was quoting his damned Vazir again. He was so obsessed by the new premier that there was even talk of him marrying the man into the royal *anderoun*.

But there were surely other ways less crude, she purred, to exert his majesty's sovereign rights. There were other means his majesty might use, less vulgar than this. She paused.

The Shah waited for her to continue. She did not. His Mother always managed to have him ask her to interfere in his affairs. What ways, he finally said. What means?

This allegation of heresy, for example, continued the queen. If her son exploited it more intelligently, he could befriend the priests instead of causing offence; he could use the charge to win their support instead of antagonizing them. Should she make discreet inquiries, perhaps, from a few carefully chosen members of the religious community? Could she inquire on his behalf about the possibilities of re-education? Intelligence could sometimes be misguided—

Discreet? he repeated. What kind of re-education? He did not altogether trust his Mother's definitions of intelligence. What was she suggesting that they could do to the female prisoner, exactly, he inquired, and why was she so keen to butter up the priests?

She smiled soothingly. She was only offering to make preliminary inquiries, seek some sort of compromise on his behalf. She only wanted to act in his best interests. But perhaps the Shah preferred to take on the ecclesiastic courts himself and deal with the priests directly? She certainly had no intention of interfering. His father had maintained good relations with the clerics all his life. Would he like to take over the case personally?

The Shah yawned. There was no point in pursuing an argument once the queen brought his father into it, and besides, he suspected that the prisoner's husband was one of those nit-picking theologians with whom the only good relations were none at all. Jurisprudence was such a bore, he whined. Did he really have to take on the ecclesiastic courts? He would rather not.

She told him not to worry about it, then. She had her own ways to deal with nit-picking theologians. She promised to take the matter into her own hands and resolve it with the greatest discretion in the world. Let him rest assured. The Mayor was busy with his prisoners, the Grand Vazir had far more important things to do, and this was only woman's business, after all.

(15)

The private funeral and provisional burial of the Shah, which took place in the orange groves the day after the shooting in the shrine, was a high-pitched, female affair. Apart from the Prime Minister and a few well-heeled eminences, allied by marriage to the Qajars for reasons that did not bear close scrutiny, the only other participants, besides court servants, were the women.

Once they appropriated the body, the whole business was under their control. They wailed over the dead man in the gardens all afternoon. They howled as they drained the palace pools and washed him at sundown, and by the time they had laid him on the sodden mattresses, trussed up and tied in knots at both ends, they had wept themselves hoarse. Their keening punctuated the midnight watches, their sobs rent the dawn air, and since nothing encourages decomposition more rapidly than excess of human breath, putrefaction had set in before the crowing of the cock.

The Prime Minister was obliged to call in the gravediggers early the following morning. In the interests of science as well as religion, the sovereign had to be interred as soon as possible. Although the official state funeral would take place in a month, when the Crown Prince arrived in the capital, he announced that in the interim, the Shah would be buried in a temporary grave in the private gardens of the palace, beneath the orange groves of the old queen, according to the explicit wishes of the ladies of the royal *anderoun*.

Due to their proximity to the women's quarters, the private gardens of the Shah had always belonged to the harem. Ever since the early days of his reign, his palace had been mirrored in these limpid pools, its reflection shimmering upside down in these bodies of imprisoned water. Royal carp nibbled and burped between the lilting balconies of this female empire; frogspawn drifted lazily through the half-seen passageways of this underwater world within a world. The women of the harem had developed strategies of subaqueous complexity that paralleled the most sophisticated intrigues of the court. They bore grudges, harboured resentments, and nurtured ambitions that competed with the Shah's foreign policies. And over the years they vied with one another savagely, down at the muddy roots of the dreaming lotus, to be the mothers of his sons.

Motherhood is the only immortality, they shrieked, as they wended their way through the queen's apartments and stumbled through the garden doors in the wake of the dead Shah. They had draped his coffin with purple velvet and adorned it with a wreath of lilies, but after a sleepless night, their grief was already turning. They were so exhausted that they could barely remember whose funeral it was; their heads were full of sodden quilts and their legs moved slowly, like damp earth, that morning. The Mother of the Shah was much on their minds.

In the halcyon summer of her regency, her highness had presided over this honeycomb of parallel governance. Her doors had opened directly into the garden and her apartments had dominated the harem. There was no further that a concubine could go, no other aim to which a courtier could aspire, once the lamp-lit halls and palace galleries had been passed, once the anteroom of mirrors had been crossed. There was no entrance to preferment, nor any exit but through death, or her domain. Hers had been the halls beyond which there was no passing.

Why, you could hardly breathe without her knowing, howled the women as the procession straggled out onto the balconies. You could hardly move without her spying on you. And they nudged the pallbearers to straighten up the lopsided coffin and managed to maintain a steady whimper as they staggered down the steps. But despite their wails, they were beginning to raise wry brows at each other by the time the funeral procession neared the rose gardens.

For the private gardens of the palace had acquired a salacious reputation in the days of the old queen. Veiled men had trodden through these flower-beds at her bidding; ambitious lovers, disguised as women, had entered her apartments through these grounds. On one dreadful occasion, the Shah had discovered her highness sharing confidences here, with the protégé she had been cultivating to replace his Grand Vazir. Had it not been for the timely intervention of a palace eunuch, his majesty might have shot his Mother dead among these roses.

She was a salty old cat, hissed the women, until her breasts began to curdle. She was a lively whore in her time. When the procession came to a ragged stop on the edge of the orange orchards, there was a hiatus in their lamentations to allow for prayers and sighs in memory of the queen. But it

was not long before they burst into tears with renewed enthusiasm. Once
the coffin was lowered into the ground and clods of wet soil began to fall
on the planks, they had ceased to think about their royal consort or his
Mother, and were frankly crying for themselves.

It was not the first time blood would seep into this soil, for it had been
contaminated long ago. Condemned men had been dragged in here in the
past to provide entertainment for the old kings. Prisoners had been executed privately among these roses before the members of the Persian court.
The Mother of the Shah considered it salutary for courtiers to observe
blood spouting from a human torso, to note how long it took for lungs
to fill. When he first came to the throne, her son participated willingly in
this traditional sport, but soon after the capture of the poetess of Qazvin,
private tortures gave way to public executions, much to the queen's disgust.

Nothing kills as quickly as ingratitude, sobbed the women; nothing de-
moralizes like remorse. And since a widow's weeds can cover all kinds of
bereavement, they began to beat their breasts and tear their nails across
their cheeks as earth was raked over the grave. But it was not the loosening
of marriage bonds as much as the tightening of purse strings that caused
them grief now. By the time the body was covered with a little heap of
stones it was not the demise of the King of Kings but the fear of their own
impecunious widowhood that most tormented them.

The dismal truth was that the queen's garden had gradually lost its stra-
tegic uses over the course of the Shah's reign. As her influence ebbed in the
palace, his Mother had found herself pushed into a backwater. Instead of
dominating the harem, she had been imprisoned in its peripheries; instead
of holding a commanding view of the court, she had been isolated from it.
And she withdrew into strange reflections. In the late autumn of her life,
she used to lean against the balustrade of the pools, gazing sightlessly at
the stagnant waters, for hours. During her last lonely years, she talked to
herself behind locked doors. The Shah had begun to shun her by then.

About time too, wept the women, their ravaged cheeks stinging in the
east wind. About time he finally shrugged her off, they sobbed, turning their
backs on the dismal mound. They knew their own days at court were also

numbered. They too would have to leave the royal palace soon. The old Shah had more dependents than could reasonably anticipate charity from the new one, and before long, different daughters, sisters, wives, and mothers would be jostling for attention in the royal *anderoun*. If they did not want to scrape for favours, they would have to eke out their days in beggarly pride, just like the Mother of the Shah. It was cruel of his majesty to disown her in the end, they wailed, but what else could you do with a mother like that?

As irony would have it, the Mother of the Shah had also been interred in these gardens. She was also laid to rest here, at the midpoint of the Shah's reign. But she was not allowed to rot in peace for long. The king had been greatly put out by it and had bundled her bones off to Qum on his return from his grand tour to the West, saying that a garden was an unbefitting grave for the body of a queen.

Especially one so sullied by execution and copulation, sniffed the women, as they trailed back to the palace after the peremptory burial. They were pale with exhaustion and desperate for some tea, but there would be no proper wake, of course, no formal funeral feast until the re-interment of the dead sovereign in a month's time. How cloying the stink of rotting lilies! they thought, bleakly. How tedious the talk of memorials! Was it due to a blocked well, perhaps, or because of all these lugubrious obsequies, that the garden seemed suddenly to smell?

Such a shame, sighed the women, through dry lips, to violate a place redolent with love and poetry! Such a pity, they murmured, as the lamps were lit and the dusk of widowhood drew in, to sully a Persian garden with murder and scandal. For although no one mentioned her, even under cover of darkness, they were all thinking of the poetess of Qazvin.

❨ 16 ❩

When the Mother of the Shah realized that her son was serious about having an interview with the woman who had had the temerity to strip off her veil, she was appalled. The idea was almost as crazy as that of marrying his Sister to the Grand Vazir, which was the current rumour running round the court. The queen refused to countenance such folly. She was certainly not going to allow the king to meet such a woman. He must be mad to think of it, she said.

She summoned the young Shah into her presence that very evening, for a few words of maternal counsel, for a frank heart-to-heart talk with him.

He came reluctantly and sat fiddling with a pen and paper while she spoke. Drawing, she supposed, as he so often did when anyone talked to him. He said it helped him concentrate. It drove her to distraction. Was it true that he wanted to interview this so-called poetess who had just been placed under house arrest in the Mayor's residence, she inquired.

The Shah shrugged his shoulders and continued doodling.

It was hardly befitting for a head of state to undertake such an interview, she continued. He should remember his rank, she said, and his religion. He should leave such matters to his inferiors. Couldn't his minister do it?

"Of course he can," snapped the Shah. "And would." And before his Mother could respond, he reminded her, complacently, that she herself had warned him not to defer to his Grand Vazir for everything. She herself had instructed him to keep the upstart in his place. Well, continued the Shah, he had a new place in mind for the upstart and what's more, he intended to be present at the interrogation, so as to ensure the premier kept his place. "It's up to a king to judge his subjects," he scowled. "I want to know just what this woman has actually done."

His Mother eyed the smug young man from under knitted brows. His sallow cheeks were flushed and he was biting his lower lip, just like his father. She could tell from the way that he was squirming in his seat that he was drawing something scatological, as usual. She wished her only son were endowed with more manly attributes. She wished he were either more intelligent or rather less so. She drew a deep breath and began again.

By insisting on conducting such an interview, she told him, his majesty would demean himself. And by participating in it as a mere eyewitness, he would undermine his position. He should choose carefully when and why and how and where his subjects saw him. The occasion was inappropriate, the circumstances degrading. He shouldn't dangle himself at the drop of a hat before every whore in the kingdom.

The Shah put his pen down. "She's one of the most brilliant women in the kingdom," he retorted. "Perhaps even in the world," he added. "The Grand Vazir says so. She's won all kinds of honours in Karbala and Baghdad too, as well as in Qazvin. Why shouldn't I see her?"

His Mother flushed, angrily. This wonder of the world hadn't acquired much wisdom, had she? She wasn't so very clever for all her learning. What could one expect from a family of clerics that had bedded each other for generations? she spat. Her highness preferred to argue on the basis of blood rather than the Holy Book; she built her logic on lineage rather than along philosophical lines. Perhaps this woman knew how to cite the traditions, she said, coldly, but her behaviour proved how stupid she was. She was a scandal to her sex, a blot on the brow of decency. The Shah should not be exposed to the pernicious influence of such a creature.

"I've been exposed to worse," he replied, narrowing his eyes.

His Mother bit her tongue and drew her breath in, sharply. His majesty's decision was ill advised, she retorted. She strongly recommended that he change his mind.

There was a pause, as the Shah returned to his scribbles.

And what in heaven's name, she erupted, did he have to say to the woman anyway? He would never cut a royal figure in public if he had nothing to say.

Her son looked up, chewing on his pen. "I want to see her face," he said quietly.

His Mother lost her temper. That was no reason. Was he planning to gawp at the harlot like a schoolboy? To stare at her and drool? A woman's motives for unveiling were obvious. If she exposed herself in public, it was tantamount to treason; if she showed her face in private, it was an act of seduction. Either way, this creature was a danger to the state and to the Shah.

"And you know very well that you're a wimp when it comes to women," she snapped.

The Shah spat out the broken tip of his reed, morosely.

"You will cancel this ridiculous interview immediately," she repeated.

His eyes bulged the way they always did when he turned stubborn.

She reminded him of all the other times when he had been stupid and told him, in no uncertain terms, that he had better do as she asked. Now. This instant. "And will you stop chewing on your pen and look at me when I'm talking to you," she hissed, in fury.

He threw the reed down and told her, crossly, to leave him alone.

She raised her voice and ordered him not to be such a little fool.

Just at that moment, a hinge whined, the velvet drapes stirred; they heard a muffled cough from the mirrored antechamber beyond the curtained doorway of the room. It was the Sister of the Shah. The queen noted with satisfaction that her son looked distinctly put out to discover who had been eavesdropping on them. She took advantage of it, promptly.

"I can only hope," she concluded, in icy tones, "that the Mayor has enough sense to keep that woman under lock and key, or you'll be inviting her to take up residence here next! I can just imagine the havoc she could wreak in the royal *anderoun!*"

Her son stamped his foot then, and did not even wait to be dismissed from her presence, but flung out of her chambers in a fit of pique, shouting over his shoulder, so that the eunuchs, the concubines, and in particular his Sister could hear him, that he would see the poetess of Qazvin, he would, so there. He would see her when he wanted and for as long as he pleased. He would order her to be brought to him now. This instant. With her veil off.

❨ 17 ❩

Although the Shah's assassin was a man and clearly identified as such in all the historical records, those who measured power by the yard blamed women for the demise of the dynasty. It was doomed from the moment that tailors took over from astrologers in fashioning the future, they said; it declined from the instant that a Persian woman voluntarily cast off the veil.

The formal trial of the assassin did not take place until after the old Shah's funeral and the accession of the new Shah to the throne, but the link between veils and petitions featured strongly in the case brought against him. He was asked about his name and his aims, about his pistol and his politics; he was interrogated about his religious sympathies, his economic theories, and his affiliates. But above all, he was questioned about his association with corpse washers.

The assassin was outraged by such suggestions. He was an anarchist, he protested proudly, and didn't care a dried fig about dead bodies. He had never seen that beggar woman before and hoped never to see her again. He preferred to be compared with lunatics who had failed to killed the king, rather than be suspected of having links with such women. For he had used the same strategy to approach his majesty as the students had deployed the first time; he had hidden his revolver under a petition in his attempt to draw near the Shah, just as they had done.

It was considered highly significant that he had done the deed under cover of paper. He had drawn near the sovereign in the shrine as if to make a request, as if to ask a royal favour, concealing his motives beneath the traditional female hypocrisies. In fact, he had behaved just like a woman covering herself in public when he approached the Shah, the same way the students had done fifty years before. It confirmed the link between a cocked pistol and the female face.

But there was no further resemblance between the two events. There were no scenes of wholesale carnage, no rivers of blood spilled on the eve of the Shah's jubilee as in the aftermath of his coronation. The assassin was not torn to pieces on the spot, nor did he have his brains smashed with a mallet, like others who had dared offer the king petitions in the past. Although the revolver he employed was designed to shoot far more than birds, he was not condemned to verbal defamation, either, even if his right ear was ripped off in the excitement. The students who botched the first attempt were transformed to monsters in the popular imagination, but the regicide who committed the deed became a constitutional hero in the years that followed.

Conjectures still lingered on, however, as to whether his majesty died by an assassin's hand or a woman's face. Even when the regicide was put on trial, condemned, and hanged, doubts about him still remained. He had so thoroughly succeeded in doing away with the king compared to others who had tried and failed, in recent times, to shoot the Queen of England, the Tsar of Russia, and the Emperor of France, that some even hazarded he might be a woman himself. It was necessary in the weeks that followed his execution to publicize his photograph, bearded and in chains, to quell such theories. As a result, he became a sensation among the ladies, and his sullen stare attracted at least as much attention in the royal harem as did the bovine features of the new sovereign. Stories began to circulate that the plot to kill the king had actually been hatched inside the women's *anderoun*.

The Mother of the Shah had already anticipated such collaboration half a century before. Soon after the first attempt against her son, she had turned her baleful attentions from the would-be assassins to the harem. Even as she was giving orders for reprisals in the town, she had unleashed a witch-hunt in the royal *anderoun*. She scoured the bedrooms for rebellion, raked the nurseries for disobedience, and interrogated the wives and concubines of the Shah, one by one. Which among them had visited the Mayor's house during her absence in the city of Qum? Who had read the words of, written letters to, or, worse still, actually met the poetess of Qazvin?

The blood of the princesses ran cold at her questions. There was no stigma worse than this, no liaison more dangerous, no greater peril than to be tarred by the same brush as the heretic.

Naturally, they forswore all association with the woman. They denied her vehemently, protested, on the blood of their sons, that they had never put a foot in the Mayor's house, swore on their fathers' heads and their mothers' bowels that they had never met the shameful harlot in their lives. They had nothing to do with the female heretic, they cried, and cursed her to prove it. They had never read a word she had written nor heard anything she had said. If she had tried to expose hypocrisy, let her be damned for it. If she had defied custom, let her be punished for it. Let her rue the day that she'd refused to pretend, they shuddered, turning their faces to the wall.

But by a stroke of irony performed by few calligraphers, the influence of the poetess of Qazvin was remembered years after the assassin's political aims were forgotten. When the unwilling widows of the Shah finally packed up and left the royal *anderoun* half a century later, they covered their heads with modesty, swathed their bodies with decorum, and left the palace bewailing their impoverishment, their destitution. They were being sent away, they lamented, with nothing but their veils. No one could possibly suggest, for fear of arousing suspicion, that this may have been altogether too much in the circumstances. No one dared hint, in the wake of his dead majesty's official funeral, that they ought to strip off those veils immediately, given the amount of loot hidden beneath their folds. For the naked truth of it was that they were skipping away to the provinces with the spoils of the palace and the best jewels of the treasury tucked beneath their veils. They were using the privilege of sex to rob the kingdom. But no one could say a thing about it as long as women's business was synonymous with political change.

《 18 》

The Mother of the Shah was in the provincial city of Qum when her son met the poetess of Qazvin. She had been forced to undertake the journey some days before, and gossip was rife in the palace regarding the reasons why the Shah had kicked her out of town.

Had she been sent away because her criticism of the Grand Vazir had become too overt, her refusal to consent to his betrothal too obstructive? Had her accusations against the premier—of usurping her rights, of appropriating her prerogatives—become too embarrassing? Or had her plots to replace him become too obvious, perhaps, her interference in governance too great? Was the Shah simply looking for an excuse to annul his Mother's regency? For he not only exiled her to the mausoleum of dead Qajars, but demoted her as soon as her back was turned.

It was such an act of cowardice on his part that some even felt pity for her highness. He should have had the guts to tell her to her face, they murmured. Couldn't a son have at least that much respect for his mother? It had cost her so much to ensure his position, and so little for him to abuse it; it had taken so long for her to confirm her regency, and so little to lose it. But the worst of it was that she had been banished just before the Shah interviewed the poetess of Qazvin. Although the official reason given for her departure was that her highness did not wish to be in town during the execution of the prisoners arrested during the purges of the Grand Vazir, her exile in the provinces actually coincided with this woman's summons to the palace. He must have sent his Mother out of town just so that he could see the harlot, people whispered.

When two such powerful women coincide in history, the consequences to truth can be fatal. Despite the number of spies that were involved, the queen was never able to confirm if the interview actually took place between her son and the prisoner in the Mayor's house. The intelligence she received from the Chief Steward was thoroughly unsatisfactory. The protestations of the Mayor were entirely untrustworthy, and even the Secretary, her erstwhile protégé, could not persuade her that he was speaking the truth. In fact, the reports were so inconsistent and the facts so uncertain, that her highness always confounded what took place in the palace that winter with an incident that occurred in the provinces the summer before.

She was in her winter garden when she heard the news. She was seated with her back against the sunlit wall that morning, and her feet extended towards the brazier, covered with rugs and blankets under the *korsi*. She was also cross and impatient for the arrival of the couriers, having received letters full of lies and flatteries from her son, but nothing from her spies.

Her garden here could not be compared with her garden in the capital. It was a mean rectangular affair with nothing to recommend it but an ancient chestnut tree, a pool filled with dead leaves, and a dysfunctional fountain. It was surrounded by the high walls of one of the most decrepit of the Qajar palaces, built by a pious prince who came to die in Qum a century before. Whenever the queen's couriers arrived from the capital, they rode like the wind through the streets of the city to this palace, and were ushered straight in, without further ceremony, to the courtyard at the back. Here they awaited her highness' pleasure, sweating in their dust-laden and mud-caked clothes, behind a flap of a tent, as the minarets resonated overhead.

The neighbourhood had acquired not only royal but also religious prestige over the years. Four mosques had sprouted in its vicinity, which vied with one another five times a day. Since the minarets towered over her courtyard and her highness suspected the zeal of the *muezzin*, she had ordered an awning to be raised between the door of the *anderoun* and the chestnut tree, in order to protect her privacy. The arrival of a wintry sun coinciding with the season for roast chestnuts that morning, she had just settled herself under her shawls outside, when the first courier was announced. The queen questioned him from the other side of the awning.

"So did the king finally see her?"

"See her highness?" echoed the courier, in a daze. He had been riding hard, without stopping, to be the first to bring her news. She was irritated by his panting.

"Dolt! Did she step into the presence of the Potent King of Persia?"

"She did, so please you, highness," gasped the man hoarsely.

"Well? Out with it, man!" snapped the queen. "What happened? How did she do it?"

"With nothing on!" He had been advised by the others that if her highness showed any sign of irritation he should leave out the preliminaries and come straight to the point.

"Nothing?" The queen was scandalized. "And the Grand Vazir allowed it?"

"He wasn't there, highness," gulped the courier.

"You mean his majesty the Shah met this naked harridan alone?"

The man became flustered and begged to be excused. He had apparently confounded the royal interview with a different one. On closer questioning it appeared that he had muddled it up with another scandal associated with the poetess of Qazvin. Although the veracity of witnesses could hardly be credited, given the disgrace associated with their participation in the affair, the queen learned from the trembling man that on a midsummer's morning the previous year, in a remote hamlet far from the centres of power, the poetess had shown her face before a crowd of some four-score men. After issuing warnings, after announcing her intention, she had stepped into a public tent, unsolicited and uninvited, with her face completely bare. If this was how she had behaved in an obscure corner of Mazanderan, imagine what she might have done in Tehran!

The courier had evidently imagined, for he conveyed fewer facts than suppositions. But who needs to distinguish between them when both are equally sensational? If the naked ambitions of this harlot had been exposed in the past, the queen had little doubt of their existence in the present circumstances. Not only her face but her lust for power was clear, and she feared, from the courier's manifest confusion, that her son had fallen for both.

She had just ordered him to be lashed for incompetence when a second courier made his appearance. "Well?" snapped the queen. "Is it true?"

The second courier was far less anxious to rush into details than the first. He had been advised to retain as much ambiguity as possible in order to avoid blame for the bad news. And besides, he hadn't eaten anything for three days and the smell of roast chestnuts clouded his mind. No, he could not swear that his majesty the Shah had actually met the poetess of Qazvin face to face. Perhaps he had simply spied on her through a curtain, while she was being interrogated. Nor could he say for sure whether the Grand Vazir or someone else had been in the room, and could not confirm, either, whether anyone had intervened or not when the woman refused to comply with the Shah's demand to lift her veil. In fact, the more closely the queen questioned him, the more it was clear that he too appeared to have conflated the events in the palace with those which had taken place in the provinces the previous summer. He suggested, as a solution to uncertainty, that the whole scandal may well have been masterminded by foreign powers. Perhaps the Russian ambassador was involved, he said, his eyes glazing over as he snuffed the succulent air. Or maybe the British Envoy was trying to interfere in the country's domestic affairs.

Since such conspiracy theories did nothing to allay her fears, the queen ordered this man to be taken to the stables with the other, and whipped for stupidity. The backs of both were in ribbons by the time the third one showed up and was ushered into her irate presence.

He stood shifting from foot to foot on the other side of the awning, his eyes bloodshot. He had drunk rather too much *arak* in order to brave her highness and was more than a little inebriated. When she turned those dreadful green eyes on him, he was overcome with vertigo.

"So did it really happen?" she demanded.

"It did, highness," he stuttered.

"And who else witnessed the scandal?"

"One cut his throat, highness, to avoid seeing her—"

"The Vazir?" she cried.

"And ran from the garden with blood pouring down his shirt—" gabbled the man.

"What garden?" roared the queen. "I thought his majesty met her secretly, in the palace!"

It appeared that this courier too was confusing the prisoner's private meeting in the capital and her public unveiling in the provinces. The Mother of the Shah was not sure whether to credit reality or her rage on learning of what happened at one or both or neither of these events. She had no idea whether a throat had been slashed or a curtain drawn aside, whether a sword had been raised or a neck bowed in anticipation of a blow. But as the tipsy courier sank involuntarily to his knees and begged for mercy, she did hear him say, in spite of herself, that though many averted their eyes and a few stopped their ears against this woman the year before, those who remained in her presence were rewarded by a rare experience. They found themselves listening to her at the same time as seeing words form on her lips. They discovered themselves reading the lineaments of her face even as they heard her talk. And they saw gardens and rivers flowing from her mouth, as she spoke, with breath-taking eloquence, of paradise.

Paradoxes liberate the imagination but contradictions weary the mind. The Mother of the Shah had grown weary of all this nonsense. She accused the couriers of making contradictory statements and had them strung up by the heels and bastinadoed. When the fourth arrived soon after, he found his fellows languishing in the stocks and her highness visibly exhausted.

He had only one piece of news to deliver, which he presented, unadorned. He informed her highness that the King of Kings and Pivot of the Universe had been smitten by the female heretic. Whether or not he interviewed her, inside or outside the court, with or without the veil, he had granted the prisoner an instant reprieve. And he had defied the Grand Vazir to do it.

The queen experienced the most violent sensations on hearing this. She plotted slashings, killings, murders in the night; she determined on poison for the couriers and lingering torture for her spies. She wanted to throttle all the cats of Qum at the thought of her son's stupidity. She wept beneath the awning so no one could witness the ravage to her face and cursed the day that she was born a woman. And then she started writing a stream of letters to the Shah: appeals and protests; passionate accusations; demands, denials, and attempted reconciliations. For what burned her, what enraged her most was that her son was corresponding with the poetess of Qazvin behind her back. There was only one point on which all the couriers were in agreement: his majesty had sent the poetess a letter and the wretch had actually replied.

He had made an offer, extended his patronage, promised freedom to the poetess of Qazvin. He had sent her word that she could be released from prison instantly if only she complied with his desires. Against all rules of propriety, against all notions of respectability, against every standard of decency, he had invited her to be a concubine in the royal *anderoun*. And the horrid hussy had answered. She had had the presumption to respond. She had sent an impromptu quatrain scribbled on the back of his proposal, refusing him!

The verse was so admired, the queen was told, that it was doing the rounds of court as well as the royal *anderoun*. It had found its way out of the gates of the palace and was taking root in the bazaars and alleys. Some said it was even being quoted by clerics in the theological colleges. Everyone was repeating the words written to the Shah by the poetess of Qazvin.

> *Wealth, power, and lordship for thee;*
> *poverty, loss, and exile for me.*
> *Take the choice that is thine own,*
> *and let me make mine!*

❨ 19 ❩

After the attempt on her son's life, in the fifth summer of his reign, the Mother of the Shah herself repeated the verse written by the prisoner to the king. It had achieved the status of a popular saying by then, but she knew he would never forget its origins. She had bided her time for three years but was eager to settle scores with the woman she blamed for her banishment.

The Shah was still at the mercy of his French physician when she forced her way through the thronging courtiers amassed at the doors of his private chambers. The pellets had finally been extracted and the tweezers had clattered disrespectfully in the porcelain dish beside the moaning sovereign, when she pushed them all aside. The doctor had washed his hands rather too many times and given her son instructions to avoid the saddle and bridle for the following week as she laid her ear against the door. But when he began to advise his royal patient that he might wish to curtail his visits to the royal *anderoun* as well, her imperial highness lost patience. She turned the door handle and rustled in.

The King of Kings and Pivot of the Universe was lying with his buttocks in the air.

The French physician bowed low as she approached. He had just been swabbing the wounds with lint soaked in witch hazel, he informed her, coldly. It might have been less embarrassing to his majesty, he added, if her highness had remained outside. His perfunctory scorn, as he turned to leave, was not lost on the Mother of the Shah, nor was the humiliation of her son. She shuddered at the sight of him.

The king lifted his head from the cushions, his nose running and one cheek covered with a plaster. "That doctor is a brute!" he snivelled. "He's as callous as the killers!"

She gave a glance at the departing Frenchman and murmured that he would pay for it.

"I could be dead," sniffed the indignant youth, "and all he could say was that I'm lucky I wasn't a grouse!"

She said, through stiff lips, that she would make sure others were less fortunate.

"He dared to suggest that I'd have to choose where and when I sat from now on!" grumbled the Shah. "And he had the nerve to make jokes about it, at my wives' expense!"

And what, asked his Mother, in tones of ice, was his majesty's choice?

The Shah glanced up at her frowning, and then flinched, as her eyes bored down on him. He realized that she was serious. What the hell could he choose to do in his present condition?

"Do you want to sit on the throne of your forefathers," she demanded, "or ride like an imbecile on the backs of foreigners who ridicule the royal harem?"

He did not reply. Silence seemed the best alternative, in the circumstances.

"This is no time for jokes, my son," his Mother continued, grimly. "You're going to have to sit in judgement on your subjects from now on. If you can," she added.

He turned away from her, scowling into his pillows.

"And if you can't, then I will have to do it for you," she concluded. "I'm not going to stand by and let you make a fool of yourself again. Make your choice, and let me make mine!"

The Pivot of the Universe shuddered. He never dreamed that the day would actually come when his Mother would quote the words of the poetess of Qazvin. She had sworn to kill the captive in the Mayor's house when she learned that he had offered her his protection; her spies had confessed as much when they came back to the capital. She had supported all the clergy's accusations against the woman, especially after her return from Qum. And she had held her responsible for every uprising since, insisting that her doctrines had caused the insurrections in his reign. All this time, as long as it cost him nothing to do so, the Shah had extended his protection over the prisoner in the Mayor's house on the grounds that nothing had been proven against her. He had deflected his Mother's plans till now, but it was not easy to continue to do so in his present position. His Mother had caught him off guard, as it were, with his pants down.

"Take the choice that is thine own, and let me make mine!" she repeated, softly, as she leaned over him, combing her fingers through his hair. She could see that he had been frightened and she was determined to take advantage of it. Serve him right for being such a coward, she thought in disgust, as she bent down to kiss the sweaty forehead of her son.

He shrank at her touch. It looked as though she was going to carry out her threat at last.

"Don't you worry, my darling," she murmured, soothingly. "I'm not going to stand by and let you suffer! I've made my choice. That French doctor will rue the day he hurt the Shah of Persia. I'll see to his punishment. I'll see to it that everyone is punished who has dared offend the king. And that," she added, pointedly, "goes for women as well as men."

Her son winced, as the impact of gender touched his sensibilities. He knew his Mother was going to exploit this crisis to reassert her authority over the throne. When she blamed the prisoner in the Mayor's house for the incompetence of his guards, he had no choice but to submit to her pressure. He knew he could no longer extend his protection over the poetess of Qazvin.

If a woman prefers the love of God to the love of her king, what is a man supposed to do to help the stupid bitch? he had muttered to his Sister afterwards, in an attempt to justify himself.

He stared sulkily at the plateful of bloody pellets on the table beside him as his Mother droned on. She was saying that she would speak in private to the Prime Minister that evening: the ecclesiastical interrogations at the Mayor's house should be resumed immediately, she insisted. She was going to talk to the Chief Steward too about appointing the Sardar for the task: no one whose rank was below that of the Commander of the army should be put in charge of such a delicate matter, in her opinion. She also suggested that the Austrian ophthalmic specialist might be present at the execution, as an eyewitness: there should be no superstitions, no mythmaking around this affair, she said. The last thing she wanted was to encourage legends. The Shah, she concluded, should make that clear to the chief of police himself.

"You have to send for the Mayor," she concluded, "and ask his son to do the honours. It's the only way to ensure that his Wife will hold her tongue."

THE BOOK OF THE WIFE

When the Mayor was hanged, they said his Wife stopped talking. She had rarely been at a loss for words as long as he was alive, but death can have a curious impact on the garrulous. She was speechless soon after her husband was summoned to the palace, and by the time his body dangled at the city gates, his turban gone, his beard cut off, his face fixed in a grimace of surprise, she was completely mute.

It was not the first instance that the Mayor had thus been summoned, but it proved to be the last. The patronage of the Shah had never failed him before. He had presented himself at court innumerable times these dozen years, since the king's accession to the throne; he had frequently been called upon to demonstrate his faithfulness to his royal master, since his house had been transformed into the prison headquarters. On all previous occasions, which had resulted in honours, titles, and an increase of his powers, his Wife had told the whole town what she thought about it. This time, after his hanging, she said nothing.

In order to keep her safe from the marauding mob, they hauled her up the ladder to the second storey of the house where the poetess of Qazvin had been confined all those years before, but though she lingered on for several days, she never spoke again. Perhaps she had done so too many times already. Perhaps there was nobody to listen to her any more. Or perhaps she was trying not to say something, for her incontinence was something dreadful in the end. The corpse washers cast lots to avoid the task but it finally took them all to drain her. Even with the cloth tied round her chin, she kept dribbling.

(2)

The Mayor's Wife was known for her volubility. Her shrill voice was as familiar as garlic in the mosque, and rendered the veil irrelevant in the bazaar. Her words drifted over the walls and down the alleys, like the sizzling of kebabs and the smell of fried onions. Her opinions even penetrated through the palace gates at times, and lingered in the royal *anderoun* with the persistence of fenugreek. The Mother of the Shah used to tell the women of the court that if they wished to know the news, they should just shut their mouths and follow their noses into town.

For the Mayor's Wife was the queen of cuisine as well as gossip, despite her lack of court and clerical connections. Few had attained the perfection of her pickles, none achieved the orthodoxy of her rice. Her jams had the consistency of truth, according to connoisseurs, and were the despair of all but the philosophical. Her conserves, too, were suspended in pure faith, and needed no interpretation. But if the quince were sliced too thin or cut too thick, if the cardamom was crushed too much or not enough, if sugar was boiled beyond the point of belief, she was ready to damn her cooks for apostasy. She was a fundamentalist when it came to food.

Despite her provincial origins and the fact that she was not his first, the Mayor's Wife was the chief lady of his harem. Her husband had other dependents, of course, as might be expected of so prominent a citizen, but he had adorned this one with gold bangles and hooped earrings to prove she was the finest ornament in his *anderoun*. She was a pretty woman in her youth, with creamy dimples, plump white arms, and a substantial dowry. She was a witty woman too, with an intelligence that was inquisitive rather than inquiring. Above all she was a jealous woman who wielded her tongue like a kitchen knife. Unlike his deaf mother, and penurious sister, unlike his unmarried daughters and other pock-marked wives, she dominated the Mayor.

But by the time the young Shah came to the throne, she had been married long enough to have tired of cheap jewellery. Her attentions had shifted by then from her husband to her son. He was the same age as the young king, and deserved a princess, in her opinion. He was her darling, her dumpling, her adored, and just as good-looking as the Shah. In the weeks before the coronation, she nagged her husband incessantly about that pearl of a girl, that pride of a bride who would be suitable for her boy. She could only talk of marriage contracts as he was preparing to leave for the palace to offer his compliments to the new Shah.

"Everything depends on currying favour with the queen," she reminded the Mayor, "so you will do what you can, won't you, to flatter her highness during the ceremonies?"

He muttered something about earning favours before asking for them.

"Her highness has all sorts of suitable relations," his Wife continued, unperturbed.

He said something about having other priorities for the moment.

"Why, even a distant cousin would do," she persisted.

He told her something about having to serve the new Vazir from now.

"Well, the Grand Vazir seems to have his eye on a princess too," she retorted. "Wasn't he going to marry the Sister of the Shah? If he can do it, so can you," she sang.

The Mayor flinched. His Wife's voice carried. He did not want the whole neighbourhood to hear her talking of a betrothal about which the queen still violently disapproved. It would be best, he murmured, to keep quiet on that particular subject until her highness gave consent.

But nothing could keep his Wife quiet. "Precisely," she rounded on him. "I told you that a good alliance depended on the Mother of the Shah!"

The Mayor sighed as he dressed himself in preparation for the palace. He had been unable to forewarn his Wife about his plan to offer the house as a gift to the new sovereign. Each time he had tried to raise the subject over the past few weeks, she had countered with talk of marriage contracts.

Each time he had tried to speak to her, she had interrupted him to chatter about brides instead. And with each interruption he forgot completely what he was going to say.

A man can be driven to violence by words and garlic, he thought, savagely, as he strode across the courtyard towards the stables, cuffing the gatekeeper out of his way.

The Mayor had been obliged to protect his house from the attention of the envious by hiring a blockhead of a gatekeeper who let no one in or out. Security in the city had become a problem since the new Shah's accession to the throne. Not only the rabble in the streets but the rakes and rogues in court were growing increasingly dangerous. The Mayor judged it safer to buy the young king's indebtedness than to depend on his uncertain generosity. Since he might lose the house entirely if he did not act fast, he thought it best to bargain with the property before he was obliged to give it up. His decision to relinquish it, on the occasion of the coronation, was as calculated a move as his savage swipe at the gatekeeper's shaven head on leaving the premises.

He knew that his Wife would be furious once she found out. She would give him no respite when she learned of his perfidy. He had built this house in her honour, after the birth of his only son. He had constructed the second storey over the kitchens, just to satisfy her fancy for a palace. She considered it one of her chief assets in negotiating for a suitable daughter-in-law. She would never forgive him for bargaining it away before she could use it to buy a bride.

〖 3 〗

It was the winter of the bread riots when the Mayor was hanged, nine years after the attempt on the life of the Shah. The second storey of his house had been locked up all that time, and the Mayor had never crossed the threshold of the upper chamber since the summer massacres. His Wife did not let him use the premises after its last occupancy. She hid the key from him and was the only person in the house who ever entered that room. When she was stricken during the bread riots, her son found it threaded on a greasy ribbon and imbedded in the rolls of fat around her waist. They had to cut it off with a knife before they could open the door.

It was the dumb gatekeeper who found his mistress lying stupefied in the mud between the gates of the Legation and the garden up the road. When he ran back to the house, with arms circling and fingers pointing, the Mayor's son gave immediate orders that his mother be hauled home in a carpet and hidden out of sight. To die fat at a time of famine was almost as provocative as to die mute after a life of garrulity. She should be locked upstairs, he said.

"Over my dead body," his aunt retorted, when she heard of it. She suspected that her cowardly nephew had something else to hide, besides his mother.

He protested that it was the only place safe from the fury of the mob.

"If you lift her up there," warned the widow, "you'll never bring her down again alive."

But the Mayor's son ignored his aunt. She was one of those women who drooled over the past like a camel at a salt lick. The old girl thinks she can see through the back of her head, he told his wives and sisters, but the danger's right under her nose. Their father's body was still dangling over the city gates and rotting, after having been hauled by the heels all over town, he warned; the crowd was still out there and starving, its rage still unappeased. Their house would be looted next unless he could bargain to keep it safe. It would be best, he urged the women, to conceal his mother until the worst was over. Since the second storey was not easily accessible, they should carry her up there and destroy the ladder if anyone came knocking.

His sisters thought it an excellent idea. They had been itching to look inside the upper chamber for years. After the prisoner went away, the Mayor's Wife used to go up there every evening; she said that she was using the room to say her prayers, but they never believed her. Their aunt claimed that it was the only place a woman could think in the house. But the Mayor's daughters were sure their stepmother was hoarding money in the second storey and trying to cheat them of their dowries; they suspected she was keeping delicacies up there for her fat son which she did not want to share with them. Long before the bread riots overran the capital, they told the neighbours that the upper chamber was their stepmother's private granary.

Commodities were certainly scarce during the second decade of the Shah's reign. Ever since his majesty's accession to the throne, the Mayor had been fixing the price of rice at inflated levels. He had been stockpiling wheat for over a decade too, and knew exactly when to reduce its distribution to the bakers. While he made sure that the queen and her kinsmen received their shares, and shut the mouths of the clerics with their cut of the bribes, he kept the keys of the granary in his own possession, on the Shah's authority. He made good money every winter.

He had also become adept at distracting people from their hunger. The chief of police governed by the law of fear, and his thugs were a formidable alternative to the poorly paid soldiers of the king. But they too required inducements. Since the Mayor had no intention of paying them out of his own pockets, he kept wealthy merchants in his custody in the early years, to extort bribes for his men. Later, in the aftermath of the assassination attempt, he undertook reprisals on behalf of the queen to rob the sons of ministers for the same purpose. By the second decade of the Shah's reign, he needed more scapegoats to run a profitable establishment.

But the old man's meteorological instincts were not paralleled by political acumen. His son was afraid that the Mayor was pushing his luck that year and attempted to warn him against exploiting the winter weather. There was a chance of insurrections sweeping across the country, like in the old king's time, he told him, timidly. The Shah's first Vazir had attempted to crush the disturbances a decade earlier, but he had not resolved their cause. If commodities were hoarded, there might be more uprisings similar to when the Shah first came to the throne.

The Mayor scoffed at his son's warnings. There were always food shortages between the winter solstice and the spring equinox, he said, so why should it be any different this year?

In fact, it was worse. After barricading his house and placing double security at the gates, the Mayor ensured that deliveries to the capital were reduced to a trickle that winter, on the Shah's orders. There was no wheat on the market, no barley available, and no corn for sale at all. Bread, such as it was, was made of husks and rope, compounded into a grey paste with the bones of heaven knew what animal more wretched than the men who ate it. Respectable citizens were reduced to penury and scrambled for scraps in the ditches, raked the sewers, chewed on leather to survive. Rice prices rose so high that people starved for a week to eat a mouthful a day, and a thousand souls expired at the beginning of the cold season, in the attempt to stay honest.

By mid-winter, the famine was widespread. When the Shah went off on a long hunting expedition, without leaving any instructions about what should be done in a case of emergency, the city was held to ransom by robber barons and corpse washers. The only professions that thrived, besides the unscrupulous, were to be found in the cemetery. But even funerals were a masquerade that winter. Most bodies were hardly worth washing and the ground was too hard for spades. Many slept in the cemeteries at night to save their relatives the trouble of taking them there in the mornings, and famished creatures often toppled head first into the graves with those they were burying. Priests annulled the need for prayers, and only when the thawing earth gave birth to bones the following spring were the mourners and the mourned accorded any distinction.

But although the end of the cold season offered some reprieve to the dead, it promised little or no relief to the living. Plague haunted the heels of famine that year. Those who had scoured the fields for the first frail blades of corn began to sicken, their bellies bloated with cooked grass, their tongues hideously distended. Even old maids and married women became afflicted by the green sickness and expired as fast as ravenous virgins. Babes were born sucking on their thumbs, they said, and when the first thaws anticipated spring, children died with the maggots already at work on them. The month of mourning that year was interminable.

And then, at the height of the crisis, bread riots paralyzed the capital. One cold February day, the women gutted the bakers' shops. The same women, who had run in the sweltering August heat, howling for blood in the wake of the Mayor's cart after the attempt on the life of the Shah nine years before, now took to the streets and surged towards the palace, howling for bread.

The king was out hunting when it happened and summoned the Mayor to resolve the crisis, the minute he returned. But as soon as the Mayor set off for the palace, his son finally took matters into his own hands. He unlocked the granaries, and instructed his trembling sisters to barricade themselves in the cellars. He also let the concubines flee the premises and told the servants to run for their lives. He knew the riots would not be resolved without more violence. He hoped that if the rabble broke into his compound, they would loot the stores and leave the house alone.

But his aunt refused to budge from the breezeway. Even when the starving populace flooded the market square and turned down the alley, even when they began to hammer at the gates and knock on the granary doors, she just sat there, staring into space with opaque eyes. She seemed not to hear her nieces shouting and ignored her nephew's appeals. She was probably deaf as well as blind, he told his sisters, and urged them to abandon the stupid old woman to her fate. For there was nothing but the gatekeeper's brains between them and the rabble by then.

It was only when he scuttled underground that he discovered his mother's absence. She had not taken refuge in the cellars with the rest of the womenfolk, nor in the room above the terrace. She was nowhere in the house. She must have followed his father out of the gates to the palace, he thought, with horror. She must be out there in the streets, telling the howling mob what she thought of the Mayor. And he realized then that his aunt had known it all along.

〔 4 〕

Twelve years before, the Mayor's Wife had told the whole street what she thought of the female prisoner who was going to be placed in her husband's custody.

"Having a jail for a home is bad enough," she had cried, "but living with a whore is too much. Aren't there enough female prisoners in this place already?"

The Mayor could not keep her quiet. His Wife had not taken kindly to living in the prison headquarters of the king. She had been highly offended by the distinctions granted to the chief of police during the coronation ceremonies, and he had been hard-pressed to appease her ruffled pride ever since. Even the queen's good will towards her son was not enough to mollify her.

Her highness made all the overtures herself, he told her, anxiously. She was insistent about sending her gracious compliments.

His Wife gave him a liverish look. "My boy needs more than compliments," she scowled.

Her highness no doubt had the perfect princess in mind, he answered, soothingly. Wasn't it worth living in a prison in exchange for a bride?

"Quite a bargain," she rejoined. "Depending on who's paying for it."

He did his best to appease her. As long as she could believe that the men in her cellars were part of the negotiations, he was able to restrain her indignation, but when she learned that a woman was going to be placed in his custody as well, she erupted again. Her righteous anger resonated over the rooftops. Her displeasure echoed across the market square.

"Are we paying with prostitutes now?" she demanded, her cheeks flushed.

Don't cross him, whispered her son. He can be ruthless.

Don't upset him, murmured her sister-in-law, or he might take a concubine.

But the Mayor's Wife could not hold her tongue. "Is this a prison headquarters or a brothel?" she raged at the Mayor. "Are you a father or a pimp? How can I forge alliances with families of good standing," she cried, "when you invite harlots into this house?"

She treated him very coolly after that, and a mean wind blew through the prison headquarters in the weeks that followed. The couple were barely on speaking terms at the start of the winter season, and by the time the female prisoner arrived at the gates of the capital, and the frustrated crowd finally dispersed from the alley, a chilly silence had descended on the house of the Mayor. His Wife took umbrage after their public quarrel and withdrew into her tea room in a huff. She was expecting her husband to apologize and refused to have anything to do with the new prisoner until he did. But she was consumed with curiosity about the woman, nonetheless, and settled beside the frosted window to watch for her arrival.

What would the creature look like, she wondered. Would she be as filthy as the gypsies, after roving all over the countryside? Would she be flaunting her face without a veil? A peasant girl, roused by her inflammatory words, had ridden on horseback in the provinces, so they said, waving a sword and terrifying the soldiers of the Shah with her shrill cries. Housewives, inspired by her example, had cut off their braids and wrapped them around the battered muskets of their menfolk in the recent insurrections. She was accused of strutting about in brightly coloured dresses during the month of mourning, of boycotting the butchers, of teaching girls how to read. Was it possible, wondered the Mayor's Wife, that such a woman had ever been a wife?

Her estranged husband had returned to town recently, demanding that she be put to death for her misdeeds. He was a cleric, a mullah, a man of the cloth, and claimed that she had abandoned his children and dared to divorce him. The Mayor's Wife loved a good gossip, but she was as shocked by the husband's vulgar accusations as by his wife's behaviour. The wrong was never all on one side in these situations, in her opinion, and she fixed her attention on the narrow arch that connected the *birouni* to the *anderoun* below, with mounting curiousity.

Everyone was coming through the archway except the prisoner. First the idiot gatekeeper dragged a laden donkey into the women's courtyard, with the Mayor at his heels, yelling at him to take the animal back to the stables, you blockhead. Then the narrow passage was filled by a lopsided *howdah*, its curtains sagging, its cross-poles broken, borne on the back of a lumbering mule, with the Mayor hollering that surely one of you stupid grooms could hold it back? But when a bundle of rags finally tumbled out of the *howdah* into the snow, and the Mayor swore by the head of all the dead saints for her to get lost, his Wife stared. Was this the poetess of Qazvin?

The girl on her knees in the courtyard below was wearing a rough kerchief across her forehead and had scabs all over her arms. She was imploring the Mayor to let her stay, begging him to permit her to serve her mistress.

She would rather die than leave her, she said. As he loosed another volley of curses and whipped her back through the archway, along with the mule and the grooms, his Wife realized she must be the prisoner's maid. That's all we need, she muttered to herself. A prisoner with a maid! She'd better not expect to be served by a maid in this house; she'd have to do her own washing and cooking, and use her own charcoal. Whatever the weather.

The first flakes were already beginning to fall when the Mayor finally came back through the arch after ordering the *howdah* out of the premises. And this time his Wife saw, with a quickening of her pulse, that there was a veiled figure behind him. The prisoner was neither tall nor particularly short, neither too thin nor obviously fat, but that was all that could be judged of her in that unflattering travelling garb. She wore baggy trousers bunched at the ankles, with rough cloths covering her feet. Her dark cloak was caked to the knees in mud and the latticework over her face was grimy. The Mayor's Wife stared at her curiously. She was no different from anyone dressed for the street. A woman in a veil was like a book with covers closed.

But she seemed to shrink into its folds when the chief of police cursed the servants for forgetting to unload her belongings from the donkey they had dispatched to the stables; she withdrew into her cloak and bowed her head when he yelled at their slowness and damned them as fools when they finally brought it back. It was as though she were pained to have them reprimanded in her presence. After a while, as he continued to utter oaths and shout redundant orders, she removed herself to the far side of the pool. And there she stood, with her back to the wall, the flakes settling on her shoulders, as the idiot boy untied her chest from the back of the donkey with aching slowness. There she waited, black against the falling whiteness, as he unloaded the bundle of bedding and began to haul her belongings up the ladder, one by one. There she remained, like a stroke of ink against the snow, until the Mayor's Wife began to shiver just looking at her in the fading winter light.

And then there were shouts at the gate and a groom suddenly appeared in the archway.

A royal carriage had arrived, he told the Mayor, breathlessly, with a message from the palace. Would his master come? The Mayor strode out of the courtyard, cursing.

There was a momentary lull below. The servants, ill at ease at being left alone with a female prisoner, abandoned their unpacking after a few moments and trailed after their master. Everyone else in the Mayor's house stayed behind closed doors, watching through the darkened panes. The prisoner was entirely alone on the far side of the snowy courtyard. She drew near the pool. She bent down and scooped a handful of snow from its tiled edge. And then she suddenly dropped her veil. The Mayor's Wife caught her breath in surprise, as the poetess of Qazvin bent her bared head to wipe a palm of snow across her brow. Her face was still circled by a scarf, the face-cloth covering nose and mouth still knotted behind her head after she pulled off the white *ruband*. But she shook her hair free, with visible relief, as she passed a wet hand swiftly across both cheeks. Her skin glistened as she straightened her back and looked around. She gazed across the pool and at the breezeway; she glanced towards the kitchens and the doors of the women's *anderoun*. And then, she suddenly looked up towards the windows of the tea room.

The Mayor's Wife pulled back from the window sharply. She was shocked. Not only by the woman's youth, but by her air of hope. Or was it brazenness? Her eyes were shining. She had not thought the prisoner would be her own age. She had not imagined she would be so attractive. She had four children, after all. A clever woman should be less good-looking. More vulgar. A woman guilty of scandal should be less pleasing. Or was that eager look just the glance of a prostitute, the glint of a whore? The Mayor's Wife frowned. There were stories of this creature chanting on the highways, reading her poetry in the caravanserais at midnight. They said that she had caused a furor in Baghdad, that she had been crowned queen of fifty thousand Kurds in the mountains of Iraq. They said she had walked about naked in a tent full of men and invited them to bite her nipples—! Certainly, that disconcerting look she had flashed across the courtyard left the Mayor's Wife feeling naked, but nipples had nothing to do with it. It was a while before she dared peep down again, furtively, at the poetess of Qazvin.

The woman had lowered her gaze to the empty pool by then. She had a fine head of hair, the Mayor's Wife noticed, tumbling below her scarf. Her braids were shot with copper threads that glistened in the melting snow, and two curls were trained against her cheeks, according to the fashion of the day. Beautiful, the Mayor's Wife admitted to herself resentfully, with that translucent complexion and those lovely brows. Vain too, she thought, the way she smoothed the curls, pressing them down with the tips of her fingers. A right prima donna, she told herself. The prisoner looked up again from time to time, causing the Mayor's Wife to withdraw in fear. Her hands moved like birds' wings; her stillness and her movement were like a dance.

It took forever for the Mayor to return from the gates. All activity came to a stop in the women's courtyard during his absence. The prisoner's bundles lay sodden in the snow after the servants shrank away in his absence; the gatekeeper stood grinning foolishly under the arch, waiting for orders that did not come. And only once in all that time did the prisoner speak. She had evidently requested for water because the idiot brought her an urn that looked as though it had been retrieved from the outhouse. She heaved a sigh, just once too, as she stood there shifting her weight from foot to foot, and drooped, as though the snow were heavy on her shoulders. Finally she replaced her veil and sank down by the marbled lip of the pool, as though her strength had failed her. It was only when the Mayor's Wife saw her shivering that she realized, with a pang, how exhausted the wretched creature must be.

She wished then that the prisoner had been invited into the kitchens, at least, out of the cold. She wished that the servants had offered her hot tea, after her long journey. But no one had approached her; no one besides the gatekeeper had done anything for her. The mistress of the house had given no orders. As she fixed her eyes on the bowed back below her, the Mayor's Wife experienced an upheaval in her heart: she resented this criminal for invading her privacy; she felt ashamed for failing to honour this guest. She was in a turmoil of conflicting emotions.

It was dark by the time her husband came back. The woman covered herself, modestly, at his footsteps, and when ordered by him to climb the ladder, first pressed a coin in the idiot's palm to convey her thanks. The Mayor indicated, gruffly, that the gatekeeper should remove the ladder afterwards, with a savage show of unnecessary discipline. His Wife was embarrassed for him.

He was in a filthy temper that night. She was obliged to break her vow of silence just to make him talk. But when she whined about having a harlot in the house, he told her to shut her mouth. When she pouted and said that people would think he had taken a new concubine, he answered he would do so too, if she did not hold her tongue. And when she retorted, with stinging tears—for she really was upset by then—that he could take as many wives as he wanted for all she cared, he rolled over, turned his back on her and snored like a pig. He refused to tell her what the visit of the royal carriage had been about that evening. It was most unsatisfying.

But all through that lonely night, whenever she woke and glimpsed the faint light of an oil lamp flickering on the terrace, she shuddered to think that there was no brazier in the upper room. And each time she recalled those glowing eyes lifted up towards her from the courtyard, so hopefully, so eagerly, she trembled.

In fact, the Mayor's Wife half-believed the prisoner was a *jinn*.

(5)

The day the Shah ordered the hanging of the Mayor was unseasonably warm for winter. By the second day, with the air still balmy, his body was beginning to bloat above the city gates. But that evening, the temperatures suddenly dropped and a blizzard swept through the capital. When his daughters saw the flat-roofed terrace blanketed with drifts of snow on the morning of the third day since their father's death, they declared that it was impossible for them to climb the ladder to cater to his Wife's needs.

"She won't notice if the washerwoman attends to her," they assured their brother, for the Mayor's Wife just snored when they had laid her glassy eyed on the floor.

They had been bitterly disappointed by the upper chamber. Although the exterior walls of the second storey were covered with ostentatious tiles, the interior ones were made of mere wattle and daub and unfinished. The door and windows were crude, the mud floor rough, the plaster thin. The wind whistled through the high rafters, and the whitewashed walls were streaked with stains where the rain leaked in. They had forgotten that the place was so uninhabitable.

"Goodness knows what possessed her to come up here all these years," scowled the Mayor's daughters, staring around them in dismay when they brought the Mayor's Wife inside.

For the room was bare. It was as empty as on the night the prisoner moved in, more than twelve winters before, and the window overlooking the Legation gardens was thick with dust and cobwebs. A battered brass lamp still stood in the blackened niche, in one wall, and traces of candle wax stained the narrow shelf on the other. The shuttered air was tainted with mildew, and the bundle of cotton quilts rolled up against the rain-stained walls was mice-infested. But besides the threadbare prayer rug and the reed mats worn to a pale gold by pacing, the only trace of the heretic was a chest which still stood behind the door. There was also a lacquered mirror hanging on a nail above it. The chest was locked and the backing of the mirror fly-blown.

"Fancy a prisoner using a mirror," murmured the Mayor's daughters uneasily, turning away from their warped reflections in the spotted glass. And they rubbed circles in the dusty panes as they peered down to the Legation garden the way they used to, when they were young.

On the second day of the bread riots, they sent the washerwoman up alone and then changed their minds and decided to follow after her, in order to rifle through the chest in the corner of the room. There was no improvement in the condition of the Mayor's Wife. After the washerwoman had cleaned her up, the stricken woman lay staring up at the rafters and breathing hoarsely. The rattle in her throat made it difficult to concentrate as her step-daughters fiddled with the key in the rusted lock and tried to work it open. She half-choked when they lifted the lid but continued breathing once it yawned wide. But then their disappointment doubled.

Not only was the room bare but the chest was empty too. All it contained, besides dried bread crumbs and a packet of sugar crystals, was a Russian tea glass, a gold-rimmed china saucer, and a tarnished silver spoon.

Finally, on the third day, just before the Mayor's body was cut down from the gates, they discovered an odd stain behind the door. They had braved the falling snow, after the washerwoman had waddled up the ladder, and decided to make one last search of the room before giving up on it altogether. That's when they found it. The stain. The floor mats were frayed and broken and the blot had spread between the flattened reeds. It had evidently been covered by a samovar at one time. The Mayor's daughters could still see the burnt indentations of the heavy brass feet on the mats. They could distinguish the scorch marks too, caused by the scattering of hot coals, across the reeds. But they could not make head nor tail of the blot. It was green.

One of them thought that it smelled faintly of tarragon. The other believed it was more the colour of parsley. They were still arguing, on their hands and knees, and sniffing the reed mats to verify the truth, when there was a sudden uproar from across the town. They leapt to their feet, their hearts pounding. The Mayor's Wife lay between them like a stone, still staring up at the ceiling. And then the whole building was shaken by a distant cannon blast followed by another blood-curdling howl. Their brother started shouting at them from below, telling them to hurry into the cellars. The worst was yet to come. The mob had evidently been roused to a fury again, and he wanted to take the ladder down.

They had heard howls just like these after the attempt on the life of the Shah, when their father had terrorized the city, knocking on the doors of innocent citizens on his rampage of reprisals. They had listened to the same uproar echoing through the market square when the first public executions were taking place that winter, after the Mayor had tortured prisoners in the cellars of the house. And now was it his turn. The starving mob had hauled their father's mangled body through the streets three days before with shouts and execrations before hanging him at the city gates. And they were cutting him down now, with the same blood-curdling screams.

When their brother was told of the indignities being inflicted on his father's body, he panicked completely. If the hunger-crazed populace could do this to a dead man, what might they do to a living one? He ordered the gatekeeper to barricade the doors against the rabble in a bid for time and chopped the ladder to pieces. As a result, as snow blanketed the terrace above and the mob churned through the alleys of the town below, his mother was marooned in the upper chamber with no one but the washerwoman in attendance.

(6)

The royal carriage, which had stopped at the doors of the prison head-quarters on the night of the poetess' arrival, brought specific instructions from the queen. Her message had been unambiguous to the Mayor. The heretic was to remain under solitary confinement until further notice. She was not allowed to conduct correspondence with anyone. And she was to be deprived of all physical comfort, including visits to the public baths. Her imperial highness wanted the woman strictly shunned, according to the Chief Steward, who delivered these instructions.

The Mayor had been put out. He took instructions from the Grand Vazir, he told his Wife gruffly the following morning. He did not see why he should have to obey the Mother of the Shah on matters concerning the prisoner's incarceration. What did it have to do with her?

"No skin off my nose," said his Wife, when she finally learned about the Chief Steward's message. She had every intention of following the queen's commands. She suspected that whatever benefits her husband might have gained, by offering his house as a gift to the Shah, had been jeopardized the minute he deferred to the Grand Vazir. As long as there was still a way of obtaining a princess for her son, she had no scruples about imposing her highness' sanctions.

Besides, she was sufficiently jealous, after a sleepless night, to harden her heart against the prisoner. Although she sympathized in general with any woman who wanted to be clean, she was wary enough of this one to wish dirt on her head. She had no intention of wasting words or hot water on her, and gave instructions that the prisoner take care of her own laundry too, unless she had the means to pay the washerwoman for the service. If she really was a *jinn*, she did not need money or material comforts anyway. And if she wasn't, there was no need to encourage her to become a temporary wife. This woman posed a threat to the Mayor's *anderoun*.

The Wife kept close watch on her during the first weeks of her captivity, for the Mayor was too preoccupied with his other prisoners that winter. She spied on the woman surreptitiously through the tea room windows each time she came on to the flat roof of the outhouses. She observed the hour she rose at dawn to perform her ablutions, and when she swept the dust from her mats each night. She noticed how she covered her head before stepping out onto the terrace where the ogling guards could see her from the other side, and saw how quickly she retreated whenever they threw vulgar obscenities at her. She kept the prisoner under constant surveillance only to note how reluctant she was to draw attention to herself. In fact, given all the scandalous rumours, the Mayor's Wife found the poetess of Qazvin surprisingly discreet.

The same could hardly be said of the prisoner's embittered husband. After his unsatisfactory interview at the palace, the mullah from Qazvin marched over to the prison headquarters and hammered loudly at the gates, demanding in stentorian tones to see the chief of police. Since the Shah had not granted him permission to take his wife back to Qazvin, he too wanted to instruct the Mayor about the conditions of her incarceration in Tehran.

As bad luck would have it, the washerwoman had come that day, and given the definitions of uncleanliness in the Holy Book, it was the worst time of the week to be entertaining members of the clergy. The mistress of the house was exasperated. For the prisoner's husband did not hammer at the gates alone; he was attended by an entourage of ecclesiastical gentlemen, dressed in fine cashmere wool and armed to the teeth with theological proofs about his prerogatives. They were already in hot debate with the Mayor by the end of the first round of tea. It was quite evident that they intended to stay all morning and expected to be served a meal.

It was a husband's mandate to chastise his wife, they insisted. No one but her husband had the right to decide on a female prisoner's conditions of incarceration.

The Mayor shrugged. He was only following the orders of the Shah, he drawled, with an appraising glance at the clerics. It was clear to him that they were wealthy, pampered, and had food on their minds as they so vociferously objected to the rations given to female prisoners.

Even if the heretic was in the custody of the chief of police, they were saying, her diet was none of his business. Only a husband could decide what his wife should eat.

The Mayor adopted a temporizing tone, as he jingled the coins in his pockets. The prisoner's diet was certainly of no interest to him, he replied. The kitchens were not his domain. He wouldn't even dream of interfering with what his own Wife ate, he added with a laugh.

This discussion was about what a woman does *not* eat, the prisoner's husband retorted pointedly. It was about submitting to religious jurisprudence, he laboriously specified.

The Mayor noted the paunch under the priest's rich brocade. He was reputed to be a fanatic when it came to the letter of the law. Pedantry paid, he thought wryly as he cleared his throat to speak. As chief of police, he intoned, officiously, he was bound to obey his master, the Shah. But he would be glad to receive any appropriate advice suggested by his honour, the respected mullah. He would be glad, the Mayor repeated, jingling the coins in his 'aba pocket again, to consider whatever his honour offered him. If his honour wished to give him some specific counsel, he concluded, he would be more than ready to comply with his requests.

It did not take much imagination for the mullah to understand just how specific was the advice and how precise the counsel he had to offer the Mayor. The exact sum was folded neatly, in a silk purse, in the hem of his robes. Although it made him rather sore to have to pay more so that his estranged wife might eat less, he finally coughed up the required amount, counting the gold coins one by one in a well-padded palm. Since deprivation proved so expensive, he outstayed his welcome and had to be served two full meals in the course of that washing day. He used the opportunity of the evening one to elaborate on the theological basis of his demands.

The prisoner was guilty of religious as well as other crimes, he informed the Mayor, and so her incarceration should be according to canonical as well as civil law. Precedents for female heretics were rare, but certain rules and regulations did apply. According to well-documented traditions—not in the Holy Book exactly, nor in the words of the Prophet, peace be upon Him, but according to certain jurists of the past and the interpretations of individual clerics—a female heretic should be deprived of food until she relinquished her misguided opinions. The prisoner's husband wanted to ensure that this principle was upheld in the present circumstances. One piece of bread a day was quite sufficient, he said, as long as she persisted in her benighted ways.

The Mayor's Wife was scandalized when she heard of it. How could a person live on bread alone? Although she had been willing to comply with the strictures of the queen, she was less willing to submit to the cleric's demands. She suspected he was one of those men whose trousers were twisted into a turban's knot. It was not as if she were squeamish. She had been protected from the ravages of want but was perfectly accustomed to its perpetration. She was inured to the sight of famine each winter, the beggars amassed behind her gates, the children following her in the bazaar, but as long as her household was well stocked, she turned a blind eye to her husband's exploitation of the poor. What she found hard to witness was someone starved before her eyes. After two weeks of the ecclesiastical diet, the prisoner was as pale as her unleavened bread.

The Mayor's Wife finally provided the woman with an old samovar and charcoal. Even if she did not have a brazier, there was surely no harm in a mouthful of hot tea? She had already let the washerwoman to do the prisoner's laundry, for the sight of those raw and bony knuckles in the freezing pool made her nervous. A whore might have chilblains, she had thought, but would a *jinn* have so many? So it was only logical that she should ignore the payment for the laundry services. The prisoner evidently gave the washerwoman money for the market and was sharing what she bought.

They did not talk to one another, but the Mayor's Wife noticed vegetables hidden in the laundry, in their paper bundles. Since she was rather partial to the taste of bread and herbs herself, she did not see why she should tell her husband about it. All that was required to consecrate a meal of bread, tarragon, and winter parsley was a small piece of fresh white cheese.

(7)

Reports of the bread riots in Tehran did not appear in the London papers until one month after the Mayor was hanged. Mutiny was more sensational than starvation to the British public, and the recent atrocities committed in Cawnpur more relevant than the fate of wretches famished in Persian snows. When the pages of the press were not taken up with debate about the American Negro and the Civil War in the old colonies, they were filled with melancholy eulogies about the untimely demise of the Prince Consort at home. Besides, even when the news of the riots did reach London, it was hard to associate the legendary land of the Lion and the Sun with hunger. In the popular imagination, Persia positively reeled with loaves of bread and flasks of wine.

The brief notice read by the Colonel that day did, however, allude to the hanging of the Mayor. Since his retirement, the former Envoy had kept a close eye on Persia from the precincts of his London club. He had advised the Foreign Office about British interests during the Anglo-Persian war and had strong opinions on safe asylum for Armenians in that country. As his hansom cab swept through the fog that evening, he brooded over the threat posed to the Shah by women without veils and mused about the men who might be hiding behind them, inciting all this violence. He pondered over the strange story of the female heretic, which he had heard from his chargé d'affaires after coming back to Persia in the company of his bride, and remembered how he had rejected it out of hand, dismissing as preposterous the idea that an unveiled woman could threaten the stability of the country. Now, a decade later, he wondered if he had been wrong.

The Colonel had been reading a great deal of nonsense in the papers recently about women's rights. It was rather disconcerting to discover that a notorious conference on the question of universal suffrage, which took place in what used to be the American colonies the same year he resumed his post in Tehran, had been foreshadowed, that very summer, by a gathering of insurgents in the Persian countryside, about which his chargé d'affaires had tried to warn him on his return. Was it possible that words spoken by an unveiled woman to some four-score men in an obscure corner of Mazanderan had been echoed, just two weeks later, in a declaration of rights, signed in upstate New York? It sounded like a conspiracy of international dimensions! Although it was probably an injudicious topic for the dinner table, he began to hold forth on the subject of starving women that evening, just as the lamb cutlets were being served.

The political consequences of the Persian famine might prove more far-reaching than the Irish one, he trumpeted, if women became involved.

One of their dinner guests was an illustrator of a satirical journal, but the Colonel did not respond to his wife's warning glance. After a lifetime of self-restraint and cautious diplomacy, he had grown garrulous and rather deaf in his old age. She quailed for him.

It wasn't the first time the fair sex had been the cause of insurrection in that country either, he continued; they could cause a revolution the next time, if they had half a mind to do it. "These women want more than bread, I can assure you," he guffawed.

Like many shy men, the Colonel had a tendency to laugh inordinately at his poorest jokes. His wife replaced her glass with a tremulous hand and applied a napkin to the damask.

The retired ambassador's wife was known to be a reluctant hostess. A more devoted wife and mother could hardly be found between Eaton Place and Cadogan Gardens, but she was spending less time in London than she should. The curious circumstances surrounding her husband's early retirement from Iran, and her pretensions as a blue-stocking when she published her diary on her return, had somewhat lowered her ladyship's social reputation in the drawing rooms of Belgravia.

The satirist watched his hostess glance across the ranks of shining cutlery towards her husband with that air of premature exhaustion characteristic of conjugal strain. Was she worried about the danger he was posing to the old Persian porcelain, in the cabinet behind his chair, or was there some other scandal she feared he might expose? The Colonel remained oblivious to her ladyship's raised brow, however, and it looked as though they were doomed to famine and female unrest until dessert.

When she made her first courtesy call at the Qajar palace, the Colonel had instructed his wife to avoid the subject of food shortages. Stick to slaves, he had told her: it is less awkward, especially in translation. Emphasize emancipation, he advised; flatter the queen about her son's agreement to abide by international regulations. When the door of the antechamber was opened by a sinuous negress, however, the compliments died in her ladyship's throat. The conventions the Shah may have signed were clearly not in effect in the royal *anderoun*.

But what embarrassed her even more than the slave trade, what caused her to blush and be tongue-tied throughout the visit, was the queen's state of undress. Her highness was attired in a manner that quite shocked her guest. Each time her ladyship lowered her eyes, she saw a pair of naked legs sticking out beneath short skirts. Whenever she lifted them higher, she had to stare at a bare midriff, glaringly open to the waist. And when she looked straight up, she was at the mercy of that black-rimmed, brazen gaze. Under the riot of shawls, the mutiny of petticoats, and the rebellion of extravagant jewellery, the Mother of the Shah was wearing hardly anything at all.

Her ladyship had learned, in Persia, that there was little point in showing one's shoulders to advantage if one couldn't reveal one's face. And even though she did in fact show her face, she discovered, with dismay, that her husband was ill at ease with her shoulders. The Colonel was a prudish man and very pious; except for the rigorous duties of procreation, he seemed unable to distinguish between his wife and a nun. He had tried to convert her rather than court her before marriage, had invited her to rise incorruptible with him in the entirety of her restored members, and when they set out for his diplomatic post, had assured her that rebirth awaited them in the Land of the Lion and the Sun. She had not realized, at the time, the costs of such a resurrection.

On first leaving Ireland, she had imagined that she was destined for the romantic world of the Arabian Nights. But the reality of the overland route soon brought her down to earth. A fleeting glance over the high passes in the Caucasus was enough to confirm that the female sex had less relevance than the common ass in Persia. In fact, when she first crossed the borders, she thought the country was only populated by men. The welcoming ceremonies arranged for her husband were attended by men and intended for them alone, and there were as few spots of verdure to be seen en route as women's faces. She had no alternative but to hide in the *howdah*.

Her condition hardly improved after she entered the portals of the British Legation. Her every step was severely curtailed in the capital. A simple stroll across the alley involved a mounted escort. And she was not allowed to remain alone in the garden until the Colonel had ascertained that the little holes cut high in the walls on the far side were only accessible to the doves in the rafters of the house next door. Acquaintance was necessarily limited in this city and distractions few. But she noticed that the black and brown bundles flitting in and out of the bazaars were free to come and go without anyone being the wiser. She realized that the native women were exercising liberties forbidden to the wife of the British Envoy. Contrary to all appearances, this was a country effectively ruled by women.

Her visit to the Mother of the Shah proved it. She had anticipated too hopefully, perhaps, this opportunity to enter rooms which her husband had not seen. Only other women or members of the royal household were permitted inside the harem; only men related to the royal family by blood or marriage could penetrate into the intimate quarters of the Shah. In the course of her courtesy call, however, her ladyship realized that she was also out of place in the royal *anderoun*: she was excluded from the public side of the palace because of her sex and from the private side because of her foreignness. It was evident, from the shimmer of flies hovering like black lace above the cakes, that the young women who served her tea had been poised in their allotted places behind the velvet curtains ever since she had been announced at the palace gates. But when they laid all the food at her feet, she did not know where to put herself, in her confusion.

As a result, she made a *faux pas*. She managed to avoid raising the price of wheat, but inadvertently lowered the tone of the interview with her first inquiry.

Perhaps her highness might wish to talk about the ladies in this country, she began.

The Mother of the Shah gave her a level stare.

About the condition of wives and the laws of the harem, continued the ambassador's wife, uncertainly.

From her smirking, it was evident that Madame the translator had cast the question in an ironic light for there were titters all round the room. The princesses seemed highly amused.

Perhaps her ladyship might wish to talk about the English Queen, replied the Mother of the Shah, somewhat acerbically. About the number of her sons, the nature of her powers. Was it true that Her Majesty's husband was so entirely devoted?

Madame the translator proved to be a coarse creature.

Her ladyship hurriedly informed the Mother of the Shah that Her Majesty's birthday had recently been celebrated, and showed her a miniature of the Queen.

How happy the sovereign, sighed the Mother of the Shah, whose age was known to half the world. How blessed the wife whose husband served her so very faithfully. Was her ladyship so served? inquired the Mother of the Shah. Were Englishmen faithful towards their wives?

Madame the translator's wink was mortifying.

The Envoy's wife gathered up her courage. But what about Persian women, she inquired, and the laws of the harem? What about the veil? she trailed. At that the titters faded. The joke had evidently gone too far.

Madame's translation provoked a silence that could have cut the melon into slices. The queen ordered it to be served without a word. Her ladyship naturally declined to eat with her fingers, and the interview drew to a close as soon as it was decently possible to leave the room.

She never told her husband about her *faux pas* in the palace but was obliged to let him know about her encounter in the alley some weeks later.

He was very upset. The female captive, he informed her, was a danger to the state and could have caused harm to his wife. When she demurred, assuring him that the female prisoner had not been to blame, he cited instances, gave examples, illustrated how and where and when the woman had questioned norms, advocated reforms, and violated decorum all over the kingdom. But her ladyship thought that the poetess of Qazvin had probably been condemned for stating the obvious rather than for deviating from the truth. Her words seemed holy, she told the Colonel. She must have been quoting from the sacred scriptures, because she certainly resolved the congestion in the alley miraculously.

A woman surely had more important things to do than direct traffic, answered the Colonel stiffly. And no wonder the priests were upset with her, he added, if she employed religion for such purposes. But he suspected the Cossacks might be responsible for the congestion in the alley. Foreign interference, he declared, could not be ruled out.

Her ladyship was woken from her recollections of her Persian past by the presence of the gravy boat. Foreign interference, her husband was saying in stentorian tones, could not be ruled out. Russians as well as women might be responsible for the Persian famine. The Tsar was quite capable of taking advantage of a neighbour's calamities. The Legation had been flooded with appeals for sanctuary, so he had been informed, and a recent dispatch from the British attaché had just reported that one poor woman was so badly beaten that she could barely speak.

The Colonel's wife stared at the shrivelled cutlet on her plate and declined the cold gravy. There had been a gradual chilling of relations between the couple over the past decade. Although her husband had acquired a double crypt in a north London cemetery with intentions that were lugubriously clear, she had as little interest in sharing his tomb as his bed. In fact, after so many confinements, she rather fancied starting up at the trump of doom alone.

A woman so badly beaten she could barely speak, she thought. And for some reason, the poor lamb cutlet on her plate reminded her of the Wife of the Mayor.

(8)

The Mayor's Wife denied that there were any tortures taking place in her cellars, that first winter that the poetess of Qazvin was placed in her husband's custody. Although she was most upset about having prisoners on the premises and complained loudly about the groaning and moaning downstairs, she did not wish to know precisely what was going on. She was well aware that a dozen men of good family had also been captured in the purges of the Grand Vazir, but despite the cracking and the whipping and the thumping sounds below, she preferred not to dwell on their fate. It was dreadfully awkward. It was also a confounded nuisance, because the cellars were used as a refuge from the heat in the summer season and she, for one, intended to enjoy her watermelons sitting in the cool down there, in a few months' time. But above all it was a social embarrassment. How could she possibly find a wife for her son with all this hullabaloo going on? How could she talk freely with the marriage brokers? The tortures were a serious impediment to dowry discussions. The uncomfortable proximity of the woman in the upper chamber, moreover, made it very difficult to pretend that her house was not a jail.

Then, early one cold morning, three days before the public executions, the prisoner accosted her directly. She slipped out of the upper chamber, as the mistress of the house was walking down the breezeway steps towards the kitchen, and with a rapid glance in the direction of the public courtyard, threw herself flat on the icy terrace. She had obviously been waiting for a chance to talk to the Mayor's Wife without being seen by the guards patrolling on the other side.

A message for your master! she called, in a low voice.

The Mayor's Wife was startled to see the female prisoner leaning down from the terrace directly overhead. She was wrapped in a shawl and shivering in the bitter wind. The snow-capped mountains to the north rose white behind her, and her fluttering scarf was like a cloud about her head; the mid-winter wind keened in her breath and her eyes were leaden as dulled skies. The Mayor's Wife was disconcerted at the sight of her. She had never seen the woman at such close quarters, those hollow cheeks, that stark spot below her lower lip, the darkened brow above her thick-lashed, hungry look. She drew back nervously, for she knew the servants were spying from the kitchens, the maids whispering at the doors. The daughters of the Mayor had pressed their noses flat against the tea room windows; her mole of a sister-in-law was snuffing in the breezeway. She had no desire to be seen talking to a prisoner.

Tell him to stop the tortures! whispered the poetess of Qazvin.

The Mayor's Wife was speechless. The nerve of it! She hardly trusted her own voice. "What tortures?" she retorted, querulously. She had no idea what to say, how to reply.

You know what he's doing down there, murmured the woman.

The Mayor's Wife shivered. Had the others heard the question? She glanced round.

Tell him to stop! repeated the prisoner, urgently.

The Mayor's Wife bit her lip and steeled herself to speak. Who did she think she was, this harridan? How dare she ask the mistress of the house to be her go-between? "I don't know what you're talking about," she snapped, and flounced off, for the benefit of the watching women.

But she was shaken to the core. She could no longer ignore the groans in the cellars. She spoke to the Mayor that very night. Not because of the prisoner's plea but because she could not bear it herself. Enough was enough, she hissed, under cover of darkness. Wasn't there a limit to this business? Surely if he couldn't squeeze any more out of these men, it was better to just stop? She wasn't speaking on their behalf, but on her own account and her son's, she said. She would never be able to hold her head up in the neighbourhood if this nasty business continued.

"Why, even the female prisoner is complaining about it!" she added, crossly.

She could complain all she wanted, the Mayor yawned, but his Wife had no business talking to her. Perhaps she would shut her mouth if she had less in it, he added, testily.

The Mayor's Wife shut her own mouth at that and tried to ignore the harrowing sounds that continued the following day. She also avoided leaving the four walls of the house, not only because of the recent snows and a bitter wind but because she did not want to risk another confrontation with the woman in the upper chamber. But the prisoner was waiting for her. Ignoring the soldiers on the other side, she sat crouched on the edge of the terrace, watching for the Mayor's Wife. And as soon as she emerged on the breezeway, she called again, a second time.

Khanum, she mouthed, low and urgent. A word with you.

The heart of the Mayor's Wife contracted. What now? She looked up with dread.

The female prisoner was kneeling this time, her scarf pushed back, her hair unkempt. Her hands were cradled in her lap and she was shivering. The Mayor's Wife stared at her chapped fingers in order to avoid looking into her eyes. When she finally had the courage to do so, she saw, with a rush of confusion, that the woman had been weeping.

You gave him my message? she breathed. Her eyes were rimed, the lids puffy.

The Mayor's Wife did not know where to look. The prisoner's lips were chapped too. They had an unhealthy darkness about them, as though she had been sucking ink.

Did you tell him to stop the tortures? the woman insisted. He's been at it night and day for two weeks.

The Mayor's Wife struggled. What could she say? The woman was not demanding food for herself; she was not requesting relief from her own sufferings, which would have made it marginally easier to reject the plea. But she was begging for a respite on behalf of those others, those miserable wretches in the cellars of whose existence the Mayor's Wife knew only by their sudden piteous cries at night, their low, persistent, daily groans.

Shall I tell you what is being done to them? the poetess was saying, so softly that the Mayor's Wife was forced against her will, to come nearer, so intensely that she could not help but draw closer, not wanting the others to hear. Shall I describe to you, she was saying, how they are being stripped and thrown naked into the frozen pond in the other courtyard? How they are being lashed and branded with irons? Their turbans have been torn from their heads and befouled; their necks have been loaded with rusty chains. They are being forced to stand in horse dung through the night and made to eat it in the mornings. Their nails have been pulled out with metal pincers, their noses pierced with meat hooks, their bodies mutilated with knives—

"Stop!" gasped the Mayor's Wife, drawing back, horrified. The woman was mad.

But it doesn't stop, does it? continued the other, remorselessly. It goes on and on, day after day. These men will be mangled to death before the executioner can give them the coup de grace. The prisoner took a deep breath, and it seemed to the Mayor's Wife that she was burning inside, for there was such a strange, fierce light in her eyes. Tell your husband, for the love of God, to leave them alone, she urged. Tell him it's my turn now. Let him torture me instead.

The Mayor's Wife shuddered. The woman must definitely be unhinged, she thought, eating nothing but bread up there. She must have lost her mind from hunger and cold to make such a crazy appeal. But perhaps it was more of a threat than a request. Her turn now? This plea sounded like an ultimatum. Was she planning to throw herself off the ledge? thought the Mayor's Wife, in sudden panic. The terrace was high; she would break her neck if she fell!

The Mayor's Wife backed away warily from the poetess of Qazvin. There were stories going around town about this woman and her messages. There were tales told about this heretic's ultimatums. On one occasion before her capture, according to the gossip, she had sent a message to one of her students, in an orchard, in the provinces. She had insisted that the young man should come to see her in the tent pitched for the use of women only, so they said. It was against all decency, all decorum, but when the youth ignored the improper request, she had immediately sent another message, saying that if he did not comply with her wishes, she would come to him instead; she would leave her own garden and enter the orchard reserved for men. The messenger charged to convey this fearful ultimatum had been so terrified at the prospect that he had begged the young man in question to cut his throat lest he witness his mistress carry out her threat.

But even as he bared his neck, even as the sword was raised against him, she had done the impossible. She had stepped amongst them all, forced herself upon those men, naked-faced.

And she was doing it again, thought the Mayor's Wife, shrinking back in agitation. She was forcing her reversals on them, she thought in horror; she was blackmailing her, the mistress of the house! Just listen to her, raising her voice, imperiously, so everyone could hear!

"If you don't, I'll warn him myself!"

The shutters of the tea room creaked slightly, exhaling women's breath, as the Mayor's Wife turned her back against the mean wind. The kitchen doors slammed in the cold breeze behind her, pushed by ringed fingers, caught by passing skirts. The Mayor's Wife began to stumble blindly back up the breezeway steps and was shaking by the time she reached the top. She knew she had to say something to this prisoner before going indoors—a retort, a reply, anything to restore her dignity—but her response evaporated when she turned round to face her.

The woman had not moved from her position on the terrace. She was still kneeling in the middle of the snow. But tears were streaming down her ravaged cheeks. She was gazing at the Mayor's Wife with an air of infinite sorrow, of despair almost.

"Forgive me," she called out, hoarsely. "I should not have become so angry."

The Mayor's Wife flushed crimson. She felt a hand reach down and wrench at her heart.

"It is not your fault," the prisoner repeated. "I'm sorry."

Her words gave the Mayor's Wife quite a turn. She seemed to be apologizing for both of them, asking pardon for them both. It was as though she saw more reason to pity than reproach the mistress of the house. The Mayor's Wife had the impression, at that moment, that she had been stripped naked, as when the prisoner glanced up at her that first night. She felt as though she had been read through from beginning to end and found wanting. She became thoroughly flustered. She had no idea what she had done but knew it had been wrong. She was about to beg for pardon too but before she could utter a word, the prisoner rose and left. She rose to her feet in a single motion as if from prayers, rose with the grace of one acquainted with genuflection, and turned away.

For several minutes after she disappeared, like snow in a shaft of sun, the Mayor's Wife stood staring, dumbly, at her absence on the terrace roof.

She decided then that she must speak to the Mayor, come what may. The last thing she wanted was for her husband to be accosted too, by such bewildering beauty, such knowing pain. The last thing she wanted was for this woman to touch his heart, in this same unnerving way.

₵ 9 ⟆

"He had it coming to him," trumpeted the Colonel. "The man was a brute."

His wife sighed. She was grateful that the starving women had been removed from the table, along with the lamb chops and the cold gravy, but was dismayed at the prospect of eating her pudding in the company of the Mayor of Tehran. Her husband had been an outspoken critic of their neighbour while in Persia and had often railed against him since they left.

After her frightful experience in the alley, the British Envoy had forbidden his wife to visit the garden due to its proximity to the Mayor's house. Melancholy sounds were drifting over their neighbour's walls that winter. Harrowing groans could be heard from the house next door. The cellars of the chief of police were crammed with suspects, so they said, and there was talk of a plot against the new Vazir. He had unleashed purges across the land in a determined effort to wield a strong arm at the start of the reign, and her ladyship had been instructed to stay indoors until the worst was over. Her exile from the garden coincided with the queen's, to Qum.

"I tried to draw his majesty's attention to it at the time," intoned the Colonel. "The chap's commissions amounted to half the national budget. But mutual benefits, don't you know!"

His wife winced. She used to flee from the Legation, under the guise of gardening. She used to ask to be escorted over the alley just so that she could walk beneath the dreary cypresses, and breathe. And when she was not occupied with planting vegetables and pruning her roses, she used to brood as well; she used to linger beneath the poplars, by the graves of dead English infants and their puerperal mothers, just to remember who she was. Her condition often precluded too much exercise. Her three-year sojourn in Persia had been one of continuous confinement. The first child was born soon after she arrived and the third just before they quit the country.

"Exorbitant lease," the Colonel announced. "But a woman needs her daily constitutional!"

His wife was obliged to participate in the conversation at that point. Yes, gardening. A charming recreation. As it happened the Shah's gardener was an Englishman. From Staffordshire, she believed. No, she did not regret her sojourn in Persia. "Roses and nightingales," she murmured.

"I suppose," the satirist lowered his voice discreetly, "your ladyship did not mix much with the locals?"

She avoided answering his question. Most Persian ladies had only been interested in her whalebone corset and the undergarments of her Irish maid. The royal princesses wanted to know why she removed her clothes to go to bed and mocked her for sitting for half an hour in tepid water instead of spending the day in the steaming public baths. Few exchanged anything but banalities with her. The two Armenian sisters, who visited her on the grounds of Christian charity, had even less in common with her. They shared her religion but it was clear from the way they wielded their parasols that they did not like her dog. They also thought her barbaric to have planted cabbages and cauliflowers among the tuber roses. To her great disappointment, she was not permitted to cultivate the acquaintance of the wife and daughter of the Russian Minister.

"For obvious reasons," bellowed her husband from the other end of the table, for reasons that were not obvious at all, at her end.

Her only other outings had been to a covered theatre where religious pageants were performed. She had seen a passion play there during her first winter: a sacred history, she supposed. A few camels served as cavalry for the heavenly hosts, a boy in a veil performed the part of a dying girl, and Gabriel looked like a courtesan, covered in spangles. But as she watched the tawdry spectacle from the suffocating loge above the stage, she experienced a curious sensation. It was like stepping into someone else's dream and finding herself asleep in it. The symbols belonged to a different religion, but the plot was entirely familiar. The characters were unknown, but the story was the same. It was the old story of sacrifice and resurrection, the never-ending love story of the world. In spite of herself, her tears welled up in the theatre, just as they had done in the alley. Hot air and bombast, her husband called it: everybody howling and weeping and carrying on. Female members of the royal family were among the worst offenders, he told her, dismissively. He thought the holy pageants hopelessly over-emotional and would have declined the invitation to the Persian theatricals, had his attaché not offered to escort her.

"Held the city hostage for years, you know," barked the Colonel, still harking on the Mayor, she supposed. "Had the court blackmailed too. About time he got his comeuppance."

Her husband had been on bad terms with his attaché long before he married. They had begun their careers in India at the same time, conducted military training in Persia for the same period, and harboured equal high ambitions. But their temperaments were different, their tactics opposed. The Colonel was of a bookish inclination, straight-laced and tight-fisted, a stickler for facts; the Captain was popular with the stable hands for his lavish tips, enjoyed his Shiraz wines, and loved a good story. It did not ease their relationship that the former was considered astute at Whitehall while the latter was popular in the royal *anderoun*. When one became the Envoy Plenipotentiary and the other was made his chargé d'affaires, tensions mounted, and after the new ambassador returned from his leave of absence with a youthful bride, jealousies erupted.

"The fellow was a bounder," the Colonel thundered. "A proper cad."

His wife tried to catch the eye of the butler. The last course was taking an interminable length of time to be served. The domestics were probably gossiping in the kitchens. Soon after she arrived in the Persian capital, she had discovered that the *mirzas* employed at the Legation were running bets as to which of the two diplomats would call it quits. It was like the horse races: the secretaries were actually putting money on whether the Envoy or his attaché would first resign. Some were certain that the Colonel had more sticking power; others swore that the Captain would out-swagger him. But even when her husband contracted shingles that last gruelling summer, and had to take a cure of sulphur waters in the hills, he still refused to give in.

"No one could get rid of him," he boomed, from the far end of the table. "No one could force him out of office, not even the queen. His Wife was a regular harridan, one of those who should never be given the vote," he guffawed. "But it's taken six thousand of them without veils to get rid of that fellow. Dreadful business!"

Even after the attempt on the Shah's life, she remembered, her husband had hung on. He would not budge, despite fresh murders for breakfast and mayhem every night. But his attaché resigned soon after the reprisals, either because he had participated in the executions on the orders of the queen or because he had refused to do so and had to flee the consequences. She never knew which. It happened a few months after the death of the poetess of Qazvin.

"A cruel and useless deed," her ladyship said softly.

"How so, madam?" echoed the satirist.

She looked up, startled. She had not realized that she had spoken aloud.

"I assure you, sir," bellowed the Colonel, coming to her rescue. "It was exactly so. They said his cellars ran with blood. Serve him right if he became the Shah's scapegoat in the end. His body was hung at the gates for three days, and when they finally cut him down, he wasn't just drawn and quartered, I can tell you: the women hacked him to bits with their bare hands, chopped him up piece-meal with their sewing scissors apparently, after humping his carcass through the streets. Barbarians, the lot of them."

Her ladyship shuddered. The cook's retribution had arrived: stewed fruit and jellies topped by virulent yellow custard. She gripped the spoon and felt the familiar waves of nausea. Three times in Persia. Three times in England. This would be her seventh confinement.

"Just desserts, madam?" offered the satirist beside her, raising a wry brow.

〖 10 〗

The Mayor stayed in the cellars the whole day before the executions. He even remained down there after nightfall. The prisoners were to be conducted into the marketplace early the following morning, but he evidently wished to extort as much from them as he could, before relinquishing them to the executioner. They had been wealthy citizens, and well-known.

The house reeked with his exertions. The Mayor's Wife thought her husband must be boiling sheep in the cellars, wool and all; she was afraid he was frying shoes, kebabing feather quilts, stewing old turbans. She plunged into a frenzy of pickle-making that morning, to cover the stench of scorched flesh, but nothing relieved her nerves or her nostrils. And although she spent the afternoon huddled over the brazier in the tea room, sipping an infusion of fennel seeds, drinking white tea steeped with cardamom, the congestion in her chest would not lift.

She was unable to speak to her husband all that day and by the time darkness fell, she was almost hysterical. If he did not come out of that cellar soon, she thought, she would go down there and talk to him herself. Or else she would climb the ladder and give the poetess of Qazvin a piece of her mind. When the tea room finally became too suffocating to endure, she padded into the cold night air of the breezeway, wrapped in a quilt. She had to breathe or burst.

The prisoner had placed her in a very awkward position. Her challenge was outrageous, and yet her plea seemed sincere; her defiance was presumptuous but her demands were fair. The emotions she aroused were so conflicting that the Mayor's Wife felt herself go hot and cold all over, thinking about them. She had been shocked by the physical deterioration of the woman. Captivity and starvation had taken their toll. Except for the blaze in her eyes, that wretch shivering down from the terrace that morning was very different from the one who had glanced up so confidently, so brazenly from the courtyard below, on the evening of her arrival. She must have been driven against the wall to make such an appeal, thought the Mayor's Wife.

But why had she submitted to this wretchedness in the first place? Why had she put herself in this position? She was young and from a privileged family; she was educated and attractive. Why had she chosen this humiliation, instead of living in comfort and ease? She could have been mistress of her own house, in command of her own *anderoun*; she could have handled her husband cleverly, and still had her way with him, like every other woman. Did think she was different, superior to the rest of them? Did she think she was any better than the Wife of the Mayor of Tehran? Why, she had done the necessary, thought the Mayor's Wife, stoutly. She had played the game and lived the good life. And what was wrong with that, pray?

But even as she wrapped her quilts more closely round her and cursed the Mayor for taking so long, it occurred to his Wife that there might be something slightly reprehensible about her situation. Was she leading such a very good life? And what was the name of the game that let her live in ease inside her *anderoun* while others suffered below and beyond these walls? How would history judge her, pampered by the chief of police, as innocent folk were being tortured under her feet? She knew perfectly well that the prisoners were innocent; everyone did. They had been rounded up on the flimsiest pretexts and were going to be executed in the market square for the most venal reasons. In fact, she suspected that the poetess of Qazvin might have been brought to this pass for their sake. She may have accepted humiliation on principle, for their cause.

It was very disturbing to consider the reasons why the poetess of Qazvin had thrown her life away like this. Either she was truly misguided, as the priests were claiming, and had been sadly deluded by some charlatan, some manipulator of conscience—in which case, thought the Mayor's Wife, she deserved to be saved from her own folly—(a possibility which seemed somewhat contradictory in light of her evident and reputed intelligence). Or else she was mad, insane, a lunatic, like the idiot gatekeeper of the prison headquarters—(a second possibility that had several times occurred to the Mayor's Wife that morning)—in which case, she pondered, the poor woman ought to be pitied rather than punished and protected by friends and family rather than driven to such a pass. Yet if she was just mad or simply deluded, she thought, suffused by a hot flush and a shiver at the same time, then why was she considered such a danger to the state? Why had she been chased across the country and arrested by the soldiers of the Shah on the orders of the Grand Vazir? Why did her highness the queen care a fig about whether or not she had a bath? There was only one other possibility. That she was neither lunatic nor a fool. That her cause was worth suffering for, worth dying for, worth everything. If she had been driven up against the wall, was it possibly because certain people in high places had reason to fear her criticisms? For she was advocating justice; she was challenging the old ways—

The cellar doors opened at that moment. As the capped head of the Mayor rose up the shallow steps of the cellar, his Wife's heart skipped a beat. Her husband was wiping his palms on his robes as he climbed up into the courtyard of the women's *anderoun*.

Bother him, she thought, with disgust and relief. Why doesn't he go the other way round?

The Mayor's Wife was a stickler for household rules. The cellar doors leading into the women's courtyard were kept closed when police work, as she called it, was taking place below; she obliged the Mayor to come and go by the *birouni* at such times and enter through the arch. She would have scolded him for having come up the wrong way at that moment, had not a finger of light reached out from behind him, and cautioned her. The cellar door had been left open and the light came from below. She saw it pointing incongruously and with ominous significance at the stone lip of the pool where the washerwoman did the laundry. She bit her tongue, and the court-yard quivered with pain. His thugs were evidently still at work down there.

Her husband's head, emerging above ground, was as blunt as an axe beneath the clear night sky. The clouds had gusted away and the condemned would be killed under the cruel spring sun the following morning. His bulky body sliced through the shaft of light from the cellars like the executioner's axe that would fall on their necks, before the door slammed shut behind him and the finger of light withdrew. And then, he almost missed his foot-ing on the top step, as his name was called out in the darkness.

His Wife was not sure, at first, whether she had imagined or really heard the sound. She was not sure if the voice came from the terrace above

or the cellars below. And then the poetess of Qazvin blotted out the stars.
She was almost invisible against the night sky, veiled from head to toe in
blue calico, as was her habit in front of the Mayor. His Wife froze. Was she
going to fulfill her threat? Was she going to throw herself off the terrace?
What was she going to do? He was stammering a curse as he tried to regain
his balance. Her voice pared through it like a blade.

"Beware, sir Mayor," said the poetess of Qazvin.

His Wife stopped breathing.

"Beware his majesty!" she repeated.

A trickle of ice ran down between her shoulder blades and her cheeks
burned.

"Beware the king who will betray you in the end," said the prisoner.

And the Wife of the Mayor seemed to hear the roar of a far off crowd
as she continued.

"This master whom you serve so faithfully
will one day betray you.
Mark these words, sir Mayor,
for my death will prove them true."

The Mayor's Wife released her breath with a gasp. Her husband turned
round and saw her at that moment, on the breezeway, in the rainbow light
cast by the fan of glass above the tea room door. He was incensed as he
swung back towards the poetess of Qazvin.

"You!" he stammered, shaking his fist at the darkness, "you mind your
own business!"

This was her business, replied the prisoner. He had made scapegoats of
the innocent long enough. He should let the others go and turn his attention to her now.

"I'll turn you, you minx," shouted the Mayor, lunging towards her. "I'll
screw you, you whore! You bitch!" He almost missed his footing again in
his rage and staggered on the ice.

Her death, she continued quietly, would prove it. He would remember
this one day.

This woman had her own notion of logic, thought the Mayor's Wife in bewilderment. She had her own crazy reasoning for everything. Prove what? Remember when? Her head spun in the effort to understand. Why was the prisoner warning her husband like this and where had she suddenly disappeared? For by the time he gained his balance back on the ice, the Mayor was cursing the empty sky. The poetess of Qazvin had made her damnable prophecy, returned to her room, and snuffed the lamp out behind her. Her absence was as startling as her presence.

The Mayor's Wife stood transfixed. She knew her husband was beside himself with rage. He was furious, humiliated, and in a savage mood. She heard him slithering across the icy courtyard, cursing his way up the steps, stammering. Whenever he lost his temper like this and stumbled over his words, he whipped the servants afterwards within an inch of their lives. Would he order the prisoner to be hauled down from the terrace by her heels for daring to address him so presumptuously? Would he whip her? Or might he finally beat his own Wife, as he had threatened to, so often, in the past? But it wasn't her fault, was it, she thought, defensively, if the poetess had said such horrible things? Why should she be held responsible, just because she had witnessed the scene, when the whole household had also been eavesdropping?

The Mayor had reached the bottom step of the breezeway and was clambering up towards her. He was gnawing his lower lip; his jaw was jerking the way it did when he lost control. He would be on her at any moment. His Wife took a deep breath, fixed her eyes on him, and smiled.

What nonsense! she babbled, as the Mayor approached her, step by step. What a provocation! she trilled, as he drew nearer, swinging his arm. Who did that woman think she was and why would anyone believe her? She was a lunatic, a heretic, and her words showed the error of her ways. Why, it was inconceivable that his majesty should betray so faithful a servant!

But even as she chatted, the door of the tea room opened behind her. The icy air of the breezeway dissolved in a stream of female whispers. A maid was murmuring at her shoulder.

The Mayor had reached the top step. His Wife took advantage of the darkness to run swiftly towards him and throw her arms around his neck. "There's a message from the palace for you, my dear!" she cooed, in his ear. He was rigid, but she clung to him doggedly, cleaved to him. "You've been summoned by the Shah," she said softly. "I told you, he can't do anything without you." It took half a second for her to be in full control, and his fist fell to his side.

A man can be tortured by lust too, he thought, as he strode across the courtyard a short while later. And he cuffed the gatekeeper's ear violently before riding off to the palace.

(11)

The London dailies did not report on the growing deafness of the gatekeeper, the year that the Mayor was hanged. The poor idiot had been buffeted about regularly for over a decade, but when his ears began to suffer from internal bleeding during the bread riots, it did not make the news. Nor did the papers record the social demise of the washerwoman that winter. Having slipped from the rank of wet-nurse to midwife in the course of her career, she slid still further from laundress to corpse washer, as a result of the famine raging in the Persian capital. Most importantly, Fleet Street remained ignorant of the conjunction between starving women and the insufficiency of kings: the Shah's impotence did not receive universal attention either. But his Mother's remark somehow made it into print: "When the people want a whipping boy, their leaders should know who to blame." The quote was inaccurate, the source unacknowledged, and there was no reference to bread, but the need for scapegoats was noted by the British press the same year that flogging, slavery, and the death penalty were being questioned in the West.

Winters had always been the scapegoat season in Persia. Soaring bread prices invariably coincided with dropping temperatures in the capital, and the rise of mendicancy was as inevitable as mud in the streets. By the time the women revolted, at the height of the riots, exploitation had become routine. Public executions were no longer needed to divert people's attention from inflated prices; lucrative monopolies were no longer required to mollify the clerics and the queen; and concubines were no longer necessary as a distraction from starvation. If scapegoats were needed, the Mayor knew exactly where to look for them, for he had a royal mandate, a royal patron now. The chief beneficiary of these shortages was the king himself. Finally, after being under the thumb of queen and courtier for years, his majesty controlled the purse strings.

He could not, however, control the riots. The fury of the famished that year could not be deflected and swept through the city like wildfire. When his guards met with furious resistance that cold February day, as they escorted his majesty back from the chase, he was forced to admit that scapegoats, unlike mud, could not always be ignored. Although the Shah had glimpsed at gaunt-faced peasants lining the country roads to beg for alms in the course of the hunting season, he had not thought the food shortages bore any relation to himself. But when the rich barricaded themselves in their mansions and the poor gathered at the palace gates, when women began to scream for bread and mercy, howl for rice and justice in the streets, he could no longer ignore the seriousness of the situation. He was obliged to estimate the cost of the famine to his own person.

His progress through town was severely impeded. The crowd around his carriage was dense, the menace of the hungry more pressing with every passing moment. It was not long before the royal entourage, having inched through the winding alleys, and reached the roaring market square, and finally crawled with aching slowness through the packed mob to the other side, came to a complete standstill before the palace gates. The guards could not move one step further for the desperate masses surged against the coach, like a human sea. Instead of turning their faces respectfully to the walls when he passed by, according to custom, the women were using their teeth, their nails, their fists to overwhelm the guards; they were scrabbling at the carriage doors with bleeding fingers and pressing their open mouths against the glass. And their lips clouded the cold panes with the breath of starvation.

The Shah yelled at his escort to beat, to lash, to break, to shoot their way through the blockade. He ordered them to cut through the crowd whatever the consequences, to force the horses through the gates no matter how high the cost. Let them pave the pavements with broken bones if necessary in order to get him to the royal compound as fast as possible. He stopped his ears to the screams. He shut his eyes. And when the carriage crunched over the bodies to pass through, he finally looked over his shoulder and was appalled to see the wretched creatures scaling the walls, climbing the gates, impaling themselves on pikes in the attempt to follow him.

The King of Kings and Shadow of God fled into his *anderoun* then, to escape from the savage hunger of the people. He took refuge among his women. He was sure that the mob would not pursue him there; he was certain that no one, however ravenous, would have the presumption to violate the sanctuary of the royal harem.

(12)

After the Mayor left for the palace on the eve of the first public executions, his Wife ordered her trousseau chest to be opened and her matrimonial quilts to be spread in the largest chamber of the *anderoun*. She knew how to handle her husband. He was an irascible man, but also an uxorious one. If she had not yet been the object of his violence, it was because she knew exactly how to keep his love. But even she had reached her limits that evening. The Mayor might have beaten her to pulp had the king's summons not intervened. The moment had passed, perilously passed, but she was aware that his rage had only receded before another rising.

She feared for her own safety, but despite her husband's anger, she was more afraid for his. The summons of the king had protected her from the Mayor's brutality, but she dreaded lest it lead to his punishment. What if the Shah had called him to the palace to take him to task, to accuse him of embezzlement, to condemn him, finally, for extortion? What if the poetess' frightful warnings would come true? If the words of her embittered husband, the cleric, were to be believed, it would not be the first time that this heretic had anticipated the death of a man.

The prediction she had just uttered in the dark that evening haunted the Wife of the Mayor after her husband went to the palace. She could not forget it; she could not understand it. She did not dare imagine the provenance of such strange intelligence and was more than ever sure the heretic was a *jinn*. She might have wished her dead, for having given voice to such dread words, were her death not the very proof she had promised would confirm them true. What if the Shah had summoned the Mayor to the palace to order the prisoner's execution that very evening? What if her demise would lead to his, just as she had foretold? The Mayor's Wife greatly feared her own fate, then.

But she comforted herself with the thought that this late summons to the palace might not necessarily be to the detriment of the Mayor. Perhaps the Shah wished to praise her husband, not to punish him. He had extracted suitable confessions from at least half the condemned to satisfy the clergy, after all, and put enough pressure on the rest to extort profitable bribes for the court. Perhaps his majesty wished to fête him for his faithful services, for it was the royal custom, during the tedious month of fasting, to prolong banquets through the midnight watches. And maybe the queen herself was planning an even more auspicious recompense. Maybe, hazarded the Mayor's Wife, swinging from horror to hope in the effort to reassure herself, her husband had been summoned to the court in order to be granted news of a royal match for her son!

She sought to balance these extremes by resorting to the old tricks of the *anderoun*. Maintaining equilibrium in a household could not always be achieved by external means: a woman was obliged to depend on the subtle arts of internal pressure. The Mayor's Wife was an adept at such wiles. She knew how to ward off the anger, woo back the confidence, and at the same time wheedle answers out of a man. Having made the bed, she rubbed rouge on her cheeks, stripped down to her petticoats and put her gold bangles on. Then, after giving instructions for her husband's favourite food to be prepared, she ordered all the women out of the tea room and sent for silver ewers and a copper basin to be brought in.

As soon as the servants announced his arrival, she welcomed her lord and master into a room warmed by braziers and made fragrant with rose water and cardamom. She washed his feet in the copper basin herself, in water steeped with limes, to show her appreciation of his safe return.

She also served him a delectable dinner with her own hands and rubbed his stiff joints with soothing balms. And since it is always easier to ingratiate oneself by means of denigrating another, she began to attack the prisoner the minute the meal was over.

That woman was impossible, she said, as she arranged the quilts comfortably behind her husband's back. How long would they have to endure her, holed up there in the upper chamber?

The Mayor grunted. His anger had receded with his appetite; his passions had been stirred as his stomach was appeased. And he did not want to be reminded of the prisoner.

His Wife had placed herself judiciously at his feet. She was not fond of her husband's feet, but she did her best to massage them with fidelity. What she could not bear, she murmured, was to see her lord and master being abused by that woman's abominable predictions.

The Mayor stirred irritably, loosened the folds of his 'aba, and burped.

Had the Shah decided what to do with her yet? she repeated, angling for information.

The Mayor eased himself on one elbow and edged closer to his Wife. He liked the way the lamplight glowed on her henna-red hair. He enjoyed the gentle tinkle of the bangles on her white arms. But he hoped she was not going to waste her conjugal privileges by talking.

"To hell with the prisoner!" he said gruffly, reaching down to squeeze her shoulder.

When she drew back, prettily aggrieved, and stopped massaging his feet with an appealing pout, he tried to made amends. He only meant that she should not worry her dear little head about such things, he said, fondly. He really did love her very much.

But was he going to let the wretch get away with such outrageous remarks? she persisted. Hadn't he complained to the Shah about her shocking behaviour that evening?

The Mayor loved the way his Wife's little ear lobes glittered as she tossed her curls. She was wearing his favourite earrings, he noted, but he did wish that she'd stop talking.

Anyway, what was his majesty's business with her lord and master tonight? she quizzed.

Indicating that his own business lay in the region of her blouse, he leaned forward to tickle her. She was his love, he told her thickly, his own dove, his little white turnip.

But his Wife resisted. She giggled, deliciously, saying that she wanted to know what the Shah was going to do with the woman first.

He told her it was a secret and tried to stop her mouth with kisses.

But she slipped out of his arms, demanding to be told the secret first.

The Mayor was beginning to become exasperated. The Shah wanted to see her, that was all, he snapped. He would decide what to do with her afterwards. If the Grand Vazir let him. And with that, he pulled his Wife roughly down on the quilts. He had his own priorities.

She wriggled away with alacrity. "You mean she's going to court?" she cried.

Too late he realized he had let the secret out. He told her, frowning, to lower her voice. She was not to tell a soul, not to speak to anyone about it, he growled. His majesty wished the poetess to be brought to the palace in a week's time, but it was top secret, did she understand? The condemned men had already been interrogated by the Grand Vazir for their part in the recent insurgencies and it was her turn next, that's all. But no tittle-tattle, no tale-telling, he warned.

"Her turn?" echoed his Wife. And to her husband's dismay, she sat bolt upright in the bed. "Why, that's just what she said herself! Remember? That's what she said tonight."

He did not wish to remember. He told his Wife to shut up and lie down. When he had first married her, she used to let him nibble her earrings off.

She squealed. He clamped his hand over her mouth. She bit him and he pulled away, in surprise. Provoked, he pinned her back on the quilts. Her face was flushed, to his satisfaction.

But if the prisoner met the Shah, his Mother would have something to say about it, wouldn't she? she retorted hotly. The secret would be out then, wouldn't it?

The Mayor bent over her, aroused. Now why, he grunted, would her highness need to hear the secrets he was whispering in these pretty little ears?

His Wife squirmed away, reminding him that her highness had spies all over the city. She would be dreadfully upset with the Mayor if he took that woman to see the Shah.

Her husband told her there was not much he could do about that; he had been give orders.

But what, she repeated, freeing her elbow from his grasp, about the queen's orders? Didn't her son's happiness depend on his following the orders of the Mother of the Shah?

The Mayor was tired of words. "Stuff the queen," he answered, crossly. The Grand Vazir had agreed to interrogate the woman in the presence of the king. He had to obey his masters.

His Wife tinkled dangerously and narrowed her black eyes. How many masters did he actually have, she inquired. Was he obeying the Grand Vazir or the king?

"A man obeys one master at a time, my dove," he murmured. "And so should a woman."

He had better remember the prisoner's warning, she whispered back.

The Mayor stiffened. "Control your tongue, my honey girl," he said softly.

He should think of what would happen if his master betrayed him, she hissed.

"Keep your mouth shut, my beauty," the Mayor growled.

If the queen put pressure on the Grand Vazir and the Grand Vazir told the Shah to fulfill the prisoner's predictions, she persisted relentlessly, imagine the consequences for them all—

"Silence!" he roared, and lunged at her.

Too late. She shrieked, she scrambled to her feet, and ran towards the door.

She could move fast, thought the Mayor ruefully, despite her plumpness. He had tried to grab at her ankles as she scampered past but had to pull his 'aba around his shoulders instead, for just at that moment there was a scuffling and a whispering outside the door. Damn the woman; had she no shame? Couldn't she even hold her tongue in the privacy of their chamber? he thought angrily. But his Wife had no compunction about exploiting his vulnerability.

"If you are betrayed by the Shah," she wailed, "what will happen to my son?"

Nothing would happen, the Mayor said, through clenched teeth, if she would just shut up.

"That's exactly what I'm afraid of," sniffed his Wife. "Nothing will happen. My poor darling's the one that'll be betrayed!" And she began to cry noisily into her headscarf.

The boy would just have to wait to get married, the Mayor said, curtly.

"But for how long?" howled his Wife.

Until the queen returned from Qum, her husband snapped back, in exasperation.

The scuffles ceased behind the door and gave way to a shocked silence that pervaded the room. The Mayor swore. He turned away from his Wife. He could feel her eyes boring at him.

"Qum?" she breathed.

The last thing he had wanted to do was let her know about the exile of the queen. For in addition to being given instructions that evening regarding the Shah's intention to interrogate the female prisoner privately once the public executions were over, he had been informed that this meeting would have to take place during her highness' absence in the city of the dead. Whatever the other causes for her enforced exile from the capital, it was clear that the queen was strongly opposed to the interview. And the consequences of her banishment were clear enough to the Mayor. There could be no marriages, and no dowry negotiations until her return. The queen's absence from court was bound to delay the betrothal of his son. He bit his tongue and cursed himself for having spoken too soon, for he had meant to keep the news from his Wife for as long as possible. He knew she would be furious when she heard of it.

She was abominably silent. There wasn't the faintest jingle of jewellery to be heard from her direction either. He sighed. So much for the hope of pleasure, leave alone sleep, that night.

He was relieved when she finally spoke. And dismayed by her words.

Well, she said, haughtily, if she had to wait for the queen to come back from Qum before marriage negotiations could be resumed, and her son had to wait for a wife till her highness returned, then her husband would have to wait too, before she would go to bed with him.

⟨ 13 ⟩

When the Shah fled to the royal *anderoun* during the winter of the bread riots, his wives and concubines were giddy with excitement. Would he stay with them? Would he sleep with them? Who would he choose to comfort him? He had avoided their company for a whole year. But thanks to the bread riots, he had returned to them; he had stepped inside the women's quarters once again that cold February day. It was the first time they had been graced by his majesty's presence since his favourite died. They said that grief had given him an aversion.

He had taken refuge in his hunting pavilion and dined on roast pheasant to appease his sorrow while the courtesan lay dying but had been absent for her funeral. He had emptied his treasury to construct her a gilded mausoleum when she was dead and fed morsels of fried liver to his pet cat during the mourning period but gave little thought to the hunger of his people. Her bier had been attended from the capital to the shrine by a consort of eunuchs and a mule train bearing bread and rice for the poor, but it was the last meal they were to eat for many months. For his majesty ignored the signs of worsening famine around him and became markedly indifferent to the suffering of others in the months that followed. His ministers claimed his heartlessness was feigned; his people blamed surfeit for his coldness; but his wives, who suffered most intimately from his callousness, found it easier to ignore the problem than attempt a cure.

It was not the first time that his majesty had avoided the company of women. He had begun to shun his Sister long before the great famine, when he discovered her spying on him as he lay on his couch at the mercy of his French physician. He had steered clear of his Mother too and shrank from her touch after the bloodthirsty reprisals she unleashed in the wake of the attempt on his life. But the initial symptoms of his disaffection had occurred much earlier, during the queen's enforced absence in the city of Qum. He had stopped frequenting the women's quarters for the first time just after his interview with the poetess of Qazvin.

His Mother had found the Shah in a strange mood on her return from the city of the dead. His head had been turned during her absence, they said, and he no longer had any interest in his wives and concubines. The women complained that their lord and master never graced them with his royal presence, never visited them any more; they grumbled that he avoided their company for nights at a time and declined to bless their beds. Ever since he met the poetess of Qazvin, they whined, he had been brooding unnaturally over the vanity of the world and the impotence of kings. The queen was dismayed by this new fashion for abstinence. If the unveiled face of a female heretic could affect a man so profoundly, its impact on the dynasty could be fatal. And so she promptly engaged a new concubine to be his cure a few weeks after her return.

She made much of the courtesan at first, dressed her in gold brocade, and gave her cunning counsels. Dance for the king, she murmured; turn his thoughts into desires. Steal his heart if you can't win it: make him forget the poetess of Qazvin. She encouraged her to go hunting with the Shah, her veil tied like a turban round her brow, her colour high, her eyes taunting. She taught her how to tease him till he left the chase and followed her instead. As long as such bold tricks enticed her son to forget the heretic, she tolerated the trollop; she even agreed to her formal betrothal with his majesty. But though she engaged her to distract her son from the love of God, she was obliged to keep her away from him for exactly the same reason in the end.

When the favourite of the Shah fell sick less than a decade later, she was diagnosed as consumptive, but the queen told everyone that she had lost her mind. She started to rave and spit blood after her little boy's demise, accusing the queen of trying to poison her, of trying to kill her to control the king, blaming her highness of plotting against her with the help of the

Minister who used to be her lover. In the final weeks of her malady, she even charged her mother-in-law of witchcraft. If the queen had not killed so many of the innocent, the Heir Apparent might have been saved, she cried. If she had not cast the evil eye on him, her child would have survived. He died because she ordered the death of the poetess of Qazvin during the summer massacres.

"You can't take what a sick woman says too seriously," sighed the Mother of the Shah, rolling her eyes. But it did not stop the favourite from talking. She began to reiterate all the popular sayings of the poetess of Qazvin, like talismans, to ward off death; she started quoting all the predictions attributed to the heretic, like spells. And the deeper she sank in her sickness, the worse her ravings; the graver her disease, the more she echoed words which everyone knew and did not dare repeat. The queen naturally did everything to keep the Shah away from her.

"Her breath," she whispered, "is contagious; don't come too close to her. Her words," she hissed, "are full of fever: don't listen to her. The poor thing has gone mad."

And she watched with satisfaction as the Shah shrank from the flame that burned in the cheeks of his favourite. She watched with cold pleasure as her son drew away from the wasting candle of his wife. But she could not stop the fearful effluvia from spilling out of her mouth.

On the last day of her life, the favourite asked to see his majesty. It was a late autumn morning, and a keen wind was scattering the pale gold of the silver birch leaves across his path as the Shah walked through the faded gardens towards her shuttered pergola. He was feeling sorry for himself and had no inclination to speak to his Mother, who was waiting for him at the door. Nor did he fancy wasting time on his other wives and concubines, who were clotted like folded bats around her. He wanted to be gone on his hunting expedition as soon as possible.

"Don't lower the cloth from your mouth, dear," his Mother was saying as he approached.

Her son pushed her away impatiently and ignored his women fluttering nearer.

"And don't be too shocked by her condition," she persisted.

The Shah did not need to be reminded of his wife's condition, damn it.

"Calm yourself for her sake, my dear," smiled his Mother. "Don't be so agitated."

She smelled of camphor pills and her flabby cheeks were covered in liver spots.

The Shah turned away with revulsion, and opened the door.

"And don't forget to tell her that you love her," she hissed after him. The old toad!

He was sheepish as he entered the bedchamber, for he had not seen his wife for a long time. He was ashamed, and not a little afraid. She had asked them to cover the windows, extinguish the light; she had told them to leave a single oil lamp burning. But it was still a shock to see the thin cheeks flushed with fever, the hollow chest beneath the padded quilts. When the cadaver greeted him with open arms, he drew back. He had always been repulsed by thin women.

Her amber eyes glittered dangerously with something more than the old gaiety. How, she asked brightly, was her lord? Her breathing was unbearably strained. What, she inquired, was he up to these days? And where, she rasped, had he been? She had not seen him for weeks.

Hunting, mumbled the Shah.

Oh, wonderful, she trilled. She hadn't gone hunting for months.

He was going today too, he said, feebly. But wanted to see how she was feeling first.

How kind of his majesty. She was feeling tolerably well, thank you, she gasped. It was years since she felt so well. Why, she was feeling so well that she could almost dance—

Perhaps she felt strong enough to hunt, he began hesitantly, not knowing what to say.

She laughed herself into a fit of coughing. Now there's a thought, she panted. Hunting with the Shah! But no, she didn't really want to hunt that day. He could go without her, for all she cared. Or stay with her, if he preferred. It was up to him, she whispered, because there was room enough

for both of them in here. Come! she said. And to his horror she invited
him to bed.

Terrible dare. She never lost the arts of the coquette, that one.

His majesty hesitated. He dithered. And the glance that flashed from
her eyes at that moment withered his manhood forever. She bid him farewell then, with a dismissive air.

"I know the master that I serve will never betray me!" were her last
ragged words.

His majesty fled from her, his ears burning. He turned his back on her
and went hunting with his pet cat instead. Although he guessed the last
words of his favourite had first been uttered by the poetess of Qazvin, like
everything else that she had been saying these last few months, he had no
idea whether the enigmatic declaration was an act of defiance on her part
or a sign of her too devastating confidence in him. All he knew was that he
did not want to be near her when she died. And having escaped from her
deathbed, he found every excuse afterwards to stay away from the *anderoun*.

Never take a woman at her word, if you love her, said the Mother of
the Shah, and her son cursed her for it. Only love a man who stands by his
words, sighed his wives, and the Shah cursed them too. They wished they
had held their tongues in the months that followed, for the rate of child-
birth in the royal *anderoun* declined drastically from that time on.

The death of the favourite marked the end of the dynastic game. The
queen could no longer play one woman against the other as long as her
son disliked them equally. But when he returned to the starving town in
the middle of the bread riots, one year later, when he forced his way back
into the palace, sweating profusely after his narrow escape from the crowd,
when he finally stumbled through the doors of the royal *anderoun* after his
long absence, shaken, shattered and shocked by the mob, his wives and
concubines were ready to start playing all over again.

They welcomed him with hysterical ecstasy. They rushed towards him,
flocked about him, fluttered round him, fussed and fiddled with his clothes.
They stroked and caressed him, sobbing with relief, clutching at their
hearts, sighing. They pressed food on him, as though he were the one that

was famished; they insisted that he eat, meatballs, rice and lentils, eggs, and pouted with resentment when he refused. They suffocated him with their attentions and demands.

Thank heaven he had come to their aid, they cried. Thank goodness his majesty had heard their prayers. Without him, they would be bereft. Without his protection, they were in danger of instant violation, imminent rape. How could they sleep safely at night without him? How could they endure their headaches, their cramps, their lower back pains? They feared these rampaging women were going to break into the royal *anderoun* at any moment and garotte them. They were going to scratch their faces and pull their hair; they were going to hale the harem up and down and haul them by their heels into the palace pools. Given the shameless way they were behaving in the streets, these screaming harridans were probably followers of the poetess of Qazvin. They must be the heretic's disciples, they hissed, her acolytes, her devotees!

The Shah wished they would shut up about the damned poetess of Qazvin. When she had been alive, they did nothing but gossip about her. Now they couldn't stop quoting what she said. He wished they would just let him be. He was trembling and wanted to lie down, alone. The last thing he needed was to be mauled and mussed about and given a meal. Besides, he had not seen his wives and concubines for so long that he had forgotten how strident they were, how shrill; how loud the bands of black antimony were across their brows, how piercing the silly white socks on their splayed-out feet. The mint on their breath was high-pitched with mutton fat; their armpits shrieked with sweat and lavender. He could not bear their perfumed importunities. It was bad enough to have been surrounded by famished females screaming in the street, but to be trapped indoors with all these large-mouthed overfed ones was more than he could stomach.

So he took refuge from them, in his bastion tower, at the heart of the harem.

(14)

As soon as the Mayor's Wife learned that the Mother of the Shah had been sent off to Qum, she put an end to her highness' rules and regulations in the prison headquarters. She saw no point in abiding by such strict injunctions if her son's wedding was indefinitely deferred. It was evident that the queen had no intention of finding a bride for her boy as long as she was offended with her own son, and since the tensions between the Shah and his Mother had split the court, she threw her lot in with the heretic in order to avoid taking sides.

The day before the prisoner was due to go to the palace, she booked the public baths in town. She took over the entire establishment for the private use of her *anderoun*. The rates were as expensive as for a wedding party and extra bath attendants had to be hired, because in addition to the Mayor's sister and his daughters, she had invited his old mother down from the country, along with her children's children and their maids. All the nieces and cousins and aunts of the family joined the bathing party and, to the Mayor's dismay, the poetess of Qazvin was invited too.

But, he protested, the prisoner was not permitted to leave the women's quarters.

"She's not leaving the women's quarters," his Wife retorted. "The women's quarters is going out with her. And beside, a woman has the right to wash, whatever her opinions."

When he demurred, saying that he had to follow regulations, she countered with the fact that he had broken them already. The prisoner had been conducting illicit correspondence all this time, she informed him complacently, and he had not even noticed. The washerwoman had been supplying her with herbs, which she macerated into ink in her own mouth; she had been giving the prisoner vegetable paper to write on, and delivering her correspondence all over town. Did he know that one could use reeds from the floor mats as pens? she asked. And then she told him about the green stain behind the door in the upper chamber. "If the woman can write, she might as well wash," she said, triumphantly. "Hot water's hardly more heretical than words."

But, stammered the Mayor, the queen had specifically forbidden visits to the public baths.

"Well, her arm may be long, but she can't reach into the baths of Tehran from Qum," retorted his Wife, grimly, for she was very upset with the Mother of the Shah.

The Mayor gaped at her. He had never expected the influence of a heretic could be so strong. He gave up remonstrating after that and hoped the gossip would not reach the queen.

But the voice of the Mayor's Wife carried far. It gushed through the underground water channels south of the capital, rippled west beneath the Great Salt Desert, and finally gurgled up, with sour and insalubrious noises, into the sewers of the city of the dead. Her highness loathed the public baths in Qum. The drains in her private alcove were always blocked with the slime of human hairs, and being scrubbed by a bath attendant in this noisome place was the closest thing to being prepared for burial by a corpse washer. She dreaded her monthly ablutions here and greatly resented it, when the attendant, who was working on her back as she sat naked on a brass tray, informed her, in the oily tones of a professional sycophant, that the prisoner's visit to the public baths in the capital had proven to be a turning point in her fortunes. Her reputation had risen with the bath water, even as she stepped into it.

"If she's as modest as this to show her body in private," the Mayor's Wife was reported to have said, "who can believe she would ever show her face in public?"

All the ladies had agreed with her, apparently, for it was true. The prisoner had wrapped her limbs and members discreetly in cloths, before wading up to her armpits in warm water, as was the custom in the baths. And when she had stepped out several hours later, she had dressed first, so the attendant informed her highness, before braiding her hair and using the pumice stone. But the common terms of feminine evaluation—the circumference of her breasts and the curve of her belly, the length of her leg and the hollows of her thighs—did not survive the passage, despite the garrulity of the Mayor's Wife. The only detail that emerged through the steam of gossip and the vapour of conjecture drifting from the capital was that the poetess had several beauty spots. Little else about her was reported, much to the frustration of the queen.

"Well, I can assure you that she's not one of those pock-marked women, with buttocks like raw clay," the Mayor's Wife had retorted to a princess who questioned her after the visit to the baths. "And she's not one of those sallow-skinned ones either, with hips like the handles of water pots," she added smugly, for she could recognize the queen's spies a mile off.

Her highness pursed her lips when she was told what a charming bath companion the prisoner had been; the women of the Mayor's house were delighted with her, so they said. She had soaked in the baths and wallowed in the steam with them till they puckered to their fingertips. She had helped to scrub their backs and rub their heels till their calluses were gone and their suspicions all erased. And she had spoken to them with such freshness of demeanour, such lightness of touch, that by the time their skin was peeled and shining, their hair oiled and combed, all their doubts and fears were also smoothed away and gone. The bath attendants swore they had never seen so much prejudice washed down the drains in a single day.

She apologized for the dirt she had accumulated and the inconvenience she had caused since her capture and swore that she would be indebted to the Mayor's Wife forever for being this clean. Although the Shah's decree traversed the length and breadth of Persia, she confessed that she had not realized until then how closely it could be measured by the very hairs on her head. And she made them all laugh at the thought that the summons of a king could serve the same end as the services of a good washerwoman. If a sovereign was to deserve the unsullied loyalty of his subjects, she gaily said, he should ensure that they had regular baths.

Neither her highness' sense of humour nor her appetite were much aroused when she was told by her attendants, during the midday meal, that a holiday mood had prevailed in the capital the day the Mayor's Wife hired the public baths. Given her culinary reputation, several of the bath attendants there had accepted food in exchange for the price of henna, according to the gossip, and had left the premises her devotees. The prisoner, who had also been invited to join the repast, proved to have a most enthusiastic appetite. The Mayor's Wife was reported to have announced that it was a proper shame to have deprived someone of food who was so appreciative of it. Anyone who could discriminate between the first crop of winter saffron and the last could not possibly be all bad, in her opinion; a woman whose palate could distinguish the spices in a pickle must be credited with some good judgement, surely.

"How can a woman who enjoys eating so much do such dreadful things?" she had protested. When the queen was also told that the Wife of the Mayor had begun to cook for the poetess after royal leniency was extended towards her, she threw a tantrum and knocked the rice into the water bowls so that the bath attendants had to bring a fresh supply to rinse her head.

She also learned that after the strictures were officially lifted, the prisoner was granted all the comforts which had previously been withheld. She was provided with a light and spacious chamber and was no longer denied communication. She was given a brazier too and permitted an unlimited supply of ink and paper. Her nine-year-old daughter, who had been brought to court, together with her two older brothers, to justify her father's demands for revenge, was permitted to stay with her mother against the mullah's wishes, and she was allowed company from that time on, as well as correspondence. The flower of female society was flocking to the Mayor's house, so the bath attendants told the queen. Princesses from the royal palace, female relatives of ministers and state secretaries, all vied with one another to meet her. One lady, wandering around the Legation gardens at the invitation of the British Envoy's wife, claimed to have glimpsed her from the high window above the walls and wrote a poem about it, which was doing the rounds of court. The daughters of town burghers came just to ogle at her, and the wife and sister of the Secretary of the armed forces were demanding an hour of conversation with her every day. Everyone wanted to see the woman who had made such an impact on the king. They told the Mayor's Wife that she was very lucky to have such a prisoner in her house.

"Oh tush, she's actually my guest, you know!" the Mayor's Wife had gushed. When the remark reached her in the public baths of Qum, the Mother of the Shah spat into the new basin which had recently been brought, and ordered the bath attendants to change the water yet again.

The prison headquarters became as famous as the shrine south of the capital during the queen's exile in the provinces. Her highness was told that the Mayor's Wife was no longer averse to having a heretic on the premises and was taking advantage of her popularity to curry favour at court. There was talk of weddings in the air, murmured the bath attendants, not only for the Sister of the Shah but also for the Mayor's son. Despite the winter shortages and the usual threat of famine, the lavish entertainments of the Mayor's Wife had multiplied, and so had her expenses among the marriage brokers. The woman appeared to think that she could cultivate the appropriate contacts for her boy without her highness' intervention and during her absence, according to the bath attendants.

"I may not be a Qajar," she had said, tossing her head with a jangle of pride, "but my son is as good as a prince." On hearing this outrageous remark repeated, the Mother of the Shah pronounced herself so thoroughly dissatisfied with the services of her bath attendants that they were obliged to redo her feet with fresh pumice stones in order to be paid.

She was determined to put a stop to such presumptions. It was bad enough that the Grand Vazir threatened her influence in court, but if housewives arranged marriages behind her back, she would lose her influence all over the country. The poetess of Qazvin had apparently told her hostess that if her son's marriage plans were being deferred, it meant that her reputation had risen high in the estimation of the queen. If it rose any higher she might even attain the distinction of being a scapegoat, and that would prove the answer to her prayers. Since every privilege had a cost, her present sufferings, she promised, would redound to her son's happiness in the end.

"She said the queen would not forget him," the Mayor's Wife was happily telling the ladies of the town. "She said that her highness will give him special honours when she returns from Qum!"

After the last of the filthy froth from her bath water gurgled down the drains, the queen kicked over the oils and balms, and stormed out of the building in a furious temper. She also dismissed all the bath attendants in Qum and sacked the washerwomen in the premises.

There was urgent business awaiting her in the capital. Since her opposition to her daughter's wedding with the Grand Vazir had been one cause of her exile, she had no alternative but to give it her blessing in order to return. So she sent word to the Shah that the omens were at last auspicious and the priests had confirmed it. Now that public executions were over, she said, it was the time for wedding feasts. Besides, she was desperate for a proper bath, she added. It was impossible to conceive, she told her son, of the odious conditions and poor services in Qum.

Their reconciliation was deceptively easy after that. The Shah was delighted that her dear highness had benefited from the clergy's good counsel and greatly pained to hear that her special needs had not been catered for in the city of the dead. He urged her to hasten to the capital and congratulated her on the betrothal ceremony of the Princess Royal which would take place when she came back. The private baths in the palace, he said, would be specially renovated to celebrate his Sister's nuptials.

But before her return, the Mother of the Shah negotiated another nuptial contract and engaged the services of two theologians from Qum. The contract was between the Mayor's son and a squint-eyed princess, and the theologians were to undertake the re-education of the poetess of Qazvin. As a result, the Mayor's Wife learned of the great distinction conferred on her at the same time as she heard that a pair of mullahs would be joining the stream of visitors to her house.

"Do you expect me to cope with clerics as well as criminals?" she retorted when her husband announced the news, for she had been slightly dismayed to discover that the bride-to-be was squint-eyed. But a glance from her son and a bilious look from her sister-in-law cautioned her. So she pursed her lips and said nothing more on the subject.

Her relations with the Mayor had become strained recently and were a cause of some concern. He was frequenting the *anderoun* less regularly than before, and she had been told, although she refused to believe it, that he had been seen frequenting the brothels in the town. But she preferred to look on the bright side of things. Her daughter-in-law's squint was probably due to the girl's pedigree, she told herself. She had royal blood on one side and ecclesiastic connections on the other, after all, and since half a princess was better than none, she began to plan the menu for the wedding feast with great enthusiasm. Besides, sharing the honour of being a mother-in-law with her imperial highness made up for all the rancour it entailed.

❨ 15 ❩

The bastion of the Shah had long withstood the onslaught of rancour and of time and was a building of ancient and dependable construction. Its massive walls were made of rough-hewn stone, its doors were double-barred, and prisoners had been hurtled to death from its high parapets at one time. But when a woman of scandalous reputation was thrown over these ramparts recently only to float gently to the ground, buoyed up by her petticoats, the Shah had finally ordered an end to execution by gravity. And so the bastion had been turned into a sanctuary.

His majesty may have taken refuge in the tower because of its association with miracles. He was in need of a sanctuary, for he had had enough of being the pivot of attention, the axis of adoring eyes. He was weary of being scrutinized. When he withdrew into his tower, he wanted to shield himself from observation as well as insurrection. He gave orders for the barred doors to be double-bolted. He also commanded that the cannon be primed in readiness before the gates. He instructed his guards to load their muskets, mount the parapet, and stand prepared to fire as soon as the rabble pushed through the cordon of guards. Despite his partiality for historic precedence, he had no intention of submitting to civil disobedience.

But his bastion could not withstand the onslaught of women. Although the Shah managed to shut the doors on all his wives and concubines, he could not keep his Mother or his Sister out. The first insisted on accompanying him for reasons of protocol and the second simply pushed her way inside without permission. It was very annoying to be deprived of privacy in his condition.

His Mother knew about the gravity of the Shah's condition, of course, but had kept it a well-guarded secret after the death of his favourite. No one dared mention the problem in her presence, not even the Princess Royal.

No one in the royal *anderoun* was allowed to breathe a word about the dildos and the sponges, the ointments and the struts. Since the chief astrologer had warned against ominous conjunctions in the months that followed his favourite's death, no one could argue with her highness, either, when she introduced cats into the royal *anderoun* from that time on and permitted pageboys to take over from the concubines. For the naked truth of it was that despite the medical attentions of Paris and St Petersburg, the Shah could no longer thumb himself any higher than a curve of urine.

So when the starving masses charged the barricades, stormed his citadel, and surged into the palace compound, his majesty never gave the order to fire. When he finally summoned the courage to look down through an optic glass at that human sea below, he was unable to command his soldiers to shoot at the crowd. For the one thing he could not handle was an attack by women.

Six thousand female faces were staring up at him, six thousand pairs of eyes, maddened by hunger, searched for his. Six thousand starving women, carrying children with bloated stomachs in their skeletal arms, holding dead babies up for him to see, were crying piteously for food. But the worst of it was, the women had loosed their braids and rubbed mud on their foreheads to show their desperation; they had stripped their veils off, one and all, like heretics.

He panicked completely at the sight of them. The attempt on his life nine years before was far less threatening than this. It was decidedly below the belt by comparison. His impotence was manifest as he turned reluctantly to his Mother once again, and asked for counsel.

What, he said, was he supposed to do with all these angry women?

The Mother of the Shah had cultivated her own theories about impotence and women since the attempt on the life of her son. She had borne her own grudges too for over a decade, and was not someone who forgot old resentments. So she knew what to say and made sure everyone heard her say it. She advised him to find someone to take charge of the crisis, someone to control the situation. She told him to choose a faithful servant, a loyal retainer who had served him since the beginning of his reign and would be willing to serve him still. "The people need a scapegoat," she said, "and your majesty needs someone to blame."

Her highness was feeling betrayed that winter; she needed someone to blame herself. She had been deceived by men whom she believed to be loyal servants and who had been her masters all along. She had fought to keep her power for years only to see that she had been serving the ambitions instead of ministers, mullahs, and the monarch himself. They had all cheated her to achieve their own ends. And certain among them had cheated her more than others.

She had many reasons to resent the Mayor. Ever since he had offered his house as a gift without relinquishing it, the chief of police had been extorting hefty bribes as recompense. She had seen him toadying to the first Grand Vazir from the day he came into office, and had watched him currying favour with the second, too, on the grounds of family relationship. He had exploited the rich as well as the poor over the years and obeyed his masters mainly to serve himself. But the principal reason she hated him was that he had introduced the woman into the royal *anderoun* who had driven a wedge between herself and her son. Had it not been for the Mayor, the Shah's favourite courtesan would never have ousted her highness from power.

The girl had arrived at the palace gates a few days after the wedding of the Mayor's son, and been ushered straight into the royal *anderoun* and the presence of the queen. A barrage of gifts arrived for her highness at the same time—pots brimming with fragrant wedding rice and boxes stuffed with sweetmeats, fine Kashmir shawls and embroideries and a reed cage filled with colourful birds—but the dancing girl was the most important gift from the wedding feast. She was delivered by the chief of police himself. As a token of gratitude for the honour her highness had conferred on his family; as a sign of appreciation for the advantages gained by this royal alliance. He expressed a hope, through the curtains, that the courtesan would please his imperial majesty.

The queen had been quick to put the new concubine to use. She thought the girl had been an answer to her prayers at first. She even agreed to her daughter's nuptials that same year in order to stimulate the appetite of her son. But when it proved no easier to control a body than a mind and the dancing girl began to hold sway in the *anderoun*, she blamed the chief of police for her loss of power. She preferred to forget her own role in arranging the wedding of his son and, in later years, denied having anything to do with the affair.

But that winter of the bread riots, her hunger for revenge was almost as savage as the starvation in the streets. She was even willing to take advantage of her son's impotence to play her last card by then. When the Shah took refuge in the harem for the first time in a year, she suspected it might be the last time he would turn to her for counsel and so she had an answer ready on the tip of her tongue as soon as he asked her what to do with all the unveiled women.

The Mayor was obviously the man for the occasion, she told the Shah. He was the one who had raised the price of flour, so let him be responsible for lowering the tension. Call for the Mayor, she said, before these women topple the throne. If he can control that wife of his at home, she said, he'll have no trouble controlling these harridans in the street.

And so the Shah summoned the Mayor to the palace. For the last time.

❨ 16 ❩

Though both events took place in the same year, the wedding of the Mayor's son was remembered long after the marriage of the Shah's Sister was forgotten. It constituted the high-water mark of his mother's culinary career but signalled her decline in the Mayor's *anderoun*. And while it was the turning point of many lives, it came to be associated with a single woman.

Hunger satisfies the appetite more than satiety, sometimes. Days before the wedding feast, the beggars of the town had taken up permanent residence at the Mayor's doors, just to smell the odours wafting into the alley. And in the weeks that followed they were content to feed on the remaining scraps. For three days, the house throbbed with the drum and zither, thrummed with the stringed *oud* and the wailing pipe. For three nights the striped tents in the courtyards swelled and fluttered; lanterns twinkled round the double courtyards and the walls hummed with poetry and lights. Even the wife of the British ambassador leaned out of the Legation windows to hear the music, see the Mayor's house rigged up like a circus, and sniff the tempting wedding odours. The whole alley was taken up by the festivities. Wooden boards were raised to make a stage, and the dancing girls performed on the women's side of the house for the first night, on the men's for the second. By the third evening, the revels had spread all over town.

The actual marriage ceremony took place on the first day of the wedding, in the home of a relative of the bride. Since the presence of a heretic would have insulted the presiding mullah, the wedding contract was signed and sealed at the other end of town. That was where the white embroidered cloth was spread and the candles lit beside the mirror; that was where the bride was prevailed upon to whisper her consent and where the Mayor's son choked on the smoke of wild rue as he saw the squint of royal stamp for the first time.

The feast in the groom's honour took place in the Mayor's house on the second day. His Wife outdid herself for the sake of her son. She simmered and stewed and broiled and braised; she brewed ragouts and fricassees for days. Her sauces were unparalleled, her pickles stunned the palate, and people talked about her *dolmehs* and her *kooftehs* for the next decade. Her sweet saffron wedding rice of slivered almonds and shredded orange peel achieved the status of a national treasure and even the beggars grew fat on the scraps.

But despite the delectable dishes and the Shiraz wines, the guests were not satisfied. Despite all the efforts of the Mayor's Wife, the female members of the family hungered for more. Where was the poetess of Qazvin, they cried, for to everyone's surprise, the prisoner had not been permitted to join them. Where was the heretic whom all the court had seen and they had heard so much?

The fact was that the Mayor had been reluctant to let her come down from her chamber. A wedding, he had told his Wife sourly, was not the place for such a disreputable woman.

Her guests were visibly disgruntled at the end of the first day when she told them what he had said. So, they retorted, did the Mayor think a dancing girl was more reputable than a poetess? Although their sneers provoked her dreadfully and she knew what they were whispering behind her back, their hostess did not dwell long on their insinuations. She changed her strategy.

On the evening of the second day, she waylaid her husband on the breezeway steps and would not let him pass. The dancing girl was holding the *birouni* in thrall at that moment and she knew the Mayor was impatient to be gone, but she refused to give way until he changed his mind.

The ladies, she whined, were begging to see the prisoner. The guests were so disappointed. If their wishes were thwarted, the family would eat ashes. Her son's wedding would be a total failure if the poetess of Qazvin did not participate in the feast. Do let the woman come into the tea room at least, on the last day, she begged.

The Mayor scowled and said the mullah wouldn't like it.

So what, since the religious ceremony was over? she retorted.

He told her he wanted to avoid bad omens.

She would take full responsibility for omens, she said, stoutly. Please! she begged.

Perhaps, he growled. If his Wife would just stop nagging him.

Just a brief visit, she insisted. All she was asking for was that the poetess might join them for a little while when the bridal party arrived on the third day. Was that so much?

He said he would think about it and pushed past her towards the music.

She was enthusiastic when she conveyed the news to the ladies. He's thinking about it, she gushed. A distinct possibility, she called it. Her guests sucked in their breath and nudged each other in the ribs. There wasn't going to be much thinking as long as the Mayor was watching that dancing girl, they muttered to each other, giggling behind their hands.

The Mayor's breath smelled of *arak* during his son's wedding; his clothes reeked of tobacco and alley cats, but his Wife did not recognize the odour of betrayal at the time. She was so sure of her powers over him, so confident of having bent him to her will that she interpreted the gratifying absence of the dancing girl on the third day to her personal influence over her husband. She was so certain that she had won her way on the sub-ject of the poetess that when the knocking began at the gate on the last evening of the wedding feast, she did not hesitate for a moment. She sent instructions for the prisoner and her daughter to join the rest of the guests in the tea room. And as she ran to the gate, she was thinking of how she would show her gratitude to the Mayor.

The singer with the *oud* had taken over the entertainment, and the music throbbed with plaintive songs of love as the Mayor's Wife went to welcome the bride into the house. The afternoon glowed like a ripened peach through the tall windows and the dark blades of the cypress trees in the Legation garden swayed against the gold sky when she summoned one of the servants to invite the poetess downstairs. Despite the high-pitched ululating at the gates and the rattle of the tambourines of the bridal party, the cooing of doves in the breezeway could be heard as the prisoner stepped through in the doorway to join the guests. The odour of jasmine in the courtyard was sweetened by the attar of rose she brought into the room.

The guests stopped chattering; they nudged each other in eager expec-tation. There she is, they ogled. Look! There's the woman who divorced her husband!

She sat at the low end of the room, they noticed. Like a servant.

And so she should, they muttered. Very proper. She was only a prisoner after all, even though the Mayor's Wife made so much of the woman.

She was holding her daughter by the hand, fresh as a posy, dressed in flowered calico. The child wore a white kerchief and was much prettier, they thought, than the squinting bride.

But what a shame, they gusted. She'll never be one, will she? Who'd ever want to marry that child after what her mother's gone and done?

The girl was looking eagerly towards the door through which the bride would enter. It was clear from the high-pitched cries in the courtyard that the gate of the house was opened wide.

The guests gauged the prisoner appraisingly. Nicely turned out, they muttered enviously, under their breaths. No wonder she abandoned her husband; she doesn't look like the wife of a priest.

She was wearing velvet trousers of deep purple under her flounced skirts and a brocaded tunic over a pretty printed blouse of burgundy sprigs.

She might be able to recite the most Holy Book backwards, murmured the women to one another, but she was obviously no puritan. Was she as modest as she seemed? they wondered. Was she ever so slightly vain, with those arched brows and almond eyes? Who did she think she was kidding, this daughter of priests, pretending to be a scholar and dressed up to kill?

The women sucked in their breath and wagged their heads as the clapping and singing outside drew nearer. They guessed the bride had reached the foot of the breezeway by now. The poetess was certainly attractive, they acknowledged, begrudgingly. Her headscarf was finely embroidered and her face was charmingly touched with rouge. Her eyes were darkened with kohl, as was the little mole under her lip. But why was she keeping those long lashes lowered?

You'd think a woman who had run about half-naked would be less reserved, they clucked. But she's probably a hypocrite, just like everyone else, they sighed, disappointed.

The ululations reached fever pitch as the bride climbed the breezeway steps. The women swayed on their haunches and whispered in eager anticipation. They did so want the heretic to open her mouth and say something. They hoped she would tell them the bride's fortune. They wanted her to talk about matrimony so they could have a good gossip about it afterwards.

What on earth, they tittered, could a divorced woman say to a bride? What fun to hear a woman who failed in her marriage preaching about husbands and wives!

The musicians began to play a sprightly tune at that moment as the bride, weighed down with layers of pink satin and a stiff headdress of braids, finally stepped into the tea room with the Mayor's Wife. As she sat in the seat of honour, everyone shifted, shuffled, shunted on the carpets, to make place for her female relatives. The lilting welcome was chanted, the tea was served; the clapping ceased and the bird in the singer's throat quivered and came to a stop. Everyone turned towards the mistress of the house expectantly and waited for her to begin.

It was the third evening and the time for gift-giving.

The Mayor's Wife had not been ululating with the others when she stepped over the threshold with the bridal party. Her colour was livid, her broad bosom heaving, but she had not yet said a word. She was seated at the high end of the tea room opposite the poetess of Qazvin, who was beside the door, and had fixed her eyes on the prisoner. She had an odd look about her.

The guests began to whisper among themselves in surprise. What was wrong with their hostess? they wondered. Why didn't she begin the welcoming? Had the bride sat too heavily on the ceremonial tongue during the marriage ceremony? they sniggered. Had the cloth been stitched too tightly over her head, perhaps, so that she would not nag her daughter-in-law too much? Or had she had another row with her husband? Whatever was the matter with her?

They hissed in each others' ears and arched their brows. They shared knowing winks and soft sneers. Should they call on the services of the dancing girl? Just to relieve the awkwardness? But the Mayor's Wife still did not speak. They nudged each other in the ribs and giggled. The musicians fiddled themselves into a pause, the singer was hushed, but the hostess still said nothing. A rustling silence filled the room; the guests began to twitch, to crane their necks. They finally froze. The expression on the face of the Mayor's Wife was one of pure anguish.

It was the poetess of Qazvin who came to her rescue. Rising from her seat she approached the Mayor's Wife and offered her a package, wrapped in a square of silk. For her daughter-in-law, she said. And she asked that the gift be given on her behalf.

A surge of surprise swept through the room. Everyone strained forward and back and finally craned their necks round to see who was giving what to whom.

Let it come from the hands of a happy bride, the poetess said, quietly. And she kneeled and embraced the Wife of the Mayor.

At that their hostess suddenly burst into tears and began to sob uncontrollably.

Ah, clucked the women, in relief: that's more like it. Tears are to be expected, they nodded; a woman must weep when her son marries. The Mayor's Wife had always been besotted by her boy, and now he had another woman in his life. And they passed the sweetmeats round and sipped more tea; they clapped their hands, called for music, and smiled approvingly at the poetess of Qazvin. Because everything was as it should be and the gift-giving could at last begin.

Almost everything. For they could not help wondering why the heretic had given her gift to the mother-in-law instead of the bride. And they could not resist asking her about it, since the Wife of the Mayor was still crying. They pulled on the prisoner's skirts, chattering like parakeets as she returned to her seat. What, they asked, hungering for scandal, lusting for gossip, had she given the girl? Was it the secret way to satisfy her master? Was it the perfect formula to be a wife? Did she have a few little tricks up her sleeve to keep their husbands happy too? What did marriage mean anyway, and wouldn't the poetess please tell them what was in the package?

A book, she simply replied.

The wedding guests were taken aback. But the girl couldn't read!

She'll learn, laughed the poetess. We all learn literacy on our wedding nights.

Oh, if that's the kind we're talking about, sneered some, and they winked at the prisoner's daughter. Then tell us, they asked, what sort of book learning can make a wife and husband happy? For they wanted to embarrass the poetess.

The kind that helps them read each other well, she said.

But who can truly write such a story? they persisted. For they were dying to hear about her divorce.

Only themselves, she answered. No one can judge a marriage from its binding.

Now, there's droll idea, murmured the women, eyeing their hostess. They had heard of marriage being like a watermelon, but whoever thought of it as a book?

But can a husband and wife both hold the same pen? asked a cynic softly.

Between them, replied the poetess, is a barrier, thin as paper, fine as breath—

And then the women grew still. They stopped whispering. They stopped peeking surreptitiously at the Mayor's Wife and at the daughter of the poetess. And they began to listen intently, for they knew that barrier well. They had all felt it, thinner than any veil and thicker than every wall. They listened as the poetess began to tell them the old tale of impossible love between what a woman yearned to do and what she actually achieved, between what the soul longed to say and the words available to say it. They listened as she told them how languages and marriages were bridges, merely, between man and woman, tongue and ear; how they were the means by which to build, in which to house, on which to raise new meanings between human beings. When a marriage was faithful, it gave birth to poetry, she concluded. If not, it was a dead letter overnight.

The women lowered their heads. They did not dare look at the Mayor's Wife now. This kind of literacy was painful. Marriage was a tragedy in some of their books. Love and poetry had long since died in their lives. But just as they shifted from hip to hip uncomfortably and wriggled on their buttocks and tried to turn their thoughts away from such ideas, the Mayor's Wife suddenly raised her voice.

"How does a woman know if her husband will stay faithful to her?" she blurted. "How can a wife be sure that her master will not betray her in the end?" And her words seemed to rise from the bottom of a well.

The women held their breath. Their hostess had not been crying for her son, they realized; she had been weeping for herself. She had not lost her tongue but had been gathering the courage to speak. She had asked the question which no one else had dared to put in words. For it seemed that all their pain grew from its centre, like a dark, dark rose, all their disappointment sprang from its root. And, with the answer of the poetess, the rose began to bloom. It blossomed and it turned to perfume as she put words to their unspoken tribulations in that room.

Let no man be your master as long as you are unfaithful to yourselves, she said. Let no woman control you either, as long as you do not trust your own desires. "However faithfully you serve such masters," she said, "they'll all betray you in the end."

Her words were few but their sense filled the tea room, spilled down the breezeway steps, and spread across both courtyards of the Mayor's house. Her voice was low but the music in the courtyard faded as she spoke and even the cooing doves were lulled to silence, whirring and creaking across the evening sky. The wedding guests turned away from the *oud* and the pipe to listen to the prisoner; they abandoned the tabor and the drum. They left the gaudy tents and gathered round the pool to hear her; the dancing girl drew near too, and stood, spellbound, beneath the arch. Everyone was intoxicated by that rose-red voice floating out on the air. Everyone was drunk on the wine of the words of the poetess of Qazvin.

Where had she learned these truths, the women wanted to know.

She told them she was only repeating what they knew all too well themselves.

But who had taught her how to read their lives like this? they wondered.

Life was written with deeds, she replied, and read the same way.

No one reads us, they murmured, sadly; for whom was she writing her story?

She did not respond when they begged her for her reader's name.

They cajoled, they teased, they tried to provoke her. Perhaps her writing had no purpose; perhaps her tale was being told to the empty air. But she merely smiled and said no more.

Only when the Wife of the Mayor joined in their appeals, only when the mistress of the house begged her, with tears in her eyes, to say where faithfulness could be found, did she finally confess that in all her life, in all her born days, she had only discovered one true reader, one master who would not betray her. And that one, she admitted, was neither man nor woman.

And as the women held their breath to hear the name of this incredible lover, as they waited expectantly to know whom she trusted, whose mastery was worth so much, she turned and embraced them, one and all, with open arms.

The women became pensive after that. They stopped dreaming of being brides and imagined being in love. They ceased thinking of themselves as wives and pondered what it meant to be human beings. They no longer chewed on gossip but hungered for the possibility of truth. They clucked, they swayed on their haunches, they argued for days about whether or not the poetess had actually named her Beloved, and why she had given a book to a bride. They disagreed over everything about her.

Some claimed that she had read the secrets of their hearts that afternoon and others thought her a portentous prig. Most conceded that her oratory was undeniable but several added that she was probably carried away by the sound of her own voice. Many feared that she had bewitched their hostess, for she certainly knew more about the Mayor's Wife than met the eye. And not a few added, with a nudge and a wink, that she was no doubt less of a prig than she pretended and may have known about the Mayor's peccadillos too. But though those who heard her speak never forgot her, none remembered precisely what she said.

For even the fragrance of *attar* fades.

(17)

When she heard that the Mayor was going to the palace in the middle of the bread riots, his Wife threw herself heroically on the ground and emptied a vial of *attar* of roses over his feet.

The Wife of the Mayor was a substantial woman, a heavy woman, and throwing herself on the ground was not something she did often or with ease. But on this occasion, she spread her bulk out on the floor with all the grace of a fat tail of grilled lamb on a pillow of saffron rice. She lay prone at the Mayor's feet like a stuffed aubergine baked in pomegranate sauce. And as the heady perfume of roses filled the tea room, she blubbered of prophecies.

The Mayor found it hard to distinguish prophecies from recipes when his Wife was talking. Besides, he had become somewhat heavy of hearing over the years and was satiated with words by the time the bread riots shook the capital. He had long ago started introducing temporary women into the *anderoun* in order to avoid the nagging of his Wife, and so it was easy to turn a deaf ear on her now. He ignored her as he dressed himself in ostentatious robes and trimmed his beard in preparation for the palace. He liberated his ankles from her clutches as he anointed himself with pungent lavender water, for he certainly did not want to enter the presence of the Shah smelling like a rose garden. And as he left the house surrounded by his thugs, he ordered his daughters, coldly, to lift the lady off the floor. He was impervious to her warnings and stormed out into the street to quell the bread riots, brandishing a cudgel in his hands.

The Mayor found himself surrounded by starving women as he approached the Shah's citadel. Despite the best efforts of his escort, they hurled themselves against him, flung themselves at his horse, tore at his clothes, and screamed curses at him. He had to whip them out of his way as he pushed through the crowded streets; he was even obliged to kick them aside to force a path through the palace gates; and he finally threatened them with his cudgel at the doors of the citadel. He was breathless but still perfumed by the time he reached the presence of the Shah. His robes were sullied, his appearance dishevelled, but his stick was still at his side. Most importantly, he had learned how to restrain his stammer over the years.

Of course, he could curb the uprisings, he assured his majesty, smoothly; of course he would control the situation. Only a little discipline was required. As the Shah himself knew all too well, women who cause an uproar in the marketplace usually talk too much at home. He had said as much to his own Wife, he confided, with a wink that was dangerously close to a leer.

The Shah was in no mood for vulgar jokes. It was clear, from his curt response, that what the Mayor said to his wife was immaterial but what he might do with the mob would be of keen interest to the state. He was instructed to use all necessary means to restore order to the city.

It was an enigmatic mandate. All necessary means were not necessarily justified, and there was good reason to believe, from the haughty demeanour of the king, that such means would not necessarily satisfy either. The Mayor knew that if he tried to defend his personal interests, he would risk royal ire, and if he met the demands of the people, he would lose his power.

So since he had no intention of paying for peace out of his own pockets and was not a man who suffered humiliation lightly, he wreaked his frustrations on the women.

On leaving the royal presence, he stormed into the street with his cudgel already drawn. If they want bread, give them a taste of rope, he shouted; if they want grain, let them have sticks.

And he laid into the crowd, blindly. He thrashed about him, on each side, digging his spurs into his horse till it reared up against the people massing round him. He forced his way through the streets shattering bones, bruising flesh, breaking arms and legs and heads all round him. Many fainted beneath his blows; many were trampled under his horse's hooves. Dozens were maimed for life and not a few died on the spot. But one woman in the mob had the nerve to call him by his name; one harridan accosted him more loudly than the rest, and evoked his shame; one strident, domineering voice had the audacity to scream out a warning, to reiterate a prophecy, to hurl words at his head uttered by the poetess of Qazvin.

The Mayor did not know his Wife was in the crowd. He was unaware that she had thrown on her veil, and followed him out of the prison headquarters. She had been swept up in the sea of starving women as soon as she stepped into the streets. She had lost her shoes and her veil in the swell, and despite her weight and their weakness, she had been carried like a trophy on the women's shoulders. When her husband rode out of the citadel like a fury and ordered his guards to whip everyone out of his way, she found herself directly in front of him.

Her words seemed to madden the Mayor. He began to cudgel her, blow after blow. By the time he finally realized who she was, the Shah had called for his arrest.

❨ 18 ❩

The Mayor's Wife stared up at the ceiling of the upper chamber. She could not see the shivering cobwebs in the rafters despite the fact that her eyes were wide open. She could not hear the mayhem in the city streets either,

the sound of the cannon, the roar of the starving crowds. She was unaware
of the daughters of the Mayor creeping in and out of the upper chamber,
poking in and out of the chest behind the door. She did not feel the warmth
of the brazier, or the cold of the falling snow, or the sugared rose water
being spooned between her lips by the washerwoman. And she did not
know what happened when her husband's body was finally cut down from
the city gates where it had been hanging for three violated days and nights.
But she could still smell.

She smelled the rank offal in the streets, the reek of fear in the air. She
smelled the dead bodies thawing in the ditches, the ordure in the alleys,
the urine against the walls. She smelled the smoke of burning houses and
of the cannon fired in the palace square to quell the riots. She smelled the
stench of mice rot and mildew, the taint of old dust and stale dirt in the room
where she lay. And above all she smelled the odour of betrayal.

Smells had always been important to the Wife of the Mayor. Baked
fish, for example, tarnished over time to the stink of urine. Fried onions
and fenugreek should at all costs be avoided on hair-washing days. Her
worst anxiety during the famine had been to restrain the odour of lamb
kebabs from wafting over her walls, and her greatest regret, while there
was still reason for it, was that her husband did not rinse his mouth out
with mint and his feet with lemon skins before he granted her his favours.
She hated the presumptuous stink of alley cats, despised the flagrance of
brothel perfumes, and dreaded, above all, the rancid odour of betrayal on
his skin.

It was a familiar smell. The Mayor's Wife had snuffed it floating up
from the cellars and hovering at the granary doors each winter. It had pervaded the streets after the attempt on the life of the Shah and had clung to
her son's clothes the night the soldiers took the prisoner away. And now
at the height of the bread riots, nine years later, she recognized it again:
a hint of decay without forewarning, the scent of a sewer on a fine spring
morning, a trace of treachery in the air. But this time, the incriminating
odours were her own. She recognized the whiff of tea denied, of tarragon
betrayed, the tang of pickles that perverted truth and jams that congealed

remembrance. Above all, as the Mayor's Wife lay there on the floor of the upper chamber, she smelled the cheap perfume that had wafted through the gates at her son's wedding.

The music had reached a pitch of frenzy when the gates opened for the bride. She had been strewing roses in her path, with the other ululating women. The whole courtyard seemed redolent with roses, and her head was reeling. She had been full of sentimental recollections of her own wedding, giddy with nostalgia. The Mayor had been good to her, all these years, she told herself; he had given her all she wanted. He was a little gruff and not very communicative, but then it had to be admitted that she did rather nag the poor man. He was rather heartless towards others too, it was true, but he had always been kind to her, and generous. She was flooded with gratitude, as the bolts were drawn back, and felt the throb of love towards her husband as she celebrated her son's wedding. The drumming seemed to pound in her own heart. The ground seemed to sway beneath her as the idiot boy opened wide the gates to the bride.

But she was slightly disconcerted when she saw the local *kadi* standing there, along with the rest of the wedding party. What need for a jurist again, when the contracts were already signed? And she was confused to see two palanquins and two troupes of musicians standing outside the gates. Were two brides being brought to the house instead of one? She had taken the omens upon her own head, but she had not expected them to be so double-edged.

A quick nod and whisper from the mother of the bride explained everything. There was a certain codicil to be drafted in the *birouni*, a certain business deal to be completed: the Mayor had acquired the monopoly to control the price of wheat in exchange for a squint-eyed daughter-in-law for his son. And oh! Another minor matter. There was a certain contract to be signed by the jurist, a certain transaction to be concluded: the Mayor had paid the fee and ratified the bond to bed a temporary wife himself on the night of his son's wedding. When the dancing girl emerged from the second palanquin, the Mayor's Wife realized that her husband had bought two for the price of one.

She wondered afterwards whether the prisoner knew what had happened out there at the gates of the house, whether she too had smelled the odours of betrayal, even in the tea room. Had the poetess of Qazvin realized that the bride was actually a bribe when she knelt down and embraced her? Although the warning she had uttered to the Mayor the night before the public executions was too painful to remember, his Wife never forgot the stench that rose from the cellars as she uttered it. She smelled it again at the wedding of her son, and in the years that intervened she always blamed the Mayor for it. Only on the third day after his hanging as she lay helpless in the upper chamber, did she finally realize that the fetid odours were rising from herself. She too had betrayed of the poetess of Qazvin.

Of course, she was not alone to do it. Everyone in the house knew what was happening. All the women saw the prisoner challenge the Mayor to stop the tortures and heard her prediction. It was not as though the townsfolk were unaware of the prophecy, either, though no one in the city, except the favourite of the Shah, ever had the courage to repeat it until years afterwards. Why, the sinister warning had even reached the confines of the court. The Mayor's son blamed his mother's garrulity for it, of course. His sisters cursed her too, like a pair of pickled walnuts each time she opened her mouth after that, and even his aunt counselled her to prudence. But when the summons came from the Shah, she finally assumed responsibility for it. She wanted to make amends.

The women of the house thought she wanted to warn her husband at first, when she ran after him into the bread riots, repeating the words of the poetess of Qazvin. The starving wretches she met going to the market square thought she was speaking on behalf of them all, when she cried out they had been betrayed by the masters whom they had so faithfully served. But by the time she finally confronted the Mayor with those words, it was obvious that she was uttering the phrase in self-reproach, not blame. Her words were a confession of some fatal mistake, an admission of some vital truth she had repudiated. They were an acknowledgement that she had betrayed herself and had been serving false masters all along.

"Remember," she wept, as the Mayor raised his cudgel against her. "Remember that my death will prove it to you!" But he did not wish to be reminded.

❲ 19 ❳

After her husband beat her, the Mayor's Wife fell into a stupor. She managed to remain upright as she crossed the market square and was able to stagger several paces down the alley despite her condition but she never made it into the prison headquarters. She collapsed at the gates of the Legation garden, as mute as the gatekeeper who hauled her home in a carpet. Despite the fact that she was deprived of speech, her pitiful condition was interpreted as an appeal for sanctuary at the British Legation, and a protest was immediately lodged at the palace.

The Shah did not need to wait for the London papers to print the story one month later to react to the outrage. He put on his red cloak of anger that very hour. How dare a woman summon foreign powers to intervene in a domestic crisis? he roared. Who was responsible for this grotesque humiliation? It was particularly satisfying to know the answer to his questions even as he asked them.

When the guards dragged the stuttering Mayor back into his presence, he arraigned him before the entire court. He had failed in his mandate, the Shah said; he had caused the crisis rather than resolved it. He was responsible for everyone's suffering, and had brought shame upon his country. The fact that he had been found flogging his Wife in the market square only confirmed his guilt. For if he could act with such cruelty in public, how vicious must he be in private? If this was how he treated his Wife, then no wonder the people of his city were up in arms. He should be beaten himself so that they might witness the king's justice. His punishment would be the perfect substitute for all he had denied them.

"Bastinado him!" ordered the Shah.

The old man moaned pitifully as the guards approached him. The Shah was particularly irritated by way he stammered as they bound his wrists.

"Strike the fellow with sticks!" the Shah cried, "And cut off his beard!"

With that the Mayor gave a terrible groan. The guards afterwards averred that he uttered a woman's name at that moment. But his cry aroused the Shah still more.

"Strangle him!" roared the king.

At that, the executioner placed the cord around the Mayor's neck and jerked the life out of him. But the starving populace were given his body. Even though they may have preferred bread, they slaked their hunger on the dead man for the next three days.

The attaché, who was serving at the British Legation at that time, observed that the Shah had saved his capital from revolution by a hair's breadth when he made the Mayor his scapegoat. The notice in the British press one month later echoed the remark although no mention was made of his Wife's role in his demise. As his widowed sister predicted, the battered woman did not survive the bread riots. An angry mob torched the roof of the house three days later and ransacked the building. When the breezeway was ablaze, the women were in such haste to lower their mistress to the pool that she slipped from their grasp and fell head down to the courtyard.

The daughters of the Mayor swore bitterly that she weighed more dead than alive. The widow said it was because a woman's silences were double the weight of her words. And her son was guilt-ridden about the ladder. He made no mention of the prophecy, naturally, but to cover his shame he blamed the poetess of Qazvin for the fury of the mob. It was because of the notorious prisoner who had stayed in that upper chamber that the townsfolk had gone wild, he said; it was the fault of the heretic that his father's house was gutted and his mother died.

The corpse washers told strange tales afterwards. They said that although the Mayor's Wife lay cold beneath their hands, beside the marble lip of the pool, words oozed from her every pore, like rippling water, whispers spilled through her stiffened lips, like wine. Her mouth was filled with the prayers she had been whispering in the upper chamber all these years, they said, and she was mouthing a name. The corpse washers swore it was not her husband's. But when a jagged thorn bush cracked her tomb and thrust its way out through her grave some time later, no one was surprised. Everyone knew the Mayor's Wife had died of the unspoken.

The Mother of the Shah made up for her silences. She turned her into a city icon and contributed to the cost of railings round her grave, to protect her reputation. She even wrote a scrap of verse for her tomb, citing the lady's faithful service to the Mayor, her master, who had so cruelly betrayed her. The following winter, she ordered that wheat be distributed to the poor when the Shah was out hunting, in order to avoid a repetition of the riots. She justified herself on his return by saying that surely a royal master would not betray his loyal subjects twice?

The Shah was furious about it. He had had enough of that dratted phrase. It had already broken his heart when his favourite uttered it and it drove him to distraction in his Mother's mouth. He told the old queen that if he heard her moaning on about serving masters faithfully one more time, if he heard her harping on about betrayal anymore, it would be a self-fulfilling prophecy. If she ever interfered in his affairs again, he said, he would banish her to Qum for life.

Or perhaps, he added, glancing at his Sister, perhaps her highness would prefer the bath attendants from the city of the dead to come here instead, to take care of her special needs?

THE BOOK OF THE SISTER

When the Grand Vazir died in a bathhouse in the provinces, everyone knew a woman was behind it. The surly strangers who followed him into the building on the appointed day were men, of course; the special attendants who assisted with his ablutions were naturally men too. The gates to the gardens of Fin, in which the baths were situated, were secured with the seal of the most powerful man in the land, but it was not difficult to guess who broke open all the locks.

It requires a certain art to slit a man's veins as he lies stark naked in the steam. It takes a special kind of lust to thrust a towel down his throat as his body flounders in the red waters. It betrays a desire for revenge bred only in the recesses of the *anderoun*. The official gazette which reported the demise of the disgraced minister, in the fourth winter of the young Shah's reign, stated that he had been ailing for several weeks and had been suffering, ever since he left the capital two months before, from mysterious swellings in his legs. But the corpse washers told everyone that his flesh was as fresh as cheese when he fell into their hands. They confirmed that his veins had been slit open with raw razors that very morning, and his blood had drained into boiling water for just a few hours.

In later years, court chronicles insisted that the Grand Vazir had chosen his own method of execution, but everyone knew this death was woman's work. The incriminating evidence lay in a letter written to the Shah by his own Sister, so they said.

₡ 2 ₯

The Shah's first Grand Vazir had been the object of conflicting emotions in the royal *anderoun* long before his appointment. His reputation had been tugged and pulled between the folding of the palace quilts; his ambitions had been marvelled at and spat over around the samovar. Before the court even laid eyes on him, quick looks had passed between the princesses whenever he was mentioned and knowing glances flashed across the tea room at his name. Since his rise to prominence had been more rapid and his disregard for flattery more obvious than custom could allow, it was hardly surprising that he acquired enemies in the capital while still serving on the Turko-Persian borders. There had already been one attempt to murder him during the old king's reign, and though the palace reverberated with his exploits at the crowning of the new one, nobody in the queen's hearing, dared give him praise.

The Mother of the Shah had taken to this rough soldier at first and asked innumerable questions about him. She had commented favourably on his intelligence, envied his ruthlessness, and found the breadth of his shoulders pleasing. He was only a cook's son, she said, but his bearing was impressive. She even encouraged the Shah to make him head of the army during her first term of regency and went so far as to offer him her favours on condition that he respected her sphere of influence. For she wanted to win an ally as well as to restrain a potential enemy; she was willing to concede certain of her own powers to control this rising star.

But she found that the ambitions of the new Grand Vazir could not be curtailed within the orbit of her good pleasure. It was clear from the cut of his beard that no woman ruled over him, for he was barbered like a butcher and did not dye his hair. It was also evident that his tailor and his jeweller were paid for their impudence because the dazzling diamond buckle and brooch he wore on the occasion of the Shah's coronation, the unwinking paisleys and gleaming seed pearls embroidered on his ceremonial robes, were sufficient warning that this statesman had fixed his sights far beyond the confines of domestic power.

He called himself a renovator, a reformer. As soon as he was in office, he attempted to transform the army, reorganize the chancery, and eradicate what he was pleased to call dishonesty. To the horror of the queen and her kinsmen, he even tried to implement sweeping changes in the treasury. There was hardly a sinecure or stipend he did not decrease, nor a pension he did not radically reduce. But while rendering void the positions of many, her highness noticed that he often retained the benefits of the privileges he revoked. He went so far as to abrogate the customary laws of political asylum in the holy shrines and royal stables, but she thought it was only to extend the reach of his own powers. People who resisted his orders of summary arrest and arbitrary detention were hacked to pieces on the spot, as a preventive measure. He was particularly opposed to the use of legations for places of refuge, and the British and the Russian envoys soon learned that if they offered to save peoples' lives, they put themselves at even greater risk.

In fact the Grand Vazir was employing new rules to play the same old games. His ideas may have been enlightened, but his methods were not: he advised the Shah to be a perfect despot. A king should be firm, the premier counselled, to ensure the freedom of his people, cruel to be remembered for his leniency, and merciless to restore peace to his country. And he should give rein neither to a mother's whims nor to the clergy's demands. Keep clear of priests, he advised the king, and play the foreign ambassadors against each other. The people should not expect the mercy of God if they flee from the justice of his majesty.

And so the reign of the young Shah began with raids and purges. Within weeks of being sworn into office, the Grand Vazir claimed that he had exposed a plot against his life and used the so-called conspiracy as an excuse to crack down on insurgents. The prisons were soon full of idealists, the police headquarters crammed with visionaries, scholars, poets. Random arrests were made, of merchants who expressed hope for a better future, of mullahs who tried to avoid past mistakes. It was enough to interpret reform in a way that did not tally with the premier's, to be suspect. Even reading became a risky activity, because it involved interpretation, and writing, too, could justify torture and expropriation. When the poetess of Qazvin was taken captive, it was evident that literacy itself, especially among women, was a crime. No one was safe from the Grand Vazir. There was no refuge to flee to, no haven to be found from him.

The queen was not opposed to his methods, but she greatly resented his relations with the Shah. It infuriated her that her feeble-minded son sought independence from her by hiding behind his Grand Vazir. It irked her that he followed at his premier's heels like a fawning puppy, with his opinions held on a tight leash. And when he placed the female prisoner in the new prison headquarters rather than in the hands of her own protégé, she swore to take vengeance. She might have accepted the new minister's interference if he had had the good manners to respond to her proposals. But he snubbed her and rejected her advances in the most humiliating way; he rebuffed her and complained about her lewdness to his majesty. As a result, she was obliged to resort to clandestine encounters in her private gardens, to convene in secret behind sheltered arbours, in order to cultivate her influence in the court. And when her son brandished a pistol in her face in the rose gardens one day, when she was talking with the Secretary of the armed forces about the awkward problem of the poetess of Qazvin, she knew who had goaded the silly boy to it.

The problem was awkward for many reasons, not the least of which was that the king wished to meet the female prisoner. What made matters worse was that the premier appeared to support the foolhardy plan. And there was nothing the queen could do. His power equalled hers; his influence exceeded hers. Small wonder that she hated him.

But perhaps she also loved him. The Sister of the Shah was wont to say that her highness plotted the downfall of the Grand Vazir because she was so jealous of his attentions. She told those who cared to listen that her Mother turned against the Shah's first minister because he had compared her unfavourably with another woman. He admired someone else, besides the queen.

"And that person," she added, with a bruised smile, "was not me."

(3)

Not many cared to listen to the Sister of the Shah. She had a plain way of speaking, which contrasted sharply with her brother's histrionics and her Mother's grandiloquence. Her observations were weighted by common rather than political sense, and her wits posed no great challenge to the average mind. Most of the time her quiet remarks sank like pebbles in the stream of conversation, and were quickly forgotten. Her influence was absorbed rather than observed, assimilated rather than noticed, and only remembered vaguely, like a yawn, in retrospect.

They called her the Polo Ball, even before she was sent hurtling across the muddy field of ministerial politics. She looked just like one, according to the women of the royal *anderoun*, so it was hardly surprising that the Shah passed her back and forth, with a crack of his muddy mallet, from one marriage to the next for five decades. She was wed to his first, to the son of his second, to the brother and nephew of his third and fourth, and finally to the secretary of his last premier. But her value dropped steadily with each alliance. Although she served as the king's seal of approval when new-minted, her currency became worthless when accompanied by his disfavour. Her first marriage was doomed to death, her second to divorce, her third to disease, her fourth to disappointment, and her fifth to disgrace. By the time her brother was assassinated, it had become evident that whoever married his Sister suffered castration or eradication in the end.

When the wife of the British Envoy finally met her on the occasion of her second courtesy call at court, some weeks after the ignominious funeral of the murdered Grand Vazir, she thought the little widow dreadfully dull. Her ladyship had nurtured high expectations of the young maiden. She had imagined that the princess would be distinguished for her intelligence, remarkable for her independence, notable for her bearing. For she had chosen to leave the court with her two small children and accompany the old Vazir when he was banished to the provinces; she had shared his *howdah* as well as his humiliations all the way to Kashan. The gruesome details of his death, which filtered back to the capital two months after his demise, only intensified the desire of the Englishwoman to meet this

Persian heroine who had taken such a bold stand beside her husband in his hour of need. But the Princess Royal greatly disappointed her. She turned out to be a dumpy little person, unbecomingly cocooned in black taffeta, who hung her head with the air of a simpleton and did not utter a word the entire afternoon.

Ever since that autumn day when the carriage of the exiled premier and his family had clattered through the gates of the capital and headed through the wind and rain towards the gardens of Fin, everyone had been gossiping about the Sister of the Shah. Few interpreted her departure as a sign of fidelity. Most defined it as an act of folly and some even went so far as to call it heresy that she had not hesitated for a moment between her sovereign and her spouse. It had been shockingly unorthodox of her to prefer sibling disfavour to conjugal infidelity, to place matrimonial allegiance above parental scorn. It was her own fault, people murmured, if she had had such a dreadful shock a few months later, finding the Grand Vazir like that, sunk like a sack of wet flour in the baths, his veins drained of blood and his legs swollen. She had only herself to blame for it. Sisters had a fixed role in society, and she had refused to play her part.

There is little credit given to sisters in the history books, and the Shah's Sister was no exception to the rule. Whereas the shame and honour of mothers is well documented, and fame and notoriety can automatically belong to wives, that curious status granted to a woman by accident of birth rather than alliance is rarely an entitlement she enjoys. Neither her individual happiness, nor her social distinction, nor even her spiritual autonomy is necessarily enhanced by it. Had she been less dynastically significant, the Sister of the Shah might have been more socially conspicuous. But it was safer, in the end, to remain unremarkable; it was simpler to be despised rather than blamed. If she accepted self-abasement so readily it was only because she was so anxious, in the light of constant criticism, to do the right thing.

But as far as her imperial highness was concerned, her daughter was all wrong. She had caused offence by following her husband into exile only to become an even greater embarrassment at court on her return. She had trailed back to the capital with her two small children in tow, not immediately, as was expected, but reluctantly, several weeks after his funeral. The arrival of the wife of the British ambassador in the palace on this occasion only underscored the affront implied to the queen by the girl's unreasonably tragic air. The Englishwoman had come to pay her respects to the young widow without even receiving an invitation from the queen. Although the Sister of the Shah obeyed instructions and kept her mouth shut, although she clamped her lips in a hard line above the headscarf that was tied tightly around her chin, her highness was indignant at the affront she posed.

"You looked just like a corpse," she told her daughter in disgust.

The Sister of the Shah was a disappointment to the queen. Her femininity, such as it was, consisted of ponderous elements and was compounded, in her Mother's opinion, by a deplorable heaviness of mind. Her hair was so thin that it was hard to imagine a thought in her head, and her eyes were so small that her brain could barely be bigger. The straight black line of her brows, thickened with antimony according to fashion, merely emphasized her plainness, and it was assumed she had a sullen nature, for that involuntary lift of the facial muscles associated with coquetry and innocence alike, that limpid expression praised by poets and painters throughout the ages, was not in the casual repertoire of her customary graces. The Princess Royal rarely smiled.

She certainly did not smile in the course of her ladyship's second courtesy call at the palace. Nor did she frown. She appeared to have embraced orthodoxy beneath a mask of stone. Her ladyship was disconcerted. She had come to offer her condolences to the bereaved princess and had hoped to talk to the poor young widow whose plight had touched her greatly. She had been much shaken by the news of the murder and was looking forward to shared confidences in the privacy of the *anderoun*. When her husband reminded her that the death of the Vazir had been attributed to natural causes, according to the official gazette, and should not be referred to as a murder, she was dismayed to find that even sympathy had diplomatic frontiers. How could she, in all conscience, disregard a widow's grief, whatever its political cause?

It was her third winter by then, and she was used now to the local customs. She felt she understood the Persians. Although her progress in reading backwards had been slow since coming to the land of roses and nightingales, she had acquired a good grasp of the spoken language. But she owed her fluency to nannies, nursemaids, and washerwomen, for she had spent more time with female domestics over the past two years than with male secretaries in the Legation. One child had been born at the beginning of her first winter, another delivered during the summer of her second year, and she suspected the third would be on the way, before she could even master the alphabet the following spring. As a result of these happy encumbrances, she had not learned to read but hoped that she understood Persian sufficiently well this time to be relieved of the interfering services of the French translator in the royal *anderoun*.

When she was ushered once again through the mirrored antechambers of the queen, she found the ladies huddled round the covered brazier to keep warm. She had not been so taken aback at the sight of her highness' black slave this time, but when the ladies requested that she join them on the floor, she was disconcerted. Instead of sitting in the isolated splendour of a frozen chair, she was invited to lower herself beneath the communal tent of quilts to wait for the Mother of the Shah. Her highness, the ladies told her, merrily, was going to give her ladyship a tour of the palace frescoes, in the company of the Polo Ball.

Her ladyship had no great interest in a tour of the palace frescoes. But the challenge of reaching the floor in all her stays and petticoats was a test of her determination to meet the Princess Royal. It posed a far greater diplomatic predicament to sit muffled to her chin in a stupor of smoke, with her feet extended towards the brazier in the middle of the room, than to perch awkwardly on a chair discussing the forbidden subjects of slaves and female subjection.

Her discomfort intensified, however, when she attempted to speak. Madame the translator did not take kindly to being made redundant and insisted that her ladyship's accent rendered her remarks unintelligible. No one understood her nursery vocabulary, she sneered; her ladyship sounded like a common washerwoman. The giggles of the princesses seemed to confirm it, and so the Envoy's wife was reduced, once more, to the stiff formalities of interpretation.

But her worst disappointment was the Sister of the Shah. No wonder they called her the Polo Ball, for she was certainly small and round. And just as thick-skinned, muttered the ladies of the royal *anderoun*. You'd have to be, they whispered to the Envoy's wife, if you were kicked about like that; you'd have to be tough, to be bounced from bed to bed in the service of the state. Given her past, they were under no illusions about her future. There were rumours going around the court, they nudged and whispered; they had already heard hints about the little widow's fate.

But the wife of the British ambassador ignored their innuendos and asked the grieving girl solicitously about her husband's funeral. It was difficult to know what else to talk about in the circumstances. They did say that she had surpassed herself as the chief mourner at his dismal obsequies. She may have been the dullest bride the court had ever seen but everyone agreed that funerals were her forte. The Envoy's wife thought she had already heard her grief-struck howls in the covered theatre during the month of mourning, rising above the pulse of the drummers and the chant of the singers like enormous gas balloons. But she did not open her mouth as wide as a whimper on the subject of the Grand Vazir as she stood two paces behind the Envoy's wife in front of the palace frescoes.

Her Mother answered in her stead. "A widow's lot is always hard," she grimly said.

It was hard to picture the Sister of the Shah behaving like a Persian widow, as she trailed in the wake of her Mother, who was pointing out the badly rendered paintings on the palace walls. It was difficult to think of her weeping and wailing and tearing her clothes and suffering her hair to be pulled loose and scattered about her shoulders, as she stood there, meek and mute and wrapped in black, while the queen droned on and on about the idylls of nomadic life. And it was impossible to imagine, either, what she had done upon discovering her murdered husband in the baths of Fin. Where had she been when she first heard the news? Who had told her of it, and what had she said when she discovered her husband's body? Did she scream when she saw him, lying there in the red hot waters, listing like a pale whale at her feet? Did she faint? She must have known that this was going to happen, thought the Envoy's wife. She must have read the signs. So what did she feel?

The official chronicles stated that the Princess Royal was unaware of her husband's gruesome fate until long afterwards; she was apparently ignorant of the event at the time that it occurred. There was no record, either, in the history books, of who was or even whether she suspected who might be the author of the dreadful deed; it was not supposed to concern her. Although she had been taught the basic skills of literacy, like any other woman of her rank, she was not expected to read treachery. She kept this dangerous art a secret, until her Mother died.

(4)

Around the same time that rumours were first beginning to circulate in the court about the marriage of the Sister of the Shah to the Grand Vazir, a joint communiqué was delivered to the king by the foreign envoys resident in the capital. It arrived at the palace soon after his majesty's coronation ceremonies, posing an unprecedented challenge to diplomacy.

The communiqué was not flattering. It strongly recommended that public executions should replace private tortures in Persia. Although the ministers of her Britannic majesty and the Tsar began by congratulating the young Shah on his coronation while deploring the unfortunate indisposition of his regent on that auspicious occasion, they concluded by offering the hope that his reign would be distinguished by greater enlightenment than that which had characterized his predecessor. And between the two they went on and on, in the most patronizing manner, about how the custom followed by his majesty of butchering prisoners in the palace gardens after tormenting them underground was, in their civilized opinions, a revolting exhibition, a disgrace to any modern nation, an example of conduct more suited to the barbarous tribes of Africa than to a newly crowned king of an Aryan race. They wished to lodge a joint complaint about it. It was the first time these endemic rivals had ever done anything together.

The marriage rumours that were circulating in court, when this communiqué was delivered, posed an equally unprecedented challenge to the queen. The possibility of a betrothal between the new minister and her only daughter was as delicate as any question of foreign policy. His majesty was surrounded by potential heirs of varying authenticity, but none had the same claim to the throne as his Sister. Her dubious distinction was to be his closest relative, the nearest to himself in blood. She alone shared his heredity and most threatened it; she was the only one in whose turgid veins coursed the exact mixture of legitimacy, the precise blend of ineptitude, the perfect combination of pique and pride that characterized the ruling race of the Qajars. No one else was constituted of that same disastrous recipe. Such dangerous singularity, in the queen's opinion, should not be wasted on the Grand Vazir; it should not be lightly tossed aside on the son of a cook, lest he be inclined to think himself a permanent fixture in the kingdom.

The Shah had expected his Mother to oppose both issues, but was disconcerted when the Grand Vazir told him to bow beneath the envoys' pressure and submit to the queen's judgement. On previous occasions, far from accommodating to the foreigners' demands, his minister had warned him against them; instead of agreeing with her highness' position, he had invariably opposed it. This strategy of intransigence had greatly gratified the sovereign; it had mollified his adolescent pride and promoted his giddy sense of independence. So when his Vazir advised him to give way, particularly regarding his Sister's marriage, he was inclined to protest.

But why? he whined. He knew the Grand Vazir was already married, but why should a wife come between them? Think of what fun it would be to come and go freely into the royal *anderoun*, he urged. Think of what larks they could have as brothers-in-law in a united front against her highness! Such liberties could only be enjoyed if his Vazir were part of the family.

Perhaps this servant was too old for fun and larks, the premier replied, dryly, for he preferred to keep out of the confines of this particular family. Perhaps this decrepit old man would only curtail his majesty's liberties, he said, for, as a matter of fact, he was strongly attached to his wife. When the Shah brushed the thought aside with a compliment to his virility, he suggested, in that case, that perhaps the princess was too young to have the cares of state thrust on her shoulders.

But he had underestimated the king's ruthlessness. "She'll damn well do as I ask," said the Shah, thrusting out his lower lip. He was unaccustomed to considering his Sister's wishes.

The Grand Vazir calculated his alternatives. There was only one left. Perhaps his majesty should solicit the opinion of his royal Mother first, he offered. Had the queen given her consent?

The Shah snorted. Stuff his Mother, he replied irreverently. He wasn't asking the Grand Vazir to marry *her*!

But he could not budge his minister, could not bend him to his will. The Grand Vazir had become very sober on the subject, and rather dull. He had to have her highness' consent, he solemnly replied. Marriage with the Sister of the Shah should not be treated as a sport.

The Mother of the Shah proved even less flexible on the subject of public executions. When high-handed threats were veiled by hypocritical courtesies, offence could go both ways. She was outraged when the Grand Vazir advised her son to capitulate to the foreigners. It was a plot, she told the Shah, a conspiracy from within. This joint communiqué had a domestic inspiration. Far from protecting the country, the Grand Vazir would provoke insurrection if the prisoners in the Mayor's house were killed before the eyes of the rabble in the market square.

The Shah tried to convince her that foreign criticism, like local insurrection, was a ticklish problem at the outset of a reign; it should be resolved rapidly, according to his premier, before it went out of hand. Besides, these prisoners had been plotting to overthrow the Grand Vazir.

"Overthrow my foot!" she retorted. "That man invents his own plots." If the Shah allowed the Russians and the British to interfere in his domestic affairs, he would show the world that he was under the thumb of his own Vazir. "And that," she concluded grimly, "is even more ticklish!"

Since his Mother and his minister were divided over the communiqué but united in their opposition to the marriage, the Shah decided to deploy strategy to get his own way. If he could play one against the other, as his premier had taught him to with the foreign envoys, perhaps he could use their conflict regarding the first problem to undermine their unanimity over the second.

One winter's morning, soon after the capture of the notorious poetess of Qazvin, he decided to consult about public executions with the queen regent and his Grand Vazir, together. Since his Mother refused to attend any meetings on the subject, he was obliged to discuss it in her private quarters. But as it would have compromised the dignity of the harem for an unrelated male to enter this sanctuary, he had to leave the premier behind in the chilly antechamber. He wanted his Vazir to feel that pinch. He also wanted to goad his Mother with his proximity, which he knew would pro- voke agitation among the women. Nor was he averse to teasing his Sister with glimpses of the man he wanted her to marry, each time the curtains lifted and the cold air gusted in.

The *anderoun* was suffocating in order to accommodate to the queen's usual state of undress that morning, but the Sister of the Shah shivered when she glimpsed the towering figure behind her brother as he stepped through the doorway to speak with her. The Grand Vazir was as tall as a ghoul on the other side of the curtain. The royal concubines were instantly transfixed into models of modesty at his majesty's entrance, and his wives fluttered away from the door like moths out of camphor, but the queen glared at the Shah, from under heavy brows.

What did he want? she asked crossly. She had no time for him today.

He needed to talk, he replied, about the public executions.

His needs would have to wait, she said. The British Envoy's wife was due any moment. It was her first courtesy call, and the queen had no desire to give her the upper hand by being rude.

But he had to respond to the communiqué, he whined. The Grand Vazir insisted.

The Sister of the Shah caught her breath at the thought of a ghoul that insisted.

He would have to contain himself, said the queen, testily, until the British woman left.

Why did the British, pouted the Shah, always poke their noses in other peoples' affairs?

The British, she erupted, were not the only ones to poke their noses in other peoples' affairs. And she gave the Shah a piece of her mind about the Grand Vazir's new policies.

The Sister of the Shah shuddered again when her brother lifted the curtain to return to the antechamber, for she had just seen the Grand Vazir's heavy, spade-like hands on the other side.

The Shah was obliged to repeat to his premier the words uttered by his Mother. Why, he echoed thinly, was his premier letting foreigners poke their noses in domestic affairs?

The ghoul's voice rasped through the velvet like a knife. If foreigners normally so opposed expressed a sense of outrage so united, it might be best to undermine their collaboration rather than encourage it, he said. Lose a small victory to avoid a greater defeat; sacrifice freedom now for the sake of future autonomy. The wisest course would be to submit to their demands and promise to modify the customs over time. After that his majesty could do as he wished.

The queen snorted. Over time? What kind of time, precisely, was his excellency suggesting? she hissed, and as her son pushed back through the curtains, his Sister saw a grizzled, wedge-shaped beard reflected in the mirrors behind him. The ghoul looked just like a public executioner! Perhaps the Grand Vazir should modify himself first, snapped her Mother.

He's only saying it would be wise for now, her brother protested.

But his Mother pronounced that it was a poor kind of king who would toss the ancient customs of his land aside at any time.

As he lifted the curtain to the antechamber once more, his Sister saw candles flickering in the waxy sconces and a bushy brow reflected in the mirrors beyond. She felt positively faint. Why was the minister tossing his country's customs aside, she heard her parrot brother cry.

But he was vindicating the ancient customs, replied the muffled voice of the ghoul. He was showing his sovereign how to bargain with foreigners. His majesty should tell the envoys that he would only consider implementing public executions if they stopped offering diplomatic immunity to his subjects; he would only change the old practices if they no longer gave refuge to those who fled from his justice. The premier offered to carry out fair trials of the condemned himself, on condition that *bast* or sanctuary was denied; he promised to see that justice was done.

The Sister of the Shah revived as the cold air and her brother gusted back in, but the queen was incensed. Fair trials? she blazed. Did this minister imagine that he could usurp his sovereign's rights as easily as arrogate those of God? What kind of justice was he talking about? If he exposed his country's private linen in public it would cause riots, mayhem, assassinations!

It was unbearably hot in the room. The temperature was so explosive that the Sister of the Shah felt she might burst as her Mother's voice rose higher.

The Grand Vazir would be dragging females to the scaffold next, shouted the queen. Did he intend to execute women in public too? In that case, why not cut off the poetess' head while he was at it, since she had already cast off the veil!

The Shah seemed uncertain which side of the curtain he was on at that moment. By the time he fought his way back through the velvet folds, he had found his voice but lost his temper. If his Grand Vazir wanted to argue with his Mother, he announced crossly, he had better marry his Sister so he could do it face to face because he, for one, was no longer prepared to be their go-between. And by the way, he added, loudly, for the benefit of his Mother on the other side, public executions were only possible if he could see the poetess in private first.

His Sister gaped. The woman had barely been captured and the Shah was already bargaining for her. But he seemed not to notice who he was bargaining with. Having delivered his ultimatum, he stomped off just as the wife of the British ambassador was announced at the gates.

The Shah checkmated both his Mother and his minister through petulance rather than strategy that time. The Grand Vazir had no alternative but to defend his majesty's whims in order to oblige him to institute fair trials and public executions, and the queen was so indignant with her son for accommodating to the envoys' demands that she naturally took out her frustrations on her daughter. When her ladyship was ushered in from the antechamber, for her first courtesy call shortly afterwards, the queen permitted the Shah's concubines to serve the sweetmeats and allowed her son's wives to bring in the tea, but she refused to let his Sister stay in the room.

If she was going to ogle at foreigners the way she had been gawping at that Grand Vazir, said her highness, acidly, she would put the whole court to shame.

As a result the Sister of the Shah did not meet the Englishwoman face to face until she paid a second courtesy call to court, two years later. But by then the Grand Vazir was dead.

(5)

The Grand Vazir had already been dead for several hours by the time the Sister of the Shah ran across the gardens of Fin and started hammering at the entrance of the bathhouse. The place was ominously locked and deserted. The old woman who normally sat outside was not in her usual place, and the bath attendants did not open the doors when she knocked. None of the guards pacing round the central pavilion, none of the soldiers posted at the grand portico, seemed to be around. There was no one on duty near the guardhouse either. It was strange. When she pressed her ear against the wooden door, she heard nothing. Or rather, all she heard was the ubiquitous sound of running water. But she could not distinguish between the distant drip-dripping of drains in the stone basins of the bathhouse and the continuous ripple of waters, the murmur of bubbling pools, and the forever gushing fountains all around her in the winter gardens of Fin.

She felt foolish standing there, outside the bolted door of the baths, so close to the guardhouse and in full view of the central pavilion. She felt vulnerable. The Grand Vazir would have preferred to take up residence in this grander palace rather than in the small rear one, which had been allocated to his *anderoun* on their arrival. It dominated the gardens of Fin and stood in elegant isolation between the imposing portico to the north and the rear pavilion on the southern walls. Unlike the latter, which had been built more recently, it was of ancient construction and had been designed by the old kings of Persia to span a blue-green pool that fed four water channels, running from north to south, and east to west. The pavilions set amid these cypress trees and poplars were girt by massive ramparts on four sides and were hemmed in at each corner by high circular towers, manned, like a fortress, by the soldiers of the Shah. But the rippling waterways and fountains, fed by natural springs that jetted from the desert rocks outside, flowed freely through its entire length, spilling from one translucent water channel to another and plashing effortlessly over the marble steps and pebbled paths, driven by gravity alone. The central pavilion was in a bad state of repair as were the old baths to the east of the property, but a new guardhouse had been recently constructed from which three sleepy guards finally stumbled, in response to the cries and the hammering of the Sister of the Shah.

The men's faces were new to her; she could not read their intentions. They must have been recruited from the village that morning for she had not seen them the previous day. There was a constant turnover of guards at the gardens of Fin. The exiles no sooner befriended one set of men than they were replaced by another. None of them could be trusted, in the opinion of the Sister of the Shah. These had evidently been having an afternoon siesta, after a midday meal beside the guardhouse stoves. They smelled of hashish and mutton fat, of charcoal and of their own unwashed bodies.

They had been assigned to replace the portress, they said, who had been called away to a burial that day. The Sister of the Shah had thought the hag sitting at the door to be a bad omen when they first arrived two months before, for the old woman earned a pittance as a corpse washer too, when occasion required. But she would have been glad of her garrulous presence that day. The new guards were singularly unhelpful and looked blank when she asked them questions.

They had only been following instructions, they replied, defensively. The Grand Vazir himself had said that he should not be interrupted during his ablutions.

Even for the midday meal? she retorted angrily. And then she demanded that they open the doors and let her into to the bathhouse. She wished to ensure her husband's safety, she said.

They looked embarrassed then. They were very sorry, milady, they replied, shuffling from foot to foot and avoiding her eyes, but since the baths were open to men only that day, it would be out of the question, it would be more than their jobs were worth to bend the regulations. To allow a woman into the public baths on a day set aside for men was impossible, they said.

The Shah's Sister was incredulous. Were they seriously evoking such conventions when the only person in there was her husband? And then she remembered the bath attendants.

Call out the attendants, she demanded, peremptorily, so she could speak to them.

The guards looked even more sheepish. The special attendants, they said, had already left.

So his honour has no one to help him bathe? she cried, and turning back, she began to hammer on the doors and call her husband's name. That was when she saw the seals.

The doors of the bathhouse in the garden of Fin were not only bolted shut with padlocks, but knotted with string. And the string had not only been wrapped round the locks several times, but also heavily waxed. The seal on the wax was her brother's. She recognized it immediately; she read the royal insignia on it; she became hysterical.

Who gave them orders to seal these doors? she screamed.

The guards confessed that two strangers had showed up with the bath attendants that morning. They had omitted to tell milady, they mumbled. Two surly men had showed up, who had never been seen in the village before and who had stayed in an abandoned hut the previous night. They had turned up, bold as brass, and followed the attendants into the baths. Afterwards, they had locked the doors behind them, waxed them shut, and left with the keys. That's why, shrugged the guards, feebly, it was impossible to open the doors for milady.

When the Sister of the Shah realized that her husband was sealed inside the baths alone, she began to pull at the string, to break open the knots with her nails. To the consternation of the guards, she began to stamp the wax to dust beneath her feet. She demanded that the door be axed down, immediately. She wanted to be let inside the bathhouse this instant.

They were still dithering about what they should do when she began to shriek murder, foul murder, and pulled off her veil and rake her cheeks with her nails, as if she were in mourning. Only then did they comply.

And the Sister of the Shah was crying aloud as she stepped through the door of the bathhouse and down the steps. She was sobbing as she ran through the catacomb of chambers, stumbling from one to another, until she reached the last. And as she burst into that room no woman should have entered, she gave a piercing cry, and stood there, mute and breathless. Below her lay the man she loved, his face illegible beneath the still rising steam of the murky pool, his bloated body lapped and lilting imperceptibly under the blood-red waters of retribution.

〖 6 〗

The Sister of the Shah was sure it was her fault that her Mother was banished to Qum. Although the link between her crime and the queen's punishment was never clear to anyone else, she saw it visibly written in coincidences. Her brother's decision to exile the queen to the city of a thousand funerals was made public on the same day that the Grand Vazir finally accepted to marry her. The synchronization could not have been more damning.

Spring was late that year, and much to the soothsayers' concern, the palace had been invaded by crows. These raucous birds of ill omen had taken up residence in the eaves of the royal reception rooms and interrupted with impunity the most complex debates and questions of governance, all winter long. People blamed the public executions for it. According to the gossip, all the crows of the neighbourhood had flocked to the royal gardens in order to escape from the howls of tortured men in the prison headquarters that winter. Either that, or they were drawn there by witchcraft. At any rate, they made discussion very difficult.

The deliberations of the day, taking place in the hearing of half a dozen courtiers and the colony of crows, ostensibly concerned the crime and punishment of the female prisoner in the Mayor's house. What should be done with the poetess of Qazvin? Who had the right to prove her innocent or guilty? What sort of sanctions could be imposed on her and by what kind of court? Should government, monarch, or clergy decide whether she was to be condemned or be released? For the heretic was not only a person of rank and renown, but also a woman.

According to custom, the law of retaliation was generally applicable to women in cases of adultery only. Or murder. Women could be butchered with impunity when innocent, but could only be officially killed for infidelity. Or willful slaughter. According to custom, too, though violence was frequently practiced against the female sex, a woman had to be guilty of poverty to be accused of murder or adultery: it was rare for a wealthy woman or lady of rank to be thrown from the top of a tower or stoned. The only other way to merit lawful death was by apostasy. But a female heretic would have to be impervious to reform before she could be proven guilty of that sin; she would have had to influence others to her misguided ways before she could be condemned for such a crime. And only an ecclesiastic court could pronounce on such matters.

The Grand Vazir was strongly opposed to handing the poetess to the ecclesiastic courts. The priests had altogether too much power already, he told the Shah, and he suspected that they were only insisting on this case in order to gain more. Besides, there was a contradiction inherent in the matter. The existence of an unrepentant female was theologically inconceivable according to the laws of religious jurisprudence. If a woman influenced others, it would imply that she had a mind of her own; if she were denounced for maintaining her opinions, it would acknowledge her right to think. But how could this be, if a woman only reflected the thoughts of others? Certain doctors of jurisprudence, he said, even denied that women had minds at all.

The poetess of Qazvin presented an intractable dilemma for the courts, but the queen posed another that was equally problematic to her son. She had set aside the privileges of regency that day, and had effectively boycotted the debate. Nothing could be decided in her absence; no decision could be ratified without the official regent present. And her spies were in strong evidence. The Chief Steward of the royal bedchamber stood deferentially on the left side of the throne and the Secretary of the armed forces on his majesty's right. It was hardly necessary for them to speak, because everyone knew the queen's position anyway. If the clergy could not decide on the case, she certainly did not see why the Grand Vazir should take it upon himself to advise the Shah. The fate of the poetess of Qazvin was nobody's business but her own.

The discussion came to an impasse when the flock of crows rose up and converged in a cloud beneath the palace verandas. The Shah was obliged to wait for the cacophony to subside. When he finally opened his mouth, he was visibly ruffled. So what could be done with a rebellious and uncooperative woman like this? he said, fretfully. What was the proper way to punish a woman who threatened governance and refused to submit to reform?

The question bristled with possibilities. It was obvious that his majesty was referring to more than one woman. Frankly, the crimes of the heretic were less obstructive to him at that moment than the policies of the queen. Since the pause in the cawing threatened to end at any moment and both the Chief Steward and the Secretary deferred to the Grand Vazir for a reply, his only recourse in the circumstances was to answer briefly and with extreme caution.

He ventured to suggest that since theologians themselves were divided on the subject, there might be a different way to resolve the dilemma. He would interrogate the female prisoner himself and decide on her crime and punishment, under civil law. He would deal with the issue without recourse to any priests. And his smile, as he made the offer, was as heavy as the cannonballs piled by the city gates where women prayed away their barrenness.

The Shah hesitated, as the rooks intervened. He was not sure whether the proposal added to or subtracted from his powers. His Mother had always advised him not to tread on the toes of the clergy, however autocratic he wished to be. Kingship was divinely inherited but depended on the sup-port of the *'ulama*. While he was anxious to curb their influence, he did not want to usurp their rights lest they appropriate his. He knew they could rouse the people against him and was afraid his Mother might encourage them to do so. He scowled at his Grand Vazir.

The premier was aware that her imperial highness was dominating the debate despite her absence and hurriedly added reassurances. He would naturally defer to his majesty's judgement on the matter, he demurred: the-ology and jurisprudence were as complex as the female mind.

The Shah had lost patience with theology and jurisprudence. One of the courtiers was sent out to shoo the birds off. With a shotgun. There was a momentary lull after they flapped off in panic. The point is, said the king abruptly, mind or no mind, should the woman be killed?

It would dignify her existence to execute the creature, said the Grand Vazir.

So what does anyone else propose? said the Shah, swinging round to the others in the room.

The Secretary bowed deferentially. An alternative would be to lock her up indefinitely, he replied.

Ah, said the Shah, hopefully. Incarceration for life?

The Secretary shrugged. Disappearance, he suggested, could take vari-ous forms.

Are we, the Shah inquired, speaking of murder, or exile?

Neither would be appropriate to a woman of her sort, interrupted the premier. Exile would only spread her influence abroad, and death would turn her into a martyr.

She could be done away with quietly, murmured the Chief Steward, in the ensuing pause. He caressed his beard with characteristic care, combing his fingers through the tangles with lingering slowness. She could disappear unofficially, he added. Accidentally, as it were.

There was a caw from close under the eaves outside; the intrepid crows were beginning to flap their way back from across the garden. The shotgun had failed to deflect them permanently, even officially.

In which case, interrupted the Grand Vazir, raising his voice above their raucous return, why should the ecclesiastic courts need to intervene in the matter at all?

Who else, breathed the Chief Steward, had the right to read the human conscience? Who else, he simpered piously, could offer the possibility of repentance to a heretic?

His majesty yawned. He had lost interest in the discussion and was distracted by the insistent cawing. As far as he could see, neither his Mother nor the female heretic nor even the crows seemed capable of repentance. He indicated that the Grand Vazir should affect closure on the debate, whether or not a decision had been reached.

All that was required at this stage, announced his premier, was a technicality. His majesty needed to know whether or not a woman of this sort was acting on her own volition. If she was, then the case could have nothing to do with heresy. If not, then the priests should take over.

The Shah was greatly relieved to resolve the doctrinal tangle by interim stages. The premier, he announced, would oversee the matter. He hereby authorized the Grand Vazir to ascertain the woman's independence of mind, to verify whether or not she was exerting her own will. But there was one proviso, he added. The heretic could only be interrogated under one condition.

The crows gave vent to all possible provisos. The Grand Vazir murmured that he was at his majesty's disposal under all conditions. His aim in life was to be of service to the Shah.

"In that case," replied the king, "marry my Sister so that your will and mine are one."

There was a sharp intake of breath around the audience chamber. The Grand Vazir murmured something about her highness' approval but it was clear that he had been cornered.

"The queen will go to Qum," announced the Shah, "until she gives it."

The reception room fairly rippled with eddies of surprise. The Secretary of the armed forces bowed low and backed out of the Shah's presence at the announcement. The Chief Steward of the royal bedchamber soon followed suit, but the cawing did not subside. The king insisted that his Grand Vazir deploy the shotgun again. One chapter was closed, but the story was not over: the repercussions of the queen's exile to Qum was going to be noisy.

The Grand Vazir's unwillingness to marry her daughter had been as offensive to the queen as her son's insistence on it. But the reason why the premier finally submitted to the proposal made her even more furious. The Shah agreed to public executions on condition that his premier allowed him to meet the poetess of Qazvin. But the premier would only acquiesce to marriage with his Sister if he were allowed to interrogate the woman himself. The fact that everything appeared to revolve around the heretic incensed the queen.

But the Princess Royal bowed her head and said nothing when she heard of it.

(7)

On the day of his death, the Grand Vazir walked out of the rear pavilion in the gardens of Fin with his head held high. He strode under the bending poplars, through the winter sunshine, towards the bathhouse in a jocular mood. When he passed the guards and rounded the corner towards the old baths, he was whistling. His wife could hear him. His valet had to run to keep up with him. It was the first time the minister had stepped outdoors for two months.

After he fell from grace, the Sister of the Shah knew that her husband would never be safe from her brother's arbitrary temper or her Mother's implacable revenge. Before leaving the capital, she thought a cup laced with poison would be his undoing, for Qajar coffee had become notorious at court during the queen's regency. On the road to Kashan, she expected to be waylaid by bandits, ambushed by hired assassins. And in the gardens of Fin, she was sure that the guards were just waiting for the opportunity to attack the Grand Vazir under cover of darkness, to surprise him in a shady arbour, all alone. She had begged him not to leave her side for this reason, for though her brother was not averse to humiliating her, she was sure he would not put her life in danger. She was the only protection for the Grand Vazir.

But she could not go with him into the bathhouse, even though she was his wife. So she wept into the samovar that morning when she served him breakfast; she fell to her knees and clung to his robe and begged him not to leave the house. He simply smiled, indulgently, and teased her for putting too much salt in his tea. He merely wiped her tears away and lifted her gently to her feet. He was very kind but he did not listen to her. He had walked no more than half a dozen paces down the path from the rear pavilion when she sent the valet after him with clean clothes and a message to say that if he did not come back she would follow him. He ignored the message too and whistled as he walked past the staring guards. She gave up after that.

There was no possibility of reaching the bathhouse unseen because the guards were always on the lookout. The only way to avoid passing in front of them would have been to skirt the walls and walk in front of the main portico. But that meant being seen by the Shah's soldiers instead. The Grand Vazir chose the quickest way: he walked straight through the central pavilion and under the noses of the guards. After watching him turn the corner and disappear behind the trees, his wife had little alternative but to counsel herself to patience.

Her husband was a fastidious man and very particular about personal hygiene. It had been agony for him to be cooped up in the stuffy rear pavilion since their arrival, unable to leave the premises all these weeks and obliged to make do with a brass bowl and ewer of water in the back room, which she also used as a makeshift kitchen. It had been torture for him to listen to the continuous murmur of running waters in the gardens of Fin and be deprived of a proper bath. The Sister of the Shah knew his habits: he would be gone all day.

Despite her anguish, daybreak had lightened her heart. Perhaps her husband's confidence in a royal pardon was justified; he was a shrewd politician, after all. Perhaps the gifts that had arrived from court the day before were genuine and her suspicions of her Mother unfounded, for she knew that the queen secretly admired her husband. Perhaps it was a good omen that he had finally emerged from the rear pavilion, had walked directly past the guardhouse, and had entered the baths with a merry joke under the winter sun. The valet, who scuttled in the wake of the Vazir carrying a pile of fresh garments, later told the Sister of the Shah that he had never seen his honour so jovial as the day he entered the bathhouse of Fin.

There had only been one cause for concern, and it had passed as quickly as it had arisen. When the valet returned with his master's soiled robes, he told the Sister of the Shah that the usual attendant, who was the barber from the local village, had been replaced by two different men. Two special bath attendants had taken charge of his honour's needs that day.

The heart of the Sister of the Shah misgave. What special attendants? Where had they come from? she asked fearfully.

The valet looked nonplussed. Surely the Princess Royal remembered the two special attendants sent by the Shah? They had arrived with the entourage the day before.

The Sister was disconcerted. The Grand Vazir had not mentioned special attendants to her. And then she reminded herself that if they had come from the capital with the visiting princess, they must be part of the king's pardon: gifts, a letter of reconciliation, a robe of honour, and two special attendants to assist the Grand Vazir to prepare for his return. No wonder her husband wanted to go to the baths. No wonder he had ignored all her appeals.

She controlled her fears and busied herself with the household chores. It was best not to read too much into these special attendants, she thought. The Grand Vazir would doubtless prefer their services to those of the one-eyed barber from the nearby village. There was no need to worry, she told herself, and did everything to be occupied. She washed and fed her little girls herself; she swept the leaves from the steps and scrubbed her husband's soiled shirts with her own hands. She needed no attendants to prove her love. When they had arrived here, the previous autumn, these simple daily tasks had filled her with unspeakable joy. She had sung with the birds as she swept the dust from before the door; she had served her husband with religious zeal. But today, she worked in order not to think.

Her first task after her morning chores was to send her maid down the alley of cypresses to the central pavilion with a pot of left-over rice and a fresh samovar for the travellers who had arrived the previous day. They were ladies of court, and the quantity and quality of the gifts they brought from her Mother defined the nature and degree of the welcome they expected. However else she may have failed as a daughter and a sister, she had to fulfill her obligations as a hostess, and a wife. They would have to report to the queen that she received them befittingly, at least. And with that in mind, she ordered the valet to slit the throat of another chicken. The guests would need a midday meal and food had to be sent to the bathhouse for the Grand Vazir.

It was noon by the time the valet finally left the premises, with the rice pot on his head and a heated pannikin on his arm. The Grand Vazir had been in the baths for over four hours by then. She had given the man-servant strict instructions to avoid the central pavilion and to take the long path to the bathhouse. She did not want anyone to waylay him once he passed out of her sight. She did not want the guests to stop him before he arrived. It seemed to her, as she stood watching his dwindling figure through the fretted windows of the rear pavilion, appearing and disappearing along the ladder of light and shade cast by the cypresses, that it took an eternity for the servant to pass the guardhouse and skirt the southern wall. She finally lost sight of him when he entered the shade of the tall poplars that surrounded the central pavilion. She sighed then and prepared to wait another eternity before he returned.

But to her surprise he was back in less than half an hour. She heard his feet crunch on the pebbles again, and thought at first it was the sound of rippling of water; she saw his shadow slant between the sentinel trees, and thought it was a daytime owl. And to her alarm, instead of seeing a guard on his usual rounds, she recognized the lop-sided figure of the valet, edging round the garden with the rice pot still on his head and the pannikin on his arm.

Why was the fool bringing the food back so soon? Why had he not stayed till his master had finished eating? she wanted to know. And at the same time she did not want to know.

The man was flustered. His master had not wished to eat, he said. He had turned the valet away, had sent him back, saying that he was not hungry for the midday meal.

She was astonished. She could not believe it. Her husband had never refused food before. Why didn't he want to eat? she demanded. It could only mean that he had eaten already. Had someone else sent him food? she asked, worried. Had he accepted a meal from any of the guards?

His honour had sent word that he did not want to be interrupted, the valet told her, hurriedly. They told him that the master wished to continue with his ablutions undisturbed.

They? she asked, with rising fear. Who had told him this? But she knew the answer.

The valet confessed that he had been given this information by the special attendants. They had come out of the baths to give him the message, when he knocked on the doors; they had told him to take the food away because the Grand Vazir did not wish to be disturbed.

When she realized that the man had not entered the baths himself, had not spoken to his master at all, and had not even seen him, the Sister of the Shah gave way to the terror that had been building up within her since the night before. She threw a veil over her headscarf, stepped out of the rear pavilion and ran towards the bathhouse. Death was scrawled across its walls.

〖 8 〗

It was while her Mother was in Qum that the Sister of the Shah began to dream of public executions. It was hardly surprising. They were a hot topic of discussion that year, and when the ladies spent the day in the Legation gardens during the spring festival, at the invitation of the wife of the British Envoy Extraordinary and Plenipotentiary, all they could talk about, as they nibbled on carrots which they pulled up from the flower beds and sampled her ladyship's radishes among the tuber roses, was death.

Since there were not many spots of greenery in town, the Legation gardens were filled with picnickers on days when it was customary to flee the evil spirits and stay outdoors during the vernal equinox. This plot of vacant ground had always served as a public park for the townsfolk, and the Colonel was only able to lease it from the Mayor for his own use on condition that traditions be respected every thirteenth day of the New Year. As a result the grounds that flanked the prison headquarters were invaded annually by the ladies in the town who wanted to throw out the bad luck of the old year and expunge the ill fortunes of the new. But the assault was particularly brutal that spring. The visitors not only decapitated the roses and trod the narcissus to death, but ravaged the vegetable patch too, to the dismay of the wife of the British ambassador; they wreaked havoc among the fresh greens and ate mouthfuls of mint with impunity all day long. In the end, she was obliged to flee back into the Legation in order not to see the damage. An attack of locusts could not have been more thorough. She wondered if voraciousness was linked to revenge.

Although the Shah had supposedly replaced private torture with public executions in an attempt to appease the foreign envoys, everyone knew that the seven men who had been put to death in the marketplace, just before the spring festivities, were innocent. They had been accused of conspiring against the Grand Vazir, but no one believed it, least of all the queen. They were known to be decent citizens and distinguished in the town: merchants whose means had aroused envy; scholars whose interpretations had disturbed expectation; and a poet of distinction whose words had provoked thought. Since they were all deemed a danger to the state, the Grand Vazir had ordered that their heads be cut off and the spectacle of their bodies, lying in bloody embrace, be offered as a warning and a salutary example to the restless crowds who witnessed the scene from the rooftops. But the drama did not unfold entirely as expected.

The men had evinced a disconcerting dignity in dying. They had spoken to the crowds with a fervour rarely felt even in religious pageants, and had bidden farewell to life with a vitality that shamed the witnesses of their deaths. One had burst out into impromptu verse when his turban had been knocked off, expressing the wish that it might have been his head. Another had moved the crowd to tears with his wry humour. The executioner had been so moved that he had promptly quit the scene and changed his profession to become a porter. Public sympathy for the condemned had been so aroused that certain members of the clergy found it necessary to foment trouble in the wake of the executions in order to justify them. But there was a final twist to the plot. The warning of the queen had been just: the deaths of these men only added lustre to the reputation of the woman still left alive in the prison headquarters.

Would it be her turn next? wondered the ladies of the court as they wandered round the Legation garden, peering up at the little window set in the high walls of the Mayor's house. His Wife was expected to join them in the new year festivities that day, and they could not wait to question her about the female prisoner in her husband's custody. Since they were wives of wealthy burghers and from among the princesses in town, rank had deprived them of watching the men die in the public square, but they were all the more eager to know about the woman still alive next door. They had been hoping to catch a glimpse of her and were disappointed when they only saw the pinched faces of the daughters of the Mayor peering down instead, from the little window of the upper chamber of the prison headquarters.

The two sisters had been torn between spying and staying out of doors. They had not been important enough to be invited to the Legation gardens, and were consequently unable to ensure husbands for themselves by knotting a blade of grass that New Year. How envious they were of the Sister of the Shah, whose imminent betrothal was the talk of the town, and how disappointing it was not to see her among the ladies below, for she had chosen to remain within the palace grounds during her Mother's absence in Qum. It was only when they were seen staring at the petticoats spread across the flowerbeds that they withdrew from the upper chamber and scuttled down into the courtyard. They always blamed their bad luck in marriage on the fact that they had remained indoors too long that day, like the prisoner cooped up in the Mayor's house.

The ladies in the Legation gardens buzzed like wasps round the Mayor's Wife when she arrived, eager for the latest gossip about the prisoner. They were much exercised by the rights and wrongs of the case. Even before her arrest, they had been told that the notorious woman had committed a variety of crimes: she had instigated murder, committed adultery, and was suspected of heresy too. Since allegations shifted continuously, the penalty was equally uncertain. Some ladies wondered whether her crime would be tailored to fit her punishment rather than the other way round. Whatever she may have done, everyone was dying to know her fate.

Their favourite topic of conversation concerned methods of execution. What, they wondered, snapping off the tender leaves of her ladyship's cabbages, was the best way to die? Which death, they brooded, nibbling on the nuggets of cauliflowers, was the easiest? Certain of them advocated drowning because choking was too vulgar, and strangling too physical. Others insisted that being shot was surely easier than being stabbed or burned, but many were divided as to whether thirst or starvation was the worst. All of them deplored death by stoning and no one had any compunction about speaking against the indignities of poison, although it was the only death for which no retaliation was specified. No wonder her highness was so partial to it, they murmured, grateful that the queen was too far to hear them. But in the end they all agreed, through mouthfuls of mint, that death was no worse than their own lives. Would the woman locked up in the upper chamber of the Mayor's house live or die, they wondered; they asked the Mayor's Wife her opinion.

Well, the Wife of the Mayor informed them, smugly, she had some news for them. The poetess of Qazvin wasn't in the upper chamber of her house any longer.

The ladies' mouths dropped open in surprise. They had spread their picnics under the poplars after their English hostess repaired to the Legation building, but they stopped eating when the Wife of the Mayor announced her news. The poetess of Qazvin had had a secret meeting with his majesty soon after the public executions apparently, and had been moved into the main women's quarters of the Mayor's house as a result. Better not tell the queen, she smirked.

The women were agog with questions. Was the meeting really private? Had no one else been present? Had the Grand Vazir actually left his majesty alone with a woman like that?

The Mayor's Wife told them that as far as she knew the premier had interrogated the prisoner in his majesty's hearing, the same way he had done with the others whose executions he authorized.

And what questions, the ladies urged, had the Vazir asked?

The Mayor's Wife admitted that she did not know the details but added that the heretic's answers must have been outrageous, for he had condemned her to death.

Really? shrieked the ladies with relish. How did she know that?

Because the king had intervened, she said, and granted the woman an immediate reprieve. What was the point of a reprieve if a person was not first condemned to death?

The ladies were hugely impressed by her powers of deduction. But what, they begged, had the poetess of Qazvin said to the Grand Vazir to merit being so condemned?

The Mayor's Wife told them that all her husband told her on his return was that his majesty had instructed his Grand Vazir to acquit the woman. "Leave her alone and let her live," he had told his minister. For he had liked her face.

The ladies squirmed with excitement. They pressed closer to question the Mayor's Wife. They trod all over the vegetable patch in their eagerness; they wrecked the roses.

Had the Shah seen the prisoner's face, then? Perhaps the premier condemned her for showing it. But was it fair to condemn her for obeying the wishes of the king? And what did the Shah mean anyway by leaving her alone? How long did he intend to let her live? And what on earth had the poetess of Qazvin said to the Grand Vazir? they begged.

The Wife of the Mayor had to confess that she had no idea. The only additional information she could give was that the prisoner had had the gall to turn the royal offer down.

The ladies stopped chewing on their carrots, dumbfounded. To be granted a reprieve was startling enough, in the circumstances, but to reject such a royal pardon was shocking, no matter what it implied. Could his majesty's clemency save the woman from her own presumption? Or was it evidence of the very threat she posed? Was her rejection a form of heresy too, or was it a mercy, rather, to the king's other concubines? And what would be worse, in the final analysis: to be executed in public like a man or to stay locked up forever and endure a diet of bread and re-education, because one was a woman? Most importantly, what had the woman said to the Grand Vazir to provoke all this? And what would the queen say when she heard about it?

Oh, best not tell the queen, repeated the Wife of the Mayor, that the Shah has granted the woman his protection.

The Grand Vazir's only recourse now was to hand the case over to the ecclesiastic courts, and he would never do that. It would be tantamount to a renunciation of his reforms. He could hardly depend on the collaboration of the clergy now, given his policy of annulling safe asylum in mosques and holy places; he had undermined the religious courts and taken the reins of justice into his own hands, so he could no longer count on the priests' support. Nor could he depend on the queen's advocacy, since she blamed him for her exile. In fact, murmured the ladies, as they finally prepared to throw out the frail-leafed lentils they had specially grown for the spring festival; in fact, they whispered, seizing the pale stalks in fistfuls, tugging at the intertwined stems and tearing the tangled roots apart to rid themselves of the old year's curse; in fact, they hissed, tossing aside the yellowed sprouts at last, in the ditch at the garden gates on their way out, the Grand Vazir had better be careful about who was talking to whom in Qum.

The curse of the old year was not properly expunged on that thirteenth day of the new spring. The hand of execution may have been stayed but the finger of blame was pointed at the premier from that time on. And whatever the poetess might have said to the Grand Vazir, her semi-acquittal challenged his authority. He could take no initiative so long as she remained under the king's protection. And when the queen accused him of engaging in a British plot, on the strength of the rumours that had spread all the way from the Legation gardens to the city of Qum, he could not defend himself either. He had no alternative but to exacerbate the queen's ire in order to keep his power and to submit to the Shah's demands in order to retain his good graces. And that was why his betrothal to the Princess Royal was announced.

His majesty was very pleased to have checkmated both his minister and his Mother that spring. But he had not anticipated the impact of his strategies on his Sister. She could not, without violating domestic as well as court decorum, accompany the other princesses to the Legation gardens while her Mother was in Qum, but it did not stop her from pondering the fate of the poetess of Qazvin during the spring festivals. She too brooded about what the heretic might have said to the Grand Vazir in the course of her interview. And she dreamed repeatedly of death and marriage in the aftermath of the public executions.

For three consecutive nights after the thirteenth day of the New Year, she dreamed she was going to be executed. She dreamed that a tall, imposing man with a grizzled beard and spade-like fingers summoned her to rise from her couch and follow him. He seemed to move, like the damp earth, through the unlit corridors of the royal *anderoun*; he passed, like a cold breath, through the mildewed courtyards; and she walked behind him, all the way, through the private gardens of the queen to the outer gates of the palace in her dream. When he brought her there, she knew, instinctively, that the market square lay on the other side. She was standing, in her dream, before the gates leading out to the scaffold where the seven scapegoats had been executed.

It was the still hour of the night and the watchman was about to call the dawn when the tall man suddenly halted and held up his hand.

"What is the password?" he intoned.

The Sister of the Shah wracked her brains and could not remember it.

"Say the word, or the poetess will die!" he threatened.

But it was no use: the word was gone, the watchman sounded, and the gates yawned wide. Too late she realized that the secret word had been inscribed in clear characters across his palm. She had not read it and so it was her turn now. As her conductor pushed her into the daylight, the Shah's Sister recognized the Grand Vazir and knew with a fearful joy that she had to marry him.

(9)

The night before the Grand Vazir's veins were emptied in the baths of Fin, the Sister of the Shah pretended that she had had a premonitory dream. She had already tried every other way to dissuade him from going and nothing else had worked. Dreams were a woman's last resort when higher argument failed, and besides, prophecies had come into fashion since the capture of the poetess of Qazvin. When the exiles had left Tehran, two months before, the ladies at court had been busy learning how to read the signs of the time. They were taking lessons from the poetess on how to discern the future and how to interpret the past. It had become all the rage to decipher meanings in the syllables and sounds of passing events. The heretic said it was as logical as spelling.

Since the Sister of the Shah was rather poor at spelling and could not hope to appeal to her husband's reason, she had asked for his compassion instead, for his pity even. She had finally broken down, in tears, and begged him, for his children's sake, not to go out of the rear pavilion. But the Grand Vazir was an obstinate man. He was singularly obtuse and suffered from fixed opinions. Despite his intelligence, she realized he was illiterate when it came to intuitive matters. He had been toppled from power despite his cleverness, and had been exiled despite his political shrewdness. He had been unable to read the signs of danger lying ahead.

But he was infinitely tender towards her that night. The heretic even went to the baths before meeting the king, he said, gently unlocking her arms from round his neck. How could she expect him to go back to court, without visiting the barber? I have to dye my hair and trim my beard to impress your mother! he added, laughing. The Grand Vazir was a man who rarely laughed but he was so eager to return to the capital that he was jubilantly self-deluded. He seemed unable to decipher the possible inferences in the Shah's so-called pardon.

The Sister of the Shah had gone quite cold when her husband had read her brother's letter aloud to the assembled guests the evening before. She had shuddered as he intoned the hypocritical words, line by sticky line and dot by oily dot during the celebratory feast. And when he announced his intention to travel back to court with the guests and to be reconciled with the Shah, she had a hard time swallowing. As the ladies shrilled their praise about the magnanimity of the king, she had to hide her suspicion, like a bloated stomach. She had to bite her lips and hold back the bile as they flattered him. In fact, she felt thoroughly sick.

She knew it was not because of poison. The meal that she had served to the guests that night had no pretensions, but she had supervised its preparation closely. It was hardly possible with two pots and one brazier in the back room of the rear pavilion, to produce much more than smoky rice and a tepid sauce that dripped like tallow. The food had tasted awful but she knew it was safe, although she guessed from the gleam in the eye of one of the ladies that tales of her low cuisine would feed the *anderoun* with mockery for weeks to come. Their courtesies were principally aimed at her husband, but she knew that the court ladies had come to spy on her. Whatever their other motives, they had come to ogle at her and to ridicule her on their return.

She could not wait for the banquet to be over. But the tea had to be served first and the sweetmeats passed round yet another time; the final notes of the lute and the faint throb of the tabor still had to be endured. Their guests were bearers of gifts and bringers of good tidings, after all, and though she did not believe their flatteries or trust their smiles, courtesy too had its necessary hypocrisies. In fact, the Sister of the Shah was sickened by her own insincerities.

Even when they returned to the rear pavilion and were alone at last, she could not be frank with the Grand Vazir. He was so entirely taken up with the pardons of the king that she was still unable to speak honestly to him. He would not hear a word said against her brother.

He'll soon be eating out of the palm of my hand like before, he told his wife. Just wait and see.

It was the middle of the night and they were whispering. There was only a thin partition between them and the little room beyond, where the maids and the children were sleeping, and a long shaft of pebbled moonlight lay across the quilts. It seemed to the Sister of the Shah like a finger of admonishment slanting through the slatted windows towards the Grand Vazir. She could not find the words with which to caution him. She did not know what to say to him. And she found herself helpless in the face of his high optimism, speechless in the bright light of his certainty as he prepared for bed. It was painful to see the nakedness of his naivety.

I know how to handle that little brother of yours! he laughed, snuffing out the lamp.

She was unable to sleep. The night was endless, the brazier clogged and the room chill. She lay there, rolled in her quilts at the feet of the Grand Vazir, listening to the exasperating drip of the fountains spreading their ripples through the darkness; she tossed about, in an agony of suspense, hearing the footsteps of imaginary guards crunching across the pebbles, their ghostly mutterings and murmurings at the door. But it was only the gurgles and burbles of the water, the slap and spill of the garden pools. Each time she heard the cry of the nightjar or an owl winging like a dead man's spirit through the shivering trees, she started. And each time the cold wind rattled the panes, she was jolted awake. She could not stop thinking of how the Grand Vazir had wept upon reading the pardons of the Shah. She could not forget what he had said as he broke the seal to his letter. The words he uttered at that moment climbed up her throat and gagged her; they choked her. She could not bear to think of them.

She finally crept out of bed and knelt beside her husband, trembling with cold fear.

He grumbled at being woken up. What, he slurred, was the matter now? For he had drunk more wine than was his wont at the banquet the night before.

Please, she begged, don't go to the baths tomorrow. It is not wise; it is not safe.

What nonsense, he muttered, sleepily, rolling over.

Please don't listen to these women. They are poisonous, she breathed. Dangerous.

But he patted her hand and told her not to be silly. Go back to sleep, he said.

Finally she pretended that she had had a dream. It was a premonition, an omen. She urged to him take it as a warning. "I dreamed," she sobbed, "that you were going to be executed."

And so he let her creep under the warm quilts beside him, at last. She was so small, even if she was round, that she fitted under his armpit. Tell me about it, he sighed, sleepily.

She had dreamed, she whispered, of a woman standing right there, at the door of the rear pavilion. The woman had been veiled from top to toe in white, and had summoned the Grand Vazir to rise from his couch and follow her. She had moved, like the damp earth, across the pebbled paths of the gardens; she had passed, like a cold breath, through the mildewed courtyards of the central pavilion. And she had walked tall and pale as a cypress tree before the Grand Vazir, all the way down the avenue of poplars past the fountains to the main gates.

The gates were shut but the Sister of the Shah knew that death lay beyond them. She knew that if the Grand Vazir passed through he would never return. It was the still hour of the night, and the watchman was about to call the dawn when the woman suddenly halted.

"What is the password?" she had asked, holding up her hand.

But the Grand Vazir could not remember it.

"Say the word, or you will have to die!" she had threatened. For it was his turn now.

But it was no use: the Grand Vazir could not read the word inscribed in clear characters across her palm. And by the time the watchman sounded his horn, his death sentence had been passed; the gates yawned wide on a white dawn and the woman was beckoning him, inexorably.

"Her hand was like a blade of silver," whimpered the Sister of the Shah. "Her face was like the unsheathed sword. She was the poetess of Qazvin!"

But the Grand Vazir was already half-asleep. He grunted that it was only the moonlight, it was only the moon shining brightly out there, when it rose above the trees. Just the moon. And he rolled over and began to snore.

His wife lay very still at his side, as his breathing rose and fell. The shaft of moonlight on the quilts seemed to grow ever heavier on her through the night. She felt as though she were being pressed between the pages of a book whose words she could not bear to read. And she could not erase from her thoughts what the heretic had said to her husband in the presence of the Shah.

(10)

When the queen's portentous blessings for the wedding finally issued from the city of the dead, some weeks after the public executions had taken place in the capital, many said she was sacrificing her daughter to be rid of the Grand Vazir. They thought that if he had finally agreed to the ill-starred union, it was out of sheer pity for the girl.

He should have pitied himself as much, added the gossips, wryly.

The first thing that her highness did on her return from her exile in Qum was to arrange a betrothal ceremony for the Sister of the Shah. It was just after the wedding of the Mayor's son, and everyone wondered how the royal nuptials might compare. It was also the only time the queen had so honoured her daughter. The princesses were sure that the court chroniclers would keep scrupulous records of this historic event and were agog to participate in it.

The queen spared no expense in her preparations. For weeks beforehand, the palace was replastered and frescoed with exquisite arabesques, the arched niches were whitewashed and adorned with costly tapestries and carpets. The chandeliers hanging along the length of the high halls were scrubbed and rinsed in the palace pools until they glittered. And the mirrored mosaics on the ceilings and the glazed tile-work on the walls were polished till they glowed. By the time everything was done and the ladies flocked through the gates and fluttered like giddy moths towards the dazzle of the queen's banquet, a thousand candles were winking through the palace windows.

The poplar shadows were lengthening along the paths when they arrived and settled themselves in the queen's reception rooms. The level beams of sunlight were casting rainbow patterns through the rows of windows as they leaned their backs against the walls, cross-legged, or with one knee up and the other folded under flounced skirts and velvet trousers. And when they had displayed themselves to best advantage on the satin bolsters, spread out in all their finery, in their laces and their paisleys, their sequins and embroideries; when they stretched forward to pick at the tumbling grapes and nibble on sweet nectarines and plums, heaped on the rich carpets before them; when they leaned back towards the golden dishes pyramided with pastries, crenulated with trefoils of baklava and dried mulberries; and when they craned their necks this way and that to see the seats reserved for the royalty at one end, and the musicians at the other, it was evident to everyone that there was not a single space left vacant in the room.

The place was filled to capacity, crammed with the cream of aristocracy. And it brimmed with red and gold malevolence, overflowed with scandal from the seats of honour to the humbler places by the door. Ears burned as the palace maids served the incessant tea on gleaming silver trays from side to side; smiles scalded as the tiny glasses of liquid fire crossed the carpets back and forth from guest to guest. And as the laughter tinkled to and fro, as the glances sparkled and the tongues stung, the lovely ladies of the court massacred the Mother and the Sister of the Shah.

How embarrassing, to return from Qum and find everyone's attention fixed on the prison headquarters instead of the palace. How humiliating, for a queen to have to compete with a heretic for popularity! And how very amusing if the only way her highness could once again command her powers in the royal *anderoun* was to throw a party for the Sister of the Shah!

But the sweetmeats slowly dissolved the sting of gossip and music gradually blunted their malice. After a while even the most disparaging remarks began to melt with the tit-bits of sugar held between the ladies' teeth. As the flute rose and fell with the lilting singer, as the feathered drum and the subtle lute wound their arabesques in whorls around their hearts, they sighed and finally stopped talking. Imperceptibly, the mood began to change. The plaintive chant and the tender pipe, questioning and answering, calling and replying like yearning lovers in a garden of lilies, caused them to grow melancholy. They began to recall their own unspoken miseries. Having spat their poison out, they were actually moved to pity; by the time the music ceased they had even begun to shed a tear or two for the Mother of the Shah and his Sister.

The queen rose from her seat. Her daughter's betrothal, she cried, would begin with a contest of verse. Let the finest poets of the realm give praise to the Princess Royal!

A poetry contest? Everyone was surprised. Wits woke and spirits revived as the queen clapped her hands and insisted that all the ladies return to their seats. Who were the competitors and what was the prize? Who would be judge and what criteria applied? How on earth could anyone write a serious poem about that poor little turnip?

But answers to their questions must have been censored by the court chroniclers. Although ripples ran round the room at the queen's announcement, they left no trace behind. Despite the thrill experienced by the ladies regarding what they were about to hear and who they were about to see, their excitement was erased. No documents remained extant, no reports betrayed the titters heard, the smiles suppressed when her highness was urged to recite her doggerel verse before the rest. And as to what happened when the doors of the banqueting hall were opened to the finest poets of the realm, historians recorded nothing but a resounding silence.

A sudden hush. An intake of sweetened breath in the aftermath of music. The burnt tongue caught between a little rotting tooth. Who dared recount the impact of the poetess of Qazvin on all those women, as she stepped over the threshold of that room?

In later years, whenever the betrothal of the Sister of the Shah was mentioned, the ladies of the royal *anderoun* quickly changed the subject and avoided looking at each other. The Sister of the Shah? they would flutter, uncertainly, batting their lashes, arching their brows. Now which of her betrothals might that be, they would inquire, innocently. Was that one before or after the assassination attempt on the Shah? Some would even go so far as to shake their heads and say there must be a mistake. There must be some confusion between this event and the marriage of the Mayor's son. Everyone knew what happened on that occasion. But do remember, please, the difference between a wedding at the home of the chief of police and a banquet at the court of the king! Was it possible to imagine a heretic at a royal reception? Was it really feasible that a prisoner would have been invited to the betrothal ceremonies of the Princess Royal? No, that must be pure imagination.

Well, yes, the poetess of Qazvin was popular at the time, they might admit, when pressed. True, her fame was at its height. By the early summer of her first year under house arrest, she was holding court in the Mayor's house. The whole town was talking about it. The ladies of the *anderoun* were coming and going to the prison headquarters just to see her. Everyone wanted to listen to the female prisoner; everyone was quoting her words. Even the queen may have been a bit jealous of her. Why, yes, she must have been ever so slightly envious when she returned from Qum. Because the poetess of Qazvin had started giving reading lessons to the ladies—!

Reading lessons? Perhaps that's why the queen tried to disgrace the woman in public. The last thing she wanted was to encourage such dangerous literacy in the realm. The prisoner in the Mayor's house was teaching women how to read and write far more than poetry. She was showing them how to inscribe their lives on the pages of history, how to decipher motives, inscribe actions, interpret the world. She was giving them the tools by which to be autonomous. Perhaps that's why the queen was so determined to insult her, humiliate her, ruin her reputation. Why else invite a prisoner to the palace? Why else ask such a renowned scholar, such a famous poet, to stand there like a performing monkey? Yes! That's what she did. Brought her into a banquet hall where there was no place for her, no space for her to sit, no courtesy extended. To ridicule and mock her—Yes, perhaps that was her game.

And did it work—?

Oh, but, heavens who can remember such things? Who could tell what happened so long ago? No. The ladies would shake their heads; they had nothing to say. They were too young to have attended the first betrothal ceremony of the Sister of the Shah. They were out of town. They were indisposed and did not go. They did not know. The only references they may have heard of the great banquet were restricted to the music, the gold platters, and the ladies' apparel. And if the Mother of the Shah had tried to humiliate the poetess of Qazvin publicly, why who could blame her highness? Frankly, they knew nothing about heretics.

For how could they find words to describe what took place? How could they say what happened when the poetess of Qazvin stepped in the hall? The expression on the queen's face was unspeakable, the shock that rippled through the room indescribable; the verses uttered by the poetess unrepeatable, and what the Sister of the Shah did unbelievable. As the poetess began to chant, the Princess Royal, for whom the whole court was accustomed to stand, rose to her feet involuntarily, and offered her seat to the prisoner, as if she were an honoured guest.

Why did she do it? The improper gesture reflected an instinct everybody shared and none had the courage to express. What on earth was she thinking? Best not ask, muttered the ladies; best not probe too closely: you wouldn't want to know. Best not repeat what was said.

The queen intervened right away, of course, to rectify her daughter's error. Her highness could always be relied on to restore order. The Princess Royal was quickly reseated, to everyone's relief, and proper decorum rapidly reestablished. The musicians started up again, to cover the embarrassment, and the contest was deferred until after dinner. The poetess was swiftly ushered out of the room after uttering her unrepeatable words, and a new courtesan was summoned in to dance for the ladies instead. A bold-looking girl with a hard eye and a delightful shimmy, she had caused quite a stir at the recent wedding of the Mayor's son, apparently, and was rumoured to have every chance of becoming the Shah's new concubine. But it had to be admitted that despite her dancing, there was a shuffling sense of shame in the wake of the event, which quite spoiled the ladies' afternoon. And although she never repeated them, except for once, the Sister of the Shah was haunted for years afterwards by the verse chanted by the poetess as she stepped into the room.

> *Is there is no place to flee to and no refuge left for me?*
> *Is there is no safe asylum to be found nor any sanctuary?*
> *In that case seek the solace of your eyes elsewhere;*
> *She has no place among you here!*
> *"Verily, amid gardens and rivers shall the pious dwell,*
> *in the presence of the potent King!"*

{ 11 }

The Sister of the Shah was in such a state of shock, after the murder of the disgraced minister, that she sometimes wondered if she had not dreamed that her husband had been chanting verses, the night before he died. In fact, she was ready to convince herself that the whole, strange episode at the banquet of that last evening of his life had been a figment of her over-wrought imagination.

It had been a day of false hopes, a day of spurious surprises for the family of exiles in the gardens of Fin. The weather had been balmy, unusual for the month of January, and the day was like a glowing jewel set in the heart of winter, the last gift from the summer before or the first of the spring to come. Even the few birds roosting among the leafless trees seemed uncertain as to whether the nesting season had begun, and were tricked into singing with renewed hope and vigour that day, as if to compete with the cracked voice of the *muezzin* in the nearby village.

It was just after the noonday call to prayer when an unexpected convoy arrived at the garden's grand portico. A princess had come from the town of Kashan, the servants told the Sister of the Shah, after travelling all the way from the capital. She was attended by a black slave and accompanied by a mule train sent from the queen. She had brought sweets and spices, gifts and luxuries, cones of Russian sugar and fine Ceylon teas. And she was being installed like royalty, with her maids and special attendants, in the faded splendour of the central pavilion.

The waterways and arbours of the gardens of Fin were filled with florid greetings and elegant compliments that afternoon, with shrill laughter and ornate flatteries. The servants were set to scrub the marble steps and sweep the peeling plaster off the walls of the grand pavilion, to clean the mildew from the cracked mosaics and warm the rooms with braziers. The Sister of the Shah supervised the preparation of a banquet, for the Grand Vazir had called for a feast that same evening. Everything was to be as fine as if they were at court; the greatest effort was to be made to ensure a befitting welcome to their guests who had travelled all the way from the capital.

The spirits of the host were high. The messages from court seemed warm, the greetings genuine. The princess who had come to visit him had been chosen for the task by the Mother of the Shah herself, and her mandate was to deliver gifts to the exiled minister with her own hands. But more significant than the rich presents was the personal letter from the king to the exiled premier. His majesty was extending pardon to his dear Vazir. He was reinstating the ousted politician in his royal favour with a magnificent robe of ceremonial office, exquisitely embroidered with trefoils and paisleys, as a sign of his good faith. All was forgiven and forgotten, all taint of ignominy removed. The Grand Vazir was being recalled back home.

The Sister of the Shah was dismayed. The last thing she wanted was to return to court. Her spirit had grown cankers there, like a tree that should have been in the sun and found itself in the shade, like a plant that should have been in dry soil and was forced to grow in wet. She had been over-pruned at the time her most tender leaves were forming and had suffered injury of root and death of stem. She had no desire to return. But above all she did not trust her brother's unctuous tones. She did not believe in these so-called pardons. She suspected the gifts were tricks to dupe the Grand Vazir in his despair. She was afraid her Mother was behind this visit.

In fact, when she heard about the arrival of the princess and her entourage of maids, her first thought was that her Mother had sent her wet-nurse, the poisoner, to do away with her husband. The woman was a Nubian slave from the days of the old Shah and had been the queen's rival before becoming her confidante. She had known the king's Sister since she was born, and shielded her from her Mother's callousness, her brother's scorn. It was typical of the queen to instruct the woman whom she loved more than any other in the *anderoun* to come and kill the Grand Vazir.

Although she had been raised to trust the African, the Sister of the Shah knew that the slave was subtle, her knowledge of herbs deadly. She could unravel the poison of the spider, loose the sting of the scorpion, unbind the viper's bite, but she could also tie knots in human veins and strangle unborn babies with her potions. Several grasses that she picked tasted bitter when one was whole, and sweet when one was sick; her remedies misapplied could be more lethal than the poison for which they were the antidotes.

The notorious coffee of the queen, which bore the name of the dynasty, was always brewed by her slave, who, so they said, had given her highness the elixir of eternal youth. She could kill as easily as cure, and she was ageless.

The Sister of the Shah had always dreaded poisoning. She supervised every meal after their arrival in the garden of Fin, to avoid the risk of it. She insisted on taking charge of cooking and did not let the servants use the common kitchens for fear of it. She prepared food for the Grand Vazir on the premises of the small pavilion and tasted every dish herself before she served him anything, in case of poisoning.

But when the guests arrived, her anxieties doubled. The slave's attachment to her Mother was the most deadly poison of all. What if she bribed the servants and corrupted them behind her back? What if she broke a fatal phial on the food without her noticing and offered the Grand Vazir contaminated sweets which she had not tested first? She supervised the cooks fanatically all afternoon and risked her life by stuffing everything into her own mouth before her husband touched it. And although she did not voice her suspicions, she was poisoned by them.

She hardly spoke in the course of the evening. But the Grand Vazir was voluble. He was overjoyed with his guests and their messages, delighted with his gifts and pardons. With an eagerness which his wife found excruciating, he announced his intention to leave the *anderoun* the following morning. He did not mention baths, of course; it would have been tantamount to advertising his desire for sexual congress that night. But his wife was still suffused with shame at his insistence on readying himself for public office. He had not left these four walls for weeks, he said, gaily, but could do so now that his sovereign extended his protection over him.

He called for the pipe and tabor to be played that night after the evening meal; he summoned the *oud* master and clapped enthusiastically as the black slave uncoiled her old python body from the floor. And to the horror of his wife, he began, drunkenly, to sing:

The only place to flee to, the only refuge left for me—
The only safe asylum to be found, the only sanctuary
Is in the presence of the potent King!

She could hardly believe her ears. He was perverting the poetry which the prisoner had chanted as she stepped into her Mother's banquet rooms! He was debasing the verses of the most Holy Book, which she had quoted! And the worse of it was that he appeared to be completely oblivious of what he was singing, totally unaware of the inappropriate nature of his words. She wondered whether this sudden stupidity was due to the wine or because of a curse. She wanted to rise to her feet and flee the room, crying:

> Oh! seek the solace of your eyes elsewhere;
> There is no peace or safety for you here!

But she controlled herself. She restrained herself. She was imagining things; the wine fumes and the hubblebubble must have gone to her own head. For no one else seemed to notice anything strange, no one else registered the dreadful irony. The princess kept smiling like a painted mask and clapping her jewelled hands; the black slave kept swaying her withered abdomen to and fro and writhing about on the floor. The *oud* master continued plucking on the lute and the little drum fluttered. Perhaps she was only hearing her worst fears at that moment, rather than her husband's words; perhaps she had half-dreamed the whole thing and was simply remembering her self-abasement two years before. She was haunted by the force of the words which had compelled her to stand up for the heretic.

It was just as well she did not cry out aloud and did not run from the room in her extreme distress. She had learned not to commit blunders in public, by then.

⟨ 12 ⟩

After the marriage of the Sister of the Shah, it was evident to everyone in court that the feelings of the queen were marked by more than the usual loathing appropriate to a mother-in-law. The haughty scorn she had previously evinced towards the Grand Vazir yellowed with proximity to a sickly approbation. The criticism she had levelled at his reforms dissolved into a stream of cloying compliments. She employed hyperbole to undermine him and praised him to his detriment. In fact she protested her admiration of the minister so vehemently after her daughter's marriage that everyone was sure he had committed some heinous crime.

No other man ever did so much, cried the queen. It was impossible to equal his achievements. Surely the burden of his work should be alleviated, lest he collapse in the fulfillment of his duties. Surely someone should lift the pressure off his shoulders before he died of his responsibilities. The least she could do was to be his advocate.

As long as she had been able to wield power through her son, the queen Mother had ignored her daughter, but after her marriage she turned all her attentions on the girl. She made sure the Shah graced his Sister with a title suitable to her status. She insisted on the construction of a new residence in her honour, and she began to pay frequent visits to her daughter's home in the north of town. Court gossip was naturally all about the intimate life of the Grand Vazir from that time on. There was no privacy of the bed-chamber, no intimacy of conjugal life that the queen did not consider it her duty to extort from her daughter and let loose in the court. There was no detail of dress, of domestic habit, or of diet that she did not wheedle out of her, as a matter of policy.

It was of no small interest to the queen that the Grand Vazir had chosen to divorce his previous wife in order to marry the Sister of the Shah. Whether he had done this in deference to that lady, for whom it was less humiliating to be cast aside than relegated to a secondary role, or whether as a sign of respect to the Princess Royal, who would thereby be granted a unique place in his household, the decision nevertheless rankled with her highness. She interpreted it as a slight. Monogamy, she said, merely reduced the powers within the *anderoun*, and a man who had already given his affections to a childhood sweetheart did not always remain faithful to his wife.

She counselled the girl on the connubial arts throughout the first spring of her marriage. She should be aware of her husband's affairs without be-traying any knowledge of them; she should influence his decisions without appearing to be involved in them; and she should avoid raising any doubts regarding her own fidelity. She insisted that the Sister of the Shah should travel with the Grand Vazir wherever he went and never leave his side, for there were more rumours than flies on the roads, according to the queen, and truth depended on what the *anderoun* believed. In a word, she meddled in the girl's marital affairs, and by the time summer drew near, her daughter knew she had no choice but to go on the royal progress through the provinces.

The very mention of a royal progress made the Sister feel sick. This disagreeable malaise had begun the moment her brother announced his intention to visit the southern provinces some months earlier. The distance to be covered was considerable, the season already sultry, and a sojourn in the cool hills of the north would have been far more pleasant than travelling south in the heat. Especially in her present condition, thought the Sister of the Shah, fretfully. But she had no choice.

She was not alone in dreading the trip. All the ladies of the court were complaining about it. The wife of the British ambassador, who was in the last months of her second confinement, anticipated the prestigious journey with the greatest reluctance in the world. Though everyone was obliged to participate, no one was compensated for the enforced displacement. And what was even worse, the queen had decided to oversee the travel arrangements of the court. She had taken complete control of her daughter's household. The halls echoed with the shrill voices of the palace eunuchs; the corridors reeked with sweating palace porters; carpets waited for days in the dusty courtyards to be packed under the strict supervision of the queen.

She was determined that the royal progress would cost the minister dear. She wanted the Grand Vazir to pay the lion's share of the costs. She ordered new tents for the men and women, mule trains loaded with luxuries for the whole court, and dozens of gaily caparisoned horses. The entourage of the Mother of the Shah alone comprised sixty carriages and one thousand four hundred beasts of burden. Food and shelter had to be provided, tinderboxes and leggings had to be allocated, and there had to be rugs and quilts, tea and sugar, pepper and rice sufficient for an army. For the cavalry, infantry, gunners and musketeers of the escort were swelled by a retinue of bodyguards and footmen, tinsmiths and tailors; astrologers, water-carriers, cobblers and hatmakers; cooks and scullions, carpet-spreaders and bakers;

pipe-bearers, lantern-carriers, coffee-makers and grooms. This plague of locusts was dreaded by those constrained to welcome it as much as their enforced departure was deplored by the court.

The Sister of the Shah sighed, her head reeling with dust and camphor. Since a certain auspicious event would take place before their return, she was particularly vulnerable to her Mother's attentions. She should not tire herself, ordered the queen. Had she a craving for pickled cucumbers? She should not stand or walk or bend. Had she remembered to pack the special amulets? The bag containing garlic skin and salt? The charms? Every precaution must be taken lest the baby-eater slip into her womb. The tent of the Grand Vazir would be pitched beside the queen's during the royal progress, for that very purpose. Speaking of which, she added, there was an urgent matter that the Grand Vazir had to resolve before they left the town.

They were being served tea, in the midst of the upheaval, and the Sister accepted a glass reluctantly. Since the onset of pregnancy, the wicked, red-gold liquid made her nauseous.

What, the queen was saying, are the intentions of the Grand Vazir regarding this woman he's locked up in the Mayor's house?

The Sister of the Shah gulped the tea down with an involuntary shudder. The subject was taboo. She had avoided all mention of the poetess since her betrothal ceremonies. All through the time the princesses were visiting the Mayor's house during her Mother's absence in Qum, and reading lessons had become the rage in town, she kept her own widening literacy a secret. She practiced the calligraphy of the heart in private. She concealed her dark arts of interpretation under cover of seeming stupidity. But she came close to betraying herself during her betrothal ceremony. The woman's words had so perfectly reflected her own plight in the *anderoun* that she had no choice but to give her seat up to the poetess, out of sheer pity for herself.

She can't take refuge in the prison headquarters indefinitely, her Mother was saying. Can she? The queen's words hovered between a statement and the vapour of a question, coiling like a white cobra from the surface of the scalding tea. The Sister twirled the glass, unhappily.

It's an invitation to trouble to keep a woman like that in the capital while king and court are absent in the provinces, she insisted. Something has to be done before we leave, she told her daughter.

The Sister shuddered at the flickering tongue she glimpsed between her Mother's words.

This woman was dangerous, her highness continued. Her heresy was insidious. The influence of reading was subtle and spread imperceptibly. It took time to prove, and so the quicker the clerics started, the better. She had told the Shah as much, before going to Qum, but he never listened to her anymore. She sighed in a gust of maternal self-pity.

"Perhaps he'd listen to you," she concluded, turning her kohl-encircled gaze on her silent daughter.

The girl received the remark with studied blankness. Her brother barely noticed her existence. For him to listen to her was unthinkable. She hung her head and said nothing.

"He'd certainly listen to your husband," the queen added, after a pause, eyeing her with some distaste.

Her daughter looked fixedly at her tea glass. She was beginning to feel sick again.

"The trouble is, the Vazir needs a liaison with the clergy," she continued. "He needs a go-between."

The tea had definitely been a mistake, thought the Sister of the Shah. It was true that the priests were very upset with the Grand Vazir's reforms, very offended. But the queen's insinuations were making her quite nauseous. So she looked away, to avoid seeing her Mother's face.

Someone had to authorize them to begin their interrogations, the queen was saying. Nothing would happen to the heretic as long as she was pampered in the Mayor's house and fed three meals a day. "It would be best if the business were over before this autumn," she rounded, tapping her glass with the nail of her forefinger.

So soon? The Sister of the Shah glanced up in dismay.

"Can I depend on you to raise the subject with the Grand Vazir?" her Mother asked, testily. It was obvious that she had lost patience with her daughter.

The Sister of the Shah put her glass down and spilled the tea. She bit her lip, barely noticing the burning liquid in her lap for she had broken into a cold sweat at the sight of the hatred glinting on her Mother's features. This was worse than being the object of scorn herself.

"That woman is not stupid," concluded the queen. "I depend on you to make your husband understand that."

The Sister wanted to run out of the room. There was no way to reconcile her obligations to her husband and her Mother. There was no escape from the queen's expectations, or the Grand Vazir's displeasure. The former wanted her to be her go-between; the latter had forbidden it. How could she resolve such contradictory demands? She stood up abruptly, as her Mother tapped her glass again with that long, henna-coloured nail. She rose involuntarily, with bile filling her throat, while the palace porters shouted across the courtyard and eunuchs ran from room to room.

"I'm sure the Grand Vazir agrees with you," she blurted. "He thinks the prisoner is far from stupid. In fact, he told me that the poetess of Qazvin is the most intelligent woman he's ever met."

She regretted the words the minute they were out. She read the awful verdict written on her Mother's face: the hard line of those lips below the curled scorn of the nostril, in conjunction with that heavy brow, could only spell catastrophe. There was no refuge from her fury now.

❨ 13 ❩

Whirlwinds laid Persia to waste that summer. Fierce dust storms and savage rains swept through the country, leaving devastation in their wake. Rolling tempests began on the Russian borders, gathered power on the Turkish frontiers, increased in force in the Caucasus, and expired in avalanches of mud at the gates of the Persian capital. Ominous clouds of yellow sand turned day to nightmare and perpetual thunder—growling, bellowing, roaring and rolling from east to west—filled with dread the hearts of all who heard it.

When the straggling line of pack horses, mules, and camels in the royal progress of the Shah were not being hammered flat on the hot anvil of the open plains, they were pursued into the mountains by winds of terrible vehemence and siroccos of sudden intensity. The *howdahs* and the tents of the royal harem became so breathless with heat and so laden with dust on the way south across the blistering plains that tempers, pitched in close proximity, began to fester and explode. The Grand Vazir proposed brief respites every few *farsangs* to revive the ladies, and the court left the main road and repaired to higher altitudes, just to breathe.

It was in a relatively cool spot such as this, beneath a high pass, a short distance from the city of Isphahan, where disaster hit them. One hot July day, soon after the lumbering entourage had clambered up a slope to take a break beneath the shadow of a rising cliff, the Shah's scouts reported dust clouds gathering to the north. The heavens grew ominously dark and the distant horizon began to growl and threaten; a heavy stillness fell on the camp and a strange light filtered through the lowering skies. And then, quite suddenly, without further forewarning, a gale arose, a windstorm of such heat and violence struck, that it seemed the gates of hell had opened.

By a fortuitous chance arising more from envy than from acumen, the foreign envoys had pitched their tents on a more sheltered rise above the ravine that afternoon. They had been directed to this prominence by the Grand Vazir and, as a result, found themselves marooned some distance from the royal camp, eyeing one another suspiciously in the company of four donkeys and a flock of sheep. When they heard the fearful sound of thunder in the distance, they were shaken out of their torpor by reciprocal mistrust but soon found themselves groping about in the darkness of mutual terror. Before they could even perceive the origin or grasp the severity of the oncoming storm, the floodgates had opened over their heads.

The tempest's driving force was remorseless, its impact ruthless. Muddy rain fell in torrents on the camp, uprooting rocks, ravaging trees. The river burst its banks, sundering bridges in its path under flashes of furious lightning. Whole mountains were washed away and new valleys were unrolled by the storm. And when the wife of the British ambassador emerged from her dripping, makeshift shelter some hours later, as grooms ran down the hillside after petrified mules and panic-stricken horses, she saw the sodden

camp of the Shah below her, stripped down to the naked tent poles in a
field of flattened corn. For hitching posts and stakes had been ripped out
of the ground under the impact of the tempest and several tents belonging
to the royal *anderoun* had been lifted bodily in the air, exposing the screaming harem to the skies.

Many swore it was a sign of divine retribution, but the rage of the
Mother of the Shah was no less violent than that of God. Her fury had
mounted with the thermometer, and she was not slow to draw attention to
the relative security of the Russian and British encampments on the higher
slopes compared to the nameless shames inflicted on the harem of the Shah
in the valley below. She accused the Grand Vazir of bringing disaster on
the court. He was entirely responsible for the meteorological conditions, she
said. He had not only risked the life of his sovereign but had undermined the
tent poles of the kingdom.

And as if to confirm her accusations, couriers arrived just as the royal
progress prepared for the last *farsangs* of the journey. The battered camp
was barely back on its feet and making ready to depart when news reached
the Shah of another execution botched in the north. It was the last straw.
The first public executions in Tehran had already been a disaster, as far as
public relations were concerned, but this latest one, in the barrack square
of Tabriz, was far worse, according to the couriers. The heavens had
grown dark at midday, and the awestruck masses watching the scene,
had been roused to a pitch of apocalyptic expectation before the guns
had even been fired. But once the smoke had given way to rolling thunder, the whole event had turned into a fiasco. Instead of bullet-riddled
bodies lying before them, all that could be seen were the ropes by which
the condemned had been suspended, ripped to shreds against the barrack
walls. The whole town had been on the verge of revolution, convinced a
miracle had happened rather than a dust storm. Another regiment had to
be salvaged at the last minute, for the first refused to complete the task,
and even though the second volley did its job, the tempest that erupted in
the aftermath of the execution convinced many of the inhabitants that the
wrath of God was upon them.

Since the brother of the Grand Vazir had been in charge of this latest debacle, blame for the bungled execution was laid squarely at the premier's door. It was a case of calculated incompetence, according to the queen, and exposed the nefarious danger of the Grand Vazir's policies. She claimed that despite all his protestations to the contrary, he was in collusion with foreign powers. The smoke of seven hundred and fifty muskets fired by a regiment of Christian soldiers was proof positive of it. Instead of a British plot, it was a Russian one this time, she said, for the latest drama witnessed from the rooftops of the northern capital was as sensational as the "tableaux vivants" for which the wife of the Russian ambassador had such a predilection.

The royal progress had not yet reached the gates of Isphahan before slanderous accusations began to spread against the Grand Vazir. The Secretary of the armed forces was muttering that he was not to be trusted. The Chief Steward of the royal bedchamber was murmuring that his ambitions were greater than his rights and his appetite for power insatiable. His so-called reforms had incited discontent, and he had abolished safe asylum only to undermine the throne. Far from curbing unrest, they said, the Grand Vazir had drawn attention to all the injustices perpetrated in the name of the Shah.

But it was not the threat of foreign influence in his country's domestic politics that finally turned the Shah against him. It was not the executioner's axe either that sharpened his suspicions against his premier. What caused him to yield to the queen's pressure and dismiss the man who had married his Sister, was a passing remark uttered by a bystander in the bazaar, when the royal progress entered the city of Isphahan. The welcoming ceremonies were barely over and the royal escort, the ladies' *howdahs*, and the whole cumbersome cavalcade of chief falconers and coachmen, masters of the horse and keepers of the royal garment, had just passed through the gates when one of the local tinsmiths was heard to ask his neighbour who that little fellow was.

"Which little fellow?" his neighbour said.

"The one who's got the nerve to be strutting there, in front of his majesty," the man said, pointing to the king who was riding ahead of his Grand Vazir.

"Oh, he's the brother-in-law of the Shah," his neighbour replied.

The queen seized on the story. She inflated it to provoke the Shah against the Grand Vazir; she amplified it to arouse his jealousy and shake his confidence in his minister. If a tinsmith couldn't tell the difference between a cook's son and the King of Kings, she snorted, then his throne was in a sorry state indeed! Didn't the Shah realize that he was being effectively usurped in the eyes of his people? Didn't he see that he was being overshadowed by his premier? It was quite obvious that the Grand Vazir had fixed his eye on the throne itself. Oh yes! He was showing the Shah up, shaming him. Why he even had designs on the woman who had rejected the proposals of the king! Didn't his majesty know that? He should ask his Sister about it. For according to her, the premier had started praising the poetess of Qazvin after that misguided interview the king had granted, saying he'd never met anyone as clever. This presumptuous rooster should be ousted from power, she said, before he started visiting all the rest of the chickens in the coop of the Mayor's house.

A vazir should only be as grand as his sovereign made him, she murmured to her son, and a sister only as singular as her services to the throne. If one was dismissed, the other could be put to better uses.

And for once the Shah agreed with her.

❨ 14 ❩

The royal court was barely installed in Isphahan before the brother-in-law story had spread all over the city. The premier's relations with the Shah deteriorated rapidly in the course of the royal progress that summer; his attempts to be reconciled with the king were repeatedly frustrated by the plots in the *anderoun*. And by the time the court returned to the capital, early the following autumn, the Grand Vazir was terminally out of favour.

The wife of the British ambassador had been less interested in brothers-in-law than in the confinement of the Sister of the Shah. There had been a crisis among midwives and a rush on wet-nurses at their arrival in Isphahan because the young wife of the Grand Vazir had given birth to a daughter at the same time that her ladyship was being delivered of a son. On learning of this coincidence, the Envoy's wife felt an impulse of sisterly sentiment towards the Princess Royal. She wanted to pay her compliments to the young mother as soon as they returned to the capital.

But the Colonel was not at all enthusiastic about his wife's second courtesy call. It would be inappropriate, he said. The Sister of the Shah had become almost as controversial as the prisoner in the Mayor's house. Her betrothal had caused a stir, her wedding had created a scandal, and now the gender of her child had upset the queen. Besides, the court had returned from the provinces to find a congregation of clerics gathered at the capital, clamouring for the reversal of the Vazir's policies. The palace was packed with priests at the moment, and everyone was talking about the premier's imminent fall from grace. The tide was turning, power was shifting, and the status of the Grand Vazir was uncertain. A visit would be most awkward at such a time.

Her ladyship was taken aback. Was the Sister of the Shah to be treated as persona non grata just because she had given birth to a daughter? she asked.

The Colonel demurred. He was merely suggesting a delay. She should wait a while.

But the situation only worsened. Within weeks, the premier's position was precarious and everyone was openly discussing his replacement. The only thing that kept him from being banished to the provinces, they said, was his marriage to the Sister of the Shah. The Envoy Extraordinary and Plenipotentiary of her Britannic majesty told his wife that a court visit to meet the Princess Royal was out of the question now. The queen would not like it at all.

His chargé d'affaires, the Captain, laughed outright at the statement. If the queen wanted to be rid of the Grand Vazir, she could find better pretexts than the Sister of the Shah, he scoffed.

The Colonel was not amused. He wished his chargé d'affaires would kindly stick to the facts. He could not allow his wife to visit court for reasons of diplomatic protocol, he stiffly said.

Diplomatic fiddlesticks, retorted the Captain. The Colonel was just reluctant to have her ladyship use the private carriage, that's all, since the invitation had not come from the queen.

It led to an ugly argument, but even as the two men were sparring, news came that the Grand Vazir's fate was sealed. As expected, he had toppled from power. He had been deprived of his rank and titles overnight, stripped of his wealth and properties from one day to the next, and had to leave the capital the following morning. The Shah had banished him to the ignominy of the provinces, to a garden in the outskirts of Kashan. A gloomy place in a sad state of disrepair, according to the gossip; an obscure place shrouded by dismal cypress trees, and slimy water channels. It might have been a refuge from the heat and a sanctuary in the summer season, a pleasure garden in the midst of the desert where it had been built by the ancient kings of Persia, but in the dead middle of the winter season, when the wind howled and the rain turned everything to mud, the garden of Fin was dank and chill, a host to agues and perpetual damp.

But to the wonder of the court, the displeasure of the Shah, and the disgust of the queen, the young wife of the disgraced minister had decided to accompany the Grand Vazir. The Sister of the Shah had chosen to go into exile with her husband rather than to be forcibly divorced from him. The ambassador's wife became very emotional over her cup of tea when she heard about it.

News of the premier's fall had arrived late the night before at the Legation gates, and though the Colonel consulted his watch often enough the next morning, to show that he was in a hurry to leave the breakfast table, his wife delayed him by dissolving in a flood of tears. Their family quarters were located in the female section of the house, and the Mission occupied the public side of the building but it was difficult for the Colonel to step through the door with his wife in such obvious distress. She was just out of her second confinement and rather over-sentimental.

What conjugal fidelity, she sobbed. What heroism and refinement of feeling! She begged her husband to let her meet the Sister of the Shah before she was driven into exile.

The Colonel wiped his moustache with a napkin and scraped back his chair. The change of premiership had placed him in a rather delicate position, and he had several urgent letters to write before his attaché arrived.

He really had no time to talk at the moment, he told her, rising to his feet, but he would discuss the matter with her in detail that evening.

But what was going to happen to that poor young woman in the meantime? wailed her ladyship. The disgraced Vazir would have no recourse to justice, no refuge once he left the capital. His wife would endure the worst humiliations with no protector, she cried, blowing her nose.

His wife, the Colonel stated dryly, was the Sister of the Shah, and if the Shah was willing to humiliate her, there was not much a foreign minister could do about it.

But what about offering him asylum? her ladyship protested, trailing into the parlour after her husband. All sorts of other Persians had been given *bast*; why not the Grand Vazir and his wife?

He signalled her to lower her voice. The walls were porous with Persian servants and Irish maids; the secretaries of the Mission were already shuffling papers in the adjoining chambers. But his wife seemed oblivious to eavesdroppers and insisted that sanctuary should be given to the disgraced Grand Vazir. The Captain, she urged, said that immediate action should be taken.

The Captain could say what he liked, the Colonel interrupted, but it was the Vazir's own fault if he had no place to flee to now. He had abrogated the laws of safe asylum himself. Besides, he had been offered British protection already, and had rejected it in favour of a Russian offer. "He's just an opportunist," he said, coldly, "like the rest of these people."

His wife was shocked. She thought her husband dreadfully unfeeling. How could he make such generalizations? What about the poor tortured wretches last winter? What about the woman who had been under house arrest next door for almost three years without recourse to justice? The Captain, she insisted, was sure that something could be done for the Grand Vazir.

The Captain, repeated the Colonel, had no business being so sure. Innocence was relative and over-confidence dangerous. An offer of British protection at this late stage would be enough to seal the fellow's fate. He did not add that such a gesture might also compromise British interests.

He did not say that if he granted the old fox diplomatic immunity, he would undermine his prospects with the new one. He merely added that his hands were tied.

Well, at least the Russian ambassador had done something, retorted his wife. He had sent his Cossacks round to protect the house of the Grand Vazir. Was the Envoy Extraordinary and Plenipotentiary of her British majesty's government going to do even less than that?

The Colonel snorted. His chargé d'affaires had been pressing for a similar operation, a grand liberation, as he called it, but he had refused to countenance such nonsense. The Russian initiative was a blunder, he retorted. The women in the Grand Vazir's house were part of the royal harem, and to violate the sanctity of the harem was not only silly but dangerous. "Mark my words," he concluded, "if those Cossacks don't withdraw, the rabble will ransack the Russian Legation just as they did once before. Now if you'll please excuse me—"

But as he tried to withdraw himself, he noticed that his wife was brimming again. He made a great effort to employ a more placating tone, and begged her, please, not to distress herself.

She brushed away her tears, and seized on a piece of embroidery with bristling industry. The silence between them knotted and tangled.

The Colonel fidgeted, glanced at his watch again and then drew closer, lowering his voice. He had been obliged to sign a statement just a few days before, he confided to her, a secret document renouncing all future offers of British protection to the Minister. It had been sent by the Grand Vazir himself, he murmured. That was why, he repeated, his hands were tied.

"A document renouncing protection?" she swung round, her eyes huge. "But what if it was written under duress?"

The Colonel coughed. He avoided her gaze as he slipped his watch into his waistcoat. His wife's question was unpleasantly pertinent. A messenger had indeed arrived at the Legation late the previous night, with a note from the minister, written in evident haste and appealing for assistance in the most poignant terms, despite his previous renunciation. The Envoy had no intention of acknowledging the request, of course. It put him in a damned awkward position. But how could she have guessed? Who could have let her read such confidential material? Had the confounded Captain mentioned it? he wondered. He would strangle the fellow if he had.

He mumbled something about his duty to nurture a sound basis for future Anglo-Persian relations. He said that he had to be careful not to offend the Shah, who was highly strung and prone to sudden fits of violence. He mentioned the high qualifications of the Secretary of the armed forces, a favourite of her imperial highness, who was rumoured to be the successor to the premiership and with whom, he was glad to say, her Britannic majesty's government had the most cordial relations. But his wife thrust the embroidery away and rose from her seat.

"I would prefer to quit my post than to protect my country's interests by sanctioning crimes," she said abruptly. "I would prefer to leave this land than act against my conscience."

And then, to his astonishment, she suddenly requested the use of the carriage. She wished to drive out the next morning, she said. She planned to wait by the city gates through which the Grand Vazir and his wife would be passing on their way to Kashan. She wanted the disgraced minister to see the vehicle, and know that he could avail himself of it, if necessary. Even if her husband could not offer him diplomatic immunity directly, she said, she had to do something for the Sister of the Shah. "I do so feel for that poor young girl," she quivered, "going off to the gardens of Fin!"

As she burst into renewed floods of tears, the Colonel vowed at that moment to be rid of his chargé d'affaires. He was sure this lunatic scheme was the Captain's idea.

❨ 15 ❩

It proved easier to kill the Grand Vazir than to be rid of the poetess of Qazvin. The queen had succeeded in plotting the premier's downfall soon after the royal progress but had failed to initiate ecclesiastical inquiries against the prisoner at the start of autumn. She had managed to arrange for the murder of the exiled minister that winter but still could not resolve what should be done with the woman who had been in the Mayor's custody for three years. It was only after her widowed daughter returned from the provinces, early the following spring, that the pair of clerics finally arrived at the gates of the Mayor's house to investigate the case of the female heretic. Everyone knew who had summoned them.

The clerics were two of the most respected theologians of Qum, representing the highest scholarship in the land, and they had been authorized by the new Prime Minister to conduct a program of reform so as to find out if the prisoner under the Mayor's custody had been persuading others to follow her misguided ways. Their mandate was to bring her to a state of true contrition, or else prove her guilty, once and for all. For there was talk of illicit writings in all the women's quarters up and down the land; there were rumours of reading lessons, of poetry breathed from heart to heart and verses passed from hand to hand. If one were to believe her highness, the whole country was on the verge of revolution, with women deploying an artillery of inflammatory prose, wielding books like bucklers, and taking up pens as if they were swords. She believed that an ecclesiastical trial was the only way to put an end to this female heresy.

She had already exploited the anger of the priests one month before in order to induce her son to sign the death warrant of the Grand Vazir. The heretic's husband had been an outspoken member of the delegation of clerics waiting for the return of the royal progress, and had demanded a retrial of his wife under ecclesiastic law this time. Since he was blaming the exiled minister for reducing the authority of the religious courts, the queen promised to restore their powers on one condition. His majesty needed God on his side, she said, if he was going to justify the death of the Grand Vazir. If the priests could exonerate this murder, she gave her word that the demise of the Shah's first premier would mark the beginning of the interrogations against the female prisoner. She knew they wanted to put an end to this heresy of women.

She had also taken advantage of the situation to assert her authority over the Secretary of the armed forces. She had been preparing him for the premiership for several years but was only going to let him fill the vacated seat on her terms. Several of the women of his household had been frequent visitors at the Mayor's house during her exile in Qum and considered themselves students of the poetess of Qazvin. His sister, in particular, who had even vied for influence in the royal *anderoun* during the queen's enforced absence, had extended hospitality to the woman before her capture and had been her outspoken advocate ever since. Such laxity could no longer be tolerated. His *anderoun* should, by rights, be under the queen's control. And there was an easy way to ensure it. The betrothal of the Sister of the Shah to the new Prime Minister's son would pull the premier's family firmly into the queen's orbit. The precedent had been established once already and there was no harm in keeping the premiership in the family.

But it was not so easy to win the Shah's approval for the ecclesiastical interrogations. He still retained a soft spot for the heretic, and the only way to turn him against the woman was by exploiting his antipathy towards his Sister. Since he liked to see himself as having suffered in the world, his Mother probed those gaps in his nature that invited self-indulgence and filled them with resentment against the Princess Royal. Since she knew that he was prone to guilt too, and had been inclined to self-reproach after signing the death warrant of his old Vazir, she roused him against her own daughter by encouraging him to blame her for the nasty murder which had taken place in the gardens of Fin. She insinuated that if the silly girl had gone gallivanting to the provinces the previous autumn, it was probably due to the example of the heretic. She suggested too that if the sullen widow had been indulging her grief since her return to court, it was due to the influence of the heretic. The way to put them in their places, she said, was to marry one off and give permission to the priests of Qum to investigate the other.

The Shah accepted the marriage proposal because it cost him nothing to do so. But he was on his guard against the queen's insistence on ecclesiastical trials. Although he agreed, with some reluctance, to the re-education of the female prisoner, he had no intention of finding himself back under his Mother's thumb. He was afraid she was using the poetess of Qazvin to win the support of the priests and to worm her way back into power; he suspected that she had her eye on the treasury and wanted to control the decisions of the new premier. And since he knew that the latter was just

as anxious as he was to restrain her highness' political ambitions, to curb
her intrigues in court, and to put an end to her plots, he used the Princess
Royal to bribe the new Prime Minister and win his support; he used her to
shield him against his Mother's machinations.

Thus it was that the Sister of the Shah was betrothed a second time,
allied to a premier a second time early that spring, just when the clerics of
Qum began investigations into the female heresy. The queen did not realize
how determined her son was to curtail the tyranny of women.

(16)

When the Colonel told his wife that the Sister of the Shah was marrying
again, on her return from her second courtesy call at the palace, she fled
across the alley in shock. She walked about the garden for several hours
that day just to compose herself. How could a widow become a wife with
such unseemly haste? she wondered. How could this epitome of conjugal
fidelity, who had chosen exile rather than divorce, submit to a second husband so soon? The only answer to her unuttered questions was a peal of
laughter from over the walls.

The Envoy's wife fled across the alley frequently that spring. The garden
had become her sole refuge, her only sanctuary during the last year of her
sojourn in Persia. She went there to escape from the mounting tensions in
the Legation, to avoid the arguments between her husband and his attaché,
but above all, to listen to the laughter from the other side of the Mayor's
walls. Her efforts to resuscitate the roses and replant the vegetables that
year had coincided with the heresy trials in the prison headquarters, and
although she did not always understand the questions of the priests, she became familiar with the answers of the poetess of Qazvin. The garden greatly
benefited from the fact that she lingered rather longer than necessary in
the light of the heretic's laughter. As a result, she was looking forward to a
bumper crop of vegetables that year.

Relations with her husband had become particularly strained after her
abortive attempt to save the Grand Vazir and his family. When he heard
of his wife's rescue plan, the Colonel had permitted himself to raise his

voice, despite the proximity of Legation secretaries and Persian nannies on the other side of the walls; he had only agreed to give her the carriage in the end on condition that he accompany her to the city gates himself. But as he had predicted, the operation ended in an anticlimax. The couple had sat side by side in the carriage, in rigid silence, throughout the morning: he, staring fixedly in front of him; she, weeping helplessly into her handkerchief. And when the disgraced minister and his entourage were finally driven through the gates, nothing came of the expected last-minute appeal for British clemency but disappointment. The Grand Vazir, trapped in a *howdah* with his wife and children, was surrounded by a thick retinue of guards and in no position to avail himself of diplomatic immunity. Despite the ardent wish of her ladyship to gather the exiled pair into the safety of her carriage, she had to sit beside her corpse-faced husband and watch them clatter away, without pausing, in a whirlwind of dust.

After the minister's fall from power, the Colonel took offence at his attaché's every remark; he also lost his temper with the secretaries on a regular basis and even complained about his wife's daily constitutionals. But she used the spring festivals as a pretext to flee from him into the garden. She had to supervise the pruning of the roses, she told him: the princesses were due to come in just a few weeks and the grounds had to be made ready for their annual picnic; her cabbages and cauliflowers had to be protected from the appetites of the court. However, on hearing of the Sister's second marriage, she did not even look for an excuse. She fled into the garden without stopping to ask permission from her husband and paced back and forth between the cabbages and cauliflowers, brooding on the plight of women.

The laughter came to an abrupt halt in the Mayor's house as she turned pensively towards the gates. She had been half listening to the debate taking place on the other side of the walls. The theologians from Qum were classifying female roles that morning and the heretic had ridiculed their definitions. The Envoy's wife could not decide who was right. Was motherhood necessary, she wondered; did it demand humiliation? Should sisterhood involve punishment and matrimonial penance? Was the dumpy daughter of the queen, to whom she had just offered condolences, being chastised for unorthodoxy too? What else could have induced her to agree to marry the son of the second Prime Minister? According to the gossip of the wet-nurse and the maid, the new groom was a spoiled brat, a pampered youth of vulgar habits, a creature of overweening presumption and unbounded pride. How could the girl endure being allied to him?

When she had told her husband about her rather disappointing encounter with the dull little widow under the spotted frescoes, he had said that the Princess Royal was probably undergoing a program of reform. He had been rather pleased with his wife's disillusionment over her second court visit and had reminded her that he had advised against it. The Sister of the Shah was probably atoning for her misdemeanours, he repeated, like the heretic in the Mayor's house.

But there was no evidence, from the bright voice next door, that the heretic in the Mayor's house was undergoing atonement. She seemed oblivious of her misdemeanours, impervious to exhortations, gloriously unrepentant. Although the theologians from Qum droned on, hour after hour, none of their arguments appeared to have much influence. In fact, she seemed to relish the opportunity to debate with them. Far from expressing remorse, she seemed eager, even delighted, to discuss abstruse matters with the clerics. Their statements provoked such a ringing response that the Envoy's wife had the impression the poetess was doing the interrogating, rather than the other way around. On more than one occasion, the worthy gentlemen had been obliged to wrap up their sessions with unseemly haste and quit the premises with her laughter pealing in their ears. It did not seem from their offended demeanour, as they stepped out into the mud of the alley and into the midst of her escort of Ghurkha guards, that their efforts were at all productive of compliance. Nor did it appear, from the flock of ladies who replaced them to take reading lessons with the poetess, that she was taking seriously their cautionary warnings not to influence others.

The wife of the British ambassador would not have minded learning how to read herself. She felt singularly illiterate that spring and wished she could decipher what was going on between her husband and his attaché. The atmosphere in the Legation was so charged with jealousy, so electric with suspicion, that she always re-entered the building with dread after her sojourn in the garden. She tried as far as possible to keep the conversation neutral. She talked of matters that bore no relationship whatever with foreign policy. She remarked on the extraordinary fragrance of Persian roses as compared to their disappointing size. She admired the green fingers of the Parsee gardeners and contrasted their skill favourably with those of the Staffordshire gardener. And one evening, just as the Captain walked into the room carrying a bunch of urgent papers which needed to be signed by the Colonel, she raised the subject of the poetess of Qazvin.

The Envoy was incensed with his attaché for barging into the family quarters but had been obliged to give way to him at the same time, because these dispatches were urgent. They should have been ready for signature and sealed for the diplomatic pouch for Constantinople much earlier in the day, but the Captain had been dragging his heels and had left the matter unfinished till the last minute, as usual. He whistled nonchalantly as he waited. The Colonel glared at him. His wife attempted to fill the awkward pause of rustling papers and squeaking boots, by hoping, tremulously, that the prisoner next door would not be in danger of torture or execution, would she? Like the other poor wretches arrested the other year?

Her husband assured her, stiffly, that as far as he knew the new premier had no intention of harming the woman. She was still under the protection of the Shah, and was being treated like a distinguished guest in the Mayor's house. But he could not resist throwing a barbed glance at his attaché before adding that, heretic or no heretic, the woman was highly popular among the ladies. As everyone knew, he rasped, the Prime Minister had no desire to offend the ladies.

As expected, his remarks prompted a sarcastic response. The challenge facing the new premier, retorted the Captain, was how to satisfy the ladies without upsetting the priests. Because as everyone knew, the Prime Minister had no desire to upset the priests, either.

The Colonel thrust the signed papers back at his attaché. If that woman was as clever as everyone said she was, she could handle the priests without causing offence, he barked.

She was certainly clever enough to read their weaknesses, snapped the Captain.

The Envoy's wife looked from one to the other, anxiously. Were her husband and her attaché talking about the prisoner next door or about the queen? Perhaps they were referring to something completely different, something to do with whose side should be supported in the politics of the Persian court. Anger had a way of making words lose sense. What did "clever" mean anyway? she asked, as stupidly as possible. She did not dare ask for the meaning of "weakness." Did it mean the prisoner next door was guilty of heresy? she asked, anxiously.

The Captain flashed a look at her and intervened before the Colonel could reply. It meant, he said, that two men from Qum are no match for one woman in Tehran.

Her ladyship blushed uncomfortably. Perhaps she's innocent then? she hazarded. She had an uncomfortable sense of her own guilt whenever the two men argued. When she could not escape their acrimony, she felt responsible for it. But she dared to raise the subject of the heretic again that evening, because it worried her. She knew what her husband's public answer would be, but she risked asking him privately, when he did not need to keep up appearances in front of his attaché, whether, given her probable innocence, the British Envoy might not offer sanctuary to the poetess of Qazvin.

He told her brusquely that such a proposition was out of the question. She had already made a fool of herself and of him over the Grand Vazir's exile. He was certainly not going to commit another diplomatic indiscretion for the sake of a female heretic. He advised her to forget such romantic nonsense. In his opinion nothing would come of all the fuss and bother anyway. There was every reason to believe the efforts of the clerics would begin and end in words. The Prime Minister would let them question the prisoner all they wanted, re-educate her for as long as they deemed fit, and permit interrogations that were as protracted as they desired, but the whole affair was bound to be inconclusive, given the nature of female heresy. What really mattered was whether the king could convince the clergy that he was defending their rights, while avoiding the loss of his own autonomy. For it was the queen that mattered in this equation and not the heretic.

It looked as though he might be right. The early winter zeal of the theologians soon flagged, and although the interrogations continued for several weeks after the spring festivals, they slowed down and petered to a halt just before the court left for the cool hills that summer. Her highness, however, was growing frustrated by the delay. She was beginning to suspect a conspiracy. She started to wonder whether the Prime Minister was not plotting behind her back. She feared that the poetess of Qazvin might be released while she was away from the capital.

But since conspiracies of any kind generally distinguish those with power from those without, the last person that she, or anyone else, including the wife of the British ambassador, imagined might be implicated in a plot to free the heretic, was the Sister of the Shah.

❲ 17 ❳

It had already grown hot under the awnings of the palace windows, and there was a faint odour of rot floating from the pools below, when the Sister of the Shah asked her brother if he would give her the honour of a private talk in the orange groves. The sun had begun to shrivel the rose petals in the queen's gardens and preparations were well underway for the annual departure from the capital. Everyone in court was looking forward to a sojourn in the cool hills that year instead of yet another tedious royal progress, and the Shah was eager for the hunt.

He was surprised to receive the little note from the Princess Royal. She rarely asked him for anything and had never written a letter to him before. Among the many attributes that she had not inherited from her respected Mother was the presumption of aesthetic cultivation; there was little to recommend her calligraphy. It toppled forwards where it should have sloped backwards, and its contents, even if unprecedented, were banal. She had written to say that she had a favour to beg of him and requested a private interview in the queen's gardens, the day before the court left for the summer camps. The Shah had no idea why she wanted to see him.

His majesty tried not to feel nervous when he stepped into the orange groves at the appointed hour. It was the fifth spring of his reign, and he had every reason to be complacent. His first Grand Vazir had crushed the early unrest in the kingdom and had been swept from power as soon as he was no longer needed. His second Prime Minister had been satisfactorily bribed to curb his Mother's influence, and there was no reason why he should feel so edgy now, just because his Sister wanted to talk to him. The weather was still balmy and the summer's full heat had not yet hit the plains, but the Shah found himself sweating as he walked towards the Polo Ball. She was dressed in rolls of pink satin and looked like a bolster. It suited her better to be in widow's weeds than bridal robes, he thought, after their perfunctory greetings.

He knew that she was unhappy. He had heard the gossip about her wedding night: how she had been obliged to seek refuge from her boorish husband in the privacy of her chambers; how she had locked the doors against the young oaf who had drunk too much. It was hardly a place to flee to, hardly much of a sanctuary, for the brute did not tire of kicking at the door. But the gentlemen of the bedchamber were in hysterics about it; the ladies of the *anderoun* were doubled up laughing. The court was saying that since she was destined to be the royal seal for each premiership, the stamp of approval for each new minister, the Princess Royal could hardly complain if she received a pounding. He really hoped she did not intend to complain.

He also hoped she was not planning to raise the gory subject of the murder of the old Grand Vazir. He knew that she had been upset about it. He had been told the stories. He had been informed that when his Sister had found the body of the murdered minister wallowing in the red-hot baths, she had run through the gardens of Fin, crying like a madwoman. Frankly, he agreed with the queen that it was his Sister's fault that the Grand Vazir had died the way he did. By interpreting her marriage as far more than a royal convenience, she had piqued her brother dreadfully. Had it not been for her, he might have concluded the unfortunate business more discreetly. The disgraced minister would have languished in ignominy until the poison of disfavour took effect, and could have been drained of significance without recourse to razors. But as it was, the Shah had been obliged to sign his death warrant just to spite his Sister.

He eyed her askance now, as they paced through the dappled gardens. He hoped the Polo Ball was not going to start running mad in the orange groves. She had behaved like a lunatic a few times before, he thought, nervously. She had violated decorum once already and had come close to treason by leaving court. She must have been mad to do it. It was a ridiculous act of misdirected loyalty. But perhaps her worst folly, in escaping the constraints of the royal *anderoun*, had been to show how relieved she was to go. She had bloomed like a winter rose during her brief sojourn in Kashan. She had been so happy that some said she was even rather pretty. Although her charms did not inspire, her loyalty won her husband's respect in the end.

The Shah frowned. It was not as though he had not tried to make up for her losses. It was not as if he himself had not endured just as many, what with his Mother and all the cares of the state on his shoulders. His Sister had no excuses. Even if she never reconciled herself to her second marriage, he had recompensed her handsomely for it. He had announced the betrothal of her eldest daughter to his appointed heir, at the same time as she was being married off to the Prime Minister's son. Although he planned to replace the ugly boy with the baby who had just been born to his favourite concubine, it was an attempt, in part, to compensate for her humiliations. The last thing he needed at this moment was to be reproached. He gritted his teeth.

So? he inquired. To what did he owe this great pleasure?

To whom, his Sister corrected him.

A stickler for grammar, are we? he laughed.

She told him there was no other person to whom she could turn. His majesty was the only refuge for his subjects, the only sanctuary in the land.

The Shah stared. His Sister had never flattered him before. He assumed that she had been set up to it by his Mother. The queen had probably goaded her to do this, for her own purposes.

Are you telling me, he said with mock severity, that I owe this pleasure to myself?

His Sister had never been one for words but her silence was denser that day than the odour of orange blossom. She did not respond immediately when he asked her flatly what this was all about, but paused and looked up at him, hesitantly. Her small eyes held a dull glimmer in their depths and the Shah had a curious sensation of vertigo when she finally opened her mouth.

"It's about our Mother," she said, simply.

He rolled his eyes. He supposed she was going to try to wheedle money from him, on behalf of the queen. It wouldn't be the first time. He wondered, uncomfortably, if she intended to ask him for another house. He could not be supplying her with real estate every time she married.

Their Mother put great store on these interrogations in the Mayor's house, she continued.

He frowned again. He was sick and tired of these interrogations. He wished he had never agreed with the queen's plan to start them. They seemed to be going nowhere.

But perhaps the poetess should be released, continued his Sister, before they came to an end. For their Mother's sake.

The Shah gaped. Whose sake? he echoed, incredulous. He had always thought his Sister was a little stupid, but this was the limit. Everyone knew that the queen detested the heretic. Why, she had been insisting on these ecclesiastic trials for over a year. And did the silly girl really imagine that his Mother would prefer to release the prisoner? Whatever did she mean?

His Sister hung her head. This would be the first and last request she would ever make of him, she promised. She would do whatever he wished and abide by whatever he willed if he granted her this one last favour. She would accept any alliance, marry whoever he wanted, serve as the royal seal for whoever happened to be his minister from now on, on this one condition: that he stop the trials and release the poetess of Qazvin immediately.

"For our Mother's sake," she repeated, quietly. "For all our sakes, really."

The Shah halted in his tracks and burst out laughing. And then, just as abruptly, he broke off and stared at the odd little woman beside him. She had stopped walking too, and they stood there together for a moment, brother and sister, under the pale shade of the orange trees, their skin mottled by the spring leaves. Her arms were so short they could hardly reach round her, he noticed. Her legs were short too. She really was unattractive, with that sulky mouth and those heavy jowls. But maybe she was not so dumb, thought the Shah.

He was beginning to guess what this was all about. It was true that there were only two ways to resolve the quandary of keeping the heretic forever captive and both could cause considerable embarrassment to the queen. If the priests failed to prove the prisoner guilty, their Mother would be publicly humiliated, for she had insisted on these trials. And if they condemned the prisoner or touched so much as a hair of her head, there would be a hue and cry against her highness, because the prisoner was so popular. His little Sister wasn't stupid. The Shah certainly did not want to provoke an uprising in the country. Nor could he allow the queen to be ridiculed and his throne dishonoured. He might humiliate his Mother himself, but he could not let anyone else do so. If he did not want to demean his position, his only recourse was to let the poetess go.

She had been under house arrest in the capital for three years by then. Almost three years had passed too since the tortures in the Mayor's house, the executions in the public square, and his own interview with the heretic. His Sister's first betrothal ceremony had taken place three years ago as well, and although the matter had been hushed up, the Shah knew that she had been punished brutally for standing up when the poetess made her brief appearance in his Mother's reception rooms. She had been slapped in the face and accused of shaming the queen before the court. He was sure she had not forgotten the impact of the royal rings against her cheek on that occasion, for he had never heard her repeat the words of the heretic since then. Perhaps that was why she did not want to make his Mother look ridiculous again. She had borne the brunt of the queen's humiliation before and wanted to protect herself against it now, that's all.

He was preparing a non-committal answer when she suddenly spoke again. "There's no refuge save in the presence of the potent King," she said, quietly, lifting her eyes up towards his.

The Shah was not sure he heard her correctly. He attributed the slight vertigo he experienced to the orange blossom or the heady confidence he felt that morning. But he had a distinct feeling that his Sister was not asking him for the favour at all when she uttered those strange words. It seemed to him she was addressing her appeal to some higher court, some greater authority, some King more potent than himself. Was he being mocked by the Polo Ball?

He retrieved his dignity as best he could as they walked back to the palace. He assured her, loftily, that he had already agreed to extend his protection over the heretic and was not someone who went back on his word. It was only a matter of time before she would be set free, he said. In fact, he added, with a sudden flash of inspiration, a rush of magnanimity, in fact he would promise his Sister there and then, he would give her his word that by the time they returned from the camps at the end of that summer, the poetess of Qazvin would no longer be incarcerated in the Mayor's house. How about that? Was she satisfied now?

He was thoroughly pleased with himself, and casting a glance towards the queen's balconies, he whispered that he had not expected his little Sister to be part of this female heresy. It would certainly kill their Mother to know it, he sniggered, but he promised not to tell.

It was hardly to be wondered that the Princess Royal felt obscurely responsible when her brother was shot in the thigh two weeks later. By a twist of fate, she had interceded on the prisoner's behalf shortly before the attempt on the Shah's life. When the poetess was swept up in the massacres that summer, she assumed it was because she had championed her cause.

(18)

Two decades later, when the Mother of the Shah lay dying, people blamed it on her son's profligacy, rather than her daughter's advocacy of a heretic. She had grown increasingly ill at ease over the Shah's extravagance during the previous decade. By the time he betrayed his peoples' future to a railway baron and exchanged his kingdom for a metal horse, it was obvious, at least to his Sister, that the king's recklessness had seriously undermined the queen's health. She fell prey to a grave malady but kept it from her son's knowledge. It was only when he squandered his country's future on a visit to the West, that she finally succumbed and died.

The Sister had noticed the first signs of her Mother's sickness soon after the murder of the Grand Vazir. The queen had succeeded in ridding herself of a powerful enemy with his fall but had lost her son's trust in the bargain, and it affected her profoundly. She had subsequently ensured the premiership for her protégé, but began to fail visibly when she discovered that he was plotting behind her back. And with the arrival of the Shah's favourite in court, when she lost her power in the *anderoun*, it was evident that the disease had taken hold. By the time the bread riots occurred, she was sick of venal ministers, of corrupt clerics, and of her most heartless son. It made her tired just looking at them. A bitter awareness was swelling like a tumour in her, a sour suspicion was growing like a cancer in her, a consciousness was consuming her that her plots and conspiracies, even her jealousies and vengeance, had been exploited. She felt used, abused, a mere tool in the hands of men, and this deadly knowledge was slowly killing her.

Many had witnessed the public melodramas of the queen, but few were allowed to share her private terrors. She sank a fortune in cosmetics to cover up the relentless progress of the disease but was forever complaining about ephemeral ailments. She pretended so many illnesses that her son grew callous by the end. She rehearsed her last hour so often that he never guessed how close she was to death. When she asked for the English doctors to attend her, he suspected her of interfering with his foreign policies. When she fainted at the announcement of his Western tour to visit the Tsar and the English Queen, he said it was to create a scene. The years between her fall from power and her final demise were a closed book to most people. No one was aware of the real malady gnawing at her vitals, nor had any in that female labyrinth realized the extremity of her pains, except her daughter.

The women of the *anderoun* said that if the Mother of the Shah had become so dependent on her daughter, it could only be because she had championed the cause of the poetess of Qazvin. Some kind of witchcraft must have given her these strange powers, they murmured. How else would her imperial highness defer to the woman she least respected and most despised? Why else would she let her cut her horny toenails and change her dirty linen? The Princess Royal had probably cast a spell on her Mother, they whispered to each other. She was taking her revenge on her after all these years; she was punishing the old hag at last for all the humiliations she had inflicted on her. None of them guessed that the Sister of the Shah had learned to read beyond literal interpretations. It did not occur to them that she could have forgiven her mother.

Certainly, the Princess Royal was the only person who seemed able to decipher the old woman in her last years. She was the only one whom the Mother of the Shah permitted to come near her, the only one she allowed to wash her when she developed a distressing dread of the baths. Such a fuss she made, sagging like wet salt in a mulc's saddlebag! muttered the ladies of the *anderoun*. You'd think she was seeing blood, they murmured, the way she shrieked each time she stepped into hot water. Her daughter was the only one from whom her highness accepted food too, in the end, for she lost her appetite and shrank to half her size after the bread riots. When her son lost his temper with her for opening the granaries after the hanging of the Mayor, she stopped eating; she said she preferred starvation to being poisoned by remorse.

The king interpreted such acts as symptoms of senility and told his Sister he did not want any more nonsense from the old woman. He claimed that indications of late empathy in the queen were proof that her mind as well as her eyes were developing cataracts. He had no patience for what he called her sentimentality and shunned her with each succeeding year. But on the eve of his departure to the West, she summoned him peremptorily to her bedside.

"I need him," she told her daughter, wanly. "Tell him to delay his journey, if he wants his mother's blessing for it," she croaked.

The Shah suspected it was some invented urgency, some fatuous crisis when the Princess Royal conveyed the message to him. Typical! he thought. Always a scene when it suited her; always a summons at the last minute. And it had to happen now, didn't it, just as he was preparing to leave for the Western capitals, just when a sudden furor of jealousy had broken out among his wives. They were vying with one another to accompany him, and he had been obliged to offend them by choosing one among the rest. He was convinced his mother had orchestrated the debacle. He was sure she was doing this to delay his journey. He knew every plot in her book, every trick in her repertory, and he was not going to come running to her bedside again.

The Sister of the Shah was obliged to make excuses for him to the queen. Her brother would be there soon, she lied. He had promised to come and would arrive at any moment.

But the old woman was so familiar with insincerity that she could snuff its odours from a thousand leagues away. "Tell him I'm gone already," she said, bitterly, and her breath stank. "Tell him that if he cares so little for me, then I might as well be dead. Let him bury me where I want, at least, before he goes away," she said. At which point she wailed that the Shah cared more about the Tsar and the Kaiser and the English Queen than about his mother and, rolling herself up in her sheets, began to chant poetry, in a high cracked voice.

The Sister of the Shah thought that it was the fever raving, at first; she thought the drugs were singing. She also saw, with pity, that despite her efforts, a line of grime had gathered in the creases of her Mother's mouth; her heavy jowls were caked with old cosmetics, dried spit and despair. But since the words that bubbled from her lips could be heard through the walls and all the women of the *anderoun* were listening, she decided to send for her brother a second time.

"Inform his majesty," she told one of the eunuchs in the court, her small eyes glimmering dully, "that his Mother is quoting the poetess of Qazvin."

The Shah shuddered when he was given the message. This Sister, he thought, had the markings of a murderer. She had inherited the family arts.

By the time he arrived at his Mother's apartments, an ominous silence reigned behind the locked doors. His Sister was waiting for him but he avoided looking at her. He knocked on the doors and waited, with his face averted. And when the old lady did not respond, he could not help hoping, for a moment, that he had come too late. But when they forced the locks open, the scene inside the room filled him with disgust. The old queen was sitting and waiting for him, girlish and tearful on her mattresses in the middle of the floor. She was propped up among her quilts, grotesque and triumphant in rouge and china powder. She was smiling sweetly, trembling.

"I knew that you would come," she whispered, huskily. "I knew that you must love me, just a little!" Her half-blind eyes, lined with shaky kohl, were like sedge on a stagnant pool. She reeked of rose-water. "You wouldn't abandon me, would you?" she besought him. "You wouldn't leave me now, in this condition?" And before he could stop her, she threw herself forward and tried to embrace his knees.

She loved him, she whispered hoarsely. As God was her witness, she loved her son with all her heart. She begged him to forgive her for the wrongs she had done, to forget all mistakes she had committed, but it was only because she loved him. Please let him not leave her now, she implored. Please let him stay with her till the end: she would soon be gone. When he tried to disentangle her, to pull away, she lifted her hands towards him like a beggar, as though asking for alms. Mercy, for the love of God, she sobbed. She did not want to die alone.

He was so put to shame by her gesture and simultaneously so revolted that he broke free from her with unnecessary violence and took refuge by the door.

He shouted at her that she had cheated him, that she was lying, as she had always done.

She wailed in response that she was telling him the truth, that he had never believed her.

He yelled back that she had always tormented him, all her life long.

She screamed that couldn't he see she was dying?

It led to a bitter leave-taking. He was in no mood for reconciliation and she was in no condition to dissemble. Harsh words passed between them. He accused his Mother of trying to control him and was accursed in turn. She called him an ingrate and was subsequently sent to hell. He wished her a long and curdled life like the gall she had fed him from her breasts. She retorted that he deserved the bullet she had always known would bring about his downfall. Finally he wished the same fate on her that she had perpetrated on others: might she choke to death, he shouted, like the poetess of Qazvin. And at that, she fell back soundlessly on her quilts and turned her face to the wall.

But just before he walked out of her apartments, slamming the doors behind him, the Shah turned round one last time and saw his Sister standing there, at his Mother's bedside. Her narrow eyes were fixed on him as he turned to leave: she had witnessed everything.

❨ 19 ❩

The Shah never made his peace with his Mother. He left the capital on his Western tour two days later with a fanfare of trumpets and a wailing of wives but without her customary blessing. The angle at which dark brows were raised in the *anderoun* that evening, the heights to which black eyes were rolled in the days that followed, might have proven mortal, had her imperial highness cared to note them. But she was already too far gone by then. Her old saddle of a body had taken the shape of her obstinacy and its stiff straps snapped the minute the Shah turned his back on her. The women of the *anderoun* claimed that she died of a broken heart.

After all her years of sacrifice, all her proofs of love, they clucked, hypocritically.

Her limbs were rigid, the flesh already turning by the time the corpse washers carried her down and laid her with little ceremony beside the palace pools. When her daughter unwound her, wrapped like soft curds in an old curtain, she saw the old woman had died curled up like a foetus, with a ring sunk into the empty crater of her flaccid cheek. The state of her undergarments was pitiful. She had decked herself in fine silk robes to die, wrapped Kashmir shawls around her and drenched herself with rose-water, but her skin was riddled all over like the workings of wood lice. There was a sour powder, like egg shells or damp salt, gathered in her hollows. It would take hours to wash away her crimes thought her daughter wearily.

A mother deserves more than to be abandoned like an old cat on the offal heap, sighed the women. She would have died soon enough, so why kill her with callousness?

The Shah's Sister had to strip the stale garments off to wash the queen. Unlike the Grand Vazir, who had been soaked to transparency by his own bloodletting, the queen was opaque with neglect; her transgressions were ingrained. Her daughter had to instruct the corpse washers to scrub her with horsehair and use pumice stones to dislodge the dirt. But disuse as well as disease had distorted her lumpy breasts. The crusts on her elbows and heels were worn like an old leather binding; her flanks had grown thin with obsessive fingering. But it was evident from her mottled skin that though she was long-versed in dying, she had never learned to read her wrongs.

Who would have guessed how sick she'd been, or in what pain? The Cradle of the Universe deserved more respect, sighed the women of the *anderoun*, piously.

The corpse washers emptied goat pellets from her bowels but they could not dissolve the marbled tumours in her groins. The Sister of the Shah rinsed her with pail after pail of water from the palace pools, but her unforgiving smell lingered in the *anderoun* for days after her disappointments had been scrubbed from the bedding. A dirty corpse, that one. A sad corpse, for all her plots. Who could blame the Shah for razing her apartments down?

His majesty was rather hard, simpered the women of the *anderoun*, tolling their kohl-rimmed eyes, but who would have guessed his Sister could be so tender-hearted?

For she did not let the corpse washers shroud her Mother. Although they helped to strip her and to scrub her, she did not let them rub her with balm or comb her hair or wind the sere cloths round about the old queen. She performed that task alone. There are certain secrets that have to be kept back from the eyes of the *anderoun*. There are certain marvels, too, and mysteries that the ladies of the harem may not see because they would not understand. One had to be more than a wife or a mother, a sister or a daughter to forgive the crimes of womankind. The Sister of the Shah wanted to smooth away every scar and crevice in her Mother's body, caress every fold and wrinkle of her shroud so that no hatred would be left, no jealousy remain when they laid her in the coffin. She wanted the angels to read a different story about the queen.

She had tried to protect her Mother from bitterness for a quarter of a century. She had hoped to change the story of her life when she asked the Shah to release the poetess for her sake. She had already seen what the death of the Grand Vazir had done to the queen: how it had hardened her, how it had curdled her. She had lost the last vestiges of her youth when he was murdered, and her daughter dreaded what further ravages she might sustain with the death of the prisoner in the Mayor's house. Her fears were well-founded, for the attempt on the life of the Shah that summer distorted the queen's features forever. When the dust rose outside the women's enclosures and the guards cried out that the Shah had been shot, when crisis and hysteria swept through the royal camp and the tent poles were struck down in a panic, the queen stood among the trembling ladies of the *anderoun*, exultant, triumphant, with a terrible look of joy stamped on her face. The attack on the Shah was the pretext she had been waiting for, for years.

That look of jealous joy hardened over time, but was never erased. The mask she wore was never transformed by suffering. The Sister of the Shah longed for her eternal pride to soften over time, but the stubble of vanity continued to sprout into her old age. Her only hope was that death might wash away that grimace in the end. For the queen had denied herself regret until too late. She had hated the heretic more than she loved her only son.

The Sister of the Shah sighed as she combed her fingers slowly through her Mother's lustreless hair: antimony at the tips, violent henna in the middle, retreating to a sickly yellow. She wept for pity as she wove these lank locks about her Mother's head, for there was no evidence among them of remorse. She sighed as she caressed her shrunken thighs, but there were no signs of regret. She had tried to protect the queen from humiliation but she could not protect her from arrogance. There was no escape for those who took refuge in their ignorance. The only asylum lay in one's freedom from the need of it, she realized, placing her Mother's withered arms across her breasts; the only place to flee to was from fear.

She was about to give up and roll the old woman in her shroud, when she suddenly saw a glimmer at the scalp. Lifting the cloth back, nervously, unwilling to disturb the body further, jolt the brittle bones or break the skin, she discovered, with surprise, a sheen of baby curls springing beneath the headscarf of the queen. Was immortality hidden in her hair follicles? The roots were startling as innocence, pure as hope. Was another version of her story waiting to be born?

The Sister was so moved by the revelation, so touched by the thought that she sat down, after her Mother's burial, and tried to compose a letter to the Shah. It was difficult. She had to tell him of the queen's death without blaming him; she had to convey the sad news without reproach. And so to find the words she recalled those spoken by the heretic as she had stepped into the queen's reception room. She remembered what the poetess of Qazvin had said to the Grand Vazir so many years ago, which he had indiscriminatingly repeated before he died. The woman had been offered refuge in the royal *anderoun* and had declined it; she had been given sanctuary by the Shah and had rejected it. But the verse she quoted had not been intended for herself alone. She had chosen to seek another refuge, a different sanctuary, under wider skies.

Our Mother found no place among us here, she wrote to the Shah. She has sought the solace of her eyes elsewhere. Then, after repeating her highness' dying wishes regarding her place of burial, she prayed that the dead queen might finally attain a different reading of her life in their response to it, and begged for reconciliation between them.

But she never heard back from him.

When the couriers brought news of the old lady's death to the Winter Palace in the Russian capital, where the Shah was staying during the first leg of his Western tour, he stared blankly at his Sister's letter, turned on his heel, and repaired for dinner. But when he had confirmations that she had buried their Mother in the palace gardens instead of in the holy city of Qum, as requested, his majesty acted precipitously and in a wholly unexpected way. He sent his chief wife packing.

The lady was furious. It had cost her several love potions to be chosen for this trip; she had paid good money on amulets to ensure that she would accompany his majesty. She had planned to walk the arbours of Versailles with him, and meet the magnates of the coal industry in Manchester; she had harboured fond dreams of being presented to the English Queen. Why had the Shah changed his mind?

The excuses were varied. Some murmured that it was because of her lack of dinner etiquette: the Shah's chief wife was an embarrassment at the table of the Tsar. Others, more conciliatory, said that foreigners did not know how to treat the fair sex with due respect and her return was a diplomatic necessity lest the king's dignity be compromised. A few suggested that the source of the humiliation lay with the Shah's third premier in as many decades, and predicted that despite the usual tie of kinship, this minister too, like the others before him, would be swept from power on his return. One or two were even prepared to blame a corpse for the offence and thought the dead queen was responsible for the disgrace.

But the lady herself accused his Sister. She laid the blame squarely on the Princess Royal. "Only your killjoy, sour-faced Sister could humiliate me like this!" she railed. The Shah had no answer to that one.

There were several humiliating episodes in his life, which he would have preferred to bury in oblivion, and it was true that his Sister had seen them all. She had watched him beat the queen off his knees like a beggar. She had witnessed his impotence as he eyed six thousand famished women through his opera glass. She had observed him flinching under the fingers of his French physician, and eavesdropped on him lying on his couch, as he broke his promises to release the poetess of Qazvin. Her words alone could have toppled the dynasty, had she chosen to use them.

Literacy killed the poetess of Qazvin in the end. When the queen unleashed a bloodbath after the attempt on the Shah's life, proof of adultery, evidence of murder, and even heresy was no longer needed to condemn her. Literacy was crime enough. And he could see dangerous signs of it in his Sister's letter.

THE BOOK OF THE DAUGHTER

When the Mullah was found stabbed in the mosque in the last year of the old king's life, they said the daughter of the house had done it. An old woman discovered the cleric, bowed in his orisons, as she thought, and left him to his business at first. She was a regular at the mosque who swept the floors before the call to prayer each Friday and washed the dead on weekdays, and she had learned to stay clear of prostrate priests, for their daily irritation cost her more in curses than she earned in prayers over a fortnight. But when the old man remained flat on his face for as long as it took her to sweep the main hall, and when she drew near and saw the spreading darkness on the stones, and heard the gurgling in his throat, heaven preserve us from the thought, she fled into the market square.

"Foul murder!" she screamed. "Blood in his mouth and murder, just as she said!"

The daughter of the house had said too many things. If a woman put so much into words, the gossips whispered, perhaps it was because she wanted it all to happen. If she could read the future so easily, perhaps she had written it. Female literacy was dangerous and the prime suspect was nothing if not literate. Heaven only knew how many men of learning she had destroyed already, just by putting pen to paper. Her erudition could lay low several generations. But the worst of it was, if she could write, what was to stop her from reading history too, to the detriment of all mankind? The most sacrilegious crime, according to the priests, was interpretation.

(2)

Her father was blamed for it at first: he had educated his daughter like a boy, that was the problem. It was bad enough that he had allowed her to be literate from a tender age but to let her sit among her brothers and her cousins, to allow her to study philosophy and jurisprudence with them, was the worst. He should never have treated her as their equal, praised her memorization, applauded her commentaries. He should never have encouraged her to debate the nature of the soul or measure the temporal limits of justice in sentences and phrases. She had no right to interrupt theological debates from behind the curtain. It was beyond all decency, all reason. What did a woman have to do with resurrection?

That was what her uncle said. He thought his niece too clever by half, and accused her of drawing attention to herself. He insisted on an early marriage with her cousin, to curb her ambitions, and criticized her for giving more time to her studies than to her female responsibilities.

"A woman should know her place," he trumpeted, with an oath.

The patriarch had made an art of execration before he was stabbed in the throat. The eldest of three brothers, he was a shrewd and worldly man, quick to offend and slow to forgive his enemies, of which he had accumulated not a few over four-score years. The youngest brother in the family was his opposite: a poet by temperament, an ascetic with a mystical inclination, who spent more time in his library than in the courthouse or bazaar. But the middle brother, who was the father of this too brilliant daughter, tried to keep peace between the two extremities. Leaving the management of properties to the patriarch, and questions of metaphysics to the poet, he struggled for equilibrium between this world and the next and took refuge in jurisprudence, attempting to define by law what could not be resolved by debate.

The family had been distinguished as priests and clerics in the town for generations. The men had risen to positions of eminence as theologians and scholars, and the women had achieved honours at court for their erudition and calligraphy. Their illustrious forebears had built schools and hospitals, had been known for piety and charity. Their libraries were renowned, their righteousness revered, and intermarriage amongst them was to be expected, for who could merit an alliance with people of such prominence? As a result their wealth had been kept snug within the family. In recent decades, the three brothers had acquired vast properties in the region too, and enjoyed great material advantages that paralleled their spiritual standing.

The only blight on the family escutcheon, in the years before the daughter of the house stained the high front of its eminence with infamy, was that they had fallen out of favour with the court. It happened during the last decade of the old king's reign, when a certain Shaykh, who was renowned for his piety and much respected by the gouty monarch, passed through Qazvin. This saintly man had gently declined the hospitality of this prominent family, and since the gesture suggested the possibility that a different cleric might be appointed to the coveted role of spiritual authority in town, it was tantamount to an affront as far as the elder brother was concerned. He felt slighted and sought every means to castigate the Shaykh. One day, during a public discourse on spiritual resurrection, he pointedly turned his back on him to prove its physical interpretation. Later, at a meal given in his honour, he refused to share the same plate with the old man. His disrespect was so flagrant that it not only created conflict in his own family but incurred royal disfavour, causing divisions in the community at large.

The bazaar had not always been affected by theological disputes. As long as mullahs and merchants kept to their separate spheres, arguments about the boundaries of immortality, the frontiers between sex and soul, had little impact on the price of wheat, the cost of bread. But when priests began to bargain for belief in the marketplace, the currency of truth became volatile. Conflicting theories about resurrection soon started to control the grape harvest; arguments over the dissolution or reconstitution of a corpse were discovered to determine the tithes and taxes in the town, and not even prayer could stop the canker of inflation after that. The worm of opinion contaminated whole congregations, and infected entire regions. By the time the Crown Prince had acceded to his father's throne, religious debate had rotted half the kingdom.

The wealth of the three brothers was already legendary by then. Despite the loss of royal favour, their spiritual rank had been built on solid economic foundations and their theology had proven lucrative over the years. If the patriarch thundered against his niece's heresies, it was probably because his revenues depended on the orthodoxy of his flock. If he raged against her new-fangled philosophies, it may have been due to the fact that her reforms were a threat to his income. She did not mince her words: she called his theories false, his acts immoral, and was critical of his bribes as well as his beliefs. She was an advocate of change.

What made matters worse was that many agreed with her gospel. Although her sex denied her the right to practice the profession, she cited proofs with the precision of a priest. Her arguments were so persuasive that clergy as well as lay folk were convinced of the truth of her beliefs. For she defended her opinions and refuted her opponents with dazzling logic, using every dot and line of the sacred text itself to prove her point of view. She knocked on the gates of men's hearts, beat against the bars of their prejudices with a terrible persistence. She begged, urged, admonished, and finally demanded that the truth be let in.

❨ 3 ❩

Knock, knock, knock, bark, bark, knock, bark, knock, bark.

The simpleton who served as the Mayor's gatekeeper wandered out of the stables into the white blaze of the noonday sun and listened. His shaven head moved in and out of his collarless shirt, his mouth sagged. The heat hit the back of his neck like a pile of bricks as he stared blankly for a moment through the archway into the private world of women. Then he glanced back across the main courtyard towards the passage leading to the gate. The knocking would not stop, and there was a mad dog barking in the alley. The last time he had opened those gates, soldiers had knocked him senseless to stop him from making noises in the middle of the night.

The Mayor's house was full of noises. Or perhaps they were in his head. The idiot had grown accustomed to them since he began working at the prison quarters five years before. He was familiar with the chatter from the women's quarters. He was inured to the groans of prisoners, the shouts and curses of the guards, but when the knocking began at the gate after the assassination attempt, he panicked. That gate was forever knocking. It had knocked on his head three nights ago when the soldiers arrived for the poetess. It knocked on his heart these past two weeks each time the Mayor's cart rolled by. And here it was again, knocking. He began to count the blow of fists between the barks, to calculate their impact. He might be dumb but he was literate. He could read the past in the shape of bruises, the future in the sound of the lash. Threads of saliva drooled from his mouth and tears began to gather in his eyes.

After the soldiers knocked him down, he hid in the ditch to listen and to watch them. They were talking about which route to take, which back streets to use in order to avoid the main thoroughfares of the city; they were arguing about which orchard they had to find, where it was that his honour the Chief Steward had ordered them to go. He saw them spit into the palms of their hands, heard them mutter about the Commander of the army, smelt the fear of the Sardar on them. He followed them under the dim starlight as they closed ranks around the prisoner; he winced at their coarse jokes, their vulgar sniggers in the alley as they rode away with her. And his heart was in his mouth as he stumbled after them in the dark, slipping on their horse dung, choking back grunts of dismay. By the time he turned into the market square, they had already gone. The clip-clopping of their hooves faded as they headed towards the northern gates of town.

He was given strict instructions to keep the doors locked the following day. The Mayor had not been home when the soldiers came knocking, but he had returned to the prison headquarters briefly in the morning and snored out the hot afternoon. He had barely spoken to the womenfolk in the house and had distributed the usual threats and punishments to the servants before leaving again on his deadly rounds. Don't open the gates, he told the simpleton, no matter who comes knocking. Don't open the doors, on pain of being flogged. No one was allowed to enter after the poetess of Qazvin went away. It was like being the gatekeeper of a grave, thought the idiot. Without her, the house had died.

Three days had passed since her going, but it was always that day. The knocking at the gates of the Mayor's house was as always as grief too. The air hung still and heavy as always. And then there was a pause in the horns and drums, a lull in the market square for a moment. The cries of the crowd grew faint and distant; the whole city heard the knocking at that instant.

Knock, knock, bark, bark, bark, knock, bark, knock, bark.

The idiot boy began to weep then, lifting his huge fists in the air.

(4)

The daughter of the house dominated the Mullah's family. When the children were young, scurrying round the women's quarters, playing hide and seek in the cellar, squealing across the slippery tiles of the public baths, she was the one who controlled their games, who arbitrated over their disputes, even among the boys. Later, in the schoolroom, she was the one who succeeded when her brothers and cousins failed, the one who was invariably asked by the teacher to provide the correct interpretation. She not only read, but read into the Holy Book. She not only said what she thought but pitted herself against general opinion to say it, hurtling into the inexplicable dark to define each falling star of an idea. And woe betide those who contradicted her readings of the universe; woe betide any who tried to debate her understanding of eternity, for she demolished their arguments without caring about their humiliation. She was insufferable. When her male cousins protested against her ruthlessness, she was surprised.

"Don't you prefer the truth to your pride?" she would ask, wide-eyed.

The eldest amongst her cousins had always resented her. The first born of the patriarch, he found it particularly humiliating to be bested by a girl. Ever since she had been betrothed to him, in childhood, he had envied her natural superiority and intelligence; he had chafed against her conceit. She was confoundedly sure of herself. It goaded him, not only that she was always right, but that she knew it. Worst of all, she knew how to put it into words. He could have forgiven her if she had just been more hesitant, less self-assured. A girl was supposed to be talkative but not articulate; she was allowed to be a chatterbox but not eloquent. He could not bear the fact that she not only held everyone in thrall but read so much and wrote so well. His grudges against her grew; they gathered, swelled; his jealousies burgeoned and finally bore fruit in the brutal privacy of the bridal chamber. Some kinds of cruelty cannot be put into words.

But when they set off for Karbala, so that he could continue with his studies, she stepped into a wider world. She left him squirming in the bedroom as she blossomed in the schools of theology. He tried to curb her freedoms in their private life but could not prevent her from listening to his classes, could not stop her from participating in debates, from interrupting the learned priests with her comments and finally taking over the discussion entirely, from behind the curtain. Despite three pregnancies, he could not put and end to her questions. She was incorrigible. She was relentless in her hunger for what she called truth. She was voracious when it came to reading. In the end, she outshone him and won accolades from all his teachers. It was bitterly humiliating. She was honoured with laurels that, by rights, should have been his.

By the time she gave birth to her fourth child, after they returned home, the strain between the couple had reached breaking point. He took refuge in the local *madrasah* to air his opinions, to obtain praises from the provincial priests that he was being denied at home. She spent time corresponding with scholars, studying in her youngest uncle's library, giving reading lessons to the local women in the town. They had less and less in common except friction. When her uncle began to mutter about his son's need for a second wife, she begged for permission to return to Karbala. She needed to go on pilgrimage, she said, to clear her mind.

She travelled with her sister and her daughter all along the dry road to Najaf, holding a handkerchief before the child's face in the wake of a stinking caravan of the dead, brooding on resurrection. She jolted back and forth in the *howdah*, swaying on the brink of the Kurdish mountains, pondering the pendulum of renewal. And when her little girl's shoe fell over a precipice, tumbling over the rocks, somersaulting over the stones, to rest precariously, half on, half off a little ledge that jutted over the bottomless void below, she comforted the crying child through the night, assuring her that the red shoe would wait for her on that ledge till her return. There was always, she assured the child, a return. But she did not say that returns were always the same. She had determined her life's path by the time she arrived in the *'Ataba'at*, but when she left, three years later, there were far more dangerous chasms yawning at her feet.

Her interpretations had provoked an uproar in that bastion of orthodoxy. She had been damned as a heretic. The mob attacked the house where she and her companions were staying in Karbala and obliged them to leave. The priests incited the authorities to issue their deportation from Baghdad too, and the governor could do nothing to save them. Another time the rabble beat down their doors with sticks and drove them out into the wilderness on their way home, their belongings looted, their company routed. And when twelve thousand wild-looking Kurds surrounded them, on a fourth occasion, beating drums, her little girl was sure they were going to be attacked. But the tribesmen were chanting her mother's praises; they were her ardent supporters, her fervent admirers. They wanted to accompany the poetess all the way back to Qazvin.

Since fame and notoriety had gone before her, the rupture was complete by the time she reached home. The marriage had always been a stormy one but it had curdled to antipathy by then. Her husband was absolute in his condemnation of her; she, withering in her scorn. He demanded unqualified obedience, total submission to his will; she refused to live under his roof and returned to her father's house on the other side of town. In violation of every religious law and every social custom, she claimed the right to keep her children, and divorce their father.

The patriarch of the family was incensed when he heard of it. He had always been irritated by his niece. He had noted her brilliance jealously ever since she had been a child, and compared his own sons to her unfavourably and with envy; he had become increasingly resentful of her eloquence and her arrogance over time, but when she had the nerve to leave his eldest born on her return from Najaf and Karbala, his anger knew no bounds. He fulminated against the daughter of the house, swore at her through his teeth, and denounced her with a fury fed by years of frustration. He blamed her for his disappointments, accused her for his lack of court preferment, and finally stormed out of the house to give her a piece of his mind.

To the terror of the bystanders, he strode across the town, uttering violent oaths all the way to his brother's house. He pushed through the gates, roaring imprecations, calling all manner of abominations on his niece's head. And when he flung open the library doors, his brow beaded with sweat, his eyes starting out of his head, he was purple with rage. He began to throw her books on the floor, yelling that he would burn them. And he cursed her. He damned her to hell.

Since he could not condemn her parents too, without denouncing his own family, he hurled abuse at all those, including the old Shaykh, whose teachings she respected and whose theories she confirmed. He cursed the classes she attended, swore against the commentaries she studied, and even blasphemed against the books she read. He continued cursing all that week and seized the occasion of his sermon the following Friday to curse against half the town too, from the public pulpit for agreeing with her interpretations of the Holy Book. Would that the maledictions of the age might fall upon those benighted, deluded, mentally deficient fools who shared the opinions of his wretched daughter-in-law, he shouted. Would that rout and ruination might fall on whoever agreed with her heretical theories. Let them all be damned, he roared.

His curses ran deep but his niece's response to his tirade was more far-reaching still. Her father had shaken his head in sorrow when he heard it, and her younger uncle had hidden his face in his hands. Her mother had covered her mouth to stop herself from crying aloud, and her aunts, sisters, and cousins had backed hurriedly out of the room. The maid, raking the hot coals from the samovar, had bitten her own tongue and burned herself when she heard her mistress' words. But before long, those words were being repeated by maids and menservants, grooms and scholars, beggars and butchers and carpet-sellers and tea-boys all over town. Everyone, including the corpse washers, knew what the daughter of the house had said, in the ghastly pause between the old Mullah's curses, as she stood among the torn pages of the books he had just flung off her shelves.

"O uncle!" she had breathed, "I see your mouth filled with blood!"

Everyone was horrified but no one was surprised when he was found in the mosque, one week later, with his throat pierced. She had read through his curses, they whispered.

ℂ 5 ℑ

The quarrel about words tore the family apart. There had always been differences of opinion about the Holy Book amongst them, theological debates involving precedents and principles. There had always been those who placed more emphasis on literal interpretations and those who insisted on symbolic readings of the sacred texts; those who considered words in a historical context and those who read them in the light of prophecy; those who analyzed knowledge as foresight and those who believed it to be evidence of afterthought. But once the statements of the daughter of the house replaced the Holy Book, the debate split the family. It separated and severed them, it divided and cleaved them, it rent them asunder and scattered them forever. They debated her meanings hotly. They interpreted her words endlessly. They disagreed.

Was she saying that her uncle's mouth was filled with blood because his language was so violent, his curses so gory? Or had she had a fearful vision of the future, seen his throat gagged and bleeding, his tongue pierced at the root? Was she threatening him with her vengeance? Or were her words meant to be a warning to him? Was she anticipating that he would incite riots and spill blood or had she betrayed her own desire to murder the patriarch of the house? Were these words a prophecy or a plot? How had she read her uncle? How dare she read him!

The quarrel also split the town. As soon as the news of the stabbing spread across the city, everyone began to take sides. Some cried that the Mullah was a martyr and others thought him a foul-mouthed tyrant; some

protested that his son was to be pitied, and others despised him as a jealous
fool. Half the town were of the opinion that the heretic should be blamed
for the crime because her maternal relatives had raised her to be too head-
strong. The other half argued her innocence, urged the truth of her opinions,
and claimed her paternal relatives had brought disaster on their own heads.
There were those who believed that the time had come for change at last,
and that a new age of justice was about to dawn; others feared that her
fearful ideology of change would destroy society, unleash blind chaos, and
herald the end of the world.

Qazvin was in an uproar over definitions of resurrection.

⦗ 6 ⦘

Knocking. Drawing all attention to itself. Now.

The sudden sound resounded down the narrow passage past the stables
and the servants' rooms, echoed from side to side of the main courtyard and
under the archway, before rippling gently, in circles of now, across the lap-
ping pool of the women's quarters.

Who could it be now? muttered the daughters of the Mayor. Knocking.
Who had the nerve to come here under the blaze of the noonday sun?
Knocking. Who would it be knocking at such a time as this on the main
gates of the house of the Mayor?

It couldn't be their father, surely? He was still trundling that infernal
cart round the town. He was still forcing that miserable boy to point to
the houses of rich merchants, and extorting bribes for the queen. When
he knocked, even the simpleton recognized him; he could hardly open the
gates fast enough for the Mayor, to avoid a beating. Heaven forbid that
the chief of police should have come knocking on the doors of his own
home again, and in broad daylight this time.

It couldn't be their brother, either. He was on the wrong side of the
gates to be knocking, thought his sisters scornfully. Ever since the poetess
of Qazvin had been taken away three nights before, he had been in hiding.
He had taken refuge in the sweltering upper chamber after returning from
the abandoned garden outside the city gates. He was afraid his father would

arrest him for witnessing the gross incompetence of the Commander of the army that summer's night. When the knocking started, he even pulled the ladder up after him, in his terror.

There were only women in the Mayor's house when it began. The mistress dropped the kitchen knife as soon as she heard it and stared at the blade spinning round between her feet, scattering herbs all over the floor. Her sister-in-law, sewing under the limp awnings of the breezeway, pricked herself with the needle and swore. The daughter of the prisoner, in hiding since her mother had disappeared, stuffed her fingers in her ears as she crouched in the stairwell, thin elbows poking through the faded blouse worn at the wedding less than a year before, thin feet pressed one on top of the other, thin little face streaked with her silent tears. And in the cool rooms down below the breezeway, a ragged wail rose in response to the knocking at the gates. The young wife of the Mayor's son, seven months pregnant and barely fourteen, had chosen this untimely moment to go into labour. Despite the unpleasant associations of torture in the past, the daughters of the Mayor and the other female members of the household had set up the birthing bricks in the cellars and gathered down there round the squatting girl to burn wild rue and chase the *jinn* away. It was not only the coolest place in the house, but the safest at that moment.

The city was in an uproar. Enemies of the state were running rampant in the capital; godless students had attempted to assassinate the young Shah, they said. The Mayor and his men were hauling people out of their houses, herding princes and paupers into the common prisons, butchering respectable citizens, eviscerating heretics all day long. And the midwife, summoned from the other side of town, had still not come.

The daughters of the Mayor rolled their eyes. It would be a miracle if she arrived in the middle of all this mayhem. But midwife or no midwife, they had no intention of opening the gates themselves. You'd have to be mad to do it, they muttered, frowning. If the gatekeeper had any sense, he might at least find out who it was, but that poor fool did not know one side of a door from the other. If the Mayor's Wife were in less of a state, she might have taken charge of the situation, as she usually did, but the silly woman had done nothing but cry for three nights and days. Their brother, of course, could not be relied on for anything.

The daughters of the Mayor had spied on him when he came back, pale and trembling, three hours after riding away with the poetess and the soldiers in the middle of the night. They had smelt him in the tea room, reeking of *arak* and the cat odours of fear. They had eavesdropped on him whispering to his mother about what he had seen.

The Sardar was completely inebriated, he told her; his men were tippling drunk and flushed with wine when he had arrived. They had been carousing for hours, swilling the bottom of the barrel in a stupor, under the dusty leaves of the dry orchard. They had been urinating against the ruined hut in the corner, taking turns with the goat. Bring on the dancing girls, they had shouted, when the soldiers entered the garden with the poetess of Qazvin. Bring on the best Shiraz wine, they yelled, with fried chicken livers on the side. Care to join us? Supper guests of the queen, they roared with laughter, courtesy of the Chief Steward, may their lives be a sacrifice to his virile member, may they kiss his beard for tickling her imperial chin, for they owed their present pleasure to his appointment, pension promised and special benefits provided. Heave ho, to the Chief Steward of her highness' bedchamber! "I assure you gentlemen, the lady's been thrown in free, with the wine. I drink you, sirs, to the Whore of the Universe, our queen."

Hush! his mother had begged, lower your voice! But the Mayor's son wanted to continue telling the ghastly tale, despite her appeals to stop. He was overwrought.

The Sardar didn't even want to interrupt the feast, he whispered to her, hoarsely. That woman could have escaped if she wanted, without anyone being any the wiser!

His mother became hysterical then, and when he noticed that his sisters were eavesdropping behind the door, the Mayor's son finally buttoned up. He called them in peremptorily, and told them to splash water on the mistress' face, bring her salts to revive her. He seemed as upset over her blubbering as about what had happened to the poetess in the garden that night.

"For God's sake, mother," he said, "control yourself, or we'll all be slaughtered because of that woman!"

Coward, muttered the daughters of the Mayor, turning away from him in disgust. Is that all he could call the poetess of Qazvin? Shame on him, they said, primly, for they despised their half-brother bitterly. That woman, as he called her, had taught them to read. She had showed them how to hold the reed pen between finger and thumb and write their letters too. She had encouraged them to find words for their fears and had been the only one who understood their humiliations in this house. The Mayor's son wasn't worthy of her trust. She had asked him to accompany her on that last tryst. She had requested that he come with her so that the drunk guards would not strip her, would not rape her, would not violate her body; she had relied on him, confided in him, depended on him to stand by her, abide by her last wishes. And had he betrayed her request? Had unmentionable acts been perpetrated on her because of him, and was the coward now afraid of being compromised?

All through that night and the following three days, after the soldiers came, the daughters of the Mayor brooded on violations. How easy it would be to rape an undefended woman in the dark. How simple to let the drunken soldiery have their way with her. They remembered how their brother had paused as the escort turned into the square of the torpid city, how he had thrown the cloak more closely over the prisoner's shoulders, to snuff her out. They shuddered to think of his perfidy. They bit their lips then, and brushed aside their tears; they pursed their narrow little mouths and squeezed the muscles of their thighs. They tightened their skirts and fussed with their blouses, sewn according to the authentic European style, copied from the costumes of the visiting princesses, who had taken their measurements directly from the dress of the maid of the Envoy's wife when she paid a courtesy call at court. By the time the knocking began again, three days later, they had taken all the necessary precautions against violation.

Their sister-in-law was in labour and they had a good excuse. They placed an egg and a piece of charcoal near her head. They laid a knife and a pair of scissors by her. They drew a line of chalk all around the walls to protect her and hammered a piece of bread soaked in mutton fat over the lintel so that her grief, and theirs, might pass into it. And as she whimpered more loudly and her wails rose higher, they hung the talismans from the ceiling and scattered the ash across the floor so that no *jinn* could step over the threshold, no witch could come in at the doors. You never know what could happen, at times like these. They were half afraid the poetess of Qazvin might return to haunt them.

(7)

"A witch! Unfit to be the mother of my children!"

That is what the father of her children spat in her face, when he refused to let her see her two elder boys on her return from Karbala. Afterwards, he had demanded that she give him the younger children too, threatening to seize them by force if she refused. A few months later, when her father-in-law was found stabbed in the mosque, he set up such a hullabaloo in the streets that the little ones were gathered up and brought into their mother's library, for safekeeping. As the male members of the family carried the old man home in a makeshift bier, his son ran through the streets screaming that his wife was a witch. Burn her books, he had shouted; her books are the most dangerous. Ransack the house and burn the witch's library!

The daughter of the house had been given one of the best rooms in the women's quarters for her library. It was lined with bookshelves, flooded with light from three arched windows, and overlooked a courtyard where a linden tree grew beside the pool. Even after the stabbing of the Mullah, when the whole town was in an uproar, the tree stood calmly bright and decked in a secret light of its own in the courtyard of the second brother's house; its yellow leaves seemed to cast an autumnal glory over the cloth spread near the library windows where the children ate their meal. But the room itself was dim with women's whispers and the irrepressible rustle of the poetess as she paced back and forth. Each time she passed the windows, the shock of the terrible attack on the patriarch of the family seemed to fall like a shadow across the glowing carpets.

He had uttered dreadful shrieks all the way back from the mosque, they murmured. His fingers had been scrabbling on his soaked chest, as though he wanted to rip it open, his mouth had been one blood red, choking O. There was such an uproar as his sons pushed their way through shouting crowds that some people had been ready to burn down the house of the poetess of Qazvin there and then. If the old man died, the people would go wild with anger.

"If only you had not said anything," quavered the mother of the young woman who was striding silently back and forth. "If only you had held your tongue when he started cursing!"

She was rocking her grandson, who had gripped her headscarf in his tight, dimpled fist. His mouth was ringed with lentil juice but his dark-lashed eyes, smeared with customary kohl and unaccustomed fright, were bright with intelligence and fixed on his own mother, pacing.

Like a caged beast, thought the older woman, watching. Was she a panther or a daughter? She walked all the way to the corner where the bookshelves met the wall, and then walked back again, a path of fire glowing beneath her feet, from the friction almost. Her mother imagined the sparks kindling at her ankles, engulfing her body in a sheet of flame, to the last tendrils of her hair. She wished her daughter had never uttered those fatal words to her uncle but she longed for her to talk now. She yearned for her to justify herself, defend herself, argue, protest as she usually did when she was wronged. Anything but this burning silence, this prowling.

All the women fell silent in the library. The children were mute after their desultory meal. And the room grew darker, the yells in the street louder as the afternoon drew in. The eldest daughter of the house had refused to eat but her two sisters cradled their empty tea glasses and stared out at the linden tree in the courtyard as though it held an answer to the dull roar beyond the walls. The hubbub was growing: the cries in the alley were giving way to shouts. There were calls for justice, howls for vengeance, curses on the head of the poetess of Qazvin.

Say something! prayed her mother. But still the pacing continued, in silence. Sometimes her daughter was so uncompromising that it filled her mother with despair. She read too much into peoples' words, that was the trouble; she went too far, expected too much. The older woman was grateful for the warm circle of her little grandson's arm around her neck. Children were a relief at times like this: at least you knew where you were with them; at least their needs were simple. This little fellow was the youngest of the four and had been a baby when his mother left for Karbala. The poetess of Qazvin had been obliged to leave him behind because of the rigours of the journey and had only taken the little girl with her. The baby had grown fat on his grandmother's attentions.

But children were a woman's nemesis too, she thought, rocking her grandson. You loved them; you lost them. It was just as well her daughter had not allowed this youngest one to squirm his way into her affections too, because she would have to relinquish him in the end. The two older boys had already left the *anderoun* before their mother's departure on pilgrimage; they had reached the age when their father took over their supervision. How the poetess adored them! How she missed them! The older woman remembered how her daughter used to wash the smooth limbs of their wiry bodies in the public baths herself, how she used to cup her hand around their chins and lift their solemn eyes to hers and whisper prayers into the tender whorls of their little ears at night. To give them up once because of age was hard enough, but to lose them twice because of jealousy was unbearable. They had been taught to distrust her in her absence. Their father's hatred had snapped at their heels, and chased their hearts away from her. By the time all hell broke loose in the family on her return from pilgrimage, the boys had already been orphaned. They had become severe little strangers: taller, thinner shadows of their former selves.

There is nothing worse than the anguish of your child suffering anguish for her own children, thought the mother of the poetess of Qazvin. This daughter of hers, walking towards her now, she thought, with a tremulous sigh, this brilliant, beautiful, insufferably stubborn daughter with her arms so absolutely crossed, this girl who knew too much, thought too much, read far too much, and finally said too much too, why, she could have done anything she wanted had she simply behaved as a wife and a mother and a daughter should. But she had always been a rebel, thought her mother, with a catch in her throat. A heretic from the start, she thought, as the young woman turned on her heels and started moving away from her again. She had never been satisfied with her lot. There was a time when her mother had suffered for it. The other women in the family never stopped nagging her about it. They carped continuously about her having brought the girl up wrong. Too much freedom, they said. Too many privileges. Perhaps they were right. But when she was forced to return to this backwater, when her mother saw her trapped here and obliged to give up her studies, her heart had broken. It was not fair. She deserved more. Who could blame her for wanting to fly from the cage of Qazvin? So she herself had been her daughter's advocate when her son-in-law refused to let his wife return to Karbala a second time.

"For pity's sake, let her go," she had whispered to the father of the girl. "Let her accompany her sister and brother-in-law on pilgrimage. She needs to get away."

She did not add that she wanted her daughter to escape before her insufferable cousin forced another pregnancy on her. She did not say that she was afraid of the arguments that might erupt between the young woman and her bigoted brother-in-law either. But her husband was well aware of what she was too mortified to say. She did not need to insist. Pilgrimage was a respectable excuse. He gave his blessing for his daughter to go, and after convincing the rest of the family that she would return from the holy shrines with a well-tempered spirit, purged of personal desires and corrupt inclinations, he sadly watched her set off for Karbala again.

Who could have imagined the upheaval that ensued? She should have acted more wisely, thought her mother, as a thin wail rose from the corner of the room. Her granddaughter, who had been sitting with her back pressed against the bookshelves, had started to cry. Her daughter had given this child too much attention, in her opinion. She should have behaved with greater self-restraint in Karbala and held her tongue, thought the mother of the poetess, frowning at the little girl, severely. She had arrived to find her teacher dead and had immediately begun to preach in his place, at the invitation of his widow. But who was a widow to give her such rights? And how could a woman assume the authority of a leading cleric in the centre of Shi'ia orthodoxy, reading holy texts and commenting on them as if she were a man? Although her sermons attracted the highest praise, they also provoked uproar. When rumours began to spread about her readings and reforms, the three brothers were obliged to hold counsel.

They decided to recall her. Letters were sent full of accusations, denunciations; answers received full of protestation and indignation. And a commission of cousins was finally ordered to escort the rebel home. The gospel of change, thought her mother, slapping her irritating little granddaughter to make her quiet, is most effective when most silent. It works best in spite of us: like the changes in a girl's body that make her a woman; like the invisible changes in the human heart. Her daughter should never have expected the priests to give up their power overnight.

The poetess of Qazvin paused in her pacing and turned at the sound of the slap. Her little daughter had grown silent only because she was sucking on her thumb. Now there's the difficult one, thought her grandmother, disapprovingly: fractious, over-sensitive, too-thin little thing. She had reverted to this infantile habit since her return home, and no amount of gall could cure it. She hoped her daughter would slap the child again for disobedience, but the poetess knelt down suddenly on the carpet and gathered the little girl into her arms instead. Then whispering in her ear and tickling her till she laughed, she tugged on the stubborn thumb till she pulled it out of her mouth. The child was half-laughing, half-crying, eager for attention, indignant at instruction. She was radiant when her mother noticed her but as soon as the poetess rose to her feet again, she sulked and plopped the wrinkled thumb straight back into her mouth.

She's a good mother, observed the older woman, ruefully. Loving, like praying, comes naturally to her; she kneels beside her children and rises as if she had been saying prayers. Who would have thought a woman so intolerant of stupidity could be so patient with immaturity? But patience and wisdom were not always enough: a knife was needed to cut the cord at birth. The trouble was that her daughter had tried to cut the knot at the root of the turban.

There was a sudden clatter of footsteps across the courtyard and a commotion under the windows. The women froze, as someone started knocking at the library door.

"Who is it?" called the poetess of Qazvin, drawing out the key from her waist.

Her maid was trembling when she opened the door. "They say the old master is dying, *Khanum*!" she sobbed. "They say he won't last through the night!"

〔 8 〕

The knocking happened before, thought the Mayor's sister.

Three nights ago, four hours after sunset. Knocking like that can't happen twice. When the gates were opened before, it had led directly to a woman's death and one death like that is enough for a whole lifetime.

She rubbed her dim eyes and stared across the burning courtyard towards the archway of the *birouni*. The faint odour of rot reached her nostrils. The pool had been covered in scum that spring, which had dried to an ochre dust on the tiles by mid-summer, and the fragile jasmine bush by the arch had withered when the mullahs recommended their last-minute, perfunctory interrogations, after the attempt on the life of the Shah a few weeks before. There had been no pretence this time that it was a serious attempt at re-education. There had been no doubt that the two clerics had a fixed mandate when they undertook this second charade. And since the poetess refused to deny her beliefs, it only took a brief seven sessions to condemn her for apostasy.

How can you deny a demonstrable fact? she used to say. How can you refute a logical argument? She told them afterwards, when the women of the house asked her why, why in heaven's name, why she had not simply submitted to the priests' demands, that it was like denying that the earth was round or that the sun would rise. Such matters were not even questions of faith, she said: they were based on reason. If one could not follow the logic, wasn't it wiser to admit to one's ignorance first, before condemning reality?

The knocking continued unabated. A knock proved more than a gate's existence, reasoned the sister of the Mayor. Someone was there. There was no denying that. You did not need to have faith to deduce that fact. Even if you did not know, yet, who was out there, knocking.

Everyone knew that the queen was behind the massacres. She was taking advantage of the attempt on her son's life to settle scores and rid herself of age-old enemies; she was using this excuse to seize on peoples' riches and destroy their reputations. The Mayor's sister had eked out a life of genteel poverty in the past and knew something of the ways of the court. She had sewn dresses for the princesses while the petty prince to whom she had been married squandered his wealth on polo; she had embroidered petticoats for the queen to pay his debts while he complained of an insufficient stipend to go hunting. When the knocking began again she even wondered if the soldiers had come for her this time. Had her highness heard that one of the finest seamstresses in the Qajar court had been sewing a dress for the poetess of Qazvin?

There's a limit to jealousy, surely, thought the widow. To be covetous about the costumes of the British ambassador's wife was understandable, but to envy the clothes of a prisoner?

She squinted to see if the gatekeeper was going to respond to the knocking and saw a glare of darkness behind the light. Her eyesight was fading. Before the poetess of Qazvin came to this house, her sister-in-law would have been jealous if she had ever given orders to the servants. She would have called it interference. But the dynamics in the *anderoun* had changed with the heretic's arrival. She had ignored the old nonsense that insisted on wives and sisters being enemies; she had utterly disregarded the assumption of endemic envy between sisters-in-law. She treated the Mayor's sister with the same deference as his Wife, showed the widow just as much respect as anyone else, even if she was childless, dependent, and losing her eyes. She praised them equally: the cooking of the one and the sewing of the other. And they both trusted her because of it.

The widow started to remember what it was like before. Before they shot the Shah. Before the soldiers came and took the prisoner away. She knew, before the prisoner even asked her for the favour, that the white silk dress would be the last piece of sewing she would do. Despite her dimming eyes she could see that the silk was delicate, and pure. It was not a harsh white silk, bleached with lime, nor a blue or yellow silk like the Chinese kind, but the white of a jasmine: fine as gossamer and as fragile, made by the silk-worms of Milan. It lay folded carefully, in a square of cotton print, at the very bottom of the woman's chest, under her books. She had fingered it with unbounded joy, when the prisoner unfolded it for her to feel.

Could the sister of the Mayor make a dress for her from this bolt of cloth? Before she was even asked, the Mayor's sister knew that she would accept the task.

The poetess of Qazvin wanted a costume made from these five pieces of silk: one piece was for the bodice, one for the blouse, one piece was for the skirt and one for the trousers and the last piece was for her head. She did not need a scarf, she said; that she already possessed, from before. Before her capture, the Mayor's sister guessed, this woman had possessed considerably more than a white silk scarf and a phial of attar of rose.

But could the Mayor's sister sew this dress in secret? Before the poetess even had to explain, she promised that no one in the house would ever know.

Except my daughter, said the prisoner. For it seemed that the little girl was thoroughly familiar with all that was inside that chest. It would have been hard to keep a secret from her; she was much attached to her mother.

You'd think she was preparing for a wedding. The Mayor's sister even wondered whether she had not invented this device to sew a trousseau for her daughter. But she pretended, all the while, that the clothes were for her. She wanted the pantaloons with a drawstring petticoat, frilled with elegant lace-work around the ankles. She wanted the skirt tucked all round and double flounced with embroidered flowers. The blouse had to be long sleeved with puffs at the shoulders, and the bodice was garnished with rows of buttons. And the delicate veil, which framed her face, was bordered all along the edge with seed pearls and as seamless as snow. She liked pretty clothes, you could tell.

She had liked bright colours too. Before she had asked for this white dress, she had ordered her women to wear red and yellow, green and blue, during the official month of mourning, as if it were a time of celebration. The priests in Karbala had been scandalized by her attachment to her appearance. Now that the Mayor's sister thought of it, it had been rather ironic, her sewing all those seams in secret for the prisoner the previous spring while she sat on the opposite side of the curtain arguing with the sour-mouthed mullahs; her sewing a shroud for the poetess, thinking she was sewing a costume for her daughter's wedding. The sister of the Prime Minister and the Wife of the Mayor were pressing for the heretic's release, even as she was sacrificing her sight for that silk dress. She placed a sprig of jasmine in the folds when she finished it. She had half-believed the poetess was going to wear it to celebrate her freedom.

She never revealed the secret to anyone, though she was sure the Mayor's Wife guessed it. And when the soldiers came to the gate that night and the prisoner stepped out of her rooms adorned like a bride, the dress she was wearing was the widow's last glimpse of light. It gleamed like a living thing as the poetess stepped through the gate and into the alley. It dazzled so brightly that she had to be covered with a cloak so she would not blind the darkness. It shone like a lamp, its silky shimmer casting a pearly light around her as she passed through the sleeping town. She wore that dress to celebrate her freedom, all right. But it wasn't the sort of release that everyone had been working for and hoping for, praying for or expecting.

She had been adamant that no one should compel her to divest herself of her attire. When the Mayor's sister asked her nephew if her wishes had been respected, he shrugged his shoulders and turned away. She had never had much patience with that boy.

"But did you make sure no one ripped the silk off her?" she persisted, angrily, for the idea of the poetess being stripped of that lovely garment seemed suddenly worse than death itself. She may have cast aside the veil but she should not, could not have been forced to shed her clothes?

His only reply was to curse the Sardar and his lieutenants. The poetess had asked him to take over the business, he muttered, because the Commander

of the army was incapacitated. She had even provided him with a scarf for
the purpose and had asked him to induce them—that was how she put it—
to use it. "I'm disinclined to address them," she had said, "in the midst of
their revelry." And then she had stood aside and waited for the drunkards,
waited modestly to be killed. Such courtesy and consideration towards her
executioners carousing under the trees. He had shuddered as he told his
aunt about it.

The Mayor's sister forced herself to listen to the knocking, in order to
forget that scarf. She felt tears stinging her eyes and a choking in her throat.
The idiot at the gate was doing nothing to open it. A silk scarf in exchange
for being unmolested, she thought. But was it sufficient inducement? Was
it enough to bargain with, for the respect of a woman's last wishes?

Since she could not conceive of such civilities on the threshold of death,
she stood up in the breezeway and shouted out querulously to the gatekeeper. Ignoring the possibility of offending her sister-in-law, she called to
him to hurry for heaven's sake and open up the door.

(9)

When the town crier announced the dreadful news that the old Mullah was
dying, the daughter of the house insisted on paying him her last respects.
It was a basic courtesy.

He was her uncle, even if he was no longer her father-in-law. Her own
father had refused to allow her to go out of the house before. She had wanted
to speak to her estranged husband, to express her shock and sympathy, but
he obliged her to retire to her library and lock the door. It would be folly to
go out at this time, he told her; it was simply impossible now. Better wait till
the town had quietened down, till her uncle recovered and the situation was
more calm. He was hoping that if he kept his daughter out of sight, tempers
would improve in the family. He was praying that reconciliation would be
possible, in time. But when her uncle's condition worsened and news came
that he was dying, her father reluctantly permitted her to see him.

He imposed all kinds of conditions on her leaving the premises, however.
He insisted on an escort, to the considerable resentment of her siblings. He

himself would go ahead, he said; her sisters must surround her on each side, and her brothers had to bring up the rear, all the way to his brother's house.

If we were only supposed to concern ourselves with our safety in this life, she had replied, it might have been better not to be born.

He was stung by her tone. He wished she would not try to be too clever at a time like this. She was either being over-laconic or too sanctimonious. There were people blaming her for her uncle's murder out there, he said, irritably. Didn't she realize the seriousness of the situation?

It was even more serious, she retorted, that people did not think for themselves.

He told her curtly to hold her tongue; its sharpness had already cost them dear. How dare she be so flippant? How could she take her uncle's condition so lightly?

One moment he was accusing her of being smug, and another, flippant, but she was neither, she assured him. She had never been more serious in all her life, she said.

Her father was anguished. Her cousin had threatened to throttle her with his own hands, he said, his voice shaking. People were demanding her death! Wasn't that serious enough?

Death, she replied, was life's last chance to erase disharmony. If she could see her uncle now, there might be no more veils between them; they might be reconciled.

She was the daughter of priests, alright, he thought in despair, as she turned away to go; he could hardly judge her for being over-pious and self-righteous when that was what he had trained her to become. He hung his head in silence then and prayed that she might be right.

It was late in the afternoon by the time they crowded into the sick-chamber. The mattress of the dying patriarch had been unrolled in the middle of the room and he was lying propped up against his quilts on the carpet. The sick-chamber was thick with members of the family and the street outside congested with people lingering by the gates, waiting to hear the worst.

The Mullah's son rose to his feet with an oath when his wife stepped across the threshold. Her father and brothers had difficulty in restraining him. The women kneeling at the foot of the bed set up an immediate cater-wauling. The room buzzed with their fury. What kind of insolence was this? How dare their outrageous cousin come sauntering in here after behaving the way that she had done? How could she intrude on their grief when she was the cause of it? But when the Mullah's brother signalled them to give way, everyone drew back. A reluctant quiet ensued. They let him pass. They still owed him some respect, as their elder.

The air was fetid, for septicaemia had already set in. The old Mullah lay on his pillows, his face livid, his tongue black and swollen. His throat was choked with pus; the poultices and unguents had been useless. The doctors had pronounced him doomed and he was gasping for his last breaths. The sound of his wheezing penetrated the walls. One of the sisters gagged as she came into the room; her cousins had to make way for her to be taken out again.

As the poetess of Qazvin approached, her cousin ignored his uncle's cautionary warnings from the other side of the bed. "Whore!" he growled, under his breath.

Your wife has come to seek reconciliation with her uncle, pleaded the older man. I urge you, with all my heart, dear nephew, to restrain yourself.

Wife? buzzed some of the women. What kind of wife has she been?

The kind that deserves a husband like him, hissed others, in disgust.

"How could she!" exploded the Mullah's son. "How dare she—!"

She has come to give and to receive pardon, continued his uncle, let her beg for her father-in-law's forgiveness, before it is too late.

Father-in-law? hissed the women. Some daughter-in-law she has been! Some niece! snarled others.

The Mullah's son ignored his uncle's appeals. "Hell-cat," he spat at his wife as she stepped closer to the bed. "Harlot!"

The poetess of Qazvin kneeled beside the Mullah, and he gave a terrible groan. He appeared to grow more agitated and was convulsed at the sight of her.

His son lashed across the bed, incensed. "Get out!" he screamed. "Can't you see you're killing him all over again? Wasn't it enough that you attacked him with your tongue and through your wretched accomplices? Do you want to murder him now before our eyes?"

For a dreadful moment it looked as though he might throw himself across the dying man in an attempt to strike at his estranged wife, but his cousins and brothers managed to pull him back in time. The women in the room shrieked in consternation; they cried out in indignation against the poetess of Qazvin. Was she here as a wife, they wanted to know, or as a niece? If she had come as a wife, how dare she oppose her husband's will? If she had come as a niece, how dare she make her uncle suffer even more than he already had, on his deathbed?

Her father begged for calm again, for restraint once more. For the sake of peace in the family, he said, his voice quavering. For my dear brother's soul.

His daughter drew a deep breath in the brief lull that ensued. She had come to make her peace, she said, steadying her voice. She had come to see her uncle one last time in the hope that it might be easier, now, when the soul was on the threshold of other worlds—

But she never completed her prayer. At her words, the dying man seemed to have a fit and began to gurgle hideously. Turning his head towards his son, he indicated with a shaking finger and a choking noise that the daughter of the house be instantly removed from his presence.

"Let me kill her, let me strangle the she-devil!" screamed his son, and to everyone's horror, he succeeded this time in lunging over the low mattress and grabbing his wife by the wrist. She gave a cry as he jerked her towards him; she would have fallen across her uncle's body had her brothers not held her back. "Let me choke her at his feet," roared her husband. "Let my father see that she gets the punishment she deserves!"

A grotesque scene erupted at the bedside. Brothers and cousins came to blows. Sisters and wives and aunts pulled each other's hair and clothes, screamed, yelled oaths. There were shrieks and shouts across the bed of the dying man: charges and counter accusations, bitter indictments and allegations. There were desperate appeals for calm that were utterly ignored. And above the mayhem there were curses, as the Mullah's son howled that his wife was a witch, a bitch, a whore; that she was every filth he could name and more; she was a murderess—

But the commotion proved too much for the Mullah himself. Within minutes, he began to haemorrhage, his throat rasping, his tongue protruding from a blackened mouth, his only words a steaming pool of bloody feculence all over the quilts. And the last throes started. The poetess was dragged out of the room even as the Mullah's death rattle was heard in the street.

The town stopped breathing just to listen. Although the scandalous scene that took place round the dying Mullah was denied by the family forever afterwards and erased from all public records of his life, few needed further proof of resurrection. Even if the father never found his way out of his grave, they murmured, his son would keep his hate alive. There would never be any reconciliation between the members of this family. Their theology was governed by revenge.

❨ 10 ❩

The knocking must never be, thought the daughter of the prisoner. At the gate, leading into the alley, in front of the Mayor's house. Knocking.

Let there never be knocking again, she prayed.

She heard the knife fall in the kitchen and the widow curse on the breezeway and the wail from the cellars below. How trivial they sounded. She dreaded her father coming, but even that was trivial. The worst was three nights before when she heard the knocks resounding in the dark. Never knock, her heart had cried, as she leapt to her feet and ran down the stairs to hide in the cellar, but the knocking had continued.

In the midnight heart of the summer massacres, the soldiers came and took her mother away, and everything had become trivial from that time on.

Her mother had summoned the Mayor's Wife to her room the previous evening, to give her instructions. When she opened the door to her knock, her daughter saw that she was dressed in the white silk at last, which the Mayor's sister had been sewing so secretly. She had been begging her mother to wear that dress for weeks, but the poetess of Qazvin had pressed a finger to her lips and shaken her head. When she whined and asked why, her mother had told her with a twinkle in her eyes that it must be kept a secret till the right time.

What time was right? Would it have been right before all the troubles began in Qazvin, and the scandals in Karbala, and the running away of her mother in a dark bundle of laundry? Or was the time right now, at this moment in the Mayor's house? Perhaps it would be even more right afterwards, when the time came for her to marry perhaps, when she too would be a bride. Even though she had heard the whispers and the gossip of the women at the wedding of the Mayor's son, the prisoner's daughter still clung to the hope that a time might come when she too could wear a dress like that. She almost believed that the white silk might actually be for her.

There were cries of delight from the Mayor's Wife and his daughters when they saw her mother standing there, so beautiful, so radiant. Everyone gasped as she stood smiling at the open door. The prisoner's daughter flushed with pride and felt a clutch of dull pain in her heart at the same time. She loved it when people saw how beautiful her mother was, how clever, how like a queen. She hated it that the dress was not for her, that it would never be for her, that the time would never be right for her to be a bride. She wished that her mother had never worn that dress.

The room was redolent with her perfume; she had bathed that day and adorned herself as though she were to meet the king. She beckoned the Mayor's Wife inside, to talk to her privately, and closed the door firmly in her daughter's face. She had never done that before.

The girl waited until she was alone before peering through the keyhole. She did not see or hear much. Her mother spoke briefly to the Mayor's Wife, who burst into noisy tears. Her mother spent a long time comforting the Mayor's Wife, who huffed and puffed and sighed and sobbed. And her mother delivered a package into her hands, asking her for a favour. After that, she requested the Mayor's Wife to leave and lock the door behind her.

"Don't bring me food," were the last words her daughter heard. "Let no one disturb me."

No one. Not even her daughter? The girl felt her heart climbing up her throat as the Mayor's Wife backed out of the room. She was sniffling like a samovar and clutching a bundle in her arms no bigger than a baby. It was wrapped in cotton print, tied with knots. What was in it? What was the favour? The prisoner's daughter could not tell.

One brief glimpse of her mother, pacing up and down the room; one last breath of roses, and then the door was shut on her again. A second time. Let no one disturb her, she had said, but the child longed to push past the Mayor's Wife and run into her mother's room. She longed to cry, "I'm no one! Let me stay!" But it was impossible. The keys were jangling round the waist of the mistress of the house and the door was already locked. After she stumbled downstairs and crossed the breezeway and disappeared into the tea room, still sobbing and wheezing like a wet bellows, the daughter of the poetess sat on the steps outside her mother's room and brooded.

It was a long time not to disturb. She heard the night watchmen calling the hours. She heard the owls hooting in the poplars of the Legation garden. She heard her mother praying for a long time, her voice rising and falling, soaring and drooping, half singing, half weeping. She guessed she was pacing to and fro, up and down the room like she always did. It was a long time to wonder what her mother had asked the Mayor's son to do and what she had given away in exchange. Had she offered the little tea glass with the gold lip to the Mayor's Wife and the china saucer with the small rose buds on it? Had she given the pretty lacquer mirror with the doors that opened with a brass latch; had she given her the silver spoon too? The package was too flat for the brass lamp; it was too small for her prayer rug. Had she folded her precious pieces of old tapestry in there from her grandmother; had she given away her rings?

Never knock on that door, she had told her hand, though it had lifted timidly, once or twice, to try. Never knock on her mother's door. She had finally bitten on her small, balled fist and drawn blood to remind herself. She had obeyed, but she never stopped wondering about that package. And her mother had never stopped chanting, or pacing all that long time.

The previous day, around noon, there had been a sudden hue and cry in the street. A man was being whipped down to the gates of the house and back again, being driven down the alley and up again to the market square.

He was the son of the Keeper of the King's Horse, they said. He had preferred the company of silk merchants and carnelian carvers to the honour
of serving the throne, and since he never accepted bribes and had therefore
avoided the queen's control, she had given orders for his arrest. He was
wealthy and among the professed admirers of the poetess of Qazvin, the
Mayor's Wife whispered theatrically, in that loud hush of hers that you
could hear all through the house and over the neighbours' walls.

All the women, except for the prisoner, had clambered up to the terrace
to watch what they were doing to him. There was a mad dog at his heels.
When the daughter of the poetess first glimpsed him, standing on her tip-
toes on the terrace roof, she thought that the son of the Keeper of the King's
Horse was dancing. The crowd was clapping as he turned down the alley; the
tambourines and drums were beating at his approach. Except for the dog,
she thought it was a wedding, and he was the groom, for he had a strange air
of joy about him. But it was a curious dance. He moved oddly, progressed
in halts and starts, forwards and backwards, sometimes pausing as though to
catch his breath and then leaping again. Was it poetry he was singing?

Then in a brief hiatus in the drumming, he collapsed on the ground.
It was only when he rose once more that she heard the sizzling. She heard
the soft pock and splutter of the flames. There were candles licking his
open wounds in the raw flesh. They inserted fresh tapers in his body at the
Mayor's gates and then turned him round, burning, and chased him back
up the alley again. He was running to the rhythm of the whips, with candles
flickering in his wounds. He was dying as he danced, stinging and singing
like a bird. Long after the burning man had passed, the air in the courtyards
was sweet with the dreadful smell of him. Long after dusk, the poetess still
chanted in her room. And then it was the last day and after that the very
last night came.

At midnight when the knocking began, the Mayor's Wife barely
glanced at the child who was still sitting on the step behind the door. When
the door opened the poetess of Qazvin was veiled and ready and beckoned
her hostess in, but she did not call the child to her. The Mayor's Wife cried
like a funeral as she gave her the little key to her chest. Some rings, said the

prisoner, and a few other tokens; small gifts for her gracious hospitality. As a remembrance.

"Trivial things," she said, softly, as the Mayor's Wife blew her nose in her scarf.

Trivial? The poetess of Qazvin kissed the Mayor's Wife and kissed the Mayor's daughters and kissed the pregnant squint-eyed bride who had been married to the son of the Mayor. Trivial? When she turned to kiss her own daughter, the girl had vanished from the steps; they could not find her. Perhaps she was asleep? It was midnight when the soldiers had come knocking. It was late. Perhaps she was tired? Her mother said not to disturb her.

And then she left.

The child had run down to the cellars, her heart breaking. So the rings were not in the package after all—the cornelian, the ruby, and the turquoise. Her mother had given the little chest away with all her precious treasures and the Mayor's Wife had the key. She had left no tokens, no gifts, and no remembrances for her daughter. And she had never kissed her goodbye. I must be trivial too, thought the poor child, to be given away. All through the dark heart of that massacred night, she wept wracking sobs over her triviality. She cried herself dry over her utter inconsequence. She stayed in the cellar till the dirty dawn brought the Mayor's son back home. It was only when his young wife went into labour early the following morning that they found her down there. She returned to the steps by her mother's door after that, and refused to move.

Three days later, when the knocking started, she was still there, as limp as a rag. She had barely eaten, barely slept all that time. She barely noticed the whispers, the looks and nudges of the daughters of the Mayor, his sister, his Wife. She supposed they wished to be rid of her now her mother was gone. She assumed they had asked her father to come and take her away. She guessed she had become a liability in this house, which was almost as bad as being trivial. But oh! she cried, as the knocking began at the gates three days after the soldiers took her mother away, oh! let it never be her father. She could not bear to see him. Let him never take her back to Qazvin, she prayed.

It was the knocking that made her suddenly understand why her mother had not given her the rings. If that was her father at the gates, then thank heavens she did not have them. It was far less dreadful never to have had those treasures than to hear him curse her mother for giving them to her. It was far less painful to lose the rings to the Mayor's Wife than to have her father strip them off her fingers. It would be less agonizing, thought the poor girl, to have all the blazing candles of a world cut into her flesh than to see her father throw her legacy away.

❲ 11 ❳

The body of the old Mullah was barely cold, the corpse washers hardly summoned, before his furious son determined to expose his cousin's guilt and wrench a confession from her. Since he was certain that she had plotted his father's murder, he decided, in the absence of all evidence, to apply what he called justice to extract what he termed the truth. And so, a campaign of revenge followed hot on the heels of the funeral. During the nightmare days that followed the death of the Mullah, the air of the alley outside the house was filled with the smell of burning coals.

One week after they had buried their father, the dead Mullah's sons forced their way into their uncle's house with a brazier, a metal tray of branding irons, and a goat, in order to return their cousin's courtesy call. They would not have been able to enter had it not been for the collusion of the poetess' sisters. Her mother had instructed the servants to bar them from the gates; her father had placed strict control over who entered his premises. But the antagonism of her sisters allowed the Mullah's sons to insinuate their way into the women's quarters.

Loyalties in this house were bitterly divided. One of the sisters, who had travelled to Karbala with the poetess and attended her classes in the 'Ataba'at, was her ardent supporter and devoted companion. Another, who sided with her paternal cousins and had suffered from her domineering influence since childhood, was bitterly jealous. She was weary of the constant attention, the endless preference given to the eldest daughter of the house. She was sick of the way her sister's outrageous behaviour generated so much froth and confusion in the family. She was fed up with her verbosity, which invariably drew everyone's notice to herself alone, bored of her endlessly reading into everything and making a huge fuss. Why did she have to get all the attention? There were other women in this house, after all, and other interpretations beside hers!

She opened the gates to her cousins at the hour of noon. Taking advantage of their uncle's piety, his nephews crept across the courtyard while he was saying his midday prayers, climbed the stairs of the *anderoun*, and brought the implements of torture right up to the door of the poetess of Qazvin. After that they barred access to the stairwell leading up to the library; they kept everyone in the household out, except the cousin who had served as their go-between.

There was a furious argument about it between the sisters. One called it vile treachery; the other, flushed with triumph, claimed it was the exercise of justice. The first said it was pure folly; the second called on the folly to fall on her sister's head, with all her talk about right and wrong, all her fuss about reform, all that reading between the damned lines. So! She wanted to change the laws of jurisprudence, did she? Let her have a taste of real justice, in flesh and blood!

But the Mullah's son had no intention of inflicting bodily harm on his wife. He knew that she was fearless when it came to pain. She had a temperament that gloried in heroic gestures, and he was not going to encourage her to demonstrate it. She would suffer far more if she witnessed the suffering of another: torture, for her, would be to see someone tortured for her sake.

So he seized on her maid.

As soon as he had forced open the library, he thrust the trembling girl inside the room with her mistress. She was ordered to kneel, with her cheek pressed against the panelling and her hands placed under the gap of the door. Then he tied her wrists with thongs and pulled on them violently from the other side. The maid gave a sudden cry as her hands were yanked and her face was rammed against the doorjamb.

Stop! pleaded the poetess, don't do that. You're hurting the poor girl!

"We haven't even begun," sneered her husband, and pulled tighter. He wanted both hands well exposed. He told his younger cousin, stiffly, that she had better make herself useful by holding the thongs taut from this side. He wanted to make sure the maid would not draw them back when he began the branding, he added loudly.

The sister bit her lip as she took over the leather straps. She did not want to be thought a coward by her cousin. "What a melodrama!" she muttered, angrily. "What a scene!" she snapped, cursing her sister for the situation in which she found herself.

There was a whimper and another cry on the other side of the door as she yanked hard on the straps. The poetess begged them again to have mercy, not to pull so hard, to be reasonable and to talk instead of pursuing this dreadful business any further.

"Confess!" snarled her husband. "Confess that you killed my father!"

If he was accusing her of murder, she replied, where was proof of her complicity?

"Don't start discussing proofs with her, for heaven's sakes," whispered her sister, in alarm. "It'll go nowhere."

If he wanted to arraign her according to religious law, continued the poetess, earnestly, where was the court and who was the judge? Why did her cousin not allow her to refute his accusations in a proper fashion? Not like this.

"Don't get into an argument with her whatever you do," hissed her sister.

Her cousin needed no urging. He knew, at his own cost, that he would lose any debate with his wife. The only language to use with her was torture. "Confess your crime!" he shouted through the door. "Confess before the branding irons force you!"

"That'll teach her the difference between a real crisis and an inflated fuss," rejoined her sister, grimly, and she helped her cousin heap up the coals. "Let her read the branding irons!"

First they stoked the charcoal with the bellows till the hot coals were sizzling and heated the oil to drip on the maid's fingers, just to tease her, just to make her squeal.

Don't listen to me! they heard her gasping to her mistress on the other side, it's nothing, really nothing.

Then they shaved the buttocks of the goat and branded it with the red hot metal poker, just to fill the air with the terrified bleating and the stench of burnt skin.

Pray for me, they heard the maid begging her mistress behind the door, pray that I don't make a noise like that!

The poetess of Qazvin said nothing. After her initial attempts to reason with her cousin, after pleading and arguing, she did not utter another word. Other than the screams of the maid, there was an impenetrable silence inside the library.

Her sister interpreted it all as show. "Don't worry," she told her cousin, hurriedly. "She does this sort of thing for dramatic effect. She goes all quiet like that so that it's even more fearsome afterwards, when she starts up her harangue again."

Her cousin clashed the irons together and threw oil on the coals to make them sizzle more fiercely. Sparks flew and the goat bleated frantically. But there was no further sound from inside the library, except for the maid's whimpering. The poetess could not be provoked to speak.

"She'll be talking again soon enough," muttered her sister, nervously, with a frown. "She's just preparing her curses, that's all. She swears something awful once she gets going!"

But when the branding irons were finally ready and the maid pressed her forehead hard against the panelling to prepare herself for the worst, there was a sudden knocking at the gates of the house and the shrieks that arose came from outside the library door. The sister who had been watching the tortures panicked completely. She dropped the thongs and fled down the stairs. Even as the maid bit her lips and shut her eyes tight so she would not have to look at her mistress praying, pale and prostrate on the floor, she suddenly found her scalded hands were freed.

The knocking was insistent and accompanied by loud cries. The torture had to stop. The murderer, the servants shouted, had been found. The Mullah's murderer, they cried, running across the courtyard, had confessed.

⦅ 12 ⦆

The murderer gave himself up when he heard about the branding irons. He came forward and handed himself over to the authorities immediately. He was a stranger in the town, a traveller. He admitted to killing the Mullah in the mosque, and had the dagger to prove it. There was no need to torture innocent folk, he said, now that he had confessed to his crime.

"Ha!" sneered the husband of the poetess, "that proves he's an accomplice!"

The man swore on the most Holy Book that he had never met the poetess of Qazvin. He had not heard of her prophecies about her uncle, either, because he had only arrived in the town the week before. But he was devoted to the pious Shaykh, and had been appalled to hear the Mullah curse him in the mosque the previous Friday. Determined to make him eat his words, as he grimly put it, he had entered the mosque through a hole in the roof, crept up behind the priest while he was praying, and stabbed him in the throat. Then he had climbed back out the way he came and picked his way across the rooftops before the corpse washer had even started screaming. He had been hiding down by the river waiting for the uproar to be over.

The Mullah's son rejected his confession out of hand. Guilt, in his opinion, was a judgement to be pronounced by a religious court, not to be confessed by a layman. Even when the dagger of the man was found just where he said he had placed it, hidden under the parapet of the bridge some days later, the son of the murdered cleric refused to accept his attestation. "One butcher's blade is much the same as another in this town," he said. Although the stiletto was marked by recent blood and confirmed as the instrument of crime, he was still not satisfied. This creature, he said, was a tool himself; he had been incited to commit the bloody deed by the real author of it.

"Such a nonentity," he concluded, scornfully, "is not worthy to have killed my father."

And he spat on the floor and swore to appeal for justice at the highest levels. He would leave for the capital, he said, and demand audience with the old Shah. He would require restitution from him for his father's death. It was the least he could do to honour the family name.

His little daughter, cowering behind her paternal aunts as he spoke, could hardly pull her eyes away from that quivering blob of spittle on the carpet. Her father's words seemed to have transformed the whole world into a shimmering globe of hate. One kind of torture had stopped, but another began. The branding irons were only set aside because her father had found other instruments, more subtle, more probing. He no longer needed a goat and hot coals, but came to his uncle's house, a few days after the murderer's confession, armed with deadly determination.

The old man's grief redoubled at the sight of his nephew. He begged him, with tears in his eyes, to control his temper. Hadn't there been enough violence committed already? Hadn't there been enough hurt given and received? Deeds had been done that had destroyed an edifice raised by generations. Words had been uttered—and then he choked, unable to complete the phrase. Forgive and forget, he mumbled.

"Go ahead, uncle!" scoffed his nephew. "You have good reason to forget!"

The old man bowed his head meekly, and blamed himself for the situation. He assumed total responsibility for the conduct of his daughter, he said, his voice breaking. He guaranteed to keep her locked in her rooms until she recognized the error of her ways. He swore that he would not let her out from now on, nor allow her to take one step out of her library until she came to her senses. No one would be permitted in there except the maid, he promised; no one would be allowed to talk to her, including her own children. But in return, he begged his nephew to swear, on the most Holy Book, that he would not lay a finger on her.

His nephew sneered that he had no intention of polluting any of his fingers in the manner implied. His uncle should rest assured that he would not go near his cousin, if he could help it. He would not touch a hair of her pernicious body—it would be contamination to him—but his business here was with his children. He had come to fetch his children from this house, he said: his children who by the divine rights of paternity granted him in religious law were his indubitable property. Where, he thundered, were his children?

Despite his uncle's objections, despite their grandmother's appeals and the intervention of their aunts, he seized on the two youngest in the *anderoun*, dragged them forcibly through the gates and into the alley, and pulled them kicking and screaming back to his home. The townsfolk stood by and watched the scene in shock and awe. It seemed as if this family, which had debated the finer points of moral philosophy all these years, was hell-bent on dragging itself into the depths of infamy. The boy shrieked piteously all the way; it was discovered later that his elbow had been dislocated. The girl wet herself and was thrust into the cellars as a punishment until she begged to be obedient. And by the time the Mullah's son left for the capital, the wailing and lamentation in the house of the second brother was almost as loud as had been the grieving and mourning in the house of the first, some weeks before.

The daughter of the poetess stopped eating after she was dragged to her father's house. She grew thin and gawky and her aunts warned her that no one would ever want to marry her if she did not eat. But she clapped her mouth shut and shook her head stubbornly at their hovering spoons. She did not like her paternal aunts or her cousins who teased her. She did not like their secretive smiles, the way they whispered among themselves and stopped talking when she came into the room. She hated it when they said her mother was a heretic.

"My mother," she would retort, stubbornly, "is a poet."

They murmured behind her back that the poetess was a murderess and a whore.

"My mother," she would say in a silly, lilting, sing-song voice which drew scowls from her sulky brothers, "is good and beautiful, not like you!"

It was brave thing to say in the circumstances, because her father called his wife the filthiest names under the sun. It was also a foolish thing to say, because her brothers took sides with her cousins against her after that, and she was locked in the cellar again. It was also not an entirely honest thing to say. Sometimes the daughter of the poetess wished ardently that her mother were more like all the other women in the family. She wished that she were more normal, less vocal. She wished she would do more sewing than reading, less studying than cooking. She wished her mother would not talk so much about death and resurrection.

Once, on their way back from Karbala when she was seven years old, her mother had stayed for several months in a grand palace in Baghdad belonging to the pasha. Her little girl had been allowed by the servants to tickle the carp in the pond and chase the peacocks in the garden till they spread their feathers wide. Is this resurrection? she had asked the poetess of Qazvin, because it seemed like dying and going to heaven after all their shifting about, from house to house and place to place. But her mother talked as though everything—all the people in the mosques, all the dogs yapping in the crooked alleys, the flies in the meat market, the fleas on the donkeys—had to die and undergo resurrection. Even the cats? the child asked, anxiously; do they have to undergo resurrection too? Does everything in the world have to change?

Yes, her mother said. Everything. And when the little girl burst into tears and said she hated change, it wasn't kind, and she wished heartily that everything could stay just as it was, her mother took her in her lap and told her, gently, that change was one of the attributes of God and therefore, she need not fear it. The names of the days always change, she explained, but the sun of each dawn and dusk would always be the same. Her clothes changed as she grew out of them, but she would still be herself and essentially the same. Words had to change too; they had to become new to be listened to, said the poetess of Qazvin: this, she said, was the meaning of resurrection.

Her daughter pondered her mother's words. Most people said the same things over and over again and it was very boring; their words were like female relatives on a hot afternoon, like old women at a funeral, whining and moaning and complaining about the weather. Few people dared to use new ways of talking. Her mother's words seemed never to have been heard before. They were like lightning in a thunderstorm; they had a piercing cry, like sea birds, like babies wanting to be born. But her father's words were like death, without resurrection.

The spittle from his mouth left a little black spot on the carpet after it soaked into the wool: flat and cold and dead as an old word. The daughter of the poetess was tempted to press her finger on the spot to see if it was still wet, but it made her shudder to do it. Dead words were slimy as well as cold. She ran out to the courtyard to wash her finger hurriedly in the pool.

Her aunts stopped chattering when they saw her. "Is our little angel going to feed the carp?" they trilled, hypocritically, their words drifting like dead leaves on the surface of the pond.

They had been discussing food again, as usual. The women of the house were forever discussing food: what she ate, whether she ate, if she would eat and when. The child hated the way they said "she." She refused everything they gave her. There was a certain look that crossed their shadowed brows whenever they saw her, a twilight glance that passed between them in her presence. There was a puckered flabbiness to the skin of their underarms, an amphibiousness about the liver spots on their hands, and a sick tinge in the circles around their eyes that invariably reminded her of the flyblown carcasses, the stringy cadavers, the hunks of yellow and purple flesh hanging in the meat markets of Baghdad. The palace of the pasha may have been paradise but the butchers, incited by priests and clerics, transformed that city into hell. They were aroused to such a pitch of hatred against her mother that they tried to poison her.

The poetess had not died in Baghdad, because she had instructed her women to defy the butchers and eat raw vegetables to avoid the worst. She did not die in Qazvin either, though she fell deadly sick when her sisters and her female cousins tried to poison her food. But she mourned, she chafed, she grew pale in captivity in her father's house.

(13)

The poetess of Qazvin allowed her white hairs to grow when her children were taken away from her. She no longer believed in discussion or debate after the old Mullah was stabbed in the mosque. She no longer went to the public baths either, but used the little marble bathing pool in the cellar of the house. She said there was no point in using henna or words anymore.

"When no one listens," she had said, "there's no point in talking."

But everyone knew that it was because her father would not let her leave the premises. Even after the murderer gave himself up, the daughter of the house had been obliged to remain under lock and key. For her own safety, her father said.

Not only had her husband refused to accept the man's confession, not only had he responded to it by abducting his children and ranting about injustice to the king, but he had also exploited the murderer's subsequent escape from prison to hunt down other scapegoats. In the absence of the actual perpetrator of the crime, he had been allowed, by the old Shah, to choose someone else to redress the wrong done to him and his family. He was granted the right to an alternative culprit according to the law. So he seized on four. Two of his victims were slaughtered in the capital before he even returned, the first at the hand of the official executioner and the second by another, unofficial hand. The two others were brought back to Qazvin and mutilated on their arrival, the townsfolk having been roused to such a pitch that by the time their knives, swords and spears and axes had done their worst, no fragment of the bodies remained for burial. All four were innocent and all four were ardent supporters of the poetess of Qazvin. That was enough to prove their guilt for the Mullah's son.

He also commissioned a tombstone for his dead father on his return. Graven images were contrary to custom, but he was determined to carve his wife's guilt into the future. The gravestone depicted a praying mullah being stabbed in the back by two men, while a woman, holding a sheet of paper in her hand, stood half concealed by a curtain behind him. Whichever way the enigmatic image might be read, it indicated complicity, for the woman was clearly dictating the murder and was indicated as the author of the crime. The corpse washers made a killing on the strength of all the curious onlookers who came to ogle at the tombstone.

Given the mood of seething resentment and incipient violence in Qazvin, the father of the poetess felt justified in maintaining strict control over her movements. How could he allow his daughter to wander about, he said, when half the town had been aroused against her?

His daughter strongly objected to the strictures. How safe was she in this house anyway, she retorted, when servants had been bribed to kill her and her cousins had tried twice to poison her already? What was the use of keeping her locked up?

Her father wrung his hands and groaned. He had done his utmost to control who went in and out of his walls, but he could not heal the treachery within them.

She begged him to let her go. Why, she appealed, had he confined her like this? She pleaded with him to let her escape somewhere, anywhere, far away from Qazvin.

He protested that he had done everything for her comfort. Was she not in her own rooms, surrounded by her own books? Did she not have her own maid—?

But was she his prisoner or his daughter, she cried. What right had he to put her under this enforced detention, to treat her in this inhuman fashion?

Right? spluttered her father. He glared at the young woman, scandalized. She was not kneeling before him, as she should. She was not sitting with her head bowed in his presence as might be expected of a daughter of the house. She was pacing restlessly, back and forth, across the room. It was hard to glare satisfactorily at a woman in constant motion. He lost his temper with her. Had she forgotten to whom she was talking? he began, indignantly. Did she not know that he was her father? She should obey him, respect him, do her proper duty towards him. By what right was she even questioning him? He choked, then, and could hardly speak.

The daughter of the house frowned. There was no point in pursuing this line of argument. There was no way she could fulfill her father's expectations any more than that she could expect him to understand her appeals. The world changed when definitions of womankind were altered. She struggled to curb her impatience because she knew how much her father loved her. She knew he was only trying to find a compromise, trying to accommodate to the demands of her cousins, trying to protect her from their bloodlust. But she was not going to stay trapped in her library to smooth everyone's ruffled pride. She refused to be their scapegoat, she said.

Her father rocked back and forth where he was sitting for a few moments, wrapped in his 'aba, struggling to regain his composure. His daughter had stopped pacing and was standing before him, her arms defiantly crossed. He avoided looking up at her. Couldn't she understand that he would be blamed for negligence? he finally said, weakly, on the verge of tears. Couldn't she see that he would be shamed by his peers, ridiculed by everyone if he allowed her to come and go as she pleased, after all that had happened?

She was exasperated, despite her resolve to control her temper. She burned with indignation not against her father but the gossip. She knew all too well what people were saying: that he had raised a viper in the nest; that he had let a scorpion into his house; that a hen crowed instead of a rooster in this family. She was all too familiar with the vapid chatter, the usual tittle-tattle, the nonsense people said which strangled the truth. So he was keeping her locked up, she supposed, grimly, just to give everyone the impression that he was doing the right thing?

But he had sworn, protested her father, to keep her under house arrest for her own good. He had assumed this responsibility, before witnesses, for her own sake.

Or for her re-education, rather, she interrupted, angrily. And for once her bitterness got the better of her. Everyone in the ecclesiastical community would give him credit for doing that, wouldn't they? she continued. He had undertaken to reform her just to protect his own honour. But had he forgotten that he had educated her himself? Did he not remember how he had trained her to search for the truth no matter how high the cost? Did he really imagine that he could dissuade her from pursuing that path now? She had no intention of doing penance for thinking!

He was merely hoping to prevent worse punishments, her father answered, his voice cracking. These people were hell-bent on harming her; they could kill her for apostasy. "For the love of God," he begged, "I have already lost my pride, my profession, and my reputation in this town; don't let me lose you too." And he hid his face in his hands and wept.

The library walls seemed to shrink back as his wrenching sobs filled the room. The books on the shelves seemed to turn their faces away from the poetess of Qazvin, as she stared down in dismay at the bowed and bent head of her broken father. The lovely linden tree in the courtyard sighed as it scattered its golden leaves in the gust of wind that rattled the panes. She was shamed.

She kneeled at his feet then and bowed her head to beg for his forgiveness. She said nothing more to him about her desire to have her freedom for she could see that his heart was breaking, that he was aching with the fear of losing her. She became gentle and compliant after that, which was even more worrying to him, for he knew her patience to be as dangerous as her rage. But she sent a message to her cousin; she wrote a letter challenging the Mullah's son.

This situation, she stated, could not go on. The whole family was suffering because of them and it was up to them to find a resolution. If she could lay bare the falsity of his charges, would he drop all his accusations unconditionally? Would he agree to leave her alone if she was delivered from her rooms within nine days? She promised to submit to him, if she was not released, she said. Her escape would be proof of her innocence and her failure would demonstrate her guilt to all the world. He could do with her as he willed then, but at least this stalemate would end.

Her cousin ignored the dare of course; it was absurd. A typical example of his wife's grand gestures, her absurd claims, as if the whole universe were a text for exegesis and she were God's appointed commentator. Drop his accusation on the strength of a fantastical deliverance? Leave her alone if she was freed within nine days? What nonsense! He preferred his own definitions of guilt and innocence, which were far more realistic, more rational than hers.

Her father, however, redoubled his vigilance. There was something about this ultimatum that unnerved him. He had learned that when his daughter issued challenges like this, it was better to avoid their consequences. So he was hardly surprised when one chill day, soon after the last swallows had left the eaves that autumn, he knocked on the library door and heard no answer. The bird had flown.

⟨ 14 ⟩

Where had she gone?

They searched the houses all that day. They questioned the servants through the following night. She was nowhere and her maid had vanished with her. How did she do it? Who could have helped her escape? Some remembered a washerwoman who had come to fetch a bundle of laundry the evening before. Others said they had heard hooves outside the city walls late that night after a beggar had passed by the door. One of the grooms thought he had seen a muffled man with three horses waiting at the gates, but so many stories circulated in the weeks that followed that it was impossible for them all to be true. An old man, who owned an orchard several hours' journey out of the city, said he had given refuge to two veiled figures and their male escort for a night that winter. A lady of the court claimed to have offered the poetess hospitality in her own home over the spring festival. Several people insisted that they had seen her riding out, bare-faced, in broad daylight in the forests of Mazanderan the following summer. But none knew for certain how she escaped or where she took refuge the day she left her father's house. She remained at large, fleeing from place to place and town to town, running from house to house and street to street, until she was captured the following year, just after the coronation of the new king.

Whenever the daughter of the poetess thought about her mother during that time, she imagined her surrounded by rivers and gardens, she dreamed of her chanting poetry, adorned with rings: she thought of her among the pious dwelling in paradise.

"In the presence of the potent King!" she used to murmur, pressing her hands ardently across her breast, after her dawn prayers every morning.

I am the river of red wine in the mouth of death.
The crimson tale of my words trickles through your breath.

Paradise was her mother's smile with the little black mole beneath her lip; paradise was her rouged cheeks, her sparkling eyes and blackened brows, her chanting. Paradise was the stories that she told, the lessons that she taught: to read and write, to learn the difference between prayers and poems, to see the beauty of the linden tree outside the library window and watch the yellow leaves lilting delicately in the breeze, even as the old Mullah stood there in a towering rage and cursed darkly all over the red carpets.

"Trees," she had whispered to the child, "grow inside too."

I am the yellow river that sustains the infant mind.
My saffron pages offer hope to human kind.

Paradise was to be folded in her mother's arms, to slip her fingers in her mother's breast, to feel the branches of her mother's tree knocking on her heart. Paradise was her mother's hand, which she held all through one night when they were travelling and she was frightened. Whenever she woke up, during that night, she squeezed her hand and her mother had squeezed back each time. She did not mind that the rings hurt her.

"Don't be afraid," her mother had said quietly, in the darkness.

I am the river green as honey, full of life. I hold
the trusted and the trusting in my arms; I hold the seasons' strife.

Paradise was to play with her mother's rings. The first one was an intense blue, clear as childhood skies, without a fleck or blemish in the stone. The second was a warm gold, burnished with its own clear light. And the third bled like a pomegranate and a woman in her courses. The poetess of Qazvin allowed her daughter to play with the turquoise, the cornelian, and the ruby, but there had actually been four rings. The last one was hidden in the bottom of the chest between the folds of white silk.

"That one," her mother said, "you don't touch."

I am the heart's river, white water cleansed of rust.
My words of oneness yearn to drink the dust.

The fourth ring was a simple piece of chalcedony, set in silver. The polished surface of the quartz was the colour of pale water, crossed by concentric threads of brown and gold; it looked like a desert landscape in which circles of sand shimmered against an opaque sky. It was not a precious gem, like the other rings, but a stone used for sacred amulets, and when the light flashed on its flat surface, the daughter of the poetess could see that it was scored across with carved symbols and strange lines. It seemed to carry messages from distant horizons.

Where did this ring come from and what was the writing traced upon it? Did it carry counsels of comfort, messages of good cheer or fear, rather? How had her mother acquired it and when? Had she bought the stone, through some middleman, and then commissioned a jeweller to make it for her? Had she asked her brother-in-law or her trusted uncle, to bring her a selection from the agate merchant in Qazvin? Or had she searched out the ogling fellow himself as he sat sucking on his hubble-bubble in the back of the shop, with garlic on his breath and an eye on women's fingers, slipping through a sleeve to fondle the polished stones in his brass tray?

And when she had chosen it, opaque as breath on scalding tea, had she then sought out some subtle craftsman to adorn it with symbols, one who would be willing to come to the house on the pretext of selling turquoises, a grey-bearded man discreet of bearing and respected in the trade, who would slip off his shoes before being ushered into a private room where she could speak to him through the curtain? Perhaps she chose some silent Armenian who would not question the consignment too closely. Perhaps one of the Jews in town was willing to set the stone cheap in a circlet of silver and charge double for the price of saying nothing. Because what, in the name of mystery, was the meaning of these letters traced on the polished stone? What was the story of this ring?

A woman's jewels always tell a story. If she buys herself rings she must either use her dowry to do so or find the money elsewhere, and her husband would soon learn of the source. If she receives them as a gift, she would have to explain the reason for such generosity, and he would soon discover the giver. And if she earns them by her own means, which was the worst of all, she would have to justify the methods she had used to do so. There is space enough to slip the finger of imagination into the smallest band of silver or of gold. Lick a ring and you can taste the sweat and smell the blood in a woman's life. Bite it and you can see the marks of her teeth on it, see where it has worn thin with rubbing. The simplest ring contains a thousand associations.

The daughter of the poetess knew all the stories of her mother's rings. She knew the story of the black slave who sacrificed her life to acquire such a cornelian and had to sell it that very same day to buy herself a shroud. She knew the story of a jeweller who had thrown a whole saddlebag filled with turquoises as blue as this into a wayside ditch in order to merit entrance into paradise. And she knew the story of the thief too who cut off the finger of a dead woman to steal the ruby on it, only to lose his own hand for larceny. But her mother never told her the story of the fourth ring. The milky quartz scored with mysterious symbols kept its secrets, like the subsequent escape and absence of the poetess from Qazvin. All through that following year, all through the winter months, the spring festival and summer too, the little girl imagined her mother pacing through gardens and rivers, adorned with the ring's impenetrable purity.

The veil was not lifted till the end. The ring's meaning was not revealed until the night the soldiers came knocking at the gates of the Mayor's house. The carved symbols and concentric circles on its flat surface only gave their secrets up at that moment. But these contained no scandals, no crises, no swords raised, and no throats cut, as the daughter had been led to expect. They involved no dramatic demands, no threats, no rushing about, no ultimatums, as she had been told had been the case in the orchards of Mazanderan the summer her mother first unveiled her face. When the poetess stepped out of her room in the Mayor's house that last night, when she stood there before them, so beautiful, so finely decked in silk, so exquisitely perfumed, her daughter noticed the chalcedony on her fourth finger, that's all. The little girl understood the story of the ring the first and last time that she saw it. She knew then that her mother would die.

(15)

Then the knocking began again, hammering at the gates, beating at the doors, echoing through the courtyard of the Mayor's house. Again, and then again.

The daughter-in-law of the Mayor felt the knocking inside her. It was rocking her like an earthquake, locking the doors in her brain, sending shockwaves through her once more, and then again. It was impossible to think beyond each then, and then, and then again, of pain. Once the knocking started, she realized that anticipation was the worst. It was easier to expect nothing.

How could you call this birth? Babies were not uppermost in anyone's mind at that moment. Everyone had been snuffing the odours of death for days, thronging the streets to watch the executions. Death had been stalking the marketplace, haunting the public baths. Death had been tearing the old folks limb from limb in the alleys and ripping the little children from their nannies' arms. Death was torching people out of their houses, hounding them through the streets like blazing trees; they were being stoned and savaged by death from dawn till dusk. They were being hung, drawn, and quartered on the city gates. The cannons had been shaking the air ever since the Mother of the Shah had called for revenge because death had aimed birdshot at her son.

The daughter-in-law of the Mayor cried out with the pain. Wailing was no longer enough. She felt bitterly betrayed. The poetess of Qazvin had told her that children were a joy. What kind of joy was this? She had promised her that being a mother was the sweetest thing in all creation. Well, this was not sweet and she did not want to be a mother if it entailed such misery. She had also said that she would forget the pain when she had a baby. How could she possibly forget this brute suffering? The walls around her were impregnated with silent howls; the bricks were cemented with unheard screams. They said these cellars had witnessed torture the winter before she had been married to the Mayor's son. She wanted to go home. And she cried again.

This was no baby, she concluded, shaking with sobs and terror. It was a *jinn*, a monster, a seven-month-old freak that was pulling her apart like this, that was ripping her body to pieces, gripping her in a vice, tugging, jerking, dragging, tearing her limb from limb.

The daughter-in-law of the Mayor had not thought birth to be such a bloody business. Her mother had spawned babies like kittens. Her sisters, too, had dropped infants as easily as mulberries shaken off the summer trees, careless of those that died. Always more worms where those came from, the women in her family had said. They had wrapped them in rags and thrown the little bundles unceremoniously into the earth. Snuffed out with a white scarf in a garden, her husband whispered early that morning. They had wrapped the silk four times round the prisoner's throat, twisting and knotting and pulling and jerking, till she slumped to her knees. He had sobbed when he told her about it, his skin pale, his breath reeking. That was when her contractions started. That was when the twisting and knotting and pulling and jerking began inside her.

But though three days had passed since then, the young wife had still not been delivered of her burden. The pains had stopped and started and stopped again. She had walked and sat and lain down and squatted and rolled around the floor, but the unborn child was proving mulish. Her sisters-in-law had prepared the bricks and burned the rue before the cellar doors; they had placed the charms around her neck to prevent the evil eye and had cut the throat of a hen. And then, just as the knocking began at the gates, the contractions suddenly recommenced, with a renewed and far fiercer intensity. She felt as though the poetess was being strangled inside her.

She was exhausted. If dying took as long as being born, no wonder the prisoner had suffered. The Austrian doctor had told her husband that she had showed remarkable fortitude. Impressive, for a woman, he had said. As though women were not inured to suffering each time they gave birth, thought the daughter-in-law of the Mayor, bitterly. The doctor was one of the witnesses at the execution although he did not sully his hands. The Sardar's men were in such a stupor that they could not be trusted to do the job either. The Mayor's son had been obliged to bribe two of the servants to finish off the business. He had not waited for instructions but had just proceeded, using the white silk scarf she had given to him for the purpose.

"They apparently wish to strangle me," she had told him, pressing the scarf into his hands. Did he have any choice? He was only obeying her instructions, he protested, as his pregnant wife turned pale with horror and backed away from him, with a low moan.

It wasn't over, even then. When, after all their grunting and heaving, the servants found out she was still alive, when, after all their pulling and tugging and sweating and straining, they discovered that she was still faintly breathing, in and out and in again and thinly out, when the strangling proved not to be enough, they prised her mouth open and stuffed the silk scarf down her throat with the butt of a rifle. They shoved and pushed and rammed and forced it, inch by inch, into her mouth till she hung limp and there was no sign of life left in her.

The Mayor's son had been obliged to hold her upright, as they did it. He had to force her on her knees and stand behind her, holding her under her arms while she died. He felt the full force of the rifle butt through his body as the men rammed into her. Her head fell back on his shoulder, her braids were loosened, and she was so fragrant, he sobbed, she died so fragrant. After she slumped forward and they turned her over in the dust, he saw that her eyes had never closed all that time. The bruises on her neck were terrible and her teeth were all broken, her mouth butchered and bleeding. But he could not bear to bend too close to know if she was still breathing. He drenched himself with *arak* afterwards, to be rid of the attar of roses.

When the first pains started, the daughter-in-law of the Mayor thought she was smelling roses. It was like her wedding day when the whole house became redolent; it was like the time when the poetess of Qazvin spoke of her Beloved and the two courtyards seemed to bloom. She did not notice the sickening tang of the burnt rue in the cellars or the stink of the throttled chicken. She just breathed roses when the pains began.

Dying takes so long, she thought in a daze, as the contractions intensified. The knocking seemed to grow louder and louder in the courtyard; it seemed to be shaking the gates down, knocking the walls down, breaking the whole house apart. Perhaps it's the midwife at last, groaned the poor girl. If it's not the midwife, then it'll be the death of me, she thought. But perhaps the baby's dead, she cried, in terror. What if there's no sign of life and it's stillborn? No, being dead was not the worst, she realized, and her eyes widened at the other possibility. Because there was another worst, another pain then, coming hot on the heels of the last one. Oh no! What if the child were alive and a girl?

It was more than she could bear. As her body was caught in a vice and torn apart, the squint-eyed daughter-in-law of the Mayor began to scream.

(16)

How empty the library was after her going! Her father stayed in there, touching the spines of the books, caressing the pages she used to read to him. He lingered the whole day in there after her escape, murmuring and weeping. How he missed the sound of her voice, her chanting. How he deplored the silence in the *anderoun*.

She had taken her pen case with her and her reeds, but it was only after several hours had passed that he noticed the gaps on the shelves. She had chosen carefully; she had selected only the most important to her, and the spaces where the books used to be mocked him, teased him with his ignorance of their titles. He had the impression that if he could only remember which ones she had chosen, he might be able to trace where she had gone.

But try as he might, he could not summon those texts to memory nor retain why it was that they had been so important to his daughter. He recalled their passionate arguments about them; he remembered their differing interpretations of them. But the substance of the books, which were the pivot of their talks, eluded him. He realized that those gaps on the library shelves bore witness to his greatest loss of all, for without the knowledge of what had once lain on them, the mind as well as the body of his beloved daughter had slipped between his fingers.

He fell into a profound melancholy after her departure and refused to mingle with the clerics in the mosque. He assumed less and less of his responsibilities in the theological college in the months that followed. He could not bring himself to lead the debates or the congregation to prayer either. Before a year had passed, he decided to quit the city and retire to Karbala. Everyone blamed his daughter for it, of course.

Although opinion was divided as to whether her father left Qazvin because of humiliation or heartache, they all cried fie upon the daughter of the house, too, when her mother died. Some said she sickened and succumbed to sorrow soon after news came of her daughter's capture and imprisonment. Others said she failed when her son-in-law packed up his children and set off for the capital, determined to accuse his cousin yet again before the newly crowned Shah. There was no reason for her to live after that. She had already lost her husband to all intents and purposes; she had also lost two of her daughters and one son in the purges of the Grand Vazir at the beginning of the new Shah's reign. She had been an erudite woman and a scholar in her own right, but they said she broke her reed pens and never wrote another word from that time on.

Two decades later, the father of the poetess of Qazvin also died without a will. Not that he possessed much to distribute among his heirs, for he had abdicated everything. He lived in extreme indigence, in a little room, in the crumbling corner of one of the theology schools in Karbala, having washed his hands of the wealth that, in his opinion, fuelled the feud which split the family asunder. But in addition to not writing any will, there was no testament found in his private coffers either. When he died, alone and self-exiled in the *'Ataba'at*, they could find no statement of belief among his papers, no witness to his faith which might be read at his funeral. It was curious, for a scholar whose reputation was so well-established, whose piety was so well-known, to die with his lips sealed in silence. It was bruited about afterwards that the only papers, found by the corpse washers, folded secretly inside the seams of his *'aba*, were his daughter's letters. For almost two decades he had brooded on the correspondence of a heretic.

Five years after the death of the priest in Karbala, the retired Envoy Plenipotentiary of her Britannic majesty also expired, in London. The Colonel's last days were similarly marked by solitude and a contemplation of absences. He had lost his wife several years before, and his grief deepened when he had to undertake the melancholy task of going through her private papers. The couple had spent part of the year in London and the rest of the time in the family estate in Ireland, but despite the punctual birth of infants, relations between them had remained strained. When the Colonel read his dead wife's diary, he realized how little he had known her all along.

Her ladyship had kept a day journal during her three-year sojourn in Persia, which her husband had insisted that she submit for publication on their return. A glimpse of life and manners seen through female eyes, the Colonel had urged, would offer a charming alternative to similar books in circulation. He had undertaken to cull his wife's diary himself, to purge it of too much sentiment, to lard it with a few more facts. It provided him with an excellent means of airing his own opinions under cover of her name. He had added copious endnotes amplified with shrewd political commentary, in light of the recent breakdown in Anglo-Persian relations and the war in the Crimea, with only a modest reference to the source of the scholarship. But he was bitterly disappointed by the few notices it received. He was particularly upset by one, which suggested that despite all his careful censorship, his wife was thought to have gone native. How, the reviewer caustically inquired, despite their evident barbarism, could her ladyship be so sympathetic towards Persian women?

Years later, when the widower reread the original day journal, he wondered whether the criticism had not been justified. His wife certainly had sympathies he did not altogether share. He knew that his early retirement, so soon after the resignation of his attaché, had led to all manner of unsavoury speculation about them. He himself had suspected her attachment to his chargé d'affaires and had only given up his post when forced to do so because of his jealousy of the Captain. But after the other man bowed out, he followed suit to everyone's surprise. It caused quite a flurry in the Foreign Office. Why were both diplomats abandoning the Mission within six months of each other? Why had the Colonel not retired earlier and left the Captain to take over from him or else not retired at all? Despite his ill health, the Envoy was asked to delay his departure until a replacement had been found. But his wife had refused to comply.

The reasons for it were kept confidential but eyebrows had been raised. Whatever it was her ladyship had said or done at that critical hour caused something of a crisis in the Foreign Office. It was assumed that the Colonel's departure was no more due to ill health than the Captain's to thwarted ambition, but that both men had been forced to leave because of a woman. As the Colonel pondered the pages of his wife's uncensored diary nineteen years later, however, he realized that that woman may not have been the one that he and the gossip columns had supposed.

He had not taken his wife's suggestion seriously when she urged him to lend his support to the liberation of the female prisoner who had been locked up in the house next door. Her subsequent reprieve and the controversy that it provoked amply justified his decision to keep clear of the business, for he could see there was a difference of opinion between the crown's decision and the determined aims of the clergy. So after the attempt on the life of the Shah, he was equally reluctant to intervene on her behalf. The daughter of the Russian ambassador had made a similar appeal to protect victims of the reprisals, that had backfired badly on the reputation of the Tsar, and he had no intention of compromising his own government. He had no scruples, however, in using the prisoner's plight to rid himself of his attaché.

The two men had had a dreadful row, up at the camps, immediately after the assassination attempt. The Captain insisted that the Envoy should return to town on the grounds that it would undermine the British position to be far from court at such a time. The Colonel adamantly refused to go, on precisely the same grounds, saying that it would jeopardize the British position to be at court at such a time. There was a standoff between them, in the sweltering tent that night. The Captain, who had had a little too much to drink by then, said he was going back into town whether the Colonel agreed with it or not. And the Colonel said good riddance and gave him an ultimatum. If he was drawn into the bloodbath in any way, or was obliged by the queen to participate in it, the Colonel would have him promptly recalled for interference in matters of national sovereignty. He would be obliged to resign for breach of conduct as a British subject.

But the Envoy was totally unprepared for what ensued. It was her ladyship who took a stand. News had already reached them that the French physician of the Shah had been poisoned in his own dispensary, and that an Austrian captain had decided to quit the country indefinitely because he could no longer bear the sight of the massacres through the streets. But when the British attaché rode up to the camp early the next morning with news that the poetess of Qazvin had been strangled in a garden north of the city the night before, the Envoy's wife put her foot down. She gave both men an ultimatum. She refused to stay in the country, she said, if the representatives of her majesty's government were unable to stop such cruel and useless deeds. She had taken a similar stand at the time the Shah's first Grand Vazir had fallen from power. The words she had used then had been echoed, uncannily and probably insincerely, some weeks later, by his superiors, but this time neither they nor his attaché had anything to do with it.

Her decision was to prove fatal to British presence in Persia. The Captain blamed the Colonel for the death of the innocent and condemned him for being a hypocrite. Were it not for the Envoy's double standards, he sneered, many might have been saved. The Colonel responded by accusing his attaché of cowardice and of complicity in the massacres. If he had been fool enough to take part in the bloodshed it was just because he was afraid of the queen's reprisals, and if he had not done so, it was only because he was afraid of the consequences to his career, so who was the greater hypocrite? he rounded. It was an appalling scene. Although the Captain quit the field immediately, to salvage his honour, it was only because he knew that the Colonel would be obliged to follow suit himself, for the sake of his reputation. For it was evident that the Envoy had been blackmailed by his wife. Her ladyship was said to have undermined British diplomacy, according to the gossip in Whitehall. But it took almost two decades for the Colonel to admit to himself that both he and his attaché may have been forced out of Persia by a heretic.

He had often wondered why her ladyship spent so much time in the Legation gardens. She was forever asking for an escort, to cross the street. During the last torrid months before the foolhardy attempt on the life of the Shah, he even imagined that his wife might have an assignation under the cypresses, given the frequency of her sorties. Was she really going there with such alacrity just to attend to the irrigation of cabbages and cauliflowers? Afterwards, he began to suspect that she was not meeting the Captain at all, but was trying to evade the seething jealousies, the furious feuds in the Legation. He realized, with dismay, that she was running over there simply to avoid him.

But it was only after her death, when he was brooding over the elisions and inferences in her diary, that he began to perceive a third possibility. And this interpretation was far more disturbing to him than those he had originally supposed. Had his wife fled into the garden because of the poetess of Qazvin, he wondered? When she lingered for hours under those dusty cypresses, was it because of the prisoner on the other side of the garden walls? The words of the heretic seemed to throb between the lines of her ladyship's diary. According to popular belief, she had told the soldiers just before she died that they could kill her as soon as they liked but they would never stop the emancipation of women. Had her ladyship converted to the same cause?

The Colonel was obsessed by the preposterous notion; it worked on his nerves; it gnawed on him, like a tooth. The suffragettes had been ridiculed by the press on one side of the planet and the poetess of Qazvin denounced by the clergy on the other, but he could not banish from his mind that this was no coincidence and that there was some mysterious connection, some serendipitous association between them. For his wife seemed to have been influenced by both.

It was very disturbing to the Colonel to contemplate her ladyship's heresies in his last dark days in London. It was unnerving to realize she may have been a different wife from the one he thought he had known. He would almost have preferred to believe her unfaithful, than so immoderately free of him. His intention, to transfer her remains from Ireland had not, as yet, been accomplished, and he felt the unoccupied emptiness of the family vault keenly. But he feared she may have already resurrected without him, and in a wholly unexpected way.

⟨ 17 ⟩

Three days afterwards, she said, a woman would come.

That must be her now, knocking, thought the Wife of the Mayor. Too soon, she thought. Too late. She stared at the revolving knife on the kitchen floor with red eyes, for she had been chopping greens and onions as an excuse to be weeping. A dropped knife was a bad omen on a day when a child was to be born. Her daughter-in-law had gone into labour too soon, too late; the poetess of Qazvin was gone. And three days after her death, this woman had come, in the middle of the day, in heat of the noonday sun.

It was the infernal month of the year and too hot for words. The empty pool in the courtyard had wrinkled under the sun; the blue glazed tiles seemed to have been boiled brown. The sun smote the rooftops, like a drunken muleteer flogging his donkey in the bazaar, like the man at the street corner tossing roast giblets on the coals, like a woman's nagging tongue. Her husband had been gone for three nights in a row, but she asked no questions. She knew he was in the thick of it, fawning on the Chief Steward, grovelling at the feet of the Mother of the Shah, currying favour with the Prime Minister, who wanted to avoid responsibility for all the deaths in the town. The man had no scruples. An opportunist who shifted loyalties with the breeze.

Except that there was no breeze to be had in the courtyard of the Mayor's house. It was hotter than the bread ovens that summer, and the air was heavier than the cook's breath. The slabs of ice dug from the northern trenches and sold by the street vendors in the early mornings did not help either. Ice for sale, sweet ice! The day before the soldiers came for the poetess of Qazvin, the Mayor's Wife had found a dead rat in a lump of winter ice.

"Sweet, my foot," she said. "Paying good money to ruin the sherbet!"

But after they took the prisoner away, the Wife of the Mayor had concentrated on pickles to keep herself sane. She had thrown herself into a frenzy of vinegar and brine and forced the sighing cook to set about chopping herbs and onion greens in the sweltering kitchens, slicing garlic, stewing aubergine and fenugreek. She marinated everything she could lay her hands on, till the courtyard reeked and the sharp tang of pickles clung to the air. But nothing covered the smell of death in the streets and in the market square.

The knife rotated one last time and came to a slow stop, pointing towards the kitchen door, beyond which the courtyard blazed, the arch beckoned, and the passageway led past the servants quarters towards the gate. Knocking. Three days after. The voice of her sister-in-law echoed across the courtyard. She was calling out to the idiot, telling him to hurry up and open the gate. Three days after the prisoner's death and the woman had come for the packet of books.

The voice of the Mayor's Wife died in her throat when she was told to deny it afterwards. "I had never met that woman before, nor did I ever see her again," she faltered. Her son had instructed her on what to say when he learnt, several hours later, who it was that had come to the gate. Repeat it, he urged. Repeat after me—

"I had never before met that woman, nor did I ever see her again," she said.

If you so much as hint that you know her, he warned, we'll all be slaughtered. And he drew his finger across his throat. Like sheep, he added, unnecessarily.

The Mayor's son was afraid of the truth. He had good ears, her boy, nicely shaped ears close to his head, but it had to be admitted that his eyes were too small and he was easily frightened. He saw narrowly, and was too concerned with his own safety.

Her guest had always had the opposite problem. She believed that truth conquered fear. It's so obvious, she used to say, all aglow; it's as beautiful as logic. The Mayor's Wife had shrugged wryly and replied, your logic, my logic, seeing is what people want to see. Oh no! the poetess had laughed. There's a pure logic everyone accepts and anyone can understand, an eternal logic. It's like mathematics, like the movement of the stars that allows you to read truth in the universe. She just loved the truth, that was her problem. That woman never lied.

The Mayor's Wife squared her plump shoulders and took a deep breath. "I never met her before, and never saw her again," she lied, turning away from her son.

Denial was difficult in the face of proof. The poetess of Qazvin knew every quotation, every commentary, chapter and verse, back to front. They could not fault her with a reference, could not trip her on a single citation.

It drove them crazy. Her rules for debate with the clerics had been strict: stick to the text, avoid execration, and do not smoke. But the mullahs cursed her to her face after the assassination attempt on the Shah. They had been given a week to conclude their findings this second time and there was no more pretending. They had to decide whether she was fit for re-education, or whether she was unredeemable, that's how they put it. Could she be raised from her benighted condition or would she resist guidance? If she was amenable, she might live, they said. If not, well, they were to recommend other measures. And it was clear from the shifty look in their eyes which logic they intended to follow. Certainly not her kind.

The poetess laughed in their faces when they said it. If you have no compassion on yourself, the Mayor's Wife had told her, after the clerics left in high dudgeon, then at least take pity on those men. Consider their pride, she said. Tell them a few lies. But the poetess laughed all the more. The Mayor's Wife was afraid lest that dangerous laughter reached the ears of the Mother of the Shah. Humour is the worst of heresies in the kingdom of pride.

All those words wasted, she sighed, drawing her headscarf forward and preparing herself to cross the scalding courtyard: all that theological fuss and bother, all those arguments about what God means and what He says and whether He does and what He wants and everything boils down to human stupidity in the end. And pride. God has nothing to do with it, said the Mayor's Wife to herself, blinking her tears away at the breezeway steps. He doesn't give a fart.

Her guest had always been so polite. "I am preparing to meet my Beloved," she had said, "and wish to free you from the cares and anxieties of my imprisonment." No one else talked like that. She sounded as though she came out of a book. What cares, what anxieties, blubbered the Mayor's Wife, clinging to her hand. Her Beloved. Oh, for a Beloved such as hers!

The Mayor's Wife choked back a sob as she looked up and saw her husband's sister, at that moment, standing in the breezeway, red-eyed. She remembered all the words wasted about her son's marriage, all the fuss and bother, the arguments with her husband about what he wanted and what

she said and whether he would and why she did and it had all boiled down
to a betrayal in the end. And pride. Love had nothing to do with it. She
didn't care if the Mayor's sister saw her crying now. But it looked as if she
had been crying herself. Or was she just half-blind?

Her son had shaken her by the shoulders when she became hysterical.
He didn't want anyone to know. For God's sake control yourself, mother!
he muttered. If my father sees you in this condition he'll betray us. Do you
want us all killed because of that woman?

That woman? The Mayor's Wife blew her nose on the hem of her skirts,
struggling to control the tears. She was closer to me than my life's vein,
she thought. She was dearer to me than a sister, a daughter, a mother. She
was fit to meet a king and worthy of the courts of heaven and proof of the
only freedom a woman could attain. That woman was freer than the air, she
concluded, with another sniff, even though she was buried in the bottom
of a well.

She had requested that her body should be thrown into a pit after her
death. She had asked specifically that the pit be filled with earth and stones.
Afterwards, the night the soldiers took her away, the Mayor's Wife had
broken down and sobbed when her son told her what they had done; she
had almost fainted and could not bear to hear his part in it. She had been
weeping so much that she could barely breathe.

There was a well, he said, an unfinished well that had been dug and
left open in the orchard. The gardener had helped him lower her into the
open hole as the Sardar snored and his men belched under the trees. They
had dropped her body down into the darkness; she had fallen forwards,
with an unpleasant cracking sound, but the hardest thing was the stones.
Shovelling the earth. Throwing the stones into the awful, velvet softness.
They only stopped when they no longer heard her silence underneath the
clatter. Each time the Mayor's Wife thought of what lay bruised and broken in the bottom of that well, she burst into fresh tears.

The poetess of Qazvin had authored her own death, her son insisted.
She had prophesied exactly what would happen and had made sure it came
true. He could not be held responsible for it. He was washing his hands

of it, and so should his mother if she wanted to avoid trouble, he warned. "That woman willed her end," he said. "She had always wanted to die."

But the Mayor's Wife protested that no one had loved life so much. Why, you should have seen her dressing her daughter in pretty clothes, she told her son; she took pleasure in every mouthful. It wasn't because she willed her end but because she could read it coming. Knowing what's coming doesn't make it happen, she said. You can't blame a woman for sunrise, just because she anticipates the dawn. You can't accuse her of causing a flood if she sees the river rising. If the poetess of Qazvin had deciphered the logic of the stars it was only because she saw their signs in the dust. If she dipped her pen into the future it was only because she had turned the page of the past. She argued against the interpretations of the old books of men precisely because she had deciphered a different meaning in the Mother Book of her heart.

"My guest," the Mayor's Wife always used to say to the ladies who visited the house, "is a great one for books."

When she was first placed under house arrest, the poetess used to flatten out vegetable wrappings to use as paper, and chewed up herbs in her mouth for ink; she used to write with the spliced reeds she selected from the mats at her feet too. As though the whole floor was for scribbling on, the Mayor's Wife had said, scandalized, when she first discovered it. As though the whole house was there to be read. Line after line, stroke after stroke she covered the rough scraps with writing; dot after dot, curve after curve she smoothed them under her palm. From the first point to the last phrase, her letters were green with love. The laundry woman delivered them.

She was writing to her sister, she said, when the Mayor's Wife found her at it.

How could you call that heresy? she protested to her husband. Let her write to her womenfolk, she had pleaded. What's wrong with that? Nothing, nothing in the world, except that she wrote and wrote, especially after the strictures were lifted. Except that she read too, and taught others reading. Except that the Mother of the Shah heard of it and the mullahs arraigned her for spreading the heresy. She wrote to her sister, her cousins, her aunts.

She wrote on behalf of her daughter and to her mother. Books she wrote, not letters. And by the time the attempt was made on the life of the Shah, she had written a legacy to the women of the world.

The Mayor's Wife turned towards the breezeway. She was grateful that her sister-in-law had ordered the idiot to open the gates so that she would not have to lie about it. She could swear to her husband that she had never opened the gate to anyone. She would say nothing about the package. It was a grave responsibility to be left in charge of a legacy. It was a risky business.

"Three days after my death, a woman will come to visit you to whom you will give this package," the poetess had said. And the Mayor's Wife had accepted that charge.

Above all, her son pleaded afterwards, don't mention that package. Say nothing about it. Deny those books absolutely. Promise me, he begged his mother, when he had returned home to her, ashen, in the bleak hours of that terrible morning, when he had told her to stop weeping and pretend. Promise me, he said, that you won't let my father know that she left a package with you.

It had been her last request, the last favour she had asked for, such a small thing to do. The Mayor's Wife felt her throat tighten. Redolent with the perfume, wreathed in smiles, the poetess of Qazvin had delivered the package into her hands. It was wrapped in cloth, the four corners folded, one side over the other in the Persian way, wrapped and re-wrapped again, first in precious silks and tapestries, to protect the binding. Then in cotton print tied cross ways at the corners, first on one side, then on the other. She knew what it contained. Words too painful to remember, too beautiful to forget. Books that she had read, and re-read.

That package, her son was telling her, is dangerous; it is filled with heresies. If the dead woman's husband finds out about it when he comes to fetch his daughter, we'll be done for. Having the child of the heretic on the premises is already a liability, but her books are a thousand times worse. Don't you say a word about those books, said her son grimly, or it'll be our turn next.

She looked sadly at her cowardly son, when he asked her to deny the truth, to deny the books that the poetess of Qazvin had taught her how to read. She had half a mind to keep them for herself. But she could not disobey the prisoner's last request, even if she had to deny it.

She had prophesied that the soldiers would come and they came. She had said that they would kill her and they did. And she knew that a woman would arrive, three days after her death, to retrieve the books. And here she was. Knocking on the heart of the Mayor's Wife. If the Shah ever betrayed the Mayor, as the prisoner had predicted, his Wife swore that she would never lie again. She would never deny again. For even as she went upstairs to retrieve the package that the prisoner had given her, she dreaded the familiarity of the face behind those gates.

(18)

So was it all for this, Beloved? Was it all leading to this little bundle in the end, a package the size of a stillborn baby? Were the plots and conspiracies, the imprisonments and interrogations, the stabbings, poisonings, jealousies and recriminations, nothing but words wrapped in Persian silk, sentences transcribed by hand? Were kings killed and ministers murdered, mayors hanged and mullahs stabbed just for the sake of a few books, manuscripts embossed in leather, loosely bound?

Stories have no presumptions. They are not dictated by angels but written to assuage the demons. These books were not holy, I promise you. Let the priests toll those bells. None of these was the Mother Book, even if there were mothers in them. If there were daughters, sisters, wives in these pages, it's only because we cannot be read whole. We come to the last chapter split in parts, Beloved; we come scattered in fragments, torn. There is no such thing as a complete woman in this world.

But is none of it true, then? Was it all made up, invented?

There's always space between the stones for flesh and blood. What of the assignation in the dusty garden, the strangling in the dark and suffocation in the well? These were not fictions surely, fabrications only, tales told in the half-light. Remember the limp body, wrapped in white silk and thrown into a pit, without rhyme or reason? This was not just a story told to keep the *jinn* from the kitchen door! A woman's death, Beloved, is not too small a truth to prove the miracle of living.

But maybe we don't like being told all. Too much confidence is presumptuous in a woman. Why remember the bruises round her throat, the words half-heard in the dark, the breath that passed like a last faint sigh through her parted lips. We prefer the inferred. It is easier to cling to the brink of doubt than fall into such certitudes. Perhaps she was just too alive, in the last analysis. They had to roll a boulder over her to break her back, after all; they had to shovel dust over the edge of the well, to fill her lungs, to finally still her. There was too much breath in her.

But how else could she have avoided blame?

Forget that. The only breathing space down here is prayer. Relieve me, Beloved, from the craving to blame, the desire to persuade, from the hunger that gnaws at its own need, that sups on its own appetite to convince. Take from me the cup that would arouse the thirst it promises to slake, and grant instead the recompense decreed for those who forsook all that they possessed, who spoke for love, and left the rest unsaid.

But in the name of heaven, doesn't her erasure merit being recorded?

Spare me such coins. For I would rather be a beggar at your gate, Beloved. I would rather go laughing to the grave and unacknowledged, like the one whose turban rolled before the axe struck off his head. Preserve me from the prose of the marketplace that promises interest on what cannot be sold. Let me not die cursing, like a cleric in his bed, a body of text passed reverently from hand to hand, from which the soul has fled.

No marker on her grave, then? None. No sign of where that last sigh rose between the stones? They stamped the earth flat with their feet before they left. They spat on their palms as they parted at the garden gate. They avoided each other's eyes. The Austrian doctor had gone long since; only the Mayor's son lingered and saw all.

And can funeral rites be offered, at least, without offending?

But to what avail? For I would do it again, Beloved, endure it all again for this last moment. I would submit to every humiliation to lay my legacy at your door. Let it be as small a bundle as you will. It is the little truths that finally point towards the larger ones. We cast the piece of cloth off our faces only because we want to bare the soul.

I would be laid to rest, Beloved, to be free.

So raise me gently in your kind hands, and lay me on the cold trestle.
Lay me as a woman leans towards her lover without a light,
as a girl bends towards the breathing mirror.
Lay me under a cotton sheet of silence to await the dawn,
as a virgin waits with eager dread,
for the first breeze of desire to pass across the bed,
And do not leave my body long exposed.

Wash me quickly then in the soft waters of cassia and forgiving nard,
for I am fragile with the restlessness of living.
Caress me with jujube leaves and patient lavender,
for I am weary of this long, slow fast of dying.
Anoint my limbs with camphor and my brow with myrrh,
that neither spite nor malice might exploit me.
And since I have been overgenerous with my secrets,
let no man now disappoint me.

Smooth my curls with fragrant oils that were too tangled in my days.
Comb my thick hair and divide it now, and for always.
And let one braid hang over my right shoulder and another over my left,
to ensnare the angels.
And let the third lie thick behind me like a mother's hand
to cradle the nape of my neck.

And when all my clefts and crevices are rinsed
and every sore and callous smoothed,
grant me the recompense of a clean shroud.
Fold me in the fabric of endurance and wrap me in fortitude.
Wind me in the sere cloths, the warping cloths finer than any breath;
cover me in the weaving cloths, the sheer cloths that net the soul in death.
It would slip through, else, like a silver fish in the Caspian;

it would leap the waves and escape naked to the clasp of wider oceans.
We must be wrapped, they say, both coming and going, for pure mercy's sake,
that our beauty might not blind the angels.
So cover me in gossamer cloths as thin as humility will allow.
Dress me in a shroud of purest silk to go.

Strike up the drum and play the flute then, to the burial ground, and do not wail;
make music for my recompense and dance me to the sun.
Deck me with costly shawls and carry me on a silken bier then, do not fail,
For I shall give no hindrance: a woman is always ready to be gone.

Let none whom the earth is unwilling to forgive, bruise the dust for my sake.
Let no one who has groped for love blindly in the night, or lusted through the
valley of gold, or broken trust on the submissive hills of waiting long enough,
loose the shroud from my lips or try to slake too soon my eager thirst.
Grant that I might slip unseen into the silent places.
Fête my funeral like a wedding feast for I would be preserved from bitterness.
I would be lowered with gratitude into the thieving earth,
untouched by doubt, unscathed by expectation, and unmarked by grieving.

Woe betide the one who walks before or treads too close to my body.
Woe betide him who does not bow his head as I pass,
for the angel of death has spread his wings above my body;
let none wink therefore before the last brick is in place.
Let no one pay the midwife at my passing,
but she whose gnarled hands grant the last caressing.
And let none spit the date stone out before the sweet flesh is sucked away,
for a woman lingers longer than most among the dying.

Where is my mother to cradle my head, to suckle and hold me close?
For the man I married was always a child and the child that I loved is a ghost.

Where is my sister to weep at my feet and warn the world why I died?
For there'll never be peace in the grave for him who hollows a place at my side.

.   .   .

*May my daughter be free and unfettered by fear, may she treasure the days of her
life: may she think of me as a woman who loved, though I was only a wife.*

*My woes are written in crimson ink; my doubts are inscribed in black.
But the love in my heart is traced in gold and the name of my soul is light.*

❨ 19 ❩

Eternity stood at the gates of the Mayor's house.

I was nobody's sister, nobody's mother, nobody's wife but I must have been time's daughter for it seemed I had been standing at that gate forever.

One has to read forwards and backwards simultaneously in such circumstances. I was waiting there for the books, but I was prepared to drop everything and run for it, the minute that mad dog came any closer. The power of words to transform the world depended on the distance between a dog and a gate at that moment; it hovered in the gap between trust and fear. Her legacy to us was that uncertain, the future of women in Persia that precarious. It hung on a prayer.

To read is to pray, she used to tell us: to write is to trust. Illiteracy is fear. She wanted us to be fearless, to see with our own eyes, hear with our own ears and read the books of creation and revelation for ourselves. She taught us to take risks.

If a daughter cannot move for fear of error, for terror of doing wrong, she used to say, let her give her body to the northern winds a little more each day, beseeching aid from the Unfathomable, the Unknown, beseeching courage from the Uncreated.

If a daughter cannot dream at night for frustration, she used to tell us, let her sleep with her face turned south, seeking relief from the Most-Merciful, the Clear.

If a daughter tastes bile on her tongue and bitterness in swallowing, let her lift her palms to the western skies and ask assistance from the Limpid, the All-Wise.

And if a daughter cannot breathe on rising because of filial expectations, let her address her dawn prayers to the Unconstrained, the Unrestrained, the Wild.

There was no mention of dogs in the prayer, but she urged us not to be too literal-minded. It is an occupational hazard for women, she said. We have many roles but only one vocation. Wives we may be, according to dowry, decision or destiny. Mothers we can become, by accident or by design. And not every woman is a sister, even lawfully. But daughterhood comes with the casing: that we're locked in. And while there are many ways to fail the obligation, there is no way to change the fact. Only remember, she used to add, smiling, there's more to literacy than facts.

I knew that the gate of the Mayor's house on which I knocked that day was the threshold between facts and fictions. What was happening then as well as just before each knock on that door, would happen again and again. The sound of that knocking would be heard across the courtyards of the centuries. Years after the books were delivered and I was no longer midwife to them, it would still echo, it would still reverberate in our hearts. Her books were a legacy to the unborn daughters of the world.

She taught me literacy while I was still a maid, and by the time I had become a wet-nurse and a midwife, I'd learned all the different ways to handle texts. And all the dangers involved. I knew, when I finally held her legacy in my hands, that if you read a book from the feet forwards, you risk rewriting it, but if you begin with the roots of the hair and work backwards, you could erase everything read. It is a terrifying responsibility. I had no illusions about it, when I stood at the gates of the Mayor's house. The gatekeeper must have guessed my state of mind, because he was weeping when he drew back the bolts. The Mayor's Wife must have known it too, because she barely looked at me as she thrust the package in my arms. She did not even speak. She pushed the bundle through the gap and turned her back on me.

If you want to read the next word, the poetess used to tell us, let go of the last one. If you want to know what lies ahead, love and leave what came before.

There is no denying that reading is a risky business. But since I've been a washer of the living and the dead, I've understood that direction is immaterial in the last analysis. The ancient look on the face of a new-born can mirror the features of the deceased. One has to be flexible in this business. And a corpse washer has to know everything about detachment. Personally, beggar that I am, I take up the first passage that catches my eye now, and simply read by random divination.

We of the cemetery have professional standards to maintain. Detachment is part of the job and so is confidentiality. We close their eyes before we shroud the dead, to shield them from shame. We tie up their mouths, so it doesn't look as if they've been telling tales. We mop up their stains and protect their pride with cotton balls, and, depending on the fee, we tuck crutches under their arms so they can show respect to the angels and defy the accusations of the *jinn*. A perfect corpse should never put a foot wrong: that's why we knot their toes together. But we never let them suspect that we can read them. It's part of our contract to maintain illusions.

My specialty is women when it comes to corpses, and I can tell you, most of them carry their illusions to the grave. The sister of the Mayor and her nieces were buried with theirs intact, as was the daughter-in-law in the cellars who never knew she'd been delivered of a girl the same day that she died. But the Mayor's Wife lost all her illusions for love: she lied to protect the woman who spoke the truth and died to speak the truth herself. And the Mother of the Shah came to the same end: stripped of illusions no matter how reluctantly she relinquished them, a corpse herself long before she left the land of the living. Her daughter, however, had so few illusions to begin with that she gave hers up easily. All she was left with was a shroud of bitterness, which was of little value to her. Worms take no heed of cynicism.

There was no reason to hang around there at the Mayor's gates, once I received the books. As soon as the Mayor's Wife turned her back on me, I fled. I turned and ran down that alley for dear life. I ran, partly to protect the books and partly to protect my heels, because there's only one thing worse than a mad dog in this world and that's a bad conscience. Some can recognize the hyacinth of reunion from a thousand leagues away, but I could snuff the odours of separation the minute I saw the Mullah's son turning into the alley from the market square. He had arrived at the Mayor's house to take his daughter back to Qazvin, even as her mother's books were being delivered to the world.

The dead have rights too, she used to tell us. Words were once living breath.

To be honest, I was not thinking of the rights of the dead at that moment; I confess I was only thinking of myself. If the Mullah's son had found those books on me, he would have battered me to death on the spot. He would have burned the books too, afterwards. If they were not destroyed, it was because of a mad dog.

The only thing books cannot overcome is our collective cowardice.

Being literate is not easy, she used to tell us, when we invented our own fictions to avoid the facts. She knew very well how much simpler it was to pretend illiteracy. She knew when we were bluffing, when we were only reading what we memorized. Her own daughter took refuge in similar illusions. She grew into a staid and respectable woman in the end, who allowed her husband to censor everything. Since she could not say that her mother was right without admitting that her father was wrong, she denied the heresies of the former in order to defend her from the latter's orthodoxy. Although she was always haunted by the legacy she lost, she never knew the one she gave up. She did not care to read her mother's books.

Who can blame her? The poetess of Qazvin defied definition, resisted explanation. Each time we read her texts, we came up with different meanings. Each time we tried to remember what she said, we violated her all over again. She lay mute at the bottom of a well, and we pelted her with our interpretations, our denials and allegations, our distortions and perversions. We buried her daily, beneath our stones.

Corpses and books are a contradictory lot. Their vulnerability is heartrending, their detachment infuriating. They never acknowledge attention, never admit gratitude, but you would be hard pressed to find such humility among the living. They don't ask for charity either: you can read them or not, preserve them or pulp them as you will, but I dare say they all hope to receive some kindness, courtesy of the management.

It's best to beg while you still have breath, that's my motto. The compassion of the All-Merciful is infinite, but you never know who else might interpret you in the interim. On that fatal day of the royal jubilee, I had nudged my way as close as I dared to the door of the shrine without violating the premises, but I had no idea that the King of Kings was going to fall on me. Although several customers had dropped newly minted coins into my palm that morning, stamped with the sovereign's head, I never dreamed of receiving the original for my prayers. What had I done to deserve the Pivot of the Universe in my lap? Or rather what crime had I committed to warrant this punishment, other than reading the books of the poetess of Qazvin?

I could tell from the way he eyed me that the Shah knew I was a literate beggar. I could see from that look on his face as he fell that he guessed I was one of those innumerable nobodies who had inherited the legacy of the poetess. If I dropped my veil at that moment it was only because there was nothing left to conceal. But in fact, he may have misinterpreted me in the end. I'm afraid his majesty thought I was one of the angels, or a *jinn* waiting to interrogate him at the gates of eternity.

I've been reading the dead for half a century, but before that moment I had never experienced the ecstasy of being read by a dying man.

AFTERWORD

On a tombstone
in a city cemetery of Qazvin
is carved a gruesome image of a murder:
a praying mullah is being stabbed in the back by a masked man.
Half concealed by a curtain behind him, a woman looks on.
In her hand she holds a sheet of paper,
incriminating evidence
of her literacy.*

This book has been inspired by the life of a nineteenth-century Persian woman. It is a tribute to Tahirih Qurratu'l-Ayn, a renowned poet and theologian, radical and outcast, who rejected the sharia law more than a century and a half ago and was killed for daring to oppose the orthodoxy of her times. It is also a *memento mori* on the deaths of certain prominent men in Qajar history, a meditation on a monarch, a mayor, a minister, and the murdered mullah himself, who still lies beneath the marbled tombstone, which condemns Tahirih to eternity. Finally, it retrieves a buried history backwards, from the assassination of Nasiru'd-Din Shah in 1896 to the first attempt against his life in 1852, in order to reconstruct the world of Qajar women and tell the unrecorded stories of mothers, daughters, sisters, and wives in nineteenth-century Iran. In so doing, I hope it also shows the relevance of these lost stories for today.

The facts about the life of Tahirih Qurratu'l-Ayn are few and far between.

---

* By kind permission of Farzaneh Milani, taken from *Veils and Words: Emerging Voices of Iranian Women Writers*, Syracuse University Press, 1992.

Although her name may be familiar to more people than that of her powerful contemporary, Mahd-i-Olya, the mother of the Shah, very little is actually known about her. In fact, we know more about what is not known than what is. Her date of birth, for example, is uncertain. The exact circumstances of her death are equally unclear. The details of her marriage and divorce are ambiguous, as is the question of whether she abandoned her children or they were taken from her. Nor do we know if she was to blame for the ideological split in her family or if it had already occurred in the previous generation. Did her espousal of the faith of Siyyid Ali Muhammad, the Bab, cause more outrage or her presumption in assuming theological leadership in Karbala and Baghdad? How did she escape from the confines of Qazvin, and where did she spend her years of wandering before her final capture? Did she really have an interview with Nasiru'd-Din Shah in the capital or meet his mother? And what precisely happened that led to her decision, if it was her independent decision, to cast aside her veil in public at Badasht? These are all questions without answers or rather with too many of them. Even her name changed several times. At a time when most women were formally labelled according to relationships either to husbands, fathers, brothers, or sons, she had a variety of appellations, as if indicative of the multiple perspectives needed to analyze the course of her life. Which of these women—Umm Salma, Zarrin Taj, Fatimih Baraghani Qurratu'l-Ayn, or Tahirih—are we talking about?

When basic elements are missing from a story, conjecture is inevitable. When there are gaps in a history, assumptions invariably ensue. But fiction feeds on the gaps; it thrives on conjecture. I wrote a fiction inspired by the life of Tahirih rather than a biography based on her life because literature allows for contrary interpretations to exist simultaneously. I cast this story in quasi-allegorical form because metaphor seemed a more appropriate way to explore the world of a poet. Besides, I am neither a historian nor a biographer, and the only way I knew how to unite the shifting points of view about this woman was through literature.

Tahirih was a paradox. Her courage was unquestionable, but was it because she was heroic or foolhardy? Her suffering proves her humanity, but was it imposed or perhaps self-inflicted? Was she a visionary who lived ahead of her age or just a fanatical follower of a doomed cause? Her intelligence and erudition were certainly intimidating to her contemporaries, but would we respond to her with less prejudice today? The dilemmas she faced, as a daughter and mother, as a sister and wife, are entirely familiar to us, but did she push idealism to the point of callous indifference? Might she have survived if she had been less absolute? Perhaps we make so much of her only because she was a woman. In the end, it is hard to know the truth about Qurratu'l-Ayn because her sympathizers and critics have both distorted it.

During her lifetime, Tahirih's name was synonymous with scandal. And since her death, she has been appropriated by causes with which she may have had little in common. While the majority of her countrymen denounced her in the past, on false grounds as well as true, her fame spread to the West during the nineteenth century, a phenomenon which only confirmed the worst suspicions of her opponents. Foreign diplomats, travellers, and scholars wrote of her. Sarah Bernhardt even commissioned a play about her. Her ideals were taken up enthusiastically in Austria and the Netherlands, in America, in Russia, and in France, and aspects of her life have been turned into poems, plays, tapestries, and *tableaux vivants* ever since. No doubt many scholars as well as artists will be inspired to write about her in years to come, but while there may never be a universal interpretation of her, the irony is that Tahirih has become a universal figure. She is the first modern Iranian woman to belong to the world.

In spite of this or maybe even because of it, her cultural context is of vital importance. We need to know where she came from in order to better evaluate who she was. Research on nineteenth-century Persia began decades ago, and though the general public may still be unaware of it, the patterns woven into this complex carpet have become familiar to scholars and academics. But their appreciation has been selective, for the loops and knots of women's lives in this period were largely invisible and not often recorded. Although women in the West were scribbling themselves into popular consciousness at the time, the personal confessions of their Persian counterparts are less well-known. In fact, the subject was as unorthodox as Qurratu'l-Ayn herself until relatively recently. It is only in the twentieth century that Iranian women have begun to publish their autobiographies, and only in the last decade that personal archives relating to the world of Qajar women have been available in the public sphere.*

Much of this background material naturally belongs to the more privileged members of that society, but what is missing still stimulates conjecture, invites invention. So I structured this novel on the characters of real mothers, daughters, sisters, and wives in an attempt to recuperate the lives that have disappeared between the lines of history. I hoped by this means to create a foil against which to contrast how Tahirih defied these traditional roles herself, and to invite readers to appreciate the impact she had on her culture and her times. The ordinary women who inspired these fictive characters were part of this world. What we know about them may be sparse or contradictory, minimal and ambiguous, but the act of imaginative recuperation can, I hope, revive them. They are not named, but they were alive.

* http://www.qajarwomen.org/en/

The lack of names is also important in this novel. Names in Qajar society, whether of men or women, more often covered than distinguished individual identity. So many of them were emblematic of iconic figures from Islamic history that the actual person behind these common appellations often disappeared. This is one of the reasons why the characters in this novel have been identified by roles instead of names and by their various titles in Qajar society. They have been stripped of that cloth of common piety they wore in life, in order to achieve a greater universality.

Stripping away the veil will always be a rich metaphor in Tahirih's story, though not for the reasons we attach to it today. We define it as an emblem of sexual identity, of religious faith, of cultural expression. She saw it as evidence of prejudice, literalism, and uniformity. We have turned it into a political icon, a bargaining chip, a sign of democratization. She rejected it because it represented manipulation, and oppression. We may associate the veil with threatened identity and cultural anxiety at a time of change. She recognized the birth of a new epoch in these signs, and deployed the veil to symbolize the decline of the old one. But in the last analysis Tahirih saw beyond materialistic and theological interpretations. We are obsessed with the veil because it draws attention to the body which it covers. Tahirih cast it aside to prove that she had a soul.

If the future of this worn theme is to be less conflicted than its past, perhaps we also need to redefine our understanding of time. This is why the prophetic insights of Qurratu'l-Ayn also inspired me in this novel, and her ability to see beyond her epoch is one of its central themes. Its chronology has been reversed in order to trace the links between her prophetic words and the men who held power over her contemporaries. Although the action moves forwards from the moment of her capture to the time of her death, three-and-a-half years later, it is simultaneously moving backwards from the assassination of a monarch at the end of the nineteenth century, through the hanging of a mayor, the death of a minister, and finally the murder of a mullah at its midway point. Tahirih Qurrat'ul-Ayn was innocent of their downfall, but there is no doubt that her demand for justice, her defiance of norms, and her determination to demonstrate the truth of her ideas through reasoned argument, was perceived as a direct threat by each of them. Her words, some of which have survived in popular sayings, proved this, and they retained such power that she was often accused of creating the crisis she anticipated and of masterminding the catastrophes against which she warned her contemporaries.

Since she refused orthodoxy, this novel too had to be somewhat unorthodox. Her heresy arose from religious beliefs; mine may have contravened literary genres. She embraced the cause of Siyyid Ali Muhammad, the Bab, whose teachings about the relativity, the continuity, and the progressive nature of religious truth offended the religious canon of the times. I have written neither a strictly historical novel nor one which obeys the conventions of the commercial market by following the Western literary tradition of psychological realism. It is a challenge to translate the dilemma that Tahirih posed over a hundred years ago in a form that would appeal to readers today, to capture the timbre and texture of her voice in a language different from her own.

In the end, anyone who writes about her has to try to follow her example, for Tahirih was, in effect, the symbolic mother of women's literature in modern Iran. According to certain sources, she pioneered the spread of female literacy during her brief life. Although the women of her own family were unusually privileged in this regard and had been raised, under its clerical influence, to read and write like the princesses of the court, most women in Qajar Persia were not given any such education. But Tahirih is said to have run literacy classes, in Qazvin as well as in Karbala and Baghdad; she taught wives of merchants and daughters of tradesmen how to read and write for themselves, how to think and question the Quranic traditions. A few women who were her students became poets in their own right over time, and left records for the future. It was a revolutionary act, and a precious legacy inherited by whoever has attempted since to tell her tale.

Tahirih cannot be contained in a single story. Each time someone writes about her, it will inspire another to do so differently, because in the end her many paradoxes hold a mirror to our faces that shows us contradictory aspects of ourselves. As Henry James has said, there is always a seed of truth from which each story springs, a small hard fact that germinates into fiction under the influence of the imagination. And there are enough ambiguous and contradictory details associated with the life of Tahirih to fill a never-ending library.

The germ of this particular tale lies in the story recalled by the wife of the Kalantar, or Mayor of Tehran, in whose house Tahirih spent the last three-and-a-half years of her life. When this woman describes the circumstances of that last summer of 1852, she says that in the midst of the bloody reprisals after the attempt on the life of the Shah, the prisoner placed a bundle in her hands and told her to give it to the person who would come to the door, three days after her death. She did not tell her what the bundle contained. And the Mayor's Wife does not tell us if she asked; she does not say any more about it. But when she concludes her story by revealing that a woman did indeed come to her door to receive the bundle, just as predicted, she adds an enigmatic disclaimer: "I had never seen that woman before," she says, "nor did I ever see her again."

I built my story on this disclaimer.

Was the Mayor's Wife telling the truth or was that statement simply intended to protect herself and her family? Who was the woman, and were there indeed books in that bundle? If so, what happened to them? Were they destroyed or hidden? Might they still be found, or were they lost, erased, and forgotten? Texts were dangerous for the early Babis. They were often obliged to burn, bury, and obliterate their books. Sometimes, they washed the ink off the paper to avoid persecution. They were even driven to chew, swallow, and ingest their sacred texts. Or else, oblivion and denial saved them. If the corpse washer serves any purpose in this story, it is to link us with these forgotten texts, to reclaim these buried words. She is not only a symbol of the reader but also of the writer who retrieves and tries to honour the body of the past.

Tahirih Qurratu'l-Ayn was never given proper funeral rites. Her figure may have been carved in stone, but she was never granted the honour of an epitaph. Her bones lie lost beneath the traffic of modern-day Tehran. But her dramatic life and death, her fearless eloquence and idealism, have left deep marks on her country's psyche. The cause for which she died still affects millions today. Her struggles were the same as ours, her belief in her rights, to speak and to be heard, anticipated ours, and she faced many of the issues that we have still not resolved in the East or in the West today. She raises the same questions, rouses the same violence and uncertainty, stirs the same fanaticism and hope about the role of women and the purpose of religion as we witness in our own times. The cause for which she died is no longer an arcane matter for scholars or theologians to debate. It concerns us all. She is the everywoman of our age.

Since the history behind this story may be unfamiliar to some readers, a chronology of corpses and a selection of titles for further reading have been provided in the following pages. These materials are intended to help readers distinguish between orthodox facts and fictional heresies in this novel. The chronology provides basic information about the most significant corpses that have littered its pages. But I also owe a debt of gratitude to the living as well as to the dead, to people as well as to books. My appreciation goes, first and foremost, to Farzaneh Milani and Abbas Milani, to Shidan Taslimi and Mehran Taslimi, and to Helenka Fuglewicz and Ros Edwards, without whose unstinting support this book would never have seen the light of print. I also owe special thanks to Christine LeBoeuf, Marie Catherine Vacher, Pippa Tristram, Angela Livingstone, and Fionnuala McMahamon, without whose patient reading there would have been even more infelicities scattered in these pages. In addition, I wish to thank my daughter, Mary, and my parents, Ali and Violette, and in particular my uncle Amin Banani, without whose encouragement it would never have been written at all.

CHRONOLOGY OF CORPSES

1847   Shaykh Mullah Muhammad Taqi Baraghani, uncle of Tahirih Qurratu'l-Ayn, dies of stab wounds after being attacked by an unknown assailant before Friday prayers in a mosque in the provincial city of Qazvin.

1848   Muhammad Shah, third king of the Qajar dynasty, dies and is succeeded on the throne by Nasiru'd-Din, whose mother, Mahd-i-Olya, becomes regent for her youthful son.

1849   Seven Babis, later known as the Seven Martyrs of Tehran, are victims of the first public execution in Persia on the orders of Amir Kabir, the first Grand Vazir of Nasiru'd-Din Shah, and are decapitated in the market square after being tortured at the hands of Mahmud Khan-i-Kalantar, chief of police and mayor of Tehran.

1850   Siyyid Ali Muhammad, prophet founder of the Babi faith, is shot to death for apostasy in a barrack square in Tabriz by the soldiers of the Shah, on the orders of Amir Kabir, his body riddled with the bullets from 750 muskets after the first attempt by an Armenian regiment fails.

1851   Amir Kabir, the first Grand Vazir of Nasiru'd-Din Shah, is found dead in the gardens of Fin, in Kashan, his veins slashed open and drained in the water of the baths.

1852   Tahirih Qurratu'l-Ayn, poetess, scholar, and Babi leader, daughter of Mullah Muhammad Salih Baraghani and niece of the murdered Shaykh Mullah Muhammad Taqi Baraghani, is strangled in a garden north of Tehran during the summer massacres unleashed by the mother of the Shah, in which hundreds of corpses litter the streets and nameless thousands are murdered after a misguided attempt on the life of the Shah by a few fanatical Babi youths.

1860   Jayran, a courtesan who became the favourite concubine of the Shah, dies of consumption during the Shah's absence on a hunting expedition, approximately one year after the death of her little son, the Heir Apparent, from meningitis.

1861   Mahmud Khan-i-Kalantar, chief of police and mayor of Tehran, is hauled through the streets and hung naked at the city gates, before being cut to pieces by the starving crowds, after the bread riots in the capital.

1866   Mullah Muhammad Salih Baraghani, father of Tahirih, dies in retirement in the shrines of the Shi'iah Imams, apparently of a broken heart.

1869   Lady Mary Leonora Woulfe Sheil dies in Ireland, after bearing ten children, three of whom were born in Persia between 1849 and 1853.

1871   Sir Justin Sheil dies and is buried, alone, in his family vault in England.

1873   Mahd-i-Olya, the mother of the Shah, dies during her son's absence on a grand tour of the courts of the Tsar, the Kaiser, and Queen Victoria.

1896   The assassination of Nasiru'd-Din Shah, by the follower of one of the political factions in the country supporting constitutional reform, occurs in the shrine of Shah Abdu'l-Aziz, south of the capital, on the eve of his majesty's jubilee celebrations.

FURTHER READING

'Abdu'l-Baha. *Memorials of the Faithful*. Wilmette, IL: Bahá'í Publishing Trust, 1971.

Afaqi, Sabir, ed. *Tahirih in History: Perspectives on Qurratu'l-Ayn, Studies in the Bábi and Bahá'í Religions*, Vol. 16. Los Angeles: Kalimat Press, 2004.

Amanat, Abbas. *Resurrection and Renewal: The Making of the Bábi Movement in Iran, 1844–1850*. Ithaca, NY: Cornell University Press, 1989.

————. *Pivot of the Universe, Nasir al-Din Shah Qajar 1831–1896*. Washington, DC: Mage, 1997.

Amini, Iraj. *Napoleon and Persia*. Washington, DC: Mage, 1999.

Arnold, Arthur. *Through Persia by Caravan*. London: Tinsley Brothers, 1877.

Avery, Peter. *Modern Iran*. London: Praeger, 1965.

Balyuzi, Hasan M. *Edward Granville Browne and the Bahá'í Faith*. Oxford: George Ronald, 1970.

————. *The Báb*. Oxford: George Ronald, 1973.

————. *Bahá'u'lláh*. Oxford: George Ronald, 1980.

Banani, Amin. *Tahirih: A Portrait in Poetry, Studies in the Bábi and Bahá'í Religions*, Vol. 17. Los Angeles: Kalimat Press, 2004.

Bassett, James. *Persia, Land of the Imams*. London: Blackie, 1887.

Bausani, Alessandro. *The Persian*. London: Elek Books, 1971.

Bayat, Mangol. *Mysticism and Dissent*. Syracuse, NY: Syracuse University Press, 1982.

Binning, Robert B. M. *Journal of Two Years' Travel in Persia, Ceylon*. London: W. H. Allen, 1857.

Bird, Isabella. *Journeys in Persia and Kurdistan*. London: Virago Press, 1988.

Birkett, Dea. *Spinsters Abroad: Victorian Lady Explorers*. London: Victor Gollancz, 1991.

Blunt, Wilfred S. *The Future of Islam*. London: Kegan Paul, Trench, 1882.

Bon, Ottaviano. *The Sultan's Seraglio: An Intimate Portrait of Life at the Ottoman Court*. London: Saqi Books, 1996.

Brookshaw, Dominic. "Women in Praise of Women: Female Poets and Female Patrons in Qajar Iran," *Iranian Studies* 46 no. 1 (2013): 17–48

Browne, Edward G. *A Year Amongst the Persians*, reprint from the 1893 edition. Belgium: Time-Life Books, 1983.

———. *Selections from the Writings of*, ed. Moojan Momen. Oxford: George Ronald, 1987.

Burgess, Charles. *Letters from Persia*, ed. Benjamin Schwartz. New York: New York Public Library, 1942.

Chaqueri, Cosroe. *The Armenians of Iran*. Cambridge: Harvard University Press, 1998.

Cheyne, Thomas K. *The Reconciliation of Races and Religions*. London: Adam & Charles Black, 1914.

Cloquet, Ernest. "Perse," in *Revue de l'Orient*, 2nd ser., Vol. 5. Paris: Bureau de la Revue, 1849.

Clot, André. *Harun al-Rashid and the World of the Thousand and One Nights*, trans. John How. Paris: New Amsterdam Books, Fayard, 1986.

Curzon, George N. *Persia and the Persian Question*, London: Longmans Green, 1892.

De Vries, Jelle. *The Babi Question You Mentioned*. Leuven, Netherlands: Peeters, 2002.

Demas, Kathleen J. *From Behind the Veil*, Wilmette, IL: Gateway Series, 1983.

Diba, Layla S. *Royal Persian Paintings: The Qajar Epoch 1785–1925*. London: I. B. Tauris, 1998.

Dieulafoy, Jane. *La Perse, la Chaldée et la Susiane*, Paris: Hachette, 1887.

Djebar, Assia. *Fantasia: An Algerian Cavalcade*. Portsmouth, NH: Heinemann Educational, 1993.

Donaldson, Bess Allen. *The Wild Rue: A Study of Muhammadan Magic and Folklore in Iran*. London: Luzac, 1938.

Eastwick, Edward B. *Journal of a Diplomat's Three Years' Residence in Persia*. London: Smith Elder, 1864.

Eberhardt, Isabelle. *The Passionate Nomad: The Diary*. London: Virago Press, 1987.

Effendi, Shoghi. *God Passes By*. Wilmette, IL: Bahá'í Publishing Trust, 1944.

Encyclopedia Iranica, ed. E. Yarshater. London and Costa Mesa, CA: Bibliotheca Persica Press, 1982.

"Excerpts from Dispatches Written During 1848–1852 by Prince Dolgorukov, Russian Minister to Persia, *World Order* Vol. 1, No.1. Wilmette, IL: Bahá'í Publishing Trust, 1966.

Farman Farmanian, Sattareh. *Daughter of Persia*. New York: Crown, 1992.

Ferrier, Joseph. "Situation de la Perse en 1851" *Revue Orientale et Algérienne*, Vol. 1. Paris, 1852.

Floor, Willem. *Public Health in Qajar Iran*. Washington, DC: Mage, 2004.

———. *Wall Paintings and Other Figurative Mural Art in Qajar Iran*. Costa Mesa, CA: Mazda, 2005.

Friedl, Erika. *Women of Deh Koh: Lives in an Iranian Village*, Washington, DC: Penguin, 1989.

Gail, Marzieh. *Persia and the Victorians*. London: George Allen & Unwin, 1951.

———. *Summon Up Remembrance*. Oxford: George Ronald, 1987.

Gleave, Robert. *Religion and Society in Qajar Iran*. London: Routledge/Curzon, 2009.

Gobineau, J. A. de. *Les Religions et les Philosophies dans l'Asie Centrale*. Paris: Gallimard, 1983.

Hakimian, Donna. "Resistence, Resilience, and the Role of Narrative: Lessons from the Experiences of Iranian Baha'i Women Prisoners." *Enquire*, no. 3 (2009).

Hatcher, John. *The Poetry of Tahirih*. Oxford: George Ronald, 2002.

Hume-Griffith, M. E. *Behind the Veil in Persia and Turkish Arabia*. London: Lippincott, 1909.

Javadi, Hasan, and Floor, Willem. *The Education of Women & The Vices of Men*. Syracuse, NY: Syracuse University Press, 2010.

Kabbabi, Rana. *Europe's Myths of Orient*. London: Macmillan, 1986.

Kazemzadeh, Firuz. *Russia and Britain in Persia: A Study in Imperialism 1864–94*. New Haven, CT: Yale University Press, 1968.

Keddie, Nikki R. *Qajar Iran & The Rise of Reza Khan 1796–1925*. Costa Mesa, CA: Mazda, 1999.

Kelly, Laurence. *Diplomacy and Murder in Tehran*. London: I. B. Tauris, 2002.

Layard, Austin H. *Early Adventures in Persia, Susiana, and Babylonia*. London: John Murray, 1887.

Mabro, Judy. *Veiled Half-Truths: Western Travellers' Perceptions of Middle Eastern Women*. London: I. B. Tauris, 1996.

MacEoin, Denis. *Rituals in Babism and Baha'ism*. London: I.B. Tauris, 1994.

———. "The Trial of the Bab." In *Studies in Honour of Clifford Edmund Bosworth*, Vol. II, ed. Carole Hillenbrand. Boston: Brill, 2000.

Melman, Billie. *Women's Orients: English Women and the Middle East, 1718–1918.* Ann Arbor: University of Michigan Press, 1992.

Mernissi, Fatima. *Women's Rebellion & Islamic Memory.* London: Zed Books, 1996.

———. *Forgotten Queens of Islam.* Cambridge: Polity Press, 1994.

Milani, Abbas. *Lost Wisdom: Rethinking Modernity in Iran.* Washington, DC: Mage, 2004.

———. *The Shah.* New York: Palgrave Macmillan, 2011.

Milani, Farzaneh. *Veils and Words: The Emerging Voices of Iranian Women Writers.* Syracuse, NY: Syracuse University Press, 1992.

———. *Words Not Swords.* Syracuse, NY: Syracuse University Press, 2011.

Momen, Moojan. *The Bábi and Bahá'í Religions, 1844–1944.* Oxford: George Ronald, 1981.

Mottahedeh, Roy. *The Mantle of the Prophet.* New York: Simon & Schuster, 1985.

Nabil-i-A'zam. *The Dawn-Breakers: Nabil's Narrative of the Early Days of the Bahá'í Revelation.* London: Bahá'í Publishing Trust, 1953.

Nafisi, Azar. *Reading Lolita in Tehran.* New York: Random House, 2003.

Najmabdi, Afsaneh. *Women with Mustaches and Men Without Beards.* Berkeley, CA: University of California Press, 2005.

———. *Women's Worlds in Qajar Iran*, Digital Archive and Website, Harvard University, 2012, available at http://www.qajarwomen.org.

Nerval, Gérard de. *Journey to the Orient.* London: Michael Haag, 1984.

Nicolas a.-l.-M. *Massacres de Babis en Perse.* Paris: Maisonneuve, 1936.

Ramazani, Nesta. *The Dance of the Rose and the Nightingale.* Syracuse, NY: Syracuse University Press, 2002.

Robinson, Jane. *Unsuitable for Ladies.* Oxford: Oxford University Press, 1994.

Rodinson, Maxime. *Europe and the Mystique of Islam.* Seattle: University of Washington Press, 1987.

Root, Martha. *Tahirih the Pure.* Los Angeles, Kalimat Press, 1981.

Sheil, Lady Mary L. *Glimpses of Life and Manners in Persia.* London: John Murray, 1856.

Sweet, Matthew. *Inventing the Victorians.* London: Faber & Faber, 2001.

Taj Al-Saltana. *Crowning Anguish: Memoirs of a Persian Princess.* Washington, DC: Mage, 1993.

Wright, Denis. *The English Among the Persians During the Qajar Period, 1787–1921.* London: Heinemann, 1977.

———. *The Persians Among the English, Episodes in Anglo-Persian History.* London: I. B. Tauris, 1985.